London Borough of Tower Hamlets

91000008103278

KU-621-919

Pri...

Praise for Daniel Silva and the Gabriel Allon series

'Silva has now indisputably joined the ranks of Graham Greene and John le Carre' *Washingtonian*

'Silva excitingly delivers his story's twists and turns . . . Moves at a brisk clip, with clean, lucid exposition and characters who are thoughtfully drawn' *New York Times*

'Ranks among the best of the younger American spy novelists' *Washington Post*

'A passionate, intelligently crafted entry that cements the series' place among today's top spy fiction. The structure is classic' *Publishers Weekly*

'A story that seems ripped from the headlines . . . Chilling suspense' *Booklist*

'Daniel Silva confirms his position as a front-runner to succeed Tom Clancy as America's foremost source of international intrigue fiction' *Bookpage*

About the author

Daniel Silva is also the author of the bestselling thrillers *The Unlikely Spy*, *The Mark of the Assassin*, *The Marching Season*, *The Kill Artist*, *The Confessor* and *A Death in Vienna*. The *Washington Post* ranks him as 'among the best of the younger American spy novelists' and he is regularly compared to Graham Greene and John Le Carré. He lives in Washington DC. If you would like to find out more about Daniel Silva and his novels, visit his website www.danielsilvabooks.com

Prince of Fire

DANIEL SILVA

PENGUIN BOOKS

PENGUIN BOOKS

UK | USA | Canada | Ireland | Australia
India | New Zealand | South Africa

Penguin Books is part of the Penguin Random House group of companies
whose addresses can be found at global.penguinrandomhouse.com.

First published by G. P. Putnam's Sons 2005
Published in Penguin Books 2006

014

Copyright © Daniel Silva, 2005
All rights reserved

The moral rights of the author has been asserted

Set in 11.75/14 pt Monotype Garamond
Typeset by Rowland Phototypesetting Ltd, Bury St Edmunds, Suffolk
Printed in England by Clays Ltd, Elcograf S.p.A.

ISBN: 978-0-141-02415-8

www.greenpenguin.co.uk

Penguin Random House is committed to a
sustainable future for our business, our readers
and our planet. This book is made from Forest
Stewardship Council® certified paper.

For Neil Nyren, steady hand on the tiller,
Patrick Matthiesen, who gave me Isherwood,
and, as always, for my wife, Jamie, and
my children, Lily and Nicholas

If you live to seek revenge,
dig a grave for two.

Ancient Jewish Proverb

PART ONE
The Dossier

1. Rome: March 4

There had been warning signs – the Shabbat bombing of a Jewish community center in Buenos Aires that left eighty-seven people dead; the bombing of an Istanbul synagogue, precisely one year later, that killed another twenty-eight – but Rome would be his coming-out party, and Rome would be the place where he left his calling card.

Afterward, within the corridors and executive suites of Israel's vaunted intelligence service, there was considerable and sometimes belligerent debate over the time and place of the conspiracy's genesis. Lev Ahroni, the ever-cautious director of the service, would claim that the plot was hatched not long after the Israeli army knocked down Arafat's headquarters in Ramallah and stole his secret files. Ari Shamron, the legendary Israeli master spy, would find this almost laughable, though Shamron often disagreed with Lev simply as a matter of sport. Only Shamron, who had fought with the Palmach during the War of Independence and who tended to view the conflict as a continuum, understood intuitively that the outrage in Rome had been inspired by deeds dating back more than a half century. Eventually, evidence would prove both Lev and Shamron correct. In the meantime, in order to achieve peaceful working conditions, they agreed on a new starting point: the day a certain Monsieur Jean-Luc arrived in the hills of Lazio and settled himself in a rather handsome eighteenth-century villa on the shore of Lake Bracciano.

As for the exact date and time of his arrival, there was no doubt. The owner of the villa, a dubious Belgian aristocrat called Monsieur Laval, said the tenant appeared at two-thirty in the afternoon on the final Friday of March. The courteous but intense young Israeli who called on Monsieur Laval at his home in Brussels wondered how it was possible to recall the date so clearly. The Belgian produced his lavish leather-bound personal calendar and pointed to the date in question. There, penciled on the line designated for 2:30 P.M., were the words: *Meet M. Jean-Luc at Bracciano villa.*

'Why did you write *Bracciano villa* instead of just *villa*?' asked the Israeli visitor, his pen hovering over his open notebook.

'To differentiate it from our *St Tropez* villa, our *Portuguese* villa, and the *chalet* we own in the Swiss Alps.'

'I see,' said the Israeli, though the Belgian found that his visitor's tone lacked the humility adopted by most civil servants when confronted by men of great wealth.

And what else did Monsieur Laval remember of the man who rented his villa? That he was punctual, intelligent, and extremely well mannered. That he was striking good-looking, that his scent was noticeable but not obtrusive, that his clothing was expensive but restrained. That he drove a Mercedes car and had two large suitcases with gold buckles and a famous label. That he paid the entire monthlong lease in advance and in cash, which Monsieur Laval explained was not unusual in that part of Italy. That he was a good listener who didn't need to be told things twice. That he spoke French with the accent of a Parisian from a well-heeled arrondissement. That he seemed like a man who could handle himself well in a fight and who treated his women well. 'He was of noble birth,' Laval concluded, with the certainty of one who knows of what he speaks. 'He comes from a good bloodline. Write that in your little book.'

Slowly, additional details would emerge about the man called Jean-Luc, though none conflicted with Monsieur Laval's flattering portrait. He hired no cleaning woman and demanded the gardener arrive punctually at nine o'clock and leave by ten. He shopped in nearby market squares and attended Mass in the medieval lakeside village of Anguillara. He spent much time touring the Roman ruins of Lazio and seemed particularly intrigued by the ancient necropolis at Cerveteri.

Sometime in the middle of March – the date could never be reliably established – he vanished. Even Monsieur Laval could not be certain of the departure date, because he was informed after the fact by a woman in Paris who claimed to be the gentleman's personal assistant. Though two weeks remained on the lease, the handsome tenant did not embarrass himself, or Monsieur Laval, by asking for a refund. Later that spring, when Monsieur Laval visited the villa, he was surprised to discover, in a crystal bowl on the dining room sideboard, a brief thank-you note, typewritten, along with a hundred euros to pay for broken wineglasses. A thorough search of the villa's stemware collection, however, revealed nothing was missing. When Monsieur Laval tried to call Jean-Luc's girl in Paris to return the money, he found that her telephone line had been disconnected.

On the fringes of the Borghese gardens there are elegant boulevards and quiet leafy side streets that bear little resemblance to the scruffy, tourist-trodden thoroughfares of the city center. They are avenues of diplomacy and money, where traffic moves at a nearly reasonable speed and where the blare of car horns sounds like a rebellion in distant lands. One such street is a cul-de-sac. It falls away at a gentle pitch and bends to the right. For many hours each day, it is in shadow, a consequence of the towering stone pine and eucalyptus that loom over the villas. The narrow sidewalk is broken by tree roots and perpetually covered by pine needles and dead leaves. At the end of the street is a diplomatic compound, more heavily fortified than most in Rome.

Survivors and witnesses would recall the perfection of that late-winter morning: bright and clear, cold enough in the shadows to bring on a shiver, warm enough in the sun to unbutton a wool coat and dream of an alfresco lunch. The fact it was also a Friday served only to heighten the leisurely atmosphere. In diplomatic Rome, it was a morning to dawdle over a cappuccino and *cornetto*, to take stock of one's circumstances and ponder one's mortality. Procrastination was the order of the day. Many mundane meetings were canceled. Much routine paperwork was put off till Monday.

On the little cul-de-sac near the Borghese gardens there were no outward signs of the catastrophe to come. The Italian police and security agents guarding the perimeter fortifications chatted lazily in the patches of brilliant sunshine. Like most diplomatic missions in Rome, it officially contained two embassies, one dealing with the Italian government, the second with the Vatican. Both embassies opened for business at their appointed times. Both ambassadors were in their offices.

At ten-fifteen a tubby Jesuit waddled down the hill, a leather satchel in his hand. Inside was a diplomatic démarche from the Vatican Secretariat of State, condemning the Israeli army's recent incursion into Bethlehem. The courier deposited the document with an embassy clerk and puffed his way back up the hill. Afterward, the text would be made public, and its sharp language would prove a temporary embarrassment to the men of the Vatican. The

7

courier's timing would prove providential. Had he arrived five minutes later, he would have been vaporized, along with the original text of the démarche.

Not so fortunate were the members of an Italian television crew who had come to interview the ambassador on the current state of affairs in the Middle East. Or the delegation of local Jewish crusaders who had come to secure the ambassador's public condemnation of a neo-Nazi conference scheduled for the following week in Verona. Or the Italian couple, sickened by the new rise of European anti-Semitism, who were about to inquire about the possibility of emigrating to Israel. Fourteen in all, they were standing in a tight cluster at the business entrance, waiting to be body-searched by the embassy's short-haired security toughs, when the white freight truck made a right turn into the cul-de-sac and began its death run toward the compound.

Most heard the truck before they saw it. The convulsive roar of its diesel engine was a violent intrusion on the otherwise still morning. It was impossible to ignore. The Italian security men paused in mid-conversation and looked up, as did the group of fourteen strangers gathered outside the entrance of the embassy. The tubby Jesuit, who was waiting for a bus at the opposite end of the street, lifted his round head from his copy of *L'Osservatore Romano* and searched for the source of the commotion.

The gentle slope of the street helped the truck

gather speed at an astonishing rate. As it rounded the bend, the massive load in its cargo container pushed the truck heavily onto two wheels. For an instant it seemed it might topple. Then somehow it righted itself and began the final straight-line plunge toward the compound.

The driver was briefly visible through the windshield. He was young and clean-shaven. His eyes were wide, his mouth agape. He seemed to be standing atop the gas pedal, and he seemed to be shouting at himself. For some reason the wipers were on.

The Italian security forces reacted immediately. Several took cover behind the reinforced concrete barriers. Others dived for the protection of the steel-and-glass guard posts. Two officers could be seen pouring automatic fire toward the marauding truck. Sparks exploded on the grille, and the windshield shattered, but the truck continued unhindered, gathering speed until the point of impact. Afterward, the government of Israel would commend the heroism shown by the Italian security services that morning. It would be noted that none fled their positions, though if they had, their fate would have been precisely the same.

The explosion could be heard from St Peter's Square to the Piazza di Spagna to the Janiculum Hill. Those on the upper floors of buildings were treated to the remarkable sight of a red-and-orange fireball rising over the northern end of the Villa Borghese, followed quickly by a pitch-black mushroom cloud of smoke. Windows a mile from the blast point were shattered by the thunderclap of the shock wave, including the stained-glass windows in a nearby church. Plane trees were stripped of their leaves. Birds died in mid-flight. Geologists at a seismic monitoring station first feared that Rome had been shaken by a moderate earthquake.

None of the Italian security men survived the initial blast. Nor did any of the fourteen visitors waiting to be admitted to the mission, or the embassy personnel who happened to be working in offices closest to the spot where the truck exploded.

Ultimately, though, it was the second vehicle that inflicted the most loss of life. The Vatican courier, who had been knocked to the ground by the force of the blast, saw the car turn into the cul-de-sac at high speed. Because it was a Lancia sedan, and because it was carrying four men and traveling at a high rate of speed, he assumed it was a police vehicle responding to the bombing. The priest got to his feet and started toward the scene through the dense black smoke, hoping to be of assistance to the wounded and the dead alike. Instead he saw a scene from a nightmare. The doors of the Lancia opened simultaneously, and the four men he assumed to be police officers began firing into the compound. Survivors who staggered from the burning wreckage of the embassy were mercilessly cut down.

The four gunmen ceased firing at precisely the same time, then clambered back into the Lancia.

As they sped away from the burning compound, one of the terrorists aimed his automatic weapon at the Jesuit. The priest made the sign of the cross and prepared himself to die. The terrorist just smiled and disappeared behind a curtain of smoke.

2. Tiberias, Israel

Fifteen minutes after the last shot was fired in Rome, the secure telephone rang in the large, honey-colored villa overlooking the Sea of Galilee. Ari Shamron, the twice former director-general of the Israeli secret service, now special adviser to the prime minister on all matters dealing with security and intelligence, took the call in his study. He listened in silence for a moment, his eyes closed tightly in anger. 'I'm on my way,' he said, and hung up the phone.

Turning around, he saw Gilah standing in the doorway of the study. She was holding his leather bomber jacket in her hand, and her eyes were damp with tears.

'It just came on the television. How bad?'

'Very bad. The prime minister wants me to help him prepare a statement to the country.'

'Then you shouldn't keep the prime minister waiting.'

She helped Shamron into his jacket and kissed his cheek. There was simple ritual in this act. How many times had he separated from his wife after hearing that Jews had been killed by a bomb? He had lost count long ago. He had resigned himself, late in life, that it would never end.

'You won't smoke too many cigarettes?'

'Of course not.'

'Try to call me.'

'I'll call when I can.'

He stepped out the front door. A blast of cold wet wind greeted him. A storm had stolen down from the Golan during the night and laid siege to the whole of the Upper Galilee. Shamron had been awakened by the first crack of thunder, which he had mistaken for a gunshot, and had lain awake for the rest of the night. For Shamron, sleep was like contraband. It came to him rarely and, once interrupted, never twice in the same night. Usually he found himself wandering the secure file rooms of his memory, reliving old cases, walking old battlefields and confronting enemies vanquished long ago. Last night had been different. He'd had a premonition of imminent disaster, an image so clear that he'd actually placed a call to the night desk of his old service to see if anything had happened. 'Go back to sleep, Boss,' the youthful duty officer had said. 'Everything's fine.'

His black Peugeot, armored and bulletproof, waited at the top of the drive. Rami, the dark-haired head of his security detachment, stood next to the open rear door. Shamron had made many enemies over the years, and because of the tangled demographics of Israel, many lived uncomfortably close to Tiberias. Rami, quiet as a lone wolf and far more lethal, rarely left his master's side.

Shamron paused for a moment to light a cigarette,

a vile Turkish brand he'd been smoking since the Mandate days, then stepped off the veranda. He was short of stature, yet even in old age, powerful in build. His hands were leathery and liver-spotted and seemed to have been borrowed from a man twice his size. His face, full of cracks and fissures, looked like an aerial view of the Negev Desert. His remaining fringe of steel-gray hair was cropped so short as to be nearly invisible. Infamously hard on his eyeglasses, he had resigned himself to ugly frames of indestructible plastic. The thick lenses magnified blue eyes that were no longer clear. He walked as though anticipating an assault from behind, with his head down and his elbows out defensively. Within the corridors of King Saul Boulevard, the headquarters of his old service, the walk was known as 'the Shamron shuffle.' He knew of the epithet and he approved.

He ducked into the backseat of the Peugeot. The heavy car lurched forward and headed down the treacherously steep drive to the lakeshore. It turned right and sped toward Tiberias, then west, across the Galilee toward the Coastal Plain. Shamron's gaze, for much of the journey, was focused on the scratched face of his wristwatch. Time was now his enemy. With each passing minute the perpetrators were slipping farther and farther away from the scene of the crime. Had they attempted an attack such as this in Jerusalem or Tel Aviv, they would have been snared in a web of checkpoints and roadblocks. But it had occurred in Italy, not Israel, and Shamron was at the mercy of the Italian police. It had been a long time since the Italians had dealt with a major act of terrorism. What's more, Israel's link to the Italian government – its embassy – was in ruins. So, too, Shamron suspected, was a very important station of the Israeli secret service. Rome was the regional headquarters for southern Europe. It was led by a *katsa* named Shimon Pazner, a man whom Shamron had personally recruited and trained. It was quite possible the Office had just lost one of its most competent and experienced officers.

The journey seemed to last an eternity. They listened to the news on Israel Radio, and with each update the situation in Rome seemed to grow worse. Three times, Shamron anxiously reached for his secure cellular phone and three times he snapped it back into its cradle without dialing a number. *Leave them to it,* he thought. *They know what they're doing. Because of you, they're well trained.* Besides, it was no time for the special adviser to the prime minister on matters of security and terrorism to be weighing in with helpful suggestions.

Special Adviser . . . How he loathed the title. It stank of ambiguity. He had been the *Memuneh*: the one in charge. He had seen his blessed service, and his country, through triumph and adversity. Lev and his band of young technocrats had regarded him as a liability and had banished him to the Judean wilderness of retirement. He would have remained there were it not for the lifeline thrown to him by the prime minister. Shamron, master manipulator and puppeteer, had learned that he could exercise nearly as much power from the prime minister's office as he could from the executive suite of King Saul Boulevard. Experience had taught him to be patient. Eventually it would end up in his lap. It always seemed to.

They began the ascent toward Jerusalem. Shamron could not make this remarkable drive without thinking of old battles. The premonition came to him again. Was it Rome he had seen the night before or something else? Something bigger than even Rome? An old enemy, he was sure of it. A dead man, risen from his past.

The office of the Israeli prime minister is located at 3 Kaplan Street, in the Kiryat Ben-Gurion section of West Jerusalem. Shamron entered the building through the underground parking garage, then went up to his office. It was small but strategically located on the hallway that led to the prime minister's, which allowed him to see when Lev, or any of the other intelligence and security chiefs, were making their way into the inner sanctum for a meeting. He had no personal secretary, but shared a girl named Tamara with three other members of the security staff. She brought him coffee and switched on the bank of three televisions.

'Varash is scheduled to meet in the prime minister's office at five o'clock.'

Varash was the Hebrew-language acronym for the Committee of the Heads of the Services. It included the director-general of Shabak, the internal security service; the commander of Aman, military intelligence; and, of course, the chief of Israel's secret intelligence service, which was referred to only as 'the Office.' Shamron, by charter and reputation, had a permanent seat at the table.

'In the meantime,' Tamara said, 'he wants a briefing in twenty minutes.'

'Tell him a half hour would be better.'

'If you want a half hour, *you* tell him.'

Shamron sat down at his desk and, remote in hand, spent the next five minutes scanning the world's television media for as many overt details as he could. Then he picked up the telephone and made three calls, one to an old contact at the Italian Embassy named Tommaso Naldi; the second to the Israeli Ministry of Foreign Affairs, located a short distance away on Yitzhak Rabin Boulevard; and the third to Office headquarters on King Saul Boulevard.

'He can't talk to you now,' said Lev's secretary. Shamron had anticipated her reaction. It was easier to get through an army checkpoint than Lev's secretary.

'Put him on the phone,' Shamron said, 'or the next call will be from the prime minister.'

Lev kept Shamron waiting five minutes.

'What do you know?' Shamron asked.

'The truth? Nothing.'

'Do we have a Rome station any longer?'

'Not to speak of,' said Lev, 'but we do have a Rome *katsa*. Pazner was in Naples on business. He just checked in. He's on his way back to Rome now.'

Thank God, thought Shamron. 'And the others?'

'It's hard to tell. As you might imagine, the situation is rather chaotic.' Lev had a grating passion for understatement. 'Two clerks are missing, along with the communications officer.'

'Is there anything in the files that might be compromising or embarrassing?'

'The best we can hope for is that they went up in smoke.'

'They're stored in cabinets built to withstand a missile strike. We'd better get to them before the Italians do.'

Tamara poked her head inside the door. 'He wants you. Now.'

'I'll see you at five o'clock,' Shamron said to Lev, and rang off.

He collected his notes, then followed Tamara along the corridor toward the prime minister's office. Two members of his Shabak protective detail, large boys with short-cropped hair and shirts hanging outside their trousers, watched Shamron's approach. One of them stepped aside and opened the door. Shamron slipped past and went inside.

The shades were drawn, the room cool and in semidarkness. The prime minister was seated behind his large desk, dwarfed by a towering portrait of the Zionist leader Theodor Herzl that hung on the wall at his back. Shamron had been in this room many times, yet it never failed to quicken his pulse. For Shamron this chamber represented the end of a remarkable journey, the reconstitution of Jewish sovereignty in the Land of Israel. Birth and death, war and Holocaust – Shamron, like the prime minister, had played a leading role in the entire epic. Privately, they regarded it as their State, their creation, and they guarded it jealously against all those – Arab, Jewish, or Gentile – who sought to weaken or destroy it.

The prime minister, without a word, nodded for Shamron to sit. Small at the head and very wide at the waist, he looked rather like a formation of volcanic rock. His stubby hands lay folded on the desktop; his heavy jowls hung over his shirt collar.

'How bad, Ari?'

'By the end of the day, we'll have a clearer picture,' Shamron said. 'I can say one thing for certain. This will go down as one of the worst acts of terrorism ever committed against the State, if not *the* worst.'

'How many dead?'

'Still unclear.'

'The ambassadors?'

'Officially, they're still listed as unaccounted for.'

'And unofficially?'

'It's believed they're dead.'

'Both?'

Shamron nodded. 'And their deputies.'

'How many dead for certain?'

'The Italians report twelve police and security personnel dead. At the moment, the Foreign Ministry is confirming twenty-two personnel killed, along with thirteen family members from the residence complex. Eighteen people remain unaccounted for.'

'Fifty-two dead?'

'At least. Apparently there were several visitors standing at the entrance waiting to be admitted to the building.'

'What about the Office station?'

Shamron repeated what he'd just learned from Lev. Pazner was alive. Three Office employees were feared to be among the dead.

'Who did it?'

'Lev hasn't reached any –'

'I'm not asking Lev.'

'The list of potential suspects, unfortunately, is long. Anything I might say now would be speculation, and at this point, speculation does us no good.'

'Why Rome?'

'Hard to say,' Shamron said. 'Perhaps it was just a target of opportunity. Maybe they saw a weakness, a chink in our armor, and they decided to exploit it.'

'But you don't believe that?'

'No, Prime Minister.'

'Could it have something to do with that affair at the Vatican a couple of years ago – that business with Allon?'

'I doubt it. All the evidence thus far suggests it

was a suicide attack carried out by Arab terrorists.'

'I want to make a statement after Varash meets.'

'I think that would be wise.'

'And I want you to write it for me.'

'If you wish.'

'You know about loss, Ari. We both do. Put some heart into it. Tap that reservoir of Polish pain you're always carrying around with you. The country will need to cry tonight. Let them cry. But assure them that the animals who did this will be punished.'

'They will, Prime Minister.'

Shamron stood.

'Who did this, Ari?'

'We'll know soon enough.'

'I want his head,' the prime minister said savagely. 'I want his head on a stick.'

'And you shall have it.'

Forty-eight hours would pass before the first break in the case, and it would come not in Rome but in the northern industrial city of Milan. Units of the Polizia di Stato and Carabinieri, acting on a tip from a Tunisian immigrant informant, raided a *pensione* in a workers' quarter north of the city center where two of the four surviving attackers were thought to be hiding. The men were no longer there, and based on the condition of the room, they had fled in a hurry. Police discovered a pair of suitcases filled with clothing and a half-dozen cellular telephones, along with false passports and stolen credit cards.

The most intriguing item, however, was a compact disk sewn into the lining of one of the bags. Italian investigators at the national crime laboratory in Rome determined that the disk contained data but were unable to penetrate its sophisticated security firewall. Eventually, after much internal debate, it was decided to approach the Israelis for help.

And so it was that Shimon Pazner received his summons to the headquarters of the Servizio per le Informazioni e la Sicurezza Democratica, Italy's Intelligence and Democratic Security Service. He arrived a few minutes after ten in the evening and was shown immediately into the office of the deputy chief, a man named Martino Bellano. They were a mismatched pair: Bellano, tall and lean and dressed as though he had just stepped off the pages of an Italian fashion magazine; Pazner, short and muscular with hair like steel wool and a crumpled sports jacket. 'A pile of yesterday's laundry' is how Bellano would describe Pazner after the encounter, and in the aftermath of the affair, when it became clear that Pazner had behaved less than forthrightly, Bellano routinely referred to the Israeli as 'that kosher shylock in a borrowed blazer.'

On that first evening, however, Bellano could not have been more solicitous of his visitor. Pazner was not the type to elicit sympathy from strangers, but as he was shown into Bellano's office, his eyes were heavy with exhaustion and a profound case of survivor's guilt. Bellano spent several moments expressing his 'profound grief' over the bombing before getting round to the reason for Pazner's late-night summons: the computer disk. He placed it ceremoniously on the desktop and slid it toward Pazner with the tip of a manicured forefinger. Pazner accepted it calmly, though later he would confess to Shamron that his heart was beating a chaotic rhythm against his breastbone.

'We've been unable to pick the lock,' Bellano said. 'Perhaps you'll have a bit more luck.'

'We'll do our best,' replied Pazner modestly.

'Of course, you'll share with us any material you happen to find.'

'It goes without saying,' said Pazner as the disk disappeared into his coat pocket.

Another ten minutes would elapse before Bellano saw fit to conclude the meeting. Pazner remained stoically in his seat, gripping the arms of his chair like a man in the throes of a nicotine fit. Those who witnessed his departure down the grandiose main corridor took note of his unhurried pace. Only when he was outside, descending the front steps, was there any hint of urgency in his stride.

Within hours of the attack, a team of Israeli bomb specialists, regrettably well experienced in their trade, had arrived in Rome to begin the task of sifting the wreckage for evidence of the bomb's composition and origin. As luck would have it, the military charter that had borne them from Tel Aviv was still on the apron at Fiumicino. Pazner, with Shamron's approval, commandeered the plane to take him back to Tel Aviv. He arrived a few minutes after sunrise and walked directly into the arms of an Office greeting party. They headed immediately to King Saul Boulevard, driving at great haste but with no recklessness, for the cargo was too precious to risk on that most dangerous element of Israeli life: its roadways. By eight that morning, the computer disk was the target of a coordinated assault by the best minds of the service's Technical division, and by nine the security barriers had been successfully breached. Ari Shamron would later boast that the Office computer geniuses cracked the code in the span of an average Italian coffee break. Decryption of the material took another hour, and by ten a printout of the disk's contents was sitting on Lev's immaculate desk. The material remained there for only a few moments, because Lev immediately tossed it into a secure briefcase and headed to Kaplan Street in Jerusalem to brief the prime minister. Shamron, of course, was at his master's side.

'Someone needs to bring him in,' said Lev. He spoke with the enthusiasm of a man offering his own eulogy. Perhaps, thought Shamron, that was precisely how he felt, for he viewed the man in question as a rival, and Lev's preferred method of dealing with rivals, real or potential, was exile. 'Pazner is heading back to Italy tonight. Let him take along a team from Extraction.'

Shamron shook his head. 'He's mine. I'll bring

him home.' He paused. 'Besides, Pazner has something more important to do at the moment.'

'What's that?'

'Telling the Italians we couldn't break the lock on that disk, of course.'

Lev made a habit of never being the first to leave the room, and so it was with great reluctance that he uncoiled himself from his chair and moved toward the exit. Shamron looked up and saw that the prime minister's eyes were on him.

'He'll have to stay here until this blows over,' the prime minister said.

'Yes, he will,' agreed Shamron.

'Perhaps we should find something for him to do to help pass the time.'

Shamron nodded once, and it was done.

3. London

The quest for Gabriel was nearly as intense as the search for the perpetrators of the massacre in Rome. He was a man who never telegraphed his movements and was no longer under Office discipline, so it surprised no one, least of all Shamron, that he'd left Venice without bothering to tell anyone where he was going. As it turned out, he'd gone to England to see his wife, Leah, who was living in a private psychiatric hospital in a secluded corner of Surrey. His first stop, however, was New Bond Street, where, at the behest of a London art dealer named Julian Isherwood, he'd agreed to attend an Old Master sale at Bonhams auction house.

Isherwood arrived first, clutching a battered attaché case in one hand and the throat of his Burberry raincoat with the other. A few other dealers were huddled in the lobby. Isherwood murmured an insincere greeting and loped off to the cloakroom. A moment later, relieved of his sodden Burberry, he took up watch near the window. Tall and precarious, he was clad in his customary auction attire, a gray chalk-stripe suit and his lucky crimson necktie. He arranged his windblown gray locks to cover his bald spot and briefly examined his own face reflected in the glass. Hungover, a stranger might have assumed, perhaps a bit drunk. Isherwood was neither. He was stone-cold sober. Sharp as his mother's tongue. He flung out his arm, pushed his French cuff from his wrist, and shot a glance at his watch. Late. Not like Gabriel. Punctual as the Nine O'clock News. Never one to keep a client cooling his heels. Never one to fall behind on a restoration – unless, of course, it was due to circumstances beyond his control.

Isherwood straightened his necktie and lowered his narrow shoulders, so that the figure peering back at him had the easy grace and confidence that seemed the birthright of Englishmen of a certain class. He moved in their circles, disposed of their collections, and acquired new ones on their behalf, yet he would never truly be one of them. And how could he? His backbone-of-England surname and lanky English bearing concealed the fact that he was not, at least technically, English at all. English by nationality and passport, yes, but German by birth, French by upbringing, and Jewish by religion. Only a handful of trusted friends knew that Isherwood had staggered into London as a child refugee in 1942 after being carried across the snowbound Pyrenees by a pair of Basque shepherds. Or that his father, the renowned Berlin art dealer Samuel Isakowitz, had ended his days on the edge of a Polish forest, in a place called Sobibor.

There was something else Julian Isherwood kept secret from his competitors in the London art world

– and from nearly everyone else, for that matter. Over the years he had done the occasional favor for a certain gentleman from Tel Aviv named Shamron. Isherwood, in the Hebrew-based jargon of Shamron's irregular outfit, was a *sayan*, an unpaid volunteer helper, though most of his encounters with Shamron had been closer to blackmail than voluntarism.

Just then Isherwood spotted a flash of leather and denim amid the fluttering mackintoshes of New Bond Street. The figure vanished for a moment, then reappeared suddenly, as though he had stepped through a curtain onto a lighted stage. Isherwood, as always, was taken aback by his unimpressive physical stature – five-eight, perhaps, a hundred and fifty pounds fully clothed. His hands were thrust into the pockets of a car-length black-leather jacket, his shoulders were slumped slightly forward. His walk was smooth and seemingly without effort, and there was a slight outward bend to his legs that Isherwood always associated with men who could run very fast or were good at football. He wore a pair of neat suede brogues with rubber soles and, despite the steady rain, carried no umbrella. The face came into focus – long, high at the forehead, narrow at the chin. The nose looked as though it had been carved from wood, the cheekbones were wide and prominent, and there was a hint of the Russian steppes in the green, restless eyes. The black hair was cropped short and very gray at the temples. It was a face of many possible national origins, and Gabriel had the linguistic gifts to put it to good use. Isherwood never quite knew who to expect when Gabriel walked through the door. He was no one, he lived nowhere. He was the eternal wandering Jew.

Suddenly he was standing at Isherwood's side. He offered no greeting, and his hands remained jammed in his coat pockets. The manners Gabriel had acquired working for Shamron in the secret world had left him ill-equipped to function in the overt one. Only when he was playing a role did he appear animated. In those rare flashes when an outsider glimpsed the real Gabriel – such as now, thought Isherwood – the man they saw was silent and sullen and clinically shy. Gabriel made people supremely uncomfortable. It was one of his many gifts.

They walked across the lobby toward the registrar's desk. 'Who are we today?' Isherwood asked sotto voce, but Gabriel just leaned over and scrawled something illegible in the logbook. Isherwood had forgotten that he was left-handed. Signed his name with his left hand, held a paintbrush with his right, handled his knife and fork with either. And his Beretta? Thankfully, Isherwood did not know the answer to that.

They climbed the stairs, Gabriel at Isherwood's shoulder, quiet as a bodyguard. His leather coat did not rustle, his jeans did not whistle, his brogues seemed to float over the carpet. Isherwood had to brush against Gabriel's shoulder to remind himself he was still there. At the top of the stairs a security guard asked Gabriel to open his leather shoulder bag. He unzipped the flap and showed him the contents: a Binomag visor, an ultraviolet lamp, an infrascope, and a powerful halogen flashlight. The guard, satisfied, waved them forward.

They entered the salesroom. Hanging from the walls and mounted on baize-covered pedestals were a hundred paintings, each bathed in carefully focused light. Scattered amid the works were roving bands of dealers – jackals, thought Isherwood, picking over the bones for a tasty morsel. Some had their faces pressed to the paintings, others preferred the long view. Opinions were being formed. Money was on the table. Calculators were producing estimates of potential profit. It was the unseemly side of the art world, the side Isherwood loved. Gabriel seemed oblivious. He moved like a man accustomed to the chaos of the souk. Isherwood did not have to remind Gabriel to keep a low profile. It came naturally to him.

Jeremy Crabbe, the tweedy director of Bonhams' Old Master department, was waiting near a French school landscape, an unlit pipe wedged between his yellowed incisors. He shook Isherwood's hand joylessly and looked at the younger man in leather at his side. 'Mario Delvecchio,' Gabriel said, and as always, Isherwood was astonished by the pitch-perfect Venetian accent.

'Ahhh,' breathed Crabbe. 'The mysterious Signore Delvecchio. Know you by reputation, of course, but we've never actually met.' Crabbe shot Isherwood a conspiratorial glance. 'Something up your sleeve, Julian? Something you're not telling me?'

'He cleans for me, Jeremy. It pays to have him look before I leap.'

'This way,' Crabbe said skeptically, and led them into a small, windowless chamber just off the main saleroom floor. The exigencies of the operation had required Isherwood to express a modicum of interest in other works – otherwise Crabbe might be tempted to let it slip to one of the others that Isherwood had his eye on a particular piece. Most of the pieces were mediocre – a lackluster Madonna and child by Andrea del Sarto, a still life by Carlo Magini, a Forge of Vulcan by Paolo Pagani – but in the far corner, propped against the wall, was a large canvas without a frame. Isherwood noticed that Gabriel's well-trained eye was immediately drawn to it. He also noticed that Gabriel, the consummate professional, immediately looked the other way.

He started with the others first and spent precisely two minutes on each canvas. His face was a mask, betraying neither enthusiasm nor displeasure. Crabbe gave up trying to read his intentions and passed the time chewing his pipe stem instead.

Finally he turned his attention to Lot No. 43, *Daniel in the Lions' Den*, Erasmus Quellinus, 86 inches by 128 inches, oil on canvas, abraded and extremely dirty. So dirty, in fact, that the cats at the edge of the image seemed entirely concealed by shadow. He crouched and tilted his head in order to view the canvas with raked lighting. Then he licked three fingers and scrubbed at the figure of Daniel, which caused Crabbe to cluck and roll his bloodshot eyes. Ignoring him, Gabriel placed his face a few inches from the canvas and examined the manner in which Daniel's hands were folded and the way one leg was crossed over the other.

'Where did this come from?'

Crabbe removed his pipe and looked into the bowl. 'A drafty Georgian pile in the Cotswolds.'

'When was it last cleaned?'

'We're not quite sure, but by the looks of it, Disraeli was prime minister.'

Gabriel looked up at Isherwood, who in turn looked at Crabbe. 'Give us a moment, Jeremy.'

Crabbe slipped from the room. Gabriel opened his bag and removed the ultraviolet lamp. Isherwood doused the lights, casting the room into pitch darkness. Gabriel switched on the lamp and shone the bluish beam toward the painting.

'Well?' asked Isherwood.

'The last restoration was so long ago it doesn't show up in ultraviolet.'

Gabriel removed the infrascope from his bag. It bore an uncanny resemblance to a pistol, and Isherwood felt a sudden chill as Gabriel wrapped his hand around the grip and switched on the luminescent green light. An archipelago of dark blotches appeared on the canvas, the retouching of the last restoration. The painting, though extremely dirty, had suffered only moderate losses.

He switched off the infrascope, then slipped on his magnifying visor and studied the figure of Daniel in the searing white glow of the halogen flashlight.

'What do you think?' asked Isherwood, squinting.

'Magnificent,' Gabriel replied distantly. 'But Erasmus Quellinus didn't paint it.'

'Are you sure?'

'Sure enough to bet two hundred thousand pounds of your money.'

'How reassuring.'

Gabriel reached out and traced his forefinger along the muscular, graceful figure. 'He was here, Julian,' he said, 'I can feel him.'

They walked to St James's for a celebratory lunch at Green's, a gathering place for dealers and collectors in Duke Street, a few paces from Isherwood's gallery. A bottle of chilled white burgundy awaited them in their corner booth. Isherwood filled two glasses and pushed one across the tablecloth toward Gabriel.

'Mazel tov, Julian.'

'Are you sure about that?'

'I won't be able to make a positive authentication until I get a look beneath the surface with infrared reflectography. But the composition is clearly based on Rubens, and I have no doubt the brushwork is his.'

'I'm sure you'll have a wonderful time restoring it.'

'Who said I was going to restore it?'

'You did.'

'I said I'd authenticate it, but I said nothing about restoring it. That painting needs at least six months of work. I'm afraid I'm in the middle of something.'

'There's one person I trust with that painting,' said Isherwood, 'and that's you.'

Gabriel accepted the professional compliment with a slight cock of his head, then resumed his apathetic examination of the menu. Isherwood had meant what he said. Gabriel Allon, had he been brought into this world under a different star, might very well have been one of his generation's finest artists. Isherwood thought of the first time they had met – a brilliant September afternoon in 1978, a bench overlooking the Serpentine in Hyde Park. Gabriel had been little more than a boy then, though his temples, Isherwood remembered, were already shot with gray. The stain of a boy who'd done a man's job, Shamron had said.

'He left the Bezalel Academy of Art in seventy-two. In seventy-five, he went to Venice to study restoration under the great Umberto Conti.'

'Umberto's the best there is.'

'So I'm told. It seems our Gabriel made quite an impression on Signore Conti. He says Gabriel's hands are the most talented he's ever seen. I would have to concur.'

Isherwood had made the mistake of asking what exactly Gabriel had been doing between 1972 and 1975. Gabriel had turned to watch a pair of lovers walking hand in hand along the edge of the lake. Shamron had absently picked a splinter from the bench.

'Think of him as a stolen painting that has been quietly returned to its rightful owner. The owner doesn't ask questions about where the painting has been. He's just happy to have it hanging on his wall again.'

Then Shamron had requested his first 'favor.'

'There's a certain Palestinian gentleman who's taken up residence in Oslo. I fear this gentleman's intentions are less than honorable. I'd like Gabriel to keep an eye on him, and I'd like you to find him some respectable work. A simple restoration, perhaps – something that might take two weeks or so. Can you do that for me, Julian?'

Isherwood was brought back to the present by the appearance of the waiter. He ordered bisque and a boiled lobster, Gabriel green salad and plain grilled sole with rice. He'd been living in Europe for the better part of the last thirty years, but he still had the simple tastes of a Sabra farm boy from the Jezreel Valley. Food and wine, fine clothing and fast cars – these things were lost on him.

'I'm surprised you were able to make it today,' Isherwood said.

'Why is that?'

'Rome.'

Gabriel kept his eyes on the menu. 'That's not my

portfolio, Julian. Besides, I'm retired. You know that.'

'*Please*,' said Isherwood in a confessional murmur. 'So what *are* you working on these days?'

'I'm finishing the San Giovanni Crisostomo altarpiece.'

'Another Bellini? You're going to make quite a name for yourself.'

'I already have.'

Gabriel's last restoration, Bellini's San Zaccaria altarpiece, had ignited a sensation in the art world and set the standard against which all future Bellini restorations would be judged.

'Isn't Tiepolo's firm handling the Crisostomo project?'

Gabriel nodded. 'I'm working exclusively for Francesco now, more or less.'

'He can't afford you.'

'I like working in Venice, Julian. He pays me enough to make ends meet. Don't worry, I'm not exactly living the way I did when I was doing my apprenticeship with Umberto.'

'From what I hear, you've been a busy boy lately. According to the rumor mill, they nearly took the San Zaccaria altarpiece away from you because you left Venice on a *personal* matter.'

'You shouldn't listen to rumors, Julian.'

'Oh, really. I also hear that you're shacked up in a palazzo in Cannaregio with a lovely young woman named Chiara.'

The sharp look, delivered over the rim of a wine-glass, confirmed for Isherwood that the rumors of Gabriel's romantic entanglement were true.

'Does the child have a last name?'

'Her family name is Zolli, and she's not a child.'

'Is it true her father is the chief rabbi of Venice?'

'He's the *only* rabbi in Venice. It's not exactly a thriving community. The war ended that.'

'Does she know about your other line of work?'

'She's Office, Julian.'

'Just promise me you're not going to break this girl's heart like all the others,' Isherwood said. 'My God, the women you've let slip through your fingers. I still have the most marvelous fantasies about that creature Jacqueline Delacroix.'

Gabriel leaned forward across the table, his face suddenly quite serious. 'I'm going to marry her, Julian.'

'And Leah?' Isherwood asked gently. 'What are you planning to do about Leah?'

'I have to tell her. I'm going to see her tomorrow morning.'

'Will she understand?'

'To be honest, I'm not sure, but I owe it to her.'

'God forgive me for saying this, but you owe it to yourself. It's time you got on with your life. I don't need to remind you that you're not a boy of twenty-five anymore.'

'You're not the one who has to look her in the eye and tell her that you're in love with another woman.'

'Forgive my impertinence. It's the burgundy talking – *and* the Rubens. Want some company? I'll drive you down.'

'No,' said Gabriel. 'I need to go alone.'

The first course arrived. Isherwood tucked into his bisque. Gabriel speared a piece of lettuce.

'What kind of fee did you have in mind for the Rubens cleaning?'

'Off the top of my head? Somewhere in the neighborhood of a hundred thousand pounds.'

'Too bad,' Gabriel said. 'For two hundred, I'd consider taking it on.'

'All right, two hundred, you bastard.'

'I'll call you next week and let you know.'

'What's stopping you from making a commitment now? The Bellini?'

No, thought Gabriel. It wasn't the Bellini. It was Rome.

The Stratford Clinic, one of the most prestigious and private psychiatric hospitals in Europe, was located an hour's drive from the center of London on a rambling old Victorian estate in the hills of Surrey. The patient population included a distant member of the British royal family and the second cousin of the current prime minister, and so the staff were accustomed to unusual demands by visitors. Gabriel passed through the front security gate after identifying himself as 'Mr Browne.'

He parked his rented Opel in the visitors' carpark

in the forecourt of the old redbrick manor house. Leonard Avery, Leah's physician, greeted him in the entrance hall, a windblown figure dressed in a Barbour coat and Wellington boots. 'Once a week I lead a select group of patients on a nature walk in the surrounding countryside,' he said, explaining his appearance. 'It's extremely therapeutic.' He shook Gabriel's hand without removing his glove and inquired about the drive from London as if he did not truly wish to know the answer. 'She's waiting for you in the solarium. She still likes the solarium the best.'

They set out down a corridor with a pale linoleum floor, Avery as though he were still pounding along a Surrey footpath. He was the only one at the hospital who knew the truth about the patient named Lee Martinson – or at least part of the truth. He knew that her true family name was Allon and that her terrible burns and near-catatonic state were not the result of a motor accident – the explanation that appeared in Leah's hospital records – but of a car bombing in Vienna. He also knew that the bombing had claimed the life of her young son. He believed Gabriel was an Israeli diplomat and did not like him.

As they walked, he provided Gabriel with a terse update on Leah's condition. There had been no change to speak of – Avery did not seem overly concerned by this. He was never one for false optimism and had always maintained low expectations about Leah's prognosis. He had been proven correct. In the thirteen years since the bombing, she had never once uttered a word to Gabriel.

At the end of the corridor was a set of double doors, with round porthole-like windows clouded by moisture. Avery opened one and led Gabriel into the solarium. Gabriel, greeted by the oppressive humidity, immediately removed his coat. A gardener was watering the potted orange trees and chatting with a nurse, an attractive dark-haired woman whom Gabriel had never before seen.

'You can go now, Amira,' Dr Avery said.

The nurse went out, followed by the gardener.

'Who's that?' Gabriel asked.

'She's a graduate of the King's College school of nursing and a specialist in the care of the acutely mentally ill. Very accomplished at what she does. Your wife is quite fond of her.'

Avery gave Gabriel an avuncular pat on the shoulder, then saw himself out as well. Gabriel turned around. Leah was seated in a straight-backed wrought-iron chair, her eyes lifted toward the dripping windows of the solarium. She wore white trousers made from flimsy institutional cotton and a high-necked sweater that helped conceal her frail body. Her hands, scarred and twisted, held a sprig of blossom. Her hair, once long and black as a raven's wing, was cropped short and nearly all gray. Gabriel leaned down and kissed her cheek. His lips fell upon cool, firm scar tissue. Leah seemed not to sense his touch.

He sat down and took hold of what remained of

Leah's left hand. He felt no life within. Her head swiveled slowly round until her eyes found his. He searched for some sign of recognition, but saw nothing. Her memory had been stolen. In Leah's mind only the bombing remained. It played ceaselessly, like a loop of videotape. All else had been erased or pushed to some inaccessible corner of her brain. To Leah, Gabriel was no more important than the nurse who had brought her here or the gardener who cared for the plants. Leah had been punished for his sins. Leah was the price a decent man had paid for climbing into the sewer with murderers and terrorists. For Gabriel, a man blessed with the ability to heal beautiful things, Leah's situation was doubly painful. He longed to strip away the scars and restore her glory. But Leah was beyond repair. Too little remained of the original.

He spoke to her. He reminded her that he was living in Venice these days, working for a firm that restored churches. He did not tell her that, occasionally, he still ran the odd errand for Ari Shamron, or that two months previously he had engineered the capture of an Austrian war criminal named Erich Radek and returned him to Israel to face justice. When finally he screwed up the nerve to tell her that he was in love with another woman and wished to dissolve their marriage so he could marry her, he could not go through with it. Talking to Leah was like talking to a gravestone. There seemed no point.

When a half hour had elapsed, he left Leah's side and poked his head into the corridor. The nurse was waiting there, leaning against the wall with her arms folded across the front of her tunic.

'Are you finished?' she asked.

Gabriel nodded. The woman brushed past and went wordlessly inside.

It was late afternoon when the flight from Heathrow Airport touched down in Venice. Gabriel, riding into town in a water taxi, stood in the cockpit with the driver, his back to the cabin door, watching the channel markers of the lagoon rising out of the mist like columns of defeated soldiers returning home from the front. Soon the edges of Cannaregio appeared. Gabriel felt a fleeting sense of tranquillity. Venice, crumbling, sagging, sodden Venice, always had that effect on him. *She's an entire city in need of restoration,* Umberto Conti had said to him. *Use her. Heal Venice, and she'll heal you.*

The taxi dropped him at the Palazzo Lezze. Gabriel walked westward across Cannaregio along the banks of a broad canal called the Rio della Misericordia. He came to an iron bridge, the only one in all of Venice. In the Middle Ages there had been a gate in the center of the bridge, and at night a Christian watchman had stood guard so that those imprisoned on the other side could not escape. Gabriel crossed the bridge and entered an underground *sottoportego*. At the other end of the passageway a broad square opened before him: the Campo di Ghetto Nuovo, the center of the ancient ghetto of Venice. At its height it had been the cramped home to more than five thousand Jews. Now only twenty of the city's four hundred Jews lived in the old ghetto, and most of those were elderly who resided in the Casa Israelitica di Riposo.

Gabriel made for the modern glass doorway at the opposite side of the square and went inside. To his right was the entrance to a small bookstore that specialized in books dealing with Jewish history and the Jews of Venice. It was warm and brightly lit, with floor-to-ceiling windows overlooking the canal that encircled the ghetto. Behind the counter, seated atop a wooden stool in a cone of halogen light, was a girl with short blond hair. She smiled at him as he entered and greeted him by his work name.

'She left about an hour ago.'

'Really? Where is she?'

The girl shrugged elaborately. 'Didn't say.'

Gabriel looked at his wristwatch. Four-fifteen. He decided to put in a few hours on the Bellini before dinner.

'If you see her, tell her I'm at the church.'

'No problem. *Ciao*, Mario.'

He walked to the Rialto Bridge. One street over from the canal he turned to the left and headed for a small terra-cotta church. He paused. Standing at the entrance of the church, in the shelter of the lunette, was a man Gabriel recognized, an Office security agent named Rami. His presence in Venice could mean but one thing. He caught Gabriel's eye and glanced toward the doorway. Gabriel slipped past and went inside.

The church was in the final stages of restoration. The pews had been removed from the Greek Cross nave and pushed temporarily against the eastern wall. The cleaning of Sebastiano del Piombo's main altarpiece was complete. Unlit, it was barely visible in the late-afternoon shadow. The Bellini hung in the Chapel of Saint Jerome, on the right side of the church. It should have been concealed behind a tarpaulin-draped scaffold, but the scaffolding had been moved aside and the painting was ablaze with harsh fluorescent lights. Chiara turned to watch Gabriel's approach. Shamron's hooded gaze remained fixed on the painting.

'You know something, Gabriel, even I have to admit it's beautiful.'

The old man's tone was grudging. Shamron, an Israeli primitive, had no use for art or entertainment of any kind. He saw beauty only in a perfectly conceived operation or the destruction of an enemy. But Gabriel took note of something else – the fact that Shamron had just spoken to him in Hebrew and committed the unpardonable sin of uttering his real name in an insecure location.

'Beautiful,' he repeated, then he turned to Gabriel and smiled sadly. 'It's a pity you'll never be able to finish it.'

4. Venice

Shamron eased his body wearily onto a church pew and, with a liver-spotted hand, motioned for Gabriel to adjust the angle of the fluorescent lights. From a metal briefcase he removed a manila envelope and from the envelope three photographs. He placed the first wordlessly into Gabriel's outstretched hand. Gabriel looked down and saw himself walking in the Campo di Ghetto Nuovo with Chiara at his side. He examined the image calmly, as if it were a painting in need of restoration, and tried to determine when it had been taken. Their clothing, the sharp contrast of the afternoon light, and the dead leaves on the paving stones of the square suggested late autumn. Shamron held up a second photo – Gabriel and Chiara again, this time in a restaurant not far from their house in Cannaregio. The third photograph, Gabriel leaving the Church of San Giovanni Crisostomo, turned his spinal cord to ice. How many times? he wondered. How many times had an assassin been waiting in the *campo* when he left work for the night?

'It couldn't last forever,' Shamron said. 'Eventually they were going to find you here. You've made too many enemies over the years. We *both* have.'

Gabriel handed the photographs back to Shamron. Chiara sat down next to him. In this setting, in this light, she reminded Gabriel of Raphael's Alba Madonna. Her hair, dark and curly and shimmering with highlights of chestnut and auburn, was clasped at the nape of her neck and spilled riotously about her shoulders. Her skin was olive and luminous. Her eyes, deep brown with flecks of gold, shone in the lamplight. They tended to change color with her mood. Gabriel, in Chiara's dark gaze, could see there was more bad news to come.

Shamron reached into the briefcase a second time. 'This is a dossier, summarizing your career, uncomfortably accurate, I'm afraid.' He paused. 'Seeing one's entire life reduced to a succession of deaths can be difficult. Are you sure you want to read it?'

Gabriel held out his hand. Shamron had not bothered to have the dossier translated from Arabic into Hebrew. The Jezreel Valley contained many Arab towns and villages. Gabriel's Arabic, while not fluent, was good enough to read a recitation of his own professional exploits.

Shamron was right – somehow his enemies had managed to assemble a tellingly complete account of his career. The dossier referred to Gabriel by his real name. The date of his recruitment was correct, as was the reason, though it credited him with killing eight members of Black September when in truth he had killed only six. Several pages were devoted to Gabriel's assassination of Khalil el-Wazir, the PLO's second-in-command, better known by his nom de guerre Abu Jihad. Gabriel had killed him inside his seaside villa in Tunis in 1988. The description of the operation had been provided by Abu Jihad's wife, Umm Jihad, who had been present that night. The entry for Vienna was terse and noteworthy for its one glaring factual error: *Wife and son killed by car bomb, Vienna, January 1991. Reprisal ordered by Abu Amar.* Abu Amar was none other than Yasir Arafat. Gabriel had always suspected Arafat's personal involvement. Until now he had never seen evidence confirming it.

He held up the pages of the dossier. 'Where did you get this?'

'Milan,' Shamron said. He then told Gabriel about the raid on the *pensione* and the computer disk found in one of the suspects' bags. 'When the Italians couldn't break the security code, they turned to us. I suppose we should consider ourselves fortunate. If they'd been able to get inside that disk they would have been able to solve a thirty-year-old Roman murder in a matter of minutes.'

Contained in the dossier was the fact that he had killed a Black September operative named Wadal Abdel Zwaiter in a Rome apartment house in 1972. It was that killing, Gabriel's first, which had caused his temples to gray virtually overnight. He handed the dossier back to Shamron.

'What do we know about the men who were hiding in that *pensione*?'

'Based on fingerprints discovered on the material

and in the room, along with the photos in the false passports, we've managed to identify one of them. His name is Daoud Hadawi, a Palestinian, born in the Jenin refugee camp. He was a ringleader during the first intifada and was in and out of prison. At seventeen he joined Fatah, and when Arafat came to Gaza after Oslo, Hadawi went to work for Al-Amn Al-Ra'isah, the Presidential Security Service. You may know that organization by its previous name, the name it used before Oslo: Force 17, Arafat's praetorian guard. Arafat's favorite killers.'

'What else do we know about Hadawi?'

Shamron reached into his coat pocket for his cigarettes. Gabriel stopped him and explained that the smoke was harmful to the paintings. Shamron sighed and carried on with his briefing.

'We were convinced he was involved in terror operations during the second intifada. We placed him on a list of wanted suspects, but the Palestinian Authority refused to hand him over. We assumed he was hiding inside the Mukata with Arafat and the rest of the senior men.' The Mukata was the name of Arafat's walled, militarized compound in Ramallah. 'But when we smashed into the Mukata during Operation Defense Shield, Hadawi was not among the men we found hiding there.'

'Where was he?'

'Shabak and Aman assumed he'd fled to Jordan or Lebanon. They turned the case file over to the Office. Unfortunately, locating Hadawi was not high on Lev's list of priorities. It turned out to be a very costly mistake.'

'Is Hadawi still a member of Force 17?'

'Unclear.'

'Does he still have links to Arafat?'

'We simply don't know yet.'

'Does Shabak think Hadawi was capable of pulling off something like this?'

'Not really. He was considered a foot soldier, not a mastermind. Rome was planned and executed by a class act. Someone very smart. Someone capable of pulling off a shocking act of terrorism on the world stage. Someone with experience in this sort of thing.'

'Like who?'

'That's what we want you to find out.'

'Me?'

'We want you to find the animals who carried out this massacre, and we want you to put them down. It will be just like seventy-two, except this time you'll be the one in command instead of me.'

Gabriel shook his head slowly. 'I'm not an investigator. I was the executioner. Besides, this isn't my war any longer. It's Shabak's war. It's the Sayaret's war.'

'They've come back to Europe,' Shamron said. 'Europe is Office turf. This *is* your war.'

'Why don't you lead the team?'

'I'm a mere adviser with no operational authority.' Shamron's tone was heavy with irony. He enjoyed playing the role of the downtrodden civil servant who'd been put out to pasture before his time, even if the reality was far different. 'Besides, Lev wouldn't hear of it.'

'And he would let *me* lead the team?'

'He doesn't have a choice. The prime minister has already spoken on the matter. Of course I was whispering in his ear at the time.' Shamron paused. 'Lev did make one demand, however, and I'm afraid I was in no position to challenge it.'

'What's that?'

'He insists that you come back on the payroll and return to full-time duty.'

Gabriel had left the Office after the bombing in Vienna. His missions in the intervening years had been essentially freelance affairs orchestrated by Shamron. 'He wants me under Office discipline so he can keep me under his control,' Gabriel said.

'His motives are rather transparent. For a man of the secret world, Lev does a terrible job covering his own tracks. But don't take it personally. It's *me* who Lev despises. You, I'm afraid, are guilty by association.'

A sudden clamor rose from the street, children running and shouting. Shamron remained silent until the noise dissipated. When he spoke again, his voice took on a new tone of gravity.

'That disk contains more than just your dossier,' he said. 'We also found surveillance photographs and detailed security analyses of several potential future targets in Europe.'

'What sorts of targets?'

'Embassies, consulates, El Al offices, major synagogues, Jewish community centers, schools.' Shamron's final word echoed in the apses of the church for a moment before dying away. 'They're going to hit us again, Gabriel. You can help us stop them. You know them as well as anyone at King Saul Boulevard.' He turned his gaze toward the altarpiece. 'You know them like the brushstrokes of that Bellini.'

Shamron looked at Gabriel. 'Your days in Venice are over. There's a plane waiting on the other side of the lagoon. You're getting on it, whether you like it or not. What you do after that is your business. You can sit around a safe flat, pondering the state of your life, or you can help us find these murderers before they strike again.'

Gabriel could muster no challenge. Shamron was right: he had no choice but to leave. Still, there was something in the self-satisfied tone of Shamron's voice that Gabriel found irritating. Shamron had been pleading with him for years to forsake Europe and return to Israel, preferably to assume control of the Office, or at least Operations. Gabriel couldn't help but feel Shamron, in his Machiavellian way, was deriving a certain satisfaction from the situation.

He stood and walked to the altarpiece. Attempting to hurriedly finish it was out of the question. The figure of Saint Christopher, with the Christ Child straddling his shoulders, still required substantial inpainting. Then the entire piece required a new coat of varnish. Four weeks minimum, probably more like six. He supposed Tiepolo would have to give it to someone else to finish, a thought that made Gabriel's stomach churn with acid. But there was something else: Israel wasn't exactly flooded with Italian Old Master paintings. Chances were he would never again touch a Bellini.

'My work is here,' Gabriel said, though his voice was heavy with resignation.

'No, your work *was* here. You're coming home' – Shamron hesitated – 'to King Saul Boulevard. To Eretz Yisrael.'

'Leah, too,' Gabriel said. 'It's going to take some time to make the arrangements. Until then, I want a man at the hospital. I don't care if the dossier says she's dead.'

'I've already dispatched a Security agent from London station.'

Gabriel looked at Chiara.

'She's coming, too,' Shamron said, reading his thoughts. 'We'll leave a team from Security in Venice as long as necessary to look after her family and the community.'

'I have to tell Tiepolo that I'm leaving.'

'The fewer people who know, the better.'

'I don't care,' said Gabriel. 'I owe it to him.'

'Do what you need to do. Just do it quickly.'

'What about the house? There are things –'

'Extraction will see to your things. By the time

they finish, there'll be no trace of you here.' Shamron, in spite of Gabriel's admonition against smoking, lit a cigarette. He held the match aloft for a moment, then ceremoniously blew it out. 'It will be as though you never existed.'

Shamron granted him one hour. Gabriel, with Chiara's Beretta in his pocket, slipped from the back door of the church and made his way to Castello. He had lived there during his apprenticeship and knew the tangled streets of the *sestière* well. He walked in a section where tourists never went and many of the houses were uninhabited. His route, deliberately circuitous, took him through several underground *sottoportegi*, where it was impossible for a pursuer to hide. Once he purposely led himself into an enclosed *corte*, from which there was only one way to enter and leave. After twenty minutes, he was certain no one was following him.

Francesco Tiepolo kept his office in San Marco, on the Viale 22 Marzo. Gabriel found him seated behind the large oaken table he used as his desk, his large body folded over a stack of paperwork. Were it not for the notebook computer and electric light, he might have been a figure in a Renaissance painting. He looked up at Gabriel and smiled through his tangled black beard. On the streets of Venice, tourists often mistook him for Luciano Pavarotti. Lately he'd taken to posing for photographs and singing a few lines of 'Non ti scordar di me' very badly.

He had been a great restorer once; now he was a businessman. Indeed, Tiepolo's was the most successful restoration firm in the entire Veneto. He spent most of his day preparing bids for various projects or locked in political battles with the Venetian officials charged with the care of the city's artistic and architectural treasures. Once a day he popped into the Church of San Crisostomo to prod his gifted chief restorer, the recalcitrant and reclusive Mario Delvecchio, into working faster. Tiepolo was the only person in the art world other than Julian Isherwood who knew the truth about the talented Signore Delvecchio.

Tiepolo suggested they walk around the corner for a glass of prosecco, then, confronted with Gabriel's reluctance to leave the office, he fetched a bottle of *ripasso* from the next room instead. Gabriel scanned the framed photographs arrayed on the wall behind the Venetian's desk. There was a new photograph of Tiepolo with his good friend, His Holiness Pope Paul VII. Pietro Lucchesi had been the Patriarch of Venice before reluctantly moving to the Vatican to become leader of the world's one billion Roman Catholics. The photo showed Tiepolo and the pope seated in the dining room of Tiepolo's gloriously restored palazzo overlooking the Grand Canal. What it didn't show was that Gabriel, at that moment, had been seated to the pope's left. Two years earlier, with a bit of help from Tiepolo, he had saved the pope's life and destroyed a grave threat to his papacy. He hoped that Chiara and the team from Extraction had found the Hanuka card the Holy Father had sent him in December.

Tiepolo poured out two glasses of the blood-red *ripasso* and slid one across the tabletop toward Gabriel. Half of his own wine disappeared in one swallow. Only in his work was Tiepolo meticulous. In all other things – food, drink, his many women – Francesco Tiepolo was prone to extravagance and excess. Gabriel leaned forward and quietly told Tiepolo the news – that his enemies had found him in Venice, that he had no choice but to leave the city immediately, *before* he could finish the Bellini. Tiepolo smiled sadly and closed his eyes.

'Is there no other way?'

Gabriel shook his head. 'They know where I live. They know where I work.'

'And Chiara?'

Gabriel answered the question truthfully. Tiepolo, in Italian, was an *uomo di fiducia*, a man of trust.

'I'm sorry about the Bellini,' Gabriel said. 'I should have finished it months ago.' He would have, were it not for the Radek affair.

'To hell with the Bellini! It's you I care about.' Tiepolo stared into his wine. 'I'm going to miss Mario Delvecchio, but I'm going to miss Gabriel Allon more.'

Gabriel raised his glass in Tiepolo's direction. 'I know I'm not in any position to ask for a favor ...' His voice trailed off.

Tiepolo looked at the photograph of the Holy Father and said, 'You saved my friend's life. What do you want?'

'Finish the Bellini for me.'

'*Me?*'

'We shared the same teacher, Francesco. Umberto Conti taught you well.'

'Yes, but do you know how long it's been since I've put a brush to a painting?'

'You'll do just fine. Trust me.'

'That's quite a vote of confidence, coming from a man like Mario Delvecchio.'

'Mario's dead, Francesco. Mario never was.'

Gabriel made his way back to Cannaregio through the gathering darkness. He took a short detour so he could walk, one final time, through the ancient ghetto. In the square, he watched proprietarily as a pair of boys, clad all in black with wispy untrimmed beards, hurried across the paving stones toward the yeshiva. He looked at his watch. An hour had elapsed since he'd left Shamron and Chiara in the church. He turned and started walking toward the house that would soon bear no trace of him, and the plane that would carry him home again. As he walked, two questions ran ceaselessly in his mind. Who had found him in Venice? And why was he being allowed to leave alive?

5. Tel Aviv: March 10

Gabriel arrived at King Saul Boulevard at eight o'clock the following morning. Two officers from Personnel were waiting for him. They wore matching cotton shirts and matching smiles – the tight, humorless smiles of men who are empowered to ask embarrassing questions. In the eyes of Personnel, Gabriel's return to discipline was long overdue. He was like fine wine, to be savored slowly and with much commentary. He placed himself in their hands with the melancholy air of a fugitive surrendering after a long time on the run and followed them upstairs.

There were declarations to sign, oaths to swear, and unapologetic questions about the state of his bank account. He was photographed and issued an identification badge, which was hung like an albatross around his neck. New fingerprints were taken because no one could seem to find the originals from 1972. He was examined by a medical doctor who, upon seeing the scars all over his body, seemed surprised to find a pulse in his wrist and blood pressure in his veins. He even endured a mind-numbing session with an Office psychologist, who jotted a few notes in Gabriel's file and hurriedly fled the room.

Motor Pool granted him temporary use of a Skoda sedan; Housekeeping assigned him a windowless cell in the basement and living accommodations until he could find a place of his own. Gabriel, who wished to maintain a buffer between himself and King Saul Boulevard, chose a disused safe flat on Narkiss Street in Jerusalem, not far from the old campus of the Bezalel Academy of Art.

At sunset he was summoned to the executive suite for the final ritual of his return. The light above Lev's door shone green. His secretary, an attractive girl with suntanned legs and hair the color of cinnamon, pressed an unseen button, and the door swung silently open under its own power like the entrance of a bank vault.

Gabriel stepped inside and paused before advancing farther. He felt a peculiar sense of dislocation, like a man who returns to his childhood bedroom only to find it turned into his father's den. The office had been Shamron's once. Gone were the scarred wooden desk and steel file cabinets and the German shortwave radio on which he had monitored the bellicose voices of his enemies. Now the motif was modern and monochrome gray. The old linoleum floor had been torn up and covered by a plush executive rug. Strategically placed around the room were several expensive-looking Oriental carpets. From high in the ceiling a recessed halogen bulb shone down upon a seating area of contemporary black leather furniture that reminded Gabriel of a first-class airport lounge. The wall nearest the seating area had been transformed into a giant plasma video display, from which the world's media flickered silently in high definition. The remote control, resting on the glass coffee table, was the size of a prayer book and looked as though it required an advanced engineering degree to operate.

Whereas Shamron had placed his desk barrier-like in front of the door, Lev had chosen to reside near the windows. The pale gray blinds were drawn but angled in such a way that it was just possible to make out the ragged skyline of downtown Tel Aviv and a large orange sun sinking slowing into the Mediterranean. Lev's desk, a large expanse of smoky glass, was vacant except for a computer and a pair of telephones. He was seated before the monitor, with his hands folded praying mantis–like beneath his defiant chin. His bald head glowed softly in the restrained light. Gabriel noted that Lev's eyeglasses cast no reflection. He wore special lenses so that his enemies – meaning anyone within the Office who opposed him – could not see what he was reading.

'Gabriel,' he said, as though surprised by his presence. He came out from behind the desk and shook Gabriel's hand carefully, then, with a bony finger pressed to Gabriel's spine like a pistol, guided him across the room to the seating area. As he was lowering himself into a chair, one of the images on the video wall caught his attention, which one

Gabriel could not tell. He sighed heavily, then turned his head slowly and studied Gabriel with a predatory gaze.

The shadow of their last meeting fell between them. It had taken place not in this room but in Jerusalem, in the office of the prime minister. There had been but one item on the agenda: whether the Office should capture Erich Radek and bring him back to Israel to face justice. Lev had steadfastly opposed the idea, despite the fact that Radek had very nearly killed Gabriel's mother during the death march from Auschwitz in January 1945. The prime minister had overruled Lev and mandated that Gabriel be placed in charge of the operation to seize Radek and spirit him out of Austria. Radek now resided in a police detention facility in Jaffa, and Lev had spent much of the last two months trying to undo the damage caused by his initial opposition to Radek's capture. Lev's standing among the troops at King Saul Boulevard had fallen to dangerously low levels. In Jerusalem, some were beginning to wonder whether Lev's time had come and gone.

'I've taken the liberty of assembling your team,' said Lev. He pressed the intercom button on the telephone and summoned his secretary. She entered the room with a file beneath her arm. Lev's meetings were always well choreographed. He adored nothing more than standing before a complicated chart, pointer in hand, and decoding its secrets for a mystified audience.

As the secretary headed toward the door, Lev looked at Gabriel to see if he was watching her walk away. Then he handed the files wordlessly to Gabriel and turned his gaze once more toward the video wall. Gabriel lifted the cover and found several sheets of paper, each containing the thumbnail sketch of a team member: name, section, area of expertise. The sun had slipped below the horizon, and the office had grown very dark. Gabriel, in order to read the file, had to lean slightly to his left and hold the pages directly beneath the halogen ceiling lamp. After a few moments he looked up at Lev.

'You forgot to add representatives from Hadassah and the Maccabee Youth Sports League.'

Gabriel's irony bounced off Lev like a stone thrown at a speeding freight train.

'Your point, Gabriel?'

'It's too big. We'll be tripping over each other.' It occurred to Gabriel that perhaps Lev wanted precisely that. 'I can carry out the investigation with half these people.'

Lev, with a languid wave of his long hand, invited Gabriel to reduce the size of the team. Gabriel began removing pages and placing them on the coffee table. Lev frowned. Gabriel's cuts, while random, had clearly dislodged Lev's informant.

'This will do,' Gabriel said, handing the personnel files back to Lev. 'We'll need a place to meet. My office is too small.'

'Housekeeping has set aside Room 456c.'

61

Gabriel knew it well. Three levels belowground, 456C was nothing more than a dumping ground for old furniture and obsolete computer equipment, often used by members of the night staff as a spot for romantic trysts.

'Fine,' said Gabriel.

Lev crossed one long leg over the other and picked a piece of invisible lint from his trousers. 'You've never worked at headquarters before, have you, Gabriel?'

'You know exactly where I've worked.'

'Which is why I feel I should give you a helpful reminder. The progress of your investigation, assuming you make any, is not to be shared with anyone outside this service. You will report to me and only me. Is that clear?'

'I take it you're referring to the old man.'

'You know exactly who I'm referring to.'

'Shamron and I are personal friends. I won't cut off my relationship with him just to put your mind at ease.'

'But you will refrain from discussing the case with him. Have I made myself clear?'

Lev had neither mud on his boots nor blood on his hands, but he was a master in the art of boardroom thrust and parry.

'Yes, Lev,' Gabriel said. 'I know exactly where you stand.'

Lev got to his feet, signaling that the meeting had ended, but Gabriel remained seated.

'There's something else I needed to discuss with you.'

'My time is limited,' said Lev, looking down.

'It won't take but a minute. It's about Chiara.'

Lev, rather than suffer the indignity of retaking his seat, walked over to the window and looked down at the lights of Tel Aviv. 'What about her?'

'I don't want her used again until we determine who else saw the contents of that computer disk.'

Lev rotated slowly, as if he were a statue on a pedestal. With the light behind him, he appeared as nothing more than a dark mass against the horizontal lines of the blinds.

'I'm glad you feel comfortable enough to walk into this office and make demands,' he said acidly, 'but Chiara's future will be determined by Operations and, ultimately, by me.'

'She's only a *bat leveyha*. Are you telling me you can't find any other girls to serve as escort officers?'

'She's got an Italian passport, and she's damned good at her job. You know that better than anyone.'

'She's also burned, Lev. If you put her in the field with an agent, you'll put the agent at risk. I wouldn't work with her.'

'Fortunately, most of our field officers aren't as arrogant as you.'

'I never knew a good field man who wasn't arrogant, Lev.'

A silence fell between them. Lev walked over to his desk and pressed a button on his telephone. The door swung open automatically, and a wedge of bright light entered from Lev's reception area.

'It's been my experience that field agents don't take well to the discipline of headquarters. In the field, they're a law unto themselves, but in here, I'm the law.'

'I'll try to keep that in mind, sheriff.'

'Don't fuck this up,' Lev said as Gabriel headed toward the open door. 'If you do, not even Shamron will be able to protect you.'

They convened at nine o'clock the following morning. Housekeeping had made a halfhearted attempt at putting the room in order. A chipped wooden conference table stood in the center, surrounded by several mismatched chairs. The excess debris had been piled against the far wall. Gabriel, as he entered, was reminded of the pews stacked against the wall of the Church of San Giovanni Crisostomo. Everything about the setting suggested impermanence, including the misleading paper sign, affixed to the door with packing tape, that read: TEMPORARY COMMITTEE FOR THE STUDY OF TERROR THREATS IN WESTERN EUROPE. Gabriel embraced the disarray. From adversity, Shamron always said, comes cohesion.

His team numbered four in all, two boys and two girls, all eager and adoring and unbearably young. From Research came Yossi, a pedantic but brilliant intelligence analyst who had read Greats at Oxford; from History, a dark-eyed girl named Dina who could recite the time, place, and butcher's bill of every act of terrorism ever committed against the State of Israel. She walked with a very slight limp and was treated with unfailing tenderness by the others. Gabriel found the reason why in her personnel file. Dina had been standing in Tel Aviv's Dizengoff Street the day in October 1994 when a Hamas suicide bomber turned the Number 5 bus into a coffin for twenty-one people. Her mother and two of her sisters were killed that day. Dina had been seriously wounded.

The two other members of the team came from outside the Office. The Arab Affairs Department of Shabak lent Gabriel a pockmarked tough named Yaakov, who had spent the better part of the last decade trying to penetrate the Palestinian Authority's apparatus of terror. Military Intelligence gave him a captain named Rimona, who was Shamron's niece. The last time Gabriel had seen Rimona, she'd been tearing fearlessly down Shamron's steep driveway on a kick scooter. These days Rimona could usually be found in a secure aircraft hangar north of Tel Aviv, poring over the papers seized from Yasir Arafat's compound in Ramallah.

Instinctively, Gabriel approached the case as though it were a painting. He was reminded of a restoration he had performed not long after his apprenticeship, a crucifixion by an early Renaissance Venetian named Cima. Gabriel, after removing the yellowed varnish, had discovered that virtually nothing remained of the original. He had then spent the next three months piecing together filaments of the obscure painter's life and work. When finally he began the retouching, it was as if Cima was standing at his shoulder, guiding his hand.

The artist, in this case, was the one member of the terrorist team who had been positively identified: Daoud Hadawi. Hadawi was their porthole onto the operation, and slowly, over the next several days, his brief life began to take shape on the walls of Gabriel's lair. It ran from a ramshackle refugee camp in Jenin, through the stones and burning tires of the first intifada, and into the ranks of Force 17. No corner of Hadawi's life remained unexplored: his schooling and his religious fervor, his family and his clan, his associations and his influences.

Known Force 17 personnel were located and accounted for. Those thought to possess the skills or education necessary to build the bomb that leveled the Rome embassy were singled out for special attention. Arab informants were called in and questioned from Ramallah to Gaza City, from Rome to London. Communications intercepts stretching two years into the past were filtered through the computers and sifted for any reference to a large-scale operation in Europe. Old surveillance and watch reports were reexamined, old airline passenger lists scoured again. Rimona returned to her hangar each morning to search for traces of Rome in the captured files of Arafat's intelligence services.

Gradually, Room 456C began to resemble the command bunker of a besieged army. There were so many photographs pinned to the walls it seemed their search was being monitored by an Arab mob. The girls from the data rooms took to leaving their deliveries outside in the corridor. Gabriel requisitioned the room next door, along with cots and bedding. He also requested an easel and a chalkboard. Yossi contemptuously pointed out that no one had seen a chalkboard inside King Saul Boulevard in twenty years, and for his impertinence he was ordered to find one. It came the next morning. 'I had to call in a lot of favors,' said Yossi. 'The stone tablets and carving tools arrive next week.'

Gabriel began each day by posing the same series of questions: Who built the bomb? Who conceived and planned the attack? Who directed the teams? Who secured the safe houses and the transport? Who handled the money? Who was the mastermind? Was there a state sponsor in Damascus or Tehran or Tripoli?

A week into the investigation, none of the questions had been answered. Frustration began to set in. Gabriel instructed them to change their approach. 'Sometimes these puzzles are solved by the piece you discover, and sometimes they're solved by finding the piece that's missing.' He stood before his chalkboard and wiped it until it was a blank slate. 'Start looking for the piece that's missing.'

*

They ate supper together each night as a family. Gabriel encouraged them to set aside the case to talk about something else. He naturally became the focus of their curiosity, for they had studied his exploits at the Academy and even read about some of them in their history books at school. He was reticent at first, but they coaxed him from his shell, and he played the role that Shamron, on countless other occasions, had played before him. He told them about Black September and Abu Jihad; his foray into the heart of the Vatican and his capture of Erich Radek. Rimona drew him out on the role restoration had played in his cover and the maintenance of his sanity. Yossi started to ask about the bombing in Vienna, but Dina, scholar of terror and counter-terror, placed a restraining hand on Yossi's arm and adroitly changed the subject. Sometimes, when Gabriel was speaking, he would see Dina gazing at him as though he were a hero's monument come to life. He realized that he, like Shamron before him, had crossed the line between mortal and myth.

Radek intrigued them the most. Gabriel understood the reason for this all too well. They lived in a country where it was not safe to eat in a restaurant or to ride a bus, yet it was the Holocaust that occupied a special place in their nightmares. *Is it true you made him walk through Treblinka? Did you touch him? How could you stand the sound of his voice in that place? Were you ever tempted to take matters into your own hands?* Yaakov wanted to know only one thing: 'Was he sorry he murdered our grandmothers?' And Gabriel, though he was tempted to lie, told him the truth. 'No, he wasn't sorry. In fact, I had the distinct impression he was still rather proud of it.' Yaakov nodded grimly, as if this fact seemed to confirm his rather pessimistic view of mankind.

On Shabbat, Dina lit a pair of candles and recited the blessing. That night, instead of wandering Gabriel's dark past, they spoke of their dreams. Yaakov wanted only to sit in a Tel Aviv café without fear of the *shaheed*. Yossi wanted to trek the Arab world from Morocco to Baghdad and chronicle his experiences. Rimona longed to turn on the radio in the morning and hear that no one had been killed the night before. And Dina? Gabriel suspected that Dina's dreams, like his own, were a private screening room of blood and fire.

After dinner Gabriel slipped from the room and wandered off down the corridor. He came to a flight of stairs, climbed them, then became disoriented and was pointed in the right direction by a night janitor. The entrance was under guard. Gabriel tried to show his new ID badge, but the Security officer just laughed and opened the door to him.

The room was dimly lit and, because of the computers, unbearably cold. The duty officers wore fleece pullovers and moved with the quiet efficiency of night staff in an intensive care ward. Gabriel climbed up to the viewing platform and leaned his weight against the aluminum handrail. Arrayed before him was a massive computer-generated map of the world, ten feet in height, thirty in width. Scattered across the globe were pinpricks of light, each depicting the last known location of a terrorist on Israel's watch list. There were clusters in Damascus and Baghdad and even in supposedly friendly places like Amman and Cairo. A river of light flowed from Beirut to the Bekaa Valley to the refugee camps along Israel's northern border. The West Bank and Gaza were ablaze. A string of lights lay across Europe like a diamond necklace. The cities of North America glowed seductively.

Gabriel felt a sudden weight of depression pushing down against his shoulders. He had given his life to the protection of the State and the Jewish people, and yet here, in this frigid room, he was confronted with the stark reality of the Zionist dream: a middle-aged man, gazing upon a constellation of enemies, waiting for the next one to explode.

Dina was waiting for him in the corridor in her stocking feet.

'It feels familiar to me, Gabriel.'

'What's that?'

'The way they carried it off. The way they moved. The planning. The sheer audacity of the thing. It feels like Munich and Sabena.' She paused and pushed a loose strand of dark hair behind her ear. 'It feels like Black September.'

'There is no Black September, Dina — not anymore, at least.'

'You asked us to look for the thing that's missing. Does that include Khaled?'

'Khaled is a rumor. Khaled is a ghost story.'

'I believe in Khaled,' she said. 'Khaled keeps me awake at night.'

'You have a hunch?'

'A *theory*,' she said, 'and some interesting evidence to support it. Would you like to hear it?'

6. Tel Aviv: March 20

They reconvened at ten that evening. The mood, Gabriel would recall later, was that of a university study group, too exhausted for serious enterprise but too anxious to part company. Dina, in order to add credence to her hypothesis, stood behind a small tabletop lectern. Yossi sat cross-legged on the floor, surrounded by his precious files from Research. Rimona, the only one in uniform, propped her sandaled feet on the back of Yossi's empty chair. Yaakov sat next to Gabriel, his body still as granite.

Dina switched off the lights and placed a photograph on the overhead projector. It showed a child, a young boy, with a beret on his head and a kaffiyeh draped over his shoulders. The boy was seated on the lap of a distraught older man: Yasir Arafat.

'This is the last confirmed photograph of Khaled al-Khalifa,' Dina said. 'The setting is Beirut, the year is 1979. The occasion is the funeral of his father, Sabri al-Khalifa. Within days of the funeral, Khaled vanished. He has never been seen again.'

Yaakov stirred in the darkness. 'I thought we were going to deal with reality,' he grumbled.

'Let her finish,' snapped Rimona.

Yaakov appealed his case to Gabriel, but Gabriel's

gaze was locked on the accusatory eyes of the child.

'Let her finish,' he murmured.

Dina removed the photograph of the child and dropped a new one in its place. Black and white and slightly out of focus, it showed a man on horseback with bandoliers across his chest. A pair of dark defiant eyes, barely visible through the small opening in his kaffiyeh, stared directly into the camera lens.

'To understand Khaled,' Dina said, 'one must first know his celebrated lineage. This man is Asad al-Khalifa, Khaled's grandfather, and the story begins with him.'

Turkish-ruled Palestine: October 1910

He was born in the village of Beit Sayeed to a desperately poor fellah who had been cursed with seven daughters. He named his only son Asad: Lion. Doted on by his mother and sisters, cherished by his weak and aging father, Asad al-Khalifa was a lazy child who never learned to read or write and refused his father's demand to memorize the Koran. Occasionally, when he wanted a bit of spending money, he would walk up the rutted track that led to the Jewish settlement of Petah Tikvah and work all day for a few piasters. The Jewish foreman was named Zev. 'It's Hebrew for wolf,' he told Asad. Zev spoke Arabic with a strange accent and always asked Asad questions about life in Beit Sayeed. Asad hated the Jews, as did everyone in Beit Sayeed, but the work wasn't backbreaking, and he was happy to take Zev's money.

Petah Tikvah made an impression on the young Asad. How was it that the Zionists, newcomers to this land, had made so much progress when most of the Arabs were still living in squalor? After seeing the stone villas and clean streets of the Jewish settlement, Asad felt ashamed when he returned to Beit Sayeed. He wanted to live well, but he knew he would never become a rich and powerful man working for the Jew named Wolf. He stopped going to Petah Tikvah and devoted his time to thinking about a new career.

One evening, while playing dice in the village coffeehouse, he heard an older man make a lewd remark about his sister. He walked over to the man's table and calmly asked if he had heard the remark correctly. 'You did indeed,' the man said. 'And what's more, the unfortunate girl has the face of a donkey.' With that the coffeehouse erupted into laughter. Asad, without another word, walked back to his table and resumed his game of dice. The next morning, the man who had insulted his sister was found in a nearby orchard with his throat slit and a shoe stuffed into his mouth, the ultimate Arab insult. A week later, when the man's brother publicly vowed to avenge the death, he too was found in the orchard in the same state. After that, no one dared insult young Asad.

The incident in the coffeehouse helped Asad find his calling. He used his newfound notoriety to recruit an army of bandits. He chose only men from his tribe and clan, knowing that they would never betray him. He wanted the ability to strike far from Beit Sayeed, so he stole a stable full of horses from the new rulers of Palestine, the British army. He wanted the ability to intimidate rivals, so he stole guns from the British as well. When his raids began they were like nothing Palestine had seen for generations. He and his band struck towns and villages from the Coastal Plain to the Galilee to the hills of Samaria and then vanished without a trace. His victims were mostly other Arabs, but occasionally he would raid a poorly defended Jewish settlement – and sometimes, if he was in the mood for Jewish blood, he would kidnap a Zionist and kill him with his long, curved knife.

Asad al-Khalifa soon became a wealthy man. Unlike other successful Arab criminals, he did not draw attention to himself by flaunting his newfound riches. He wore the galabia and kaffiyeh of an ordinary fellah and spent most nights in his family's mud-and-straw hut. To ensure his protection he spread money and loot among his clan. To the world outside Beit Sayeed, he appeared to be just an ordinary peasant, but inside the village he was now called Sheikh Asad.

He would not remain a mere bandit and highwayman for long. Palestine was changing – and from the vantage point of the Arabs, not for the better. By the mid-1930s, the Yishuv, the Jewish population of Palestine, had reached nearly a half million, compared with approximately a million Arabs. The official emigration rate was sixty thousand per year, but Sheikh Asad had heard the actual rate was far higher than that. Even a poor boy with no formal schooling could see that the Arabs would be a minority in their own country. Palestine was like a tinder-dry forest. A single spark might set it ablaze.

The spark occurred on April 15, 1936, when a gang of Arabs shot three Jews on the road east of Tulkarm. Members of the Jewish Irgun Bet retaliated by killing two Arabs not far from Beit Sayeed. Events spiraled rapidly out of control, culminating with an Arab rampage through the streets of Jaffa that left nine Jews dead. The Arab Revolt had begun.

There had been periods of unrest in Palestine, times when Arab frustration would boil over into rioting and killing, but never had there been anything like the coordinated violence and unrest that swept the land that spring and summer of 1936. Jews all across Palestine became targets of Arab rage. Shops were looted, orchards uprooted, homes and settlements burned. Jews were murdered on buses and in cafés, even inside their own homes. In Jerusalem, the Arab leaders convened and demanded an end to all Jewish immigration and the immediate installation of an Arab-majority government.

Sheikh Asad, though a thief, considered himself first and foremost a *shabab*, a young nationalist, and he saw the Arab Revolt as a chance to destroy the Jews once and for all. He immediately ceased all his criminal activities and transformed his gang of bandits into a *jihaddiyya*, a secret holy war fighting cell. He then unleashed a series of deadly attacks against Jewish and British targets in the Lydda district of central Palestine, using the same tactics of stealth and surprise he'd employed as a thief. He attacked the Jewish settlement of Petah Tikvah, where he'd worked as a boy, and killed Zev, his old boss, with a gunshot to the head. He also targeted the men he viewed as the worst traitors to the Arab cause, the effendis who had sold large tracts of land to the Zionists. Three such men he killed himself with his long, curved knife.

Despite the secrecy surrounding his operations, the name Asad al-Khalifa was soon known to the men of the Arab Higher Council in Jerusalem. Haj Amin al-Husseini, the grand mufti and chairman of the council, wanted to meet this cunning Arab warrior who had shed so much Jewish blood in the Lydda district. Sheikh Asad traveled to Jerusalem disguised as a woman and met the red-bearded mufti in an apartment in the Old City, not far from the Al-Aksa mosque.

'You are a great warrior, Sheikh Asad. Allah has given you great courage – the courage of a lion.'

'I fight to serve God,' Sheikh Asad said, then quickly added: 'And you, of course, Haj Amin.'

Haj Amin smiled and stroked his neat red beard. 'The Jews are united. That is their strength. We Arabs have never known unity. Family, clan, tribe –

that is the Arab way. Many of our warlords, like you, Sheikh Asad, are former criminals, and I'm afraid many of them are using the Revolt as a means of enriching themselves. They're raiding Arab villages and extorting tribute from the elders.'

Sheikh Asad nodded. He had heard of such things. To ensure that he maintained the loyalty of the Arabs in the Lydda district, he had forbidden his men to steal. He'd gone so far as to lop off the hand of one of his own men for the crime of taking a chicken.

'I fear that as the Revolt wears on,' Haj Amin continued, 'our old divisions will begin to tear us apart. If our warlords act on their own, they will be mere arrows against the stone wall of the British army and the Jewish Haganah. But together' – Haj Amin joined his hands – 'we can knock down their walls and liberate this sacred land from the infidels.'

'What is it you want me to do, Haj Amin?'

The grand mufti supplied Sheikh Asad with a list of targets in the Lydda district, and the sheikh's men attacked them with ruthless efficiency: Jewish settlements, bridges and power lines, police outposts. Sheikh Asad soon became Haj Amin's favorite warlord, and just as the grand mufti had predicted, other warlords grew envious of the accolades being heaped on the man from Beit Sayeed. One of them, a brigand from Nablus called Abu Fareed, decided to lay a trap. He dispatched an emissary to meet with a Jew from the Haganah. The emissary told the Jew that Sheikh Asad and his men would attack the

Zionist settlement of Hadera in three nights' time. As Sheikh Asad and his men approached Hadera that night, they were ambushed by Haganah and British forces and torn to pieces in a murderous cross fire.

Sheikh Asad, badly wounded, managed to make his way on horseback across the border into Syria. He recuperated in a village on the Golan Heights and pieced together what had gone wrong at Hadera. Obviously, he had been betrayed by someone within the Arab camp, someone who had known when and where he was going to strike. He had two choices, to remain in Syria or return to the battlefield. He had no men and no weapons, and someone close to Haj Amin wanted him dead. Returning to Palestine to fight on was the courageous thing to do, but hardly the wise course of action. He remained in the Golan for a week longer, then he went to Damascus.

The Arab Revolt was soon in tatters, torn from within, just as Haj Amin had predicted, by feuding and clan rivalries. By 1938 more Arabs were dying at the hands of the rebels than Jews, and by 1939 the situation had disintegrated into a tribal war for power and prestige among the warlords themselves. By May 1939, three years after it had begun, the great Arab Revolt was over.

Wanted by the British and Haganah, Sheikh Asad decided to remain in Damascus. He bought a large apartment in the city center and married the daughter of another Palestinian exile. She bore him a son, whom he named Sabri. She became barren after that and gave him no more children. He considered divorcing her or taking another wife, but by 1947 his thoughts were occupied by things other than women and children.

Once again Sheikh Asad was summoned by his old friend, Haj Amin. He too was living in exile. During the Second World War the mufti had thrown in his lot with Adolf Hitler. From his lavish palace in Berlin, the Islamic religious leader had served as a valuable Nazi propaganda tool, exhorting the Arab masses to support Nazi Germany and calling for the destruction of the Jews. An acquaintance of Adolf Eichmann, the architect of the Holocaust, the mufti had even planned to construct a gas chamber and crematoria in Palestine to exterminate the Jews there. As Berlin was falling, he boarded a Luftwaffe plane and flew to Switzerland. Refused entry, he went next to France. The French realized that he could be a valuable ally in the Middle East and granted him sanctuary, but by 1946, with pressure mounting to put the mufti on trial for war crimes, he was permitted to 'escape' to Cairo. By the summer of 1947 the mufti was living in Alayh, a resort in the mountains of Lebanon, and it was there that he met his trusted warlord, Sheikh Asad.

'You've heard the news from America?'

Sheikh Asad nodded. The special session of the new world body called the United Nations had convened to take up the issue of the future of Palestine.

'Clearly,' said the mufti, 'we are going to be made

to suffer for the crimes of Hitler. Our strategy for dealing with the United Nations will be a complete boycott of the proceedings. But if they decide to award one square inch of Palestine to the Jews, we must be prepared to fight. Which is why I need you, Sheikh Asad.'

Sheikh Asad asked Haj Amin the same question he'd put to him eleven years earlier in Jerusalem. 'What do you want me to do?'

'Return to Palestine and prepare for the war that is surely coming. Raise your fighting force, draw up your battle plans. My cousin, Abdel-Kader, will be responsible for the Ramallah area and the hills east of Jerusalem. You will be in command of the central district: the Coastal Plain, Tel Aviv and Jaffa, and the Jerusalem Corridor.'

'I'll do it,' Sheikh Asad said, then he quickly added: 'On one condition.'

The grand mufti was taken aback. He knew that Sheikh Asad was a fierce and proud man, but no Arab ever dared to speak to him like that, especially a former fellah. Still, he smiled and asked the warlord to name his price.

'Tell me the name of the man who betrayed me in Hadera.'

Haj Amin hesitated, then answered truthfully. Sheikh Asad was more valuable to his cause than Abu Fareed.

'Where is he?'

That night Sheikh Asad traveled to Beirut and slit

the throat of Abu Fareed. Then he returned to Damascus to bid farewell to his wife and son and see to their financial needs. A week later he was back in his old straw-and-mud cottage in Beit Sayeed.

He spent the remaining months of 1947 raising his force and planning his strategy for the coming conflict. Frontal assaults against heavily defended Jewish population centers would prove futile, he concluded. Instead, he would strike the Jews where they were most vulnerable. Jewish settlements were scattered around Palestine and dependent on the roads for supplies. In many cases, such as the vital Jerusalem Corridor, those roads were dominated by Arab towns and villages. Sheikh Asad immediately understood the opportunity before him. He could strike soft targets with complete tactical surprise; then, when the engagement was over, his forces could melt into the sanctuaries of the villages. The settlements would slowly whither, and so too would the Jewish will to remain in Palestine.

On November 29, the United Nations declared that British rule in Palestine would soon end. There were to be two states in Palestine, one Arab, the other Jewish. For the Jews, it was a night of celebration. The two-thousand-year-old dream of a state in the ancient home of the Jews had come true. For the Arabs, it was a night of bitter tears. Half of their ancestral home was to be given to the Jews. Sheikh Asad al-Khalifa spent that night planning his first strike. The following morning, his men attacked a bus as it made its way from Netanya to Jerusalem, killing five people. The battle for Palestine had begun.

Throughout the winter of 1948, Sheikh Asad and the other Arab commanders turned the roads of central Palestine into a Jewish graveyard. Buses, taxis, and supply trucks were attacked, drivers and passengers massacred without mercy. As winter turned to spring, Haganah losses in men and materiel mounted at an alarming rate. During a two-week span in late March, Arab forces killed hundreds of the Haganah's best fighters and destroyed the bulk of its fleet of armored vehicles. By the end of the month, the settlements of the Negev were cut off. More importantly, so too were the hundred thousand Jews of West Jerusalem. For the Jews, the situation was growing desperate. The Arabs had seized the initiative – and Sheikh Asad was almost single-handedly winning the war for Palestine.

On the night of March 31, 1948, David Ben-Gurion, leader of the Yishuv, met in Tel Aviv with senior officers of the Haganah and the elite Palmach strike force and ordered them to go on the offensive. The days of trying to protect vulnerable convoys against overwhelming odds were over, Ben-Gurion said. The entire Zionist enterprise faced imminent collapse unless the battle of the roads was won and the interior of the country secured. In order to achieve that goal, the conflict had to be taken to a new level of violence. The Arab villages that Sheikh

Asad and the other warlords used as bases for their operations had to be conquered and destroyed – and if there was no other option, the inhabitants had to be expelled. The Haganah had already drawn up a master plan for just such an operation. It was called Tochnit Dalet: Plan D. Ben-Gurion ordered it to begin in two days with Operation Nachshon, an assault on the villages lining the besieged Jerusalem Corridor. 'And one more thing,' he said to his commanders as the meeting adjourned. 'Find Sheikh Asad as quickly as possible – and kill him.'

The man chosen to hunt down Sheikh Asad, a young Palmach intelligence officer named Ari Shamron, knew that Sheikh Asad would not be easy to find. The warlord maintained no fixed military headquarters and was rumored to sleep in a different house each night. Shamron, though he had emigrated to Palestine from Poland in 1935, knew the Arab mind well. He knew that, to the Arabs, some things were more important than an independent Palestine. Somewhere during his rise to power, Sheikh Asad had surely made an enemy – and somewhere in Palestine was an Arab thirsting for revenge.

It took Shamron ten days to find him, a man from Beit Sayeed who, many years earlier, had lost two of his brothers to Sheikh Asad over an insult in the village coffeehouse. Shamron offered the Arab a hundred Palestinian pounds if he would betray the whereabouts of the warlord. A week later, on a hillside near Beit Sayeed, they met for a second time.

The Arab told Shamron where their common enemy could be found.

'I hear he's planning to spend the night in a cottage outside Lydda. It's in the middle of an orange grove. Asad, the murderous dog, is surrounded by bodyguards. They're hiding in the orchards. If you try to attack the cottage with a large force, the guards will sound the alert and Asad will flee like the coward that he is.'

'And what do you recommend?' Shamron asked, playing to the Arab's vanity.

'A single assassin, a man who can slip through the defenses and kill Asad before he can escape. For another one hundred pounds, I'll be that man.'

Shamron did not wish to insult his informant, so he spent a moment pretending to consider the offer, even though his mind was already made up. The assassination of Sheikh Asad was too important to be trusted to a man who would betray his own people for money. He hurried back to Palmach headquarters in Tel Aviv and broke the news to the deputy commander, a handsome man with red hair and blue eyes named Yitzhak Rabin.

'Someone needs to go to Lydda alone tonight and kill him,' Shamron said.

'Chances are whoever we select won't come out of that house alive.'

'I know,' Shamron said, 'that's why it has to be me.'

'You're too important to risk on a mission like this.'

'If this goes on much longer, we'll lose Jerusalem – and then we'll lose the war. What's more important than that?'

Rabin could see that there was no talking him out of it. 'What can I do to help you?'

'Make certain there's a car and driver waiting for me on the edge of that orange grove after I kill him.'

At midnight, Shamron climbed on a motorbike and rode from Tel Aviv to Lydda. He left the bike a mile from town and walked the rest of the way to the edge of the orchard. Such assaults, Shamron had learned from experience, were best carried out shortly before dawn, when the sentries were fatigued and at their least attentive. He entered the orchard a few minutes before sunrise, armed with a Sten gun and a steel trench knife. In the first gray light of the day, he could make out the faint shadows of the guards, propped against the trunks of the orange trees. One slept soundly as Shamron crept past. A single guard stood watch in the dusty forecourt of the cottage. Shamron killed him with a silent thrust of his knife, then he entered the cottage.

It had but one room. Sheikh Asad lay sleeping on the floor. Two of his senior lieutenants were seated cross-legged next to him, drinking coffee. Caught off guard by Shamron's silent approach, they did not react to the opening of the door. Only when they looked up and saw an armed Jew did they attempt to reach for their weapons. Shamron killed them both with a single burst of his Sten gun.

Sheikh Asad awakened with a start and reached for his rifle. Shamron fired. Sheikh Asad, as he was dying, gazed into his killer's eyes.

'Another will take my place,' he said.

'I know,' replied Shamron, then he fired again. He slipped from the cottage as the sentries came running. In the half-light of dawn he picked his way through the trees, until he came to the edge of the orange grove. The car was waiting; Yitzhak Rabin was behind the wheel.

'Is he dead?' Rabin asked as he accelerated away.

Shamron nodded. 'It's done.'

'Good,' said Rabin. 'Let the dogs lap up his blood.'

7. Tel Aviv

Dina had lapsed into a long silence. Yossi and Rimona, entranced, watched her with the intensity of small children. Even Yaakov seemed to have fallen under her spell, not because he had been converted to Dina's cause but because he wanted to know where the story was taking them. Gabriel, had he wished, could have told him. And when Dina placed a new image on the screen – a strikingly handsome man seated in an outdoor café wearing wraparound sunglasses – Gabriel saw it not in the grainy black-and-white of the photograph but as the scene appeared in his own memory: oil on canvas, abraded and yellowed with age. Dina began to speak again, but Gabriel was no longer listening. He was scrubbing away at the soiled varnish of his memory, watching a younger version of himself rushing across the bloodstained courtyard of a Parisian apartment building with a Beretta in his hand. 'This is Sabri al-Khalifa,' Dina was saying. 'The setting is the Boulevard St-Germain in Paris, the year is 1979. The photograph was snapped by an Office surveillance team. It was the last ever taken of him.'

Amman, Jordan: June 1967

It was eleven in the morning when the handsome young man with pale skin and black hair walked into a Fatah recruiting office in downtown Amman. The officer seated behind the desk in the lobby was in a foul mood. The entire Arab world was. The second war for Palestine had just ended. Instead of liberating the land from the Jews, it had precipitated yet another catastrophe for the Palestinians. In just six days the Israeli military had routed the combined armies of Egypt, Syria, and Jordan. Sinai, the Golan Heights, and the West Bank were now in Jewish hands, and thousands more Palestinians had been turned into refugees.

'Name?' the recruiter snapped.

'Sabri al-Khalifa.'

The Fatah man looked up, startled. 'Yes, of course you are,' he said. 'I fought with your father. Come with me.'

Sabri was immediately placed in a car and chauffeured at high speed across the Jordanian capital to a safe house. There he was introduced to a small, unimpressive-looking man named Yasir Arafat.

'I've been waiting for you,' Arafat said. 'I knew your father. He was a great man.'

Sabri smiled. He was used to hearing compliments about his father. All his life he had been told stories about the heroic deeds of the great warlord from Beit Sayeed, and how the Jews, to punish the villagers who had supported his father, razed the village and forced its inhabitants into exile. Sabri al-Khalifa had little in common with most of his refugee brethren. He had been raised in a pleasant district of Beirut and educated at the finest schools and universities in Europe. Along with his native Arabic, he spoke French, German, and English fluently. His cosmopolitan upbringing had made him a valuable asset to the Palestinian cause. Yasir Arafat wasn't about to let him go to waste.

'Fatah is riddled with traitors and collaborators,' Arafat said. 'Every time we send an assault team across the border, the Jews are lying in wait. If we're ever going to be an effective fighting force, we have to purge the traitors from our midst. I would think a job such as that would appeal to you, given what happened to your father. He was undone by a collaborator, was he not?'

Sabri nodded gravely. He'd been told that story, too.

'Will you work for me?' Arafat said. 'Will you fight for your people, like your father did?'

Sabri immediately went to work for the Jihaz al Razd, the intelligence branch of Fatah. Within a month of accepting the assignment, he'd unmasked twenty Palestinian collaborators. Sabri made a point of attending their executions and always personally fired a symbolic coup de grâce into each victim as a warning to those considering treason against the revolution.

After six months at the Jihaz al Razd, Sabri was summoned to a second meeting with Yasir Arafat. This one took place in a different safe house from the first. The Fatah leader, fearful of Israeli assassins, slept in a different bed every night. Though Sabri didn't know it then, he would soon be living the same way.

'We have plans for you,' Arafat said. 'Very special plans. You will be a great man. Your feats will rival even those of your father. Soon, the whole world will know the name Sabri al-Khalifa.'

'What sort of plans?'

'In due time, Sabri. First, we must prepare you.'

He was sent to Cairo for six months of intense terrorist training under the tutelage of the Egyptian secret service, the Mukhabarat. While in Cairo, he was introduced to a young Palestinian woman named Rima, the daughter of a senior Fatah officer. It seemed a perfect match, and the two were hastily married in a private ceremony attended only by Fatah members and officers of Egyptian intelligence. A month later, Sabri was recalled to Jordan to begin the next phase of his preparation. He left Rima in Cairo with her father, and though he didn't realize it at the time, she was pregnant with a son. The date of his birth was an ominous one for the Palestinians: September 1970.

For some time, King Hussein of Jordan had been

concerned about the growing power of the Palestinians living in his midst. The western portion of his country had become a virtual state within a state, with a chain of refugee camps ruled by heavily armed Fatah militants who openly flouted the authority of the Hashemite monarch. Hussein, who had lost half his kingdom already, feared he would lose the rest unless he removed the Palestinians from Jordanian soil. In September 1970 he ordered his fierce Bedouin soldiers to do precisely that.

Arafat's fighters were no match for the Bedouin. Thousands were massacred, and once more the Palestinians were scattered, this time to camps in Lebanon and Syria. Arafat wanted revenge against the Jordanian monarch and against all those who had betrayed the Palestinian people. He wanted to carry out bloody and spectacular acts of terrorism on the world stage – acts that would place the plight of the Palestinians before a global audience and quench the Palestinian thirst for revenge. The attacks would be carried out by a secret unit so the PLO could maintain the charade that it was a respectable revolutionary army fighting for the liberation of an oppressed people. Abu Iyad, Arafat's number two, was given overall command, but the operational mastermind would be the son of the great Palestinian warlord from Beit Sayeed, Sabri al-Khalifa. The unit would be called Black September to honor the Palestinian dead in Jordan.

Sabri recruited a small elite force from the best

units of Fatah. In the tradition of his father, he selected men like himself – Palestinians from notable families who had seen more of the world than the refugee camps. Next he set out for Europe, where he assembled a network of educated Palestinian exiles. He also established links with leftist European terror groups and intelligence services behind the Iron Curtain. By November 1971, Black September was ready to emerge from the shadows. At the top of Sabri's hit list was King Hussein's Jordan.

The blood flowed first in the city where Sabri had served his apprenticeship. The Jordanian prime minister, on a visit to Cairo, was gunned down in the lobby of the Sheraton Hotel. More attacks followed in quick succession. The car of the Jordanian ambassador was ambushed in London. Jordanian aircraft were hijacked and Jordanian airline offices were firebombed. In Bonn, five Jordanian intelligence officers were butchered in the cellar of a house.

After settling the score with Jordan, Sabri turned his attention to the true enemies of the Palestinian people, the Zionists of Israel. In May 1972, Black September hijacked a Sabena airlines jet and forced it to land at Israel's Lod Airport. A few days later, terrorists from the Japanese Red Army, acting on Black September's behalf, attacked passengers in the arrival hall at Lod with machine-gun fire and hand grenades, killing twenty-seven people. Letter bombs were mailed to Israeli diplomats and prominent Jews across Europe.

But Sabri's greatest terrorist triumph was still to come. Early on the morning of September 5, 1972, two years after the expulsion from Jordan, six Palestinian terrorists scaled the fence at the Olympic Village in Munich, Germany, and entered the apartment building at Connollystrasse 31, which housed members of the Israeli Olympic team. Two Israelis were killed in the initial assault. Nine others were rounded up and taken hostage. For the next twenty hours, with 900 million people around the world watching on television, the German government negotiated with the terrorists for the release of the Israeli hostages. Deadlines came and went, until finally, at 10:10 P.M., the terrorists and the hostages boarded two helicopters and took off for Fürstenfeldbrück airfield. Shortly after arriving, West German forces launched an ill-conceived and poorly planned rescue operation. All nine of the hostages were massacred by the Black Septembrists.

Jubilation swept the Arab world. Sabri al-Khalifa, who had monitored the operation from a safe flat in East Berlin, was greeted as a conquering hero upon his return to Beirut. 'You are my son!' Arafat said as he threw his arms around Sabri. 'You are my son.'

In Tel Aviv, Prime Minister Golda Meir ordered her intelligence chiefs to avenge the Munich eleven by hunting down and killing the members of Black September. Code-named Wrath of God, the operation would be led by Ari Shamron, the same man who had been given the task of ending Sheikh Asad's bloody reign of terror in 1948. For the second time in twenty-five years, Shamron was ordered to kill a man named al-Khalifa.

Dina left the room in darkness and told the rest of the story as though Gabriel were not seated ten feet away from her, at the opposite end of the table.

'One by one, the members of Black September were methodically hunted down and killed by Shamron's Wrath of God teams. In all, twelve members were killed by Office assassins, but Sabri al-Khalifa, the one Shamron wanted most, remained beyond his reach. Sabri fought back. He killed an Office agent in Madrid. He attacked the Israeli embassy in Bangkok and murdered the American ambassador to Sudan. His attacks became more erratic, as did his behavior. Arafat was no longer able to maintain the fiction that he had no connection to Black September, and condemnation rained down upon him, even from quarters sympathetic to his cause. Sabri had brought disgrace to the movement, but Arafat still doted on him like a son.'

Dina paused and looked at Gabriel. His face, lit by the glow of Sabri al-Khalifa's image on the projection screen, showed no emotion. His gaze was downward toward his hands, which were folded neatly on the tabletop.

'Would you care to finish the story?' she asked.

Gabriel spent a moment contemplating his hands before taking up Dina's invitation to speak.

'Shamron learned through an informant that Sabri kept a girl in Paris, a left-wing journalist named Denise who believed he was a Palestinian poet and freedom fighter. Sabri had neglected to tell Denise that he was a married man with a child. Shamron briefly considered trying to enroll her but gave up on the idea. It seemed the poor girl was truly in love with Sabri. So we sent the teams to Paris and put a watch on her instead. A month later, Sabri came to town to see her.'

He paused and looked up at the screen.

'He arrived at her apartment in the middle of the night. It was too dark to confirm his identity, so Shamron decided to take a chance and wait until we could get a better look at him. They stayed in the apartment making love until the late afternoon, then they went to lunch in a café on the Boulevard St-Germain. That's when we snapped that photo. After lunch they walked back to her apartment. It was still light, but Shamron gave the order to take him down.'

Gabriel lapsed into silence, and once more his gaze turned down, toward his hands. He closed his eyes briefly.

'I followed them on foot. He had his left arm around the girl's waist and his hand was shoved into the back pocket of her jeans. His right hand was in his jacket pocket. That's where he always kept his gun. He turned and looked at me once, but kept walking. He and the girl had drunk two bottles of wine over lunch – I suppose his senses weren't terribly sharp at the time.'

Another silence; then, after a glance at Sabri's face, another meditation over his hands. His voice, when he spoke again, had an air of detachment, as if he were describing the exploits of another man.

'They paused at the entrance. Denise was drunk and laughing. She was looking down, into her purse, looking for the key. Sabri was telling her to hurry up. He wanted to get her clothes off again. I could have done it there, but there were too many people on the street, so I slowed down and waited for her to find the damned key. I passed by them as she slid it into the lock. Sabri looked at me again, and I looked back. They stepped into the passageway. I turned and caught the door before it could close. Sabri and the girl were in the middle of the courtyard by now. He heard my footfall and turned around. His hand was coming out of his coat pocket and I could see the butt. Sabri carried a Stechkin. It was a gift from a friend in the KGB. I hadn't drawn my gun yet. Shamron's rule, we called it. "We do not walk around in the street like gangsters with our guns drawn," Shamron always said. "One second, Gabriel. That's all you'll have. One second. Only a man with truly gifted hands can get his gun off his hip and into firing position in one second."'

Gabriel looked around the room and held the gaze of each team member briefly before resuming.

'The Beretta had an eight-shot magazine, but I

discovered that if I packed the rounds in tightly, I could squeeze in ten. Sabri never got his gun into position. He was turning to face me as I fired. His target profile was reduced – I think my first and second shots hit him in the left arm. I moved forward and put him on the ground. The girl was screaming, hitting me across the back with her handbag. I put ten shots in him, then released the magazine and rammed my backup into the butt. It had only one round, the eleventh. One round for every Jew Sabri murdered at Munich. I put the barrel into his ear and fired. The girl collapsed over his body and called me a murderer. I went back through the passageway, out into the street. A motorcycle pulled up. I climbed on the back.'

Only Yaakov, who had seen his share of killing operations in the Occupied Territories, dared break the silence that had descended over the room. 'What do Asad al-Khalifa and his boy Sabri have to do with Rome?'

Gabriel looked at Dina, and with his eyes posed the same question. Dina removed the photograph of Sabri and replaced it with the one showing Khaled at his father's funeral.

'When Sabri's wife, Rima, heard that he'd been killed in Paris, she walked into the bathroom of her apartment in Beirut and slit her wrists. Khaled found his mother lying on the floor in a pool of her own blood. He was now an orphan, his parents dead, his clan scattered to the four winds. Arafat adopted the boy, and after the funeral, Khaled disappeared.'

'Where did he go?' asked Yossi.

'Arafat saw the child as a potent symbol of the revolution and wanted him protected at all costs. We think he shipped him off to Europe under an assumed name to live with a wealthy Palestinian exile family. What we do know is this: In twenty-five years, Khaled al-Khalifa has never resurfaced. Two years ago I asked Lev for permission to start a quiet search for him. I can't find him. It's as if he vanished into thin air after the funeral. It's as if he's dead, too.'

'And your theory?'

'I believe Arafat prepared him to follow in the footsteps of his famous father and grandfather. I believe he's been activated.'

'Why?'

'Because Arafat is trying to make himself relevant again, and he's doing it the only way he knows how, with violence and terrorism. He's using Khaled as his weapon.'

'You have no proof,' said Yaakov. 'There's a terrorist cell in Europe preparing to hit us again. We can't afford to waste time looking for a phantom.'

Dina placed a new photograph on the overhead projector. It showed the wreckage of a building.

'Buenos Aires, 1994. A truck bomb flattens the Jewish Community Center during a Shabbat meal. Eighty-seven dead. No claim of responsibility.'

A new slide, more wreckage.

'Istanbul, 2003. Two car bombs explode simultaneously outside the city's main synagogue. Twenty-eight dead. No claim of responsibility.'

Dina turned to Yossi and asked him to turn on the lights.

'You told me you had evidence linking Khaled to Rome,' Gabriel said, squinting in the sudden brightness. 'But thus far, you've given me nothing but conjecture.'

'Oh, but I do have evidence, Gabriel.'

'So what's the connection?'

'Beit Sayeed.'

They set out from King Saul Boulevard in an Office transit van a few minutes before dawn. The windows of the van were tinted and bulletproof, and so inside it remained dark long after the sky began to grow light. By the time they reached Petah Tikvah, the sun was peeking over the ridgeline of the Judean Hills. It was a modern suburb of Tel Aviv now, with large homes and green lawns, but Gabriel, as he peered out the tinted windows, pictured the original stone cottages and Russian settlers huddled against yet another pogrom, this one led by Sheikh Asad and his holy warriors.

Beyond Petah Tikvah lay a broad plain of open farmland. Dina directed the driver onto a two-lane road that ran along the edge of a new superhighway. They followed the road for a few miles, then turned into a dirt track bordering a newly planted orchard.

'Here,' she said suddenly. 'Stop here.'

The van rolled to a stop. Dina climbed down and hastened into the trees. Gabriel came next, Yossi and Rimona at his shoulder, Yaakov trailing a few paces behind. They came to the end of the orchard. Fifty yards in the distance lay a field of row crops. Between the orchard and field was a wasteland overgrown with green winter grass. Dina stopped and turned to face the others.

'Welcome to Beit Sayeed,' she said.

She beckoned them forward. It soon became apparent they were walking amid the remains of the village. Its footprint was clearly visible in the gray earth: the cottages and the stone walls, the little square and the circular wellhead. Gabriel had seen villages like it in the Jezreel Valley and the Galilee. No matter how hard the new owners of the land tried to erase the Arab villages, the footprint remained, like the memory of a dead child.

Dina stopped next to the wellhead and the others gathered round her. 'On April 18, 1948, at approximately seven o'clock in the evening, a Palmach brigade surrounded Beit Sayeed. After a brief firefight the Arab militiamen fled, leaving the village undefended. Wholesale panic ensued. And why not? Three days earlier, more than a hundred residents of Deir Yassin had been killed by members of the Irgun and Stern Gang. Needless to say, the Arabs of Beit Sayeed weren't anxious to meet a similar fate. It probably didn't take much encouragement to get them to pack their bags and flee. When the village was deserted, the Palmach men dynamited the houses.'

'What's the connection with Rome?' Yaakov asked impatiently.

'Daoud Hadawi.'

'By the time Hadawi was born this place had been wiped from the face of the earth.'

'That's true,' Dina said. 'Hadawi was born in the Jenin refugee camp, but his clan came from here. His grandmother, his father, and various aunts, uncles, and cousins fled Beit Sayeed the night of April 18, 1948.'

'And his grandfather?' asked Gabriel.

'He'd been killed a few days earlier, near Lydda. You see, Daoud Hadawi's grandfather was one of Sheikh Asad's most trusted men. He was guarding the sheikh the night Shamron killed him. He was the one Shamron stabbed before entering the cottage.'

'That's all?' asked Yaakov.

Dina shook her head. 'The bombings in Buenos Aires and Istanbul both took place on April eighteenth at seven o'clock.'

'My God,' murmured Rimona.

'There's one more thing,' Dina said, turning to Gabriel. 'The date you killed Sabri in Paris? Do you remember it?'

'It was early March,' he said, 'but I can't remember the date.'

'It was March fourth,' Dina said.

'The same day as Rome,' said Rimona.

'That's right.' Dina looked around at the remnants of the old village. 'It started right here in Beit Sayeed more than fifty years ago. It was Khaled who master-minded Rome, and he's going to hit us again in twenty-eight days.'

PART TWO
The Collaborator

8. Near Aix-en-Provence, France

'I think we may have found another one, Professor.'

Paul Martineau, crouched on all fours in the deep shadows of the excavation pit, twisted his head slowly round and searched for the origin of the voice that had disturbed his work. It fell upon the familiar form of Yvette Debré, a young graduate student who had volunteered for the dig. Lit from behind by the sharp mid-morning Provençal sun, she was a mere silhouette. Martineau had always considered her something of a well-concealed artifact. Her short dark hair and square features left the impression of an adolescent boy. Only when his eye traveled down her body – across the ample breasts, the slender waist, the rounded hips – was her remarkable beauty fully revealed. He had probed her body with his skilled hands, sifted the soil of its secret corners, and found hidden delights and the pain of ancient wounds. No one else on the dig suspected their relationship was anything more than professor and pupil. Paul Martineau was very good at keeping secrets.

'Where is it?'

'Behind the meeting house.'

'Real or stone?'

'Stone.'

'The attitude?'

'Face up.'

Martineau stood. Then he placed his palms on either side of the narrow pit and, with a powerful thrust of his shoulders, pushed himself back up to the surface. He patted the reddish Provençal earth from his palms and smiled at Yvette. He was dressed, as usual, in faded denim jeans and suede boots that were cut a bit more stylishly than those favored by lesser archaeologists. His woolen pullover was charcoal gray, and a crimson handkerchief was knotted rakishly at his throat. His hair was dark and curly, his eyes were large and deep brown. A colleague had once remarked that in Paul Martineau's face one could see traces of all the peoples who had once held sway in Provence – the Celts and the Gauls, the Greeks and the Romans, the Visigoths and Teutons, the Franks and the Arabs. He was undeniably handsome. Yvette Debré had not been the first admiring graduate student to be seduced by him.

Officially, Martineau was an adjunct professor of archaeology at the prestigious University of Aix-Marseille III, though he spent most of his time in the field and served as an adviser to more than a dozen local archaeological museums scattered across the south of France. He was an expert on the pre-Roman history of Provence, and although only thirty-five, was regarded as one of the finest French archaeologists of his generation. His last paper, a treatment on the demise of Ligurian hegemony in

Provence, had been declared the standard academic work on the subject. Currently he was in negotiation with a French publisher for a mass-market work on the ancient history of the region.

His success, his women, and rumors of wealth had made him the source of considerable professional resentment and gossip. Martineau, though hardly talkative about his personal life, had never made a secret of his provenance. His late father, Henri Martineau, had dabbled in business and diplomacy and failed spectacularly at both. Martineau, upon the death of his mother, had sold the family's large home in Avignon, along with a second property in the rural Vaucluse. He had been living comfortably on the proceeds ever since. He had a large flat near the university in Aix, a comfortable villa in the Lubéron village of Lacoste, and a small pied-à-terre in Montmartre in Paris. When asked why he had chosen archaeology, he would reply that he was fascinated by the question of why civilizations came and went and what brought about their demise. Others sensed in him a certain restiveness, a quiet fury that seemed to be calmed, at least temporarily, by physically plunging his hands into the past.

Martineau followed the girl through the maze of excavation trenches. Located atop a mount overlooking the broad plain of the Chaine de l'Étoile, the site was an *oppidum,* or walled hill fort, built by the powerful Celto-Ligurian tribe known as the Salyes. Initial excavations had concluded that the fort contained two distinct sections, one for a Celtic aristocracy and another for what was thought to be a Ligurian underclass. But Martineau had put forward a new theory. The hasty addition of the poorer section of the fort had coincided with a round of fighting between the Ligurians and the Greeks near Marseilles. On this dig, Martineau had proven conclusively that the annex had been the equivalent of an Iron Age refugee camp.

Now he sought to answer three questions: Why had the hill fort been abandoned after only a hundred years? What was the significance of the large number of severed heads, some real and some rendered in stone, that he had discovered in the vicinity of the central meeting house? Were they merely the battle trophies of a barbarian Iron Age people, or were they religious in nature, linked somehow to the mysterious Celtic 'severed head' cult? Martineau suspected the cult may have had a hand in the hill fort's rapid demise, which is why he had ordered the other members of the team to alert him the moment a 'head' was discovered – and why he handled the excavations personally. He had learned through hard experience that no clue, no matter how insignificant, could be ignored. What was the disposition of the head? What other artifacts or fragments were found in the vicinity? Was there trace evidence contained in the surrounding soil? Such matters could not be left in the hands of a graduate student, even one as talented as Yvette Debré.

They arrived at an excavation trench, about six feet in length and shoulder-width across. Martineau lowered himself in, careful not to disturb the surrounding earth. Protruding from the hard subsoil was the easily recognizable shape of a human nose. Martineau, from his back pocket, removed a small hand pick and a brush and went to work.

For the next six hours he did not rise from his pit. Yvette sat cross-legged at the edge. Occasionally she offered him mineral water or coffee, which he also refused. Every few minutes one of the other team members would wander by and inquire about his progress. Their questions were met by silence. Only the sound of Martineau's work emanated from the trench. *Pick, pick, brush, brush, blow. Pick, pick, brush, brush, blow . . .*

Slowly the face rose toward him from the depths of the ancient soil, mouth drawn in final anguish, eyes closed in death. As the morning wore on he probed deeper into the soil and found, as he had expected, that the head was held by a hand. Those gathered on the edge of the excavation trench did not realize that for Paul Martineau, the face represented more than an intriguing artifact from the distant past. Martineau, in the dark soil, saw the face of his enemy – and one day soon, he thought, he too would be holding a severed head in the palm of his hand.

The storm came down from the Rhône Valley at midday. The rain, cold and driven by a harsh wind, swept over the excavation site like a Vandal raiding party. Martineau climbed out of his trench and hastened up the hill, where he found the rest of his team sheltering in the lee of the ancient wall.

'Pack up,' he said. 'We'll try again tomorrow.'

Martineau bid them good day and started toward the carpark. Yvette detached herself from the others and followed after him.

'How about dinner tonight?'

'I'd love to, but I'm afraid I can't.'

'Why not?'

'Another dreary faculty reception,' Martineau said. 'The dean has demanded my presence.'

'Tomorrow night?'

'Perhaps.' Martineau touched her hand. 'See you in the morning.'

On the opposite side of the wall was a grassy carpark. Martineau's new Mercedes sedan stood out from the battered cars and motor scooters of the volunteers and the less noteworthy archaeologists working on the dig. He climbed behind the wheel and set out along the D14 toward Aix. Fifteen minutes later he was pulling into a parking space outside his apartment house, just off the cours Mirabeau, in the heart of the city.

It was a fine, eighteenth-century house, with an iron balcony on each window and a door on the left side of the facade facing the street. Martineau removed his post from the mailbox, then rode the small lift up to the fourth floor. It emptied into a small vestibule with a marble floor. The pair of Roman water vessels that stood outside his door were real, though anyone who asked about their origin was told they were clever reproductions.

The apartment he entered seemed more suited to a member of the Aixois aristocracy than an archaeologist and part-time professor. Originally it had been two apartments, but Martineau, after the untimely accidental death of his widower neighbor, had won the right to combine them into a single flat. The living room was large and dramatic, with a high ceiling and large windows overlooking the street. The furnishings were Provençal in style, though less rustic than the pieces at his villa in Lacoste. On one wall was a landscape by Cézanne; on another a pair of sketches by Degas. A pair of remarkably intact Roman pillars flanked the entrance to a large study, which contained several hundred archaeological monographs and a remarkable collection of original field notes and manuscripts from some of the greatest minds in the history of the discipline. Martineau's home was his sanctuary. He never invited colleagues here, only women – and lately only Yvette.

He showered quickly and changed into clean clothing. Two minutes later he was behind the wheel of the Mercedes once more, speeding along the cours Mirabeau. He did not drive toward the university. Instead, he made his way across the city and turned onto the A51 Autoroute toward Marseilles. He had lied to Yvette. It was not the first time.

Most Aixois tended to turn up their noses at Marseilles. Paul Martineau had always been seduced by it. The port city the Greeks had called Massalia was now the second largest in France, and it remained the point of entry for the majority of immigrants to the country, most of whom now came from Algeria, Morocco, and Tunisia. Divided roughly in half by the thunderous boulevard de la Canebière, it had two distinct faces. South of the boulevard, on the edge of the old port, lay a pleasant French city with broad pedestrian walks, exclusive shopping streets, and esplanades dotted with outdoor cafés. But to the north were the districts known as Le Panier and the Quartier Belsunce. Here it was possible to walk the pavements and hear only Arabic. Foreigners and native Frenchmen, easy prey for street criminals, rarely strayed into the Arab neighborhoods after dark.

Paul Martineau had no such misgivings about his security. He left his Mercedes on the boulevard d'Anthènes, near the base of the steps that led to the St-Charles train station, and set out down the hill toward rue de la Canebière. Before reaching the thoroughfare he turned right, into a narrow street called the rue des Convalescents. Barely wide enough to accommodate a car, it sloped downward toward the port, into the heart of the Quartier Belsunce.

It was dark in the street, and Martineau, at his back, felt the first gusts of a mistral. The night air smelled of charcoal smoke and turmeric and faintly of honey. A pair of old men, seated on spindly chairs outside the doorway of a tenement house, shared a hubble-bubble water pipe and studied Martineau indifferently as he trod past. A moment later a soccer ball, deflated and nearly the color of the pavement, bounded toward him out of the darkness. Martineau put a foot on it and sent it adroitly back in the direction from which it came. It was scooped up by a sandaled boy, who, upon seeing the tall stranger in Western clothes, turned and vanished into the mouth of an alleyway. Martineau had a vision of himself, thirty years earlier. *Charcoal smoke, turmeric, honey* ... For an instant he felt as though he was walking the streets of south Beirut.

He came to the intersection of two streets. On one corner was a *shwarma* stand, on another a tiny café that promised Cuisine Tunisienne. A trio of teenage boys eyed Martineau provocatively from the doorway of the café. In French he wished them good evening, then lowered his gaze and turned to the right.

The street was narrower than the rue des Convalescents, and most of the pavement was consumed by market stalls filled with cheap carpets and aluminum pots. At the other end was an Arab coffeehouse. Martineau went inside. At the back of the coffeehouse, near the toilet, was a narrow flight of unlit stairs. Martineau climbed slowly upward through the gloom. At the top was a door. As Martineau approached, it swung open suddenly. A man, clean-shaven and dressed in a galabia gown, stepped onto the landing.

'*Maa-salaamah,*' he said. Peace be upon you.

'*As-salaam alaykum,*' replied Martineau, as he slipped past the man and entered the apartment.

9. Jerusalem

Jerusalem is quite literally a city on a hill. It stands high atop the Judean Mountains and is reached from the Coastal Plain by a staircase-like road that climbs through the twisting mountain gorge known as the Sha'ar Ha'Gai. Gabriel, like most Israelis, still referred to it by its Arab name, the Bab al-Wad. He lowered the window of his Office Skoda and rested his arm in the opening. The evening air, cool and soft and scented with cypress and pine, tugged at his shirtsleeve. He passed the rusted carcass of an armored personnel carrier, a memorial relic of the fighting in 1948, and thought of Sheikh Asad and his campaign to sever the lifeline to Jerusalem.

He switched on the radio, hoping to find a bit of music to take his mind off the case, but instead heard a bulletin that a suicide bomber had just struck a bus in the affluent Jerusalem neighborhood of Rehavia. He listened to the updates for a time; then, when the somber music began, he switched off the radio. Somber music meant fatalities. The more music, the higher the number of dead.

Highway One changed suddenly from a four-lane motorway into a broad urban boulevard, the famed Jaffa Road that ran from the northwest corner of

Jerusalem to the walls of the Old City. Gabriel followed the road to the left, then down a long, gentle sweep, past the chaotic New Central Bus Station. In spite of the bombing, commuters streamed across the road toward the entrance. Most had no choice but to board their bus and hope that tonight the roulette ball didn't land on their number.

He passed the entrance of the sprawling Makhane Yehuda Market. An Ethiopian girl in police uniform stood watch at a metal barricade, checking the bag of each person who entered. When Gabriel stopped for a traffic light, clusters of black-coated Haredi men drifted between the cars like swirling leaves.

A series of turns brought him to Narkiss Street. There were no parking spaces to be had, so he left the car around the corner and walked slowly back to his apartment beneath the protective awning of the eucalyptus trees. He had a bittersweet memory of Venice, of gliding home upon the silken waters of a canal and tying his boat to the dock at the back of his house.

The Jerusalem limestone apartment block was set back a few meters from the street and reached by a cement walkway through a tangled little garden. The foyer was lit by a greenish light and smelled heavily of new oil-based paint. He didn't bother checking the mailbox – no one knew he lived there, and the utility bills went directly to an ersatz property management company run by Housekeeping.

The block contained no elevator. Gabriel climbed

the cement stairs wearily to the fourth floor and opened the door. The flat was large by Israeli standards – two bedrooms, a galley kitchen, a small study off the combination living room and dining room – but a far cry from the *piano nobile* of Gabriel's canal house in Venice. Housekeeping had offered to sell it to him. The value of Jerusalem apartments seemed to sink with each suicide bombing, and at the moment it could be had for a good price. Chiara had decided not to wait for a deed to make it her own. With little else to do, she spent much of her time shopping and was steadily turning the functional but cheerless place into something like a home. A new rug had appeared since Gabriel had been home; so had a circular brass coffee table with a lacquered wood pedestal. He hoped she'd bought it somewhere reputable and not from one of those hucksters who sold Holy Land air in a bottle.

He called Chiara's name but received only silence in reply. He wandered down the hall to their bedroom. It had been furnished for operatives rather than lovers. Gabriel had pushed the twin beds together, but invariably he would awaken in the middle of the night to find himself falling into the crevasse, clinging to the edge of the precipice. At the foot of the bed rested a small cardboard box. Chiara had packed away most of their things; this was all that remained. He supposed the psychologist at King Saul Boulevard would have read deep analytical insight into his failure to unpack the box.

The truth was far more prosaic – he'd been too busy at work. Still, it was depressing to think that his entire life could fit into this box, just as it is hard to fathom a small metallic urn can contain the ashes of a human being. Most of the things weren't even his. They'd belonged to Mario Delvecchio, a role he had played for some time to moderate acclaim.

He sat down and with his thumbnail sliced open the packing tape. He was relieved to find a small wooden case, the traveling restoration kit containing pigments and brushes that Umberto Conti had given him as a gift at the end of his apprenticeship. The rest was mainly rubbish, things with which he should have parted long ago: old check stubs, notes on restorations, a harsh review he'd received in an Italian art magazine for his work on Tintoretto's *Christ on the Sea of Galilee*. He wondered why he'd bothered to read it, let alone keep it.

At the bottom of the box he found a manila envelope no bigger than a checkbook. He loosened the flap and turned the envelope over. Out fell a pair of eyeglasses. They had belonged to Benjamin Stern, a former Office agent who'd been murdered. Gabriel could still make out Benjamin's oily fingerprints on the dirty lenses.

He started to place the glasses back into the envelope but noticed something lodged at the bottom. He turned it over and tapped on the base. An object fell to the floor, a strand of leather on which hung a piece of red coral shaped like a hand.

Just then he heard Chiara's footfalls on the landing. He scooped up the talisman and slipped it into his pocket.

By the time he arrived in the front room, she'd managed to get the door open and was in the process of carrying several bags of groceries over the threshold. She looked up at Gabriel and smiled, as though surprised to find him there. Her dark hair was braided into a heavy plait, and the early spring Mediterranean sun had left a trace of color across her cheeks. She looked to Gabriel like a native-born Sabra. Only when she spoke Hebrew with her outrageous Italian accent did she betray her country of origin. Gabriel no longer spoke to her in Italian. Italian was the language of Mario, and Mario was dead. Only in bed did they speak to each other in Italian, and that was a concession to Chiara, who believed Hebrew was not a proper language for lovers.

Gabriel closed the door and helped carry the plastic bags of groceries into the kitchen. They were mismatched, some white, some blue, a pinkish bag bearing the name of a well-known kosher butcher. He knew Chiara once again had ignored his admonition to stay out of the Makhane Yehuda Market.

'Everything is better there, especially the produce,' she said defensively, reading the look of disapproval on his face. 'Besides, I like the atmosphere. It's so intense.'

'Yes,' Gabriel agreed. 'You should see it when a bomb goes off.'

'Are you saying that the great Gabriel Allon is afraid of suicide bombers?'

'Yes, I am. You can't stop living, but there are sensible things you can do. How did you get home?'

Chiara looked at him sheepishly.

'Damn it, Chiara!'

'I couldn't find a cab.'

'Do you know a bus was just bombed in Rehavia?'

'Of course. We heard the explosion inside Makhane Yehuda. That's why I decided to take the bus home. I figured the odds were in my favor.'

Such macabre calculations, Gabriel knew, were a daily facet of modern Israeli life.

'From now on, take bus number eleven.'

'Which one is that?'

He pointed two fingers toward the floor and moved them in a walking motion.

'Is that an example of your fatalistic Israeli sense of humor?'

'You have to have a sense of humor in this country. It's the only way to keep from going crazy.'

'I liked you better when you were an Italian.' She pushed him gently from the kitchen. 'Go take a shower. We're having guests for dinner.'

Ari Shamron had alienated all those who loved him most. He had wagered, foolishly as it turned out, that his lifelong commitment to the defense of his country granted him immunity when it came to his children and his friends. His son, Yonatan, was a tank commander in the Israel Defense Forces and seemed gripped by an almost suicidal need to die in battle. His daughter had moved to New Zealand and was living on a chicken farm with a gentile. She avoided his calls and refused his repeated demands to return to the land of her birth.

Only Gilah, his long-suffering wife, had remained faithfully at his side. She was as calm as Shamron was temperamental and blessed with a myopic ability to see only the good in him. She was the only person who ever dared to scold him, though to spare him needless embarrassment she usually did so in Polish – as she did when Shamron tried to light a cigarette at the dinner table after finishing his plate of roasted chicken and rice pilaf. She knew only the vaguest details of her husband's work and suspected his hands were unclean. Shamron had spared her the worst, for he feared that Gilah, if she knew too much, would abandon him the way his children had. She viewed Gabriel as a restraining influence and treated him kindly. She also sensed that Gabriel loved Shamron in the turbulent way in which a son loves a father, and she loved him in return. She did not know that Gabriel had killed men on orders from her husband. She believed he was a clerk of some sort who had spent a great deal of time in Europe and knew much about art.

Gilah helped Chiara with the dishes while Gabriel and Shamron adjourned to the study to talk. Shamron, shielded from Gilah's gaze, lit a cigarette.

Gabriel opened the window. Night rain beat a gentle rhythm on the street, and the sharp scent of wet eucalyptus leaves filled the room.

'I hear you're chasing Khaled,' Shamron said.

Gabriel nodded. He had briefed Lev on Dina's findings that morning, and Lev had immediately gone to Jerusalem to see the prime minister and Shamron.

'To be honest with you, I never put much stock in the Khaled myth,' Shamron said. 'I always assumed the boy had changed his name and had chosen to live out his life free from the shadow of his grandfather and father – free of the shadow of this land.'

'So did I,' said Gabriel, 'but the case is compelling.'

'Yes, it is. Why didn't anyone ever make the connection between the dates of Buenos Aires and Istanbul?'

'It was assumed to be a coincidence,' Gabriel said. 'Besides, there wasn't enough evidence to close the circle. No one ever thought to look at Beit Sayeed until now.'

'She's very good, this girl Dina.'

'I'm afraid it's something of an obsession with her.'

'You're referring to the fact she was at Dizengoff Square the day the Number Five exploded?'

'How did you know that?'

'I took the liberty of reviewing the personnel files of your team. You chose well.'

'She knows a lot about you, including a few things you never told me.'

'Such as?'

'I never knew it was Rabin who drove the getaway car after you killed Sheikh Asad.'

'We were very close after that, Rabin and I, but I'm afraid we parted company over Oslo. Rabin believed that Arafat was down and that it was time to strike a deal. I told him Arafat was striking a deal *because* he was down, that Arafat intended to use Oslo as a way to wage war against us by other means. I was right, of course. For Arafat, Oslo was just another step in his "phased strategy" to bring about our destruction. He said so in his own words, when he was speaking in Arabic to his people.'

Shamron closed his eyes. 'I take no satisfaction in being proven correct. Rabin's death was a terrible blow to me. His opponents called him a traitor and a Nazi, and then they killed him. We *murdered* one of our own. We succumbed to the Arab disease.' He shook his head slowly. 'Still, I suppose it was all necessary, this delusional attempt to make peace with our sworn enemies. It's steeled our spine for the steps we'll need to take if we are to survive in this land.'

The next subject, the demolition of Beit Sayeed, Gabriel approached with great caution.

'It was a Palmach operation, was it not?'

'What exactly do you want to know, Gabriel?'

'Were you there?'

Shamron exhaled heavily, then nodded once. 'We had no choice. Beit Sayeed was a base of operations for Sheikh Asad's militia. We couldn't leave such a hostile village in our midst. After the sheikh's death, it was necessary to deal the remnants of his force a fatal blow.'

Shamron's gaze grew suddenly distant. Gabriel could see he wished to discuss the matter no further. Shamron drew heavily on his cigarette, then told Gabriel about the premonition of disaster he'd had the night before the bombing. 'I knew it was something like this. I could feel it the moment it happened.' Then he corrected himself. 'I could feel it *before* it happened.'

'If Khaled is trying to punish us, why didn't he kill me in Venice when he had the chance?'

'Maybe he intended to. Daoud Hadawi was only a few miles up the road in Milan when the Italians found him. Maybe Hadawi was the one who was supposed to kill you.'

'And Rome?' Gabriel asked. 'Why did Khaled choose Rome?'

'Maybe it was because Rome served as the European headquarters of Black September.' Shamron looked at Gabriel. 'Or maybe he was trying to speak directly to you.'

Wadal Abdel Zwaiter, thought Gabriel. *The Piazza Annabaliano.*

'Keep in mind something else,' Shamron said. 'Within a week of the bombing, there was a massive demonstration in central Rome, not against *Palestinian* terror, but against *us*. The Europeans are the best friends the Palestinians have. The civilized world has abandoned us to our fate. We would never have come back to this land if we weren't pushed here by the hatred of Europe's Christians, and now that we're here, they won't let us fight, lest we antagonize the Arabs in their midst.'

A silence fell between them. From the kitchen came the clatter of china and the gentle laughter of the women. Shamron sank lower into his chair. The patter of the rain and the strong scent of the eucalyptus trees seemed to have the effect of a sedative on him.

'I brought some papers for you to sign,' he said.

'What sort of papers?'

'The kind that will quietly dissolve your marriage to Leah.' Shamron placed a hand on Gabriel's forearm. 'It's been fourteen years. She's lost to you. She's never coming back. It's time for you to get on with your life.'

'It's not as easy as that, Ari.'

'I don't envy you,' Shamron said. 'When are you planning to bring her home?'

'Her doctor is opposed to the idea. He's concerned that being back in Israel will only make her condition worse. I finally managed to convey to him that it's nonnegotiable, but he's insisting she be given adequate time to prepare for the transition.'

'When?'

'A month,' Gabriel said. 'Maybe a bit less.'

'Tell her doctor she'll be well cared for here.

Unfortunately, we have a fair amount of experience when it comes to treating the victims of terrorist bombs.'

Shamron abruptly changed course. 'Are you comfortable in this flat?'

Gabriel indicated that he was.

'It's big enough for a child or two.'

'Let's not get carried away, Ari. I'll never see fifty again.'

'Chiara will want children, if you marry, of course. Besides, you have to do your patriotic duty. Haven't you heard about the demographic threat? Soon we'll be a minority people between the River Jordan and the sea. The prime minister is encouraging all of us to contribute by having more children. Thank God for the Haredim. They're the only reason we're still in the game.'

'I'll try to contribute in other ways.'

'It's yours, you know,' Shamron said.

'What?'

'The flat.'

'What are you talking about?'

'You own it now. It was purchased on your behalf by a friend of the Office.'

Gabriel shook his head. He had always been amazed at Shamron's gangster-like access to money.

'I can't accept it.'

'It's too late. The deed is being sent over in the morning.'

'I don't want to be in anyone's debt.'

'It is we who are in your debt. Accept it graciously and in the spirit with which it is given.' Shamron patted Gabriel's shoulder. 'And fill it with children.'

Gilah poked her head around the half-open door. 'Dessert is on the table,' she said, then she looked at Shamron and, in Polish, ordered him to put out his cigarette.

'April eighteenth,' he murmured, when Gilah had gone. 'That's not much time.'

'I'm already watching the clock.'

'It's occurred to me there's one person who might know where Khaled is.'

'Arafat?'

'He *is* Khaled's father. Besides, he owes you a favor. You did save his life once.'

'Yasir Arafat is the last person I want to see. Besides, he's a liar.'

'Yes, but sometimes his lies can lead us in the direction of the truth.'

'He's off-limits. Lev would never grant me authorization.'

'So don't tell him.'

'I don't think it would be wise for me to just show up and knock on Arafat's front door. And the only way I'm going to Ramallah is in an armored personnel carrier.'

'Arafat doesn't really have a door. The IDF took care of that.' Shamron permitted himself to smile at the sinking fortunes of his old adversary. 'As for the armored car, leave that to me.'

Gabriel climbed into bed and inched carefully toward the middle. He reached out in the darkness and draped his arm across Chiara's abdomen. She remained motionless.

'What were you and Ari talking about in the study?'

'The case,' he replied absently.

'Is that all?'

He told her that the apartment was now theirs.

'How did that happen?'

'Shamron and his moneyed friends. I'll tell House-keeping to remove the old furniture. Tomorrow, you can buy us a proper bed.'

Chiara's arm rose slowly. Gabriel, in the darkness, could see the talisman swinging from her fingertips.

'What is this?'

'A Corsican good-luck charm. They say it wards off the evil eye.'

'Where did you get it?'

'It's a long story.'

'Tell me.'

'It's classified.'

He reached for the talisman. Chiara, with a deft movement of her hand, twirled the talisman so that it wrapped securely around her fingertips, in the manner in which Arabs often toy with their prayer beads.

'A gift from one of your old lovers?' she asked.

'An old enemy, actually. A man who'd been hired to kill me and a woman I was protecting.'

'Anna Rolfe?'

Yes, Gabriel said, Anna Rolfe.

'Why did you keep it?' she asked. 'To remind you of her?'

'Chiara, don't be ridiculous.'

She tossed the talisman in his direction. The red-coral hand landed on his chest.

'Is something wrong, Chiara?'

'What were those papers that Shamron gave you before he left tonight? Or is that classified, too?'

Gabriel answered the question truthfully.

'Did you sign them yet?'

'I thought I should read them first.'

'You know what they say.'

'I'll sign them,' Gabriel said.

'When?'

'When I'm ready to sign them.'

Just then the apartment block shook with the clap of a thunderous explosion. Chiara climbed out of bed and rushed to the window. Gabriel remained motionless on the bed.

'It's close,' she said.

'Ben Yehuda Mall, I'd say. Probably a café.'

'Turn on the radio.'

'Just count the sirens, Chiara. You can tell how bad it is by the number of ambulances they call.'

A moment passed, still and deathly quiet. Gabriel

131

closed his eyes and imagined, with the clarity of videotape, the nightmare taking place a few blocks from his new home. The first siren sounded, then a second, a third, a fourth. After seventeen, he lost count, for the night had become a symphony of sirens. Chiara returned to bed and clung to his chest.

'Sign the papers when you're ready,' she said. 'I'll be here. I'll always be here.'

10. Jerusalem: March 22

The army colonel waiting near the walls of the Old City did not look much like Ari Shamron, but then Gabriel did not find this at all surprising. There was something about Israel – the sunlight, the intense social cohesiveness, the crackling tension of the atmosphere – that had the power to dramatically alter the appearance of its citizenry even within the space of a single generation. Yonatan Shamron was six inches taller than his famous father, strikingly handsome, and possessed none of the old man's natural physical defensiveness – a result, Gabriel knew, of having been raised here instead of Poland. Only when the colonel leapt from the armored jeep and advanced on Gabriel with his hand out like a trench knife did Gabriel catch a faint glimpse of Shamron the Elder. His gait was not so much a walk as a death charge, and when he shook Gabriel's hand fiercely and clapped him between the shoulder blades, Gabriel felt as though he'd been struck by a chunk of Herodion stone.

They set out along Road Number One, the old border between East and West Jerusalem. Ramallah, the nominal seat of Palestinian power, lay just ten miles to the north. A checkpoint appeared before them. On the opposite side lay the Kalandiya refugee camp — ten thousand Palestinians piled into a few hundred square yards of breeze-block apartments. To the right, spread over a small hill, were the orderly red roofs of the Psagot Jewish settlement. Rising above it all was an enormous portrait of Yasir Arafat. The inscription, in Arabic, read: ALWAYS WITH YOU.

Yonatan jerked his thumb toward the backseat and said, 'Put those things on.'

Gabriel, looking over his shoulder, saw an armored vest with a high collar and a metal combat helmet. He'd not worn a helmet since his brief stint in the IDF. The one Yonatan had brought along was too big, and it fell forward over his eyes. 'Now you look like a *real* soldier,' Yonatan said. Then he smiled. 'Well, almost.'

An infantryman waved them through the checkpoint, then, seeing who was behind the wheel, smiled and said, 'Hey, Yonatan.' Discipline within the ranks of the IDF, like the Office, was notoriously lax. First names were the norm, and a salute was almost unheard of.

Gabriel, through his cloudy bulletproof window, studied the scene on the other side of the checkpoint. A pair of soldiers, weapons leveled, were ordering men to open their coats and lift their shirts to make certain they weren't wearing bomb belts beneath their clothing. Women underwent the same search behind a barrier that shielded them from the eyes of their men. Beyond the checkpoint snaked a line several hundred yards in length – a wait, Gabriel calculated, of three to four hours. The suicide bombers had inflicted misery on both sides of the Green Line, but it was the honest Palestinians – the workers trying to get to jobs in Israel, the farmers who wanted only to sell their produce – who had paid the highest price in sheer inconvenience.

Gabriel looked beyond the checkpoint, toward the Separation Fence.

'What do you think of it?' Yonatan asked.

'It's certainly nothing to be proud of.'

'I think it's an ugly scar across this beautiful land of ours. It's our new Wailing Wall, much longer than the first, and different because now people are wailing on both sides of the wall. But I'm afraid we have no other choice. With good intelligence we've managed to stop most of the suicide attacks, but we'll never be able to stop them all. We *need* this fence.'

'But it's not the only reason we're building it.'

'That's true,' Yonatan said. 'When it's finished, it will allow us to turn our backs on the Arabs and walk away. That's why they're so afraid of it. It's in their interest to remain chained to us in conflict. The wall will let us disengage, and that's the last thing they want.'

Road Number One turned to Highway 60, a ribbon of smooth black asphalt that ran northward through the dusty gray landscape of the West Bank. More than thirty years had passed since Gabriel had last been to Ramallah. Then, as now, he had come by way of armored vehicle, with an IDF helmet on his head. Those early years of the occupation had been relatively calm – indeed, Gabriel's biggest challenge each week had been finding a ride from his post back home to his mother's house in the Jezreel Valley. For most West Bank Arabs, the end of Jordanian occupation had led to a marked improvement in the quality of their lives. With the Israelis had come access to a vibrant economy, running water, electricity, and education. Infant mortality rates, once among the highest in the world, plummeted. Literacy rates, among the world's lowest, increased dramatically. Radical Islam and the influence of the PLO would eventually turn the West Bank into a seething cauldron and place IDF soldiers in daily confrontations with rock-throwing children, but for Gabriel, army service had been largely an exercise in boredom.

'So you're going to see the Irrelevant One,' said Yonatan, intruding on Gabriel's thoughts.

'Your father arranged a meeting for me.'

'The man's seventy-five years old, and he's still pulling the strings like a puppet master.' Yonatan smiled and shook his head. 'Why doesn't he just retire and take it easy?'

'He'd go insane,' said Gabriel. 'And so would your poor mother. He asked me to say hello to you, by the way. He'd like you to come to Tiberias for Shabbat.'

'I'm on duty,' Yonatan said hastily.

Duty, it seemed, was Yonatan's ready-made excuse

to avoid spending time with his father. Gabriel was reluctant to involve himself in the tangled internal disputes of the Shamron family, yet he knew how badly the old man had been hurt by the estrangement of his children. He had a selfish motive for intervention as well. If Yonatan were a larger presence in Shamron's life, it might relieve some of the pressure on Gabriel. Now that Gabriel was living in Jerusalem instead of Venice, Shamron felt free to telephone at all hours to swap Office gossip or dissect the latest political developments. Gabriel needed his space back. Yonatan, if skillfully handled, could act as a sort of Separation Fence.

'He wants to see more of you, Yonatan.'

'I can only take him in small doses.' Yonatan took his eyes from the road a moment to look at Gabriel. 'Besides, he always liked you better.'

'You know that's not true.'

'All right, so it's a bit of an exaggeration. But it's not all that far from the truth. He certainly thinks of you as a son.'

'Your father's a great man.'

'Yes,' Yonatan said, 'and great men are hard on their sons.'

Gabriel glimpsed a pair of large tan-colored armored personnel carriers parked ahead of them at the edge of the road. 'It's best not to enter town without a bit of muscle,' Yonatan said. They formed a small convoy, with Yonatan's jeep in the middle position, and drove on.

The first evidence of the approaching city was the stream of Arabs walking along the edge of the highway. The *hijabs* of the women fluttered like pennants in the midday breeze. Then Ramallah, low and drab, rose out of the arid landscape. Jerusalem Street bore them into the heart of the city. The faces of the 'martyrs' glared at Gabriel from every passing lamppost. There were streets named for the dead, squares and markets for the dead. A kiosk dispensed key chains with faces of the dead attached. An Arab moved among the traffic, hawking a martyrs' calendar. The newest posters bore the seductive image of a beautiful young girl, the Arab teenager who had detonated herself in the Ben Yehuda Mall two nights previously.

Yonatan turned right into Broadcast Street and followed it for about a mile, until they reached a roadblock manned by a half-dozen Palestinian Security officers. Ramallah was technically under Palestinian control again. Gabriel had come at the invitation of the Authority's president, the equivalent of entering a Sicilian village with the blessing of the local don. There was little tension in evidence as Yonatan, in fluent Arabic, spoke to the leader of the Palestinian detail.

Several minutes elapsed while the Palestinian consulted with his superiors over a handheld radio. Then he tapped the roof of the jeep and waved them forward. 'Slowly, Colonel Shamron,' he cautioned. 'Some of these boys were here the night the Egoz

Battalion broke down the gate and started shooting up the place. We wouldn't want there to be any misunderstandings.'

Yonatan weaved his way through a maze of concrete barriers, then accelerated gently. A cement wall, about twelve feet in height and pockmarked by heavy-caliber machine-gun fire, appeared on their right. In places it had been knocked down, so that the effect was of a mouth of bad teeth. Palestinian security units, some in pickup trucks, others in jeeps, patrolled the perimeter. They eyed Gabriel and Yonatan provocatively but kept their weapons down. Yonatan braked to a halt at the entrance. Gabriel removed his helmet and body armor.

Yonatan asked, 'How long will you be?'

'That depends on him, I suppose.'

'Prepare yourself for a tirade. He's usually in a foul mood these days.'

'Who could blame him?'

'He has only himself to blame, Gabriel, remember that.'

Gabriel opened the door and climbed out. 'Are you going to be all right here alone?'

'No problem,' Yonatan said. Then he waved to Gabriel and said, 'Give him my best.'

A Palestinian Security officer greeted Gabriel through the bars of the gate. He wore an olive drab uniform, a flat cap, and a black patch over his left eye. He opened the gate wide enough for Gabriel to pass and beckoned him forward. His hand was missing the last three fingers. On the other side of the gate, Gabriel was set upon by two more uniformed men, who subjected him to a rigorous and intrusive body search while One-Eye looked on, grinning as though the whole thing had been arranged for his private amusement.

One-Eye introduced himself as Colonel Kemel and led Gabriel into the compound. It was not the first time Gabriel had set foot in the Mukata. During the Mandate period it had been a British army fortress. After the Six-Day War, the IDF had taken it over from the Jordanians and used it throughout the occupation as a West Bank command post. Gabriel, when he was a soldier, had often reported for duty in the same place Yasir Arafat now used as his headquarters.

Arafat's office was located in a square two-story building huddled against the northern wall of the Mukata. Heavily damaged, it was one of the few buildings still standing in the compound. In the lobby Gabriel endured a second search, this time at the hands of a mustachioed giant in plain clothes with a compact submachine gun across his chest.

The search complete, the security man nodded to Colonel Kemel, who prodded Gabriel up a narrow flight of stairs. On the landing, seated on a fragile-looking chair balanced precariously on two legs, was another Security man. He cast Gabriel an apathetic glance, then reached up and rapped his knuckle against the wooden door. An irritated voice on the other side said, 'Come.' Colonel Kemel turned the latch and led Gabriel inside.

The office Gabriel entered was not much larger than his own at King Saul Boulevard. There was a modest wood desk and a small camp bed with a handsome leather-bound copy of the Koran laying atop the starched white pillowcase. Heavy velveteen curtains covered the window; a desk lamp, angled severely downward toward a stack of paperwork, was the only source of light. Along one wall, almost lost in the heavy shadows, hung row upon row of framed photographs showing the Palestinian leader with many famous people, including the American president who had bestowed de facto recognition upon his miniature state and whom Arafat had rewarded by stabbing in the back at Camp David and walking away from a peace deal.

Behind the desk, elfin and sickly looking, sat Arafat himself. He wore a pressed uniform and a black-and-white checkered kaffiyeh. As usual, it was draped over his right shoulder and secured to the front of his uniform in such a way that it resembled the land of Palestine – Arafat's version of Palestine, Gabriel noted, for it looked very much like the State of Israel. His hand, when he gestured for Gabriel to sit, shook violently, as did his pouting lower lip when he asked Gabriel whether he wished to have tea. Gabriel knew enough of Arab custom to realize that a refusal would get things off on the wrong foot, so he readily accepted the tea and watched, with a certain amount of pleasure, as Arafat dispatched Colonel Kemel to fetch it.

Alone for the first time, they eyed each other silently over the small desk. The shadow of their last encounter hung over them. It had taken place in the study of a Manhattan apartment, where Tariq al-Hourani, the same man who had planted a bomb beneath Gabriel's car in Vienna, had tried to murder Arafat for his supposed 'betrayal' of the Palestinian people. Tariq, before fleeing the apartment house, had put a bullet into Gabriel's chest, a wound that very nearly killed him.

Seated now in Arafat's presence, Gabriel's chest ached for the first time in many years. No single person, other than perhaps Shamron, had influenced the course of Gabriel's life more than Yasir Arafat. For thirty years they had been swimming together in the same river of blood. Gabriel had killed Arafat's most trusted lieutenants; Arafat had ordered the 'reprisal' against Gabriel in Vienna. But were Leah and Dani the targets or had the bomb actually been meant for him? Gabriel had been obsessed by the question for thirteen years. Arafat certainly knew the answer. It was one of the reasons why Gabriel had so readily accepted Shamron's suggestion to visit Ramallah.

'Shamron said you wished to discuss an important matter with me,' Arafat said. 'I agreed to see you only as a courtesy to him. We are the same age, Shamron and I. History threw us together in this land, and unfortunately we have fought many battles. Sometimes I got the better of him, sometimes he bested me. Now we are both growing old. I had hopes we might see a few days of peace before we died. My hopes are fading.'

If that was the case, thought Gabriel, why then did you walk away from a deal that would have given you a state in Gaza and 97 percent of the West Bank with East Jerusalem as its capital? Gabriel knew the answer, of course. It was evidenced in the cloth map of 'Palestine' Arafat wore on his shoulder. He'd wanted it all.

Gabriel had no chance to respond, because Colonel Kemel returned holding a small silver tray with two glasses of tea. The colonel then settled himself in a chair and glared at Gabriel with his one good eye. Arafat explained that the aide spoke fluent Hebrew and would assist with any translation. Gabriel had hoped to meet with Arafat alone, but a translator would probably prove useful. Gabriel's Arabic, while passable, did not possess the nuance or flexibility necessary for a conversation with a man like Yasir Arafat.

Arafat, with a trembling hand, placed his glass of tea back into its saucer and asked Gabriel what had brought him to Ramallah. Gabriel's one-word answer left Arafat momentarily off balance, just as Gabriel had intended.

'Khaled?' Arafat repeated, recovering his footing. 'I know many men named Khaled. I'm afraid it is a rather common Palestinian name. You'll have to be more specific.'

Feigned ignorance, Gabriel well knew, was one of Arafat's favorite negotiating tactics. Gabriel pressed his case.

'The *Khaled* I'm looking for, Chairman Arafat, is Khaled al-Khalifa.'

'*President* Arafat,' said the Palestinian.

Gabriel nodded indifferently. 'Where is Khaled al-Khalifa?'

The blotchy skin of Arafat's face colored suddenly, and his lower lip began to tremble. Gabriel looked down and contemplated his tea. From the corner of his eye, he noticed Colonel Kemel shifting nervously in his seat. Arafat, when he spoke again, managed to keep his legendary temper in check.

'I take it you're referring to the son of Sabri al-Khalifa?'

'Actually, he's *your* son now.'

'My adopted son,' Arafat said, 'because you murdered his father.'

'His father was killed on the field of battle.'

'He was murdered in cold blood on the streets of Paris.'

'It was Sabri who turned Paris into a battlefield, President Arafat, with your blessing.'

A silence fell between them. Arafat seemed to choose his next words carefully. 'I always knew that, one day, you would come up with some sort of provocation to target Khaled for elimination. That's why, after Sabri's funeral, I sent the boy far away from here. I gave him a new life, and he took it. I haven't seen or heard from Khaled since he was a young man.'

'We have evidence to suggest Khaled al-Khalifa was involved in the attack on our embassy in Rome.'

'Nonsense,' said Arafat dismissively.

'Since Khaled had nothing to do with Rome, I'm sure you wouldn't mind telling us where we can find him.'

'As I said before, I don't know where Khaled is.'

'What's his name?'

A guarded smile. 'I went to extraordinary lengths to protect the boy from you and your vengeful service. What on earth makes you think I would tell you his name now? Do you really believe that I would play the role of Judas Iscariot and hand over my son to you for trial and execution?' Arafat shook his head slowly. 'We have many traitors in our midst, many who work right here in the Mukata, but I am not one of them. If you want to find Khaled, you'll do it without my help.'

'There was a raid on a *pensione* in Milan shortly after the bombing. One of the men hiding there was named Daoud Hadawi, a Palestinian who used to be a member of your Presidential Security Service.'

'So you say.'

'I would appreciate a copy of Hadawi's personnel file.'

'Several hundred men work in the Presidential Security Service. If this man –' He faltered. 'What was his name?'

'Daoud Hadawi.'

'Ah, yes, Hadawi. *If* he ever worked for the service, and *if* we still have a personnel file on him, I'll be glad to give it to you. But I think the odds of us finding something are rather slim.'

'Really?'

'Let me make this clear to you,' Arafat said. 'We Palestinians had nothing to do with the attack on your embassy. Maybe it was Hezbollah or Osama. Maybe it was neo-Nazis. God knows, you have many enemies.'

Gabriel placed his palms on the arms of the chair and prepared to stand. Arafat raised his hand. 'Please, Jibril,' he said, using the Arabic version of Gabriel's name. 'Don't leave yet. Stay a little longer.'

Gabriel, for the moment, relented. Arafat fidgeted with his kaffiyeh, then looked at Colonel Kemel and in quiet Arabic instructed him to leave them alone.

'You've not touched your tea, Jibril. Can I get you something else? Some sweets, perhaps?'

Gabriel shook his head. Arafat folded his tiny hands and regarded Gabriel in silence. He was smiling slightly. Gabriel had the distinct sense Arafat was enjoying himself.

'I know what you did for me in New York a few

years ago. If it weren't for you, Tariq might very well have killed me in that apartment. In another time you might have hoped for him to succeed.' A wistful smile. 'Who knows? In another time it might have been *you*, Jibril, standing there with a gun in your hand.'

Gabriel made no reply. Kill Arafat? In the weeks after Vienna, when he had been unable to picture anything but the charred flesh of his wife and the mutilated body of his son, he had thought about it many times. Indeed, at his lowest point, Gabriel would have gladly traded his own life for Arafat's.

'It's strange, Jibril, but for a brief time we were allies, you and I. We both wanted peace. We both needed peace.'

'Did you ever want peace, or was it all part of your phased strategy to destroy Israel and take the whole thing?'

This time it was Arafat who allowed a question to hang in the air unanswered.

'I owe you my life, Jibril, and so I will help you in this matter. There is no Khaled. Khaled is a figment of your imagination. If you keep chasing him, the real killers will escape.'

Gabriel stood abruptly, terminating the meeting. Arafat came out from behind the desk and placed his hands on Gabriel's shoulders. Gabriel's flesh seemed ablaze, but he did nothing to sever the Palestinian's embrace.

'I'm glad we finally met formally,' Arafat said. 'If

you and I can sit down together in peace, perhaps there's hope for us all.'

'Perhaps,' said Gabriel, though his tone revealed his pessimism.

Arafat released Gabriel and started toward the door, then stopped himself suddenly. 'You surprise me, Jibril.'

'Why is that?'

'I expected you to use this opportunity to clear the air about Vienna.'

'You murdered my wife and son,' Gabriel said, deliberately misleading Arafat over Leah's fate. 'I'm not sure we'll ever be able to "clear the air," as you put it.'

Arafat shook his head. 'No, Jibril, I didn't murder them. I ordered Tariq to kill you to avenge Abu Jihad, but I specifically told him that your family was not to be touched.'

'Why did you do that?'

'Because you deserved it. You conducted yourself with a certain honor that night in Tunis. Yes, you killed Abu Jihad, but you made certain no harm came to his wife and children. In fact, you stopped on the way out of the villa to comfort Abu Jihad's daughter and instruct her to look after her mother. Do you remember that, Jibril?'

Gabriel closed his eyes and nodded. The scene in Tunis, like the bombing in Vienna, hung in a gallery of memory that he walked each night in his dreams.

'I felt you deserved the same as Abu Jihad, to die a

soldier's death witnessed by your wife and child. Tariq didn't agree with me. He felt you deserved a more severe punishment, the punishment of watching your wife and child die, so he planted the bomb beneath their car and made certain you were on hand to witness the detonation. Vienna was Tariq's doing, not mine.'

The telephone on Arafat's desk rang, tearing Gabriel's memory of Vienna as a knife shreds canvas. Arafat turned suddenly and left Gabriel to see himself out. Colonel Kemel was waiting on the landing. He escorted Gabriel wordlessly through the debris of the Mukata. The harsh light, after the gloom of Arafat's office, was nearly unbearable. Beyond the broken gate Yonatan Shamron was playing football with a few of the Palestinian guards. They climbed back into the armored jeep and drove through streets of death. When they were clear of Ramallah, Yonatan asked Gabriel whether he had learned anything useful.

'Khaled al-Khalifa bombed our embassy in Rome,' Gabriel said with certainty.

'Anything else?'

Yes, he thought. Yasir Arafat had personally ordered Tariq al-Hourani to murder his wife and son.

11. Jerusalem: March 23

Gabriel's bedside telephone rang at 2 A.M. It was Yaakov.

'Looks like your visit to the Mukata has stirred the hornet's nest.'

'What are you talking about?'

'I'm outside in the street.'

The connection went dead. Gabriel sat up in bed and dressed in the dark.

'Who was that?' Chiara asked, her voice heavy with sleep.

Gabriel told her.

'What is it?'

'I don't know.'

'Where are you going?'

'I don't know.'

He bent to kiss her forehead. Chiara's arm rose from the blankets, curled around the back of his neck, and drew him to her mouth. 'Be careful,' she whispered, her lips against his cheek.

A moment later he was buckled into the passenger seat of Yaakov's unmarked Volkswagen Golf, racing westward across Jerusalem. Yaakov drove ludicrously fast, in true Sabra fashion, with the wheel in one hand and coffee and a cigarette in the other.

The headlamps of the oncoming traffic threw an unkind light on the pockmarked features of his uncompromising face.

'His name is Mahmoud Arwish,' Yaakov said. 'One of our most important assets inside the Palestinian Authority. He works in the Mukata. Very close to Arafat.'

'Who made the approach?'

'Arwish sent up a flare a couple of hours ago and said he wanted to talk.'

'About what?'

'Khaled, of course.'

'What does he know?'

'He wouldn't say.'

'Why do you need me? Why isn't he talking to his controller?'

'I'm his controller,' Yaakov said, 'but the person he really wants to talk to is you.'

They had reached the western edge of the New City. To Gabriel's right, bathed in the silver light of a newly risen moon, lay the flatlands of the West Bank. Old hands called it 'Shabak country.' It was a land where the usual rules did not apply – and where the few conventions that did exist could be bent or broken whenever it was deemed necessary to combat Arab terror. Men such as Yaakov were the mailed fist of Israeli security, foot soldiers who engaged in the dirty work of counterterrorism. Shabakniks had the power to arrest without cause and search without warrants, to shut down businesses and dynamite houses. They lived on nerves and nicotine, drank too much coffee and slept too little. Their wives left them, their Arab informants feared and hated them. Gabriel, though he had dispensed the ultimate sanction of the State, always considered himself fortunate that he had been asked to join the Office and not Shabak.

Shabak's methods were sometimes at odds with the principles of a democratic state, and, like the Office, public scandals had damaged its reputation both at home and abroad. The worst was the infamous Bus 300 Affair. In April 1984, bus No. 300, en route from Tel Aviv to the southern city of Ashkelon, was hijacked by four Palestinians. Two were killed during the military rescue operation; the two surviving terrorists were led into a nearby wheat field and never seen again. Later it was revealed that the hijackers had been beaten to death by Shabak officers acting under orders from their director-general. A series of scandals followed in quick succession, each exposing some of Shabak's most ruthless methods: violence, coerced confessions, blackmail, and deception. Shabak's defenders were fond of saying that interrogations of suspected terrorists cannot be conducted over a pleasant cup of coffee. Its goals, regardless of the scandals, remained unchanged. Shabak was not interested in catching terrorists *after* blood was shed. It wanted to stop the terrorists *before* they could strike, and, if possible, to frighten young Arabs from ever going the way of violence.

Yaakov applied the brakes suddenly to avoid colliding with a slow-moving transit van. Simultaneously he flashed his lights and pounded on the car horn. The van responded by changing lanes. As Yaakov shot past, Gabriel glimpsed a pair of Haredim conducting an animated conversation as though nothing had happened.

Yaakov tossed a *kippah* onto Gabriel's lap. It was larger than most and loosely knitted, with an orange-and-amber pattern against a black background. Gabriel understood the significance of its design.

'We'll cross the line as settlers, just in case anyone from PA Security or Hamas is watching the checkpoints.'

'Where are we from?'

'Kiryat Devorah,' Yaakov replied. 'It's in the Jordan Valley. We're never going to set foot there.'

Gabriel held up the skullcap. 'I take it we're not terribly popular with the local population.'

'Let's just say that the residents of Kiryat Devorah take their commitment to the Land of Israel quite seriously.'

Gabriel slipped the *kippah* onto his head and adjusted the angle. Yaakov briefed Gabriel as he drove: the procedures for crossing into the West Bank, the route they would take to the Arab village where Arwish was waiting, the method of extraction. When Yaakov finished, he reached into the backseat and produced an Uzi miniature submachine gun.

'I prefer this,' said Gabriel, holding up his Beretta.

Yaakov laughed. 'This is the *West* Bank, not the *Left* Bank. Don't be a fool, Gabriel. Take the Uzi.'

Gabriel reluctantly took the weapon and rammed a magazine of ammunition into the butt. Yaakov covered his head with a *kippah* identical to the one he'd given Gabriel. A few miles beyond Ben-Gurion Airport he exited the motorway and followed a two-lane road eastward toward the West Bank. The Separation Fence, looming before them, cast a black shadow across the landscape.

At the checkpoint a Shabak man stood among the IDF soldiers. As Yaakov approached, the Shabak man murmured a few words to the soldiers and the Volkswagen was allowed to pass without inspection. Yaakov, clear of the checkpoint, raced along the moon-washed road at high speed. Gabriel glanced over his shoulder and saw a pair of headlights. The lights floated there for a time, then receded into the night. Yaakov seemed to take no notice of them. The second car, Gabriel suspected, belonged to a Shabak countersurveillance team.

A sign warned that Ramallah lay four kilometers ahead. Yaakov turned off the road, onto a dirt track that ran through the bed of an ancient wadi. He doused his headlamps and navigated the wadi with only the amber glow of his parking lights. After a moment he brought the car to a stop.

'Open the glove box.'

Gabriel did as he was told. Inside was a pair of kaffiyehs.

'You've got to be kidding.'

'Cover your face,' Yaakov said. 'All of it, the way they do.'

Yaakov, in a practiced motion, bound his head in the kaffiyeh and tied it at his throat, so that his face was concealed except for a thin slit for his eyes. Gabriel did the same. Yaakov started driving again, plunging along the darkened wadi with both hands wrapped around the wheel, leaving Gabriel with the uncomfortable feeling he was seated next to an Arab militant on a suicide run. A mile farther on, they came to a narrow paved road. Yaakov turned onto the road and followed it north.

The village was small, even by West Bank standards, and gripped by an air of sudden desertion – a collection of squat, dun-colored houses crouched around the narrow spire of a minaret, with scarcely a light burning anywhere. In the center of the village lay a small market square. There were no other cars and no pedestrians, only a flock of goats nosing amid fallen produce.

The house where Yaakov stopped was on the northern edge. The window facing the street was shuttered. One of the shutters hung aslant from a broken hinge. A few feet from the front door was a child's tricycle. The bike was pointed toward the door, which meant the meeting was still on. Had it been pointed in the opposite direction, they would have been forced to abort and head for the backup location.

Yaakov snatched an Uzi submachine gun from the floorboard and climbed out of the car. Gabriel did the same, then pulled open the rear passenger-side door, just as Yaakov had instructed. He turned his back to the house and watched the street for any sign of movement. *'If anyone approaches the car while I'm inside, shoot in their direction,'* Yaakov had said. *'If they don't get the message, put them on the ground.'*

Yaakov hurdled the tricycle and drove his right foot against the door. Gabriel heard the crack of splintering wood but kept his eyes trained on the street. From inside came the sound of a voice shouting in Arabic. Gabriel recognized it as Yaakov's. The next voice was unfamiliar to him.

A light appeared in a nearby cottage, then another. Gabriel released the safety on his Uzi and slipped his forefinger inside the trigger guard. He heard footfalls behind him and turned in time to see Yaakov leading Arwish through the broken door, hands in the air, face shrouded by a black hood, an Uzi pressed to the back of his head.

Gabriel turned his gaze once more toward the street. A man, dressed in a pale gray galabia, had stepped outside his cottage and was shouting at Gabriel in Arabic. Gabriel, in the same language, ordered him to stay back, but the Palestinian advanced closer. 'Shoot at him!' Yaakov snapped, but Gabriel calmly held fire.

Yaakov shoved Arwish headlong into the back of the car. Gabriel scrambled in after him and drove the informant toward the floor. Yaakov ran around the front of the car to the driver's side door, pausing long enough to spray a volley of rounds a few yards from the feet of the Palestinian villager, who scurried back into the shelter of his house.

Yaakov jumped behind the wheel, then reversed down the narrow street. Reaching the market square, he turned around and sped through the village. The gunfire and the roaring of the car engine had alerted the villagers to trouble. Faces appeared in windows and doorways, but no one dared challenge them.

Gabriel kept watch out the rear window until the village vanished into the darkness. A moment later Yaakov was once again racing along the rutted wadi, this time in the opposite direction. The collaborator was still pressed to the floor, wedged into the narrow space between the backseat and the front.

'Let me up, you jackass!'

Gabriel pressed his forearm against the side of the Arab's neck and subjected his body to a rough and thorough search for weapons or explosives. Finding nothing, he pulled the Arab onto the seat and tore away the black hood. A single eye glared malevolently back at him – the eye of Yasir Arafat's translator, Colonel Kemel.

The city of Hadera, an early Zionist farm settlement turned drab Israeli industrial town, lies on the Coastal Plain halfway between Haifa and Tel Aviv. In a working-class section of the city, adjacent to a sprawling tire factory, stands a row of wheat-colored apartment buildings. One of the buildings, the one nearest the factory, stinks always of burning rubber. On the top floor of this building is a Shabak safe flat. For most officers it is a meeting place of last resort. Yaakov actually preferred it. The acrid smell, he believed, lent an air of urgency to the proceedings, for few men who came here wished to linger long. But then Yaakov was driven by other ghosts. His great-grandparents, Russian Jews from Kovno, had been among the founders of Hadera. They had turned a worthless malarial swamp into productive farmland. For Yaakov, Hadera was truth. Hadera was Israel.

The flat was devoid of comfort. The sitting room was furnished with folding metal chairs, and the linoleum floor was buckled and bare. On the kitchen counter stood a cheap plastic electric kettle; in the rust-stained basin a quartet of dirty cups. Mahmoud Arwish, alias Colonel Kemel, had turned down Yaakov's rather disingenuous offer of tea. He had also requested that Yaakov leave the lights off. The neatly pressed uniform he'd been wearing that morning at the Mukata had been replaced by a pair of gabardine trousers and a white cotton shirt, which glowed softly in the moonlight streaming through the window. Between the two remaining fingers of his right hand rested one of Yaakov's American cigarettes. With the other hand he was massaging the side of his neck. His single eye was fixed on Gabriel, who had forsaken his folding chair and was seated on the floor with his back propped against the wall and his legs crossed before him. Yaakov was a formless shadow against the window.

'I see you've learned a thing or two from your Shabak friend,' Arwish said, rubbing his jaw. 'They have a reputation of being good with their fists.'

'You said you wanted to see me,' said Gabriel. 'I don't like it when people ask to see me.'

'What did you think I was planning to do? Kill you?'

'It's not without precedent,' Gabriel replied calmly.

Shabak agents, he knew, were at their most vulnerable while meeting with assets from the other side. In recent years, several had been killed during meetings. One had been hacked to death with an ax in a Jerusalem safe flat.

'If we'd wanted to kill you, we'd have done it this morning in Ramallah. Our people would have celebrated your death. Your hands are stained with the blood of Palestinian heroes.'

'Celebration of death is what you're good at these days,' Gabriel replied. 'Sometimes it seems to be the only thing. Offer your people something instead of suicide. Lead them instead of following the most extreme elements of your society. Build something.'

'We tried to build something,' Arwish replied, 'and you tore it down with your tanks and bulldozers.'

Gabriel glimpsed Yaakov's shadow stirring in the

window. The Shabak man wanted the topic moved onto less contentious ground. Mahmoud Arwish, judging from the menacing manner in which he lit a second cigarette, was not ready to concede. Gabriel looked away from the Arab's single glaring eye and absently trailed his forefinger through the dust on the linoleum floor. Let him rant, Shamron would have counseled. Let him cast you as the oppressor and villain. It helps to assuage the guilt of betrayal.

'Yes, we celebrate death,' Arwish said, closing the lid of Yaakov's old-fashioned lighter with a snap. 'And some of us collaborate with our enemy. But that's the way it always is in war, isn't it? Unfortunately, we Palestinians are easily bought. Shabak calls it the three Ks: *kesef, kavod, kussit.* Money, respect, woman. Imagine, betraying your people for the affection of an Israeli whore.'

Gabriel, silent, continued doodling in the dust. He realized he was tracing the outline of a Caravaggio – Abraham, knife in hand, preparing to slay his own son in service to the Lord.

Arwish went on. 'Do you know why I collaborate, Jibril? I collaborate because my wife became ill. The doctor at the clinic in Ramallah diagnosed her with cancer and said she would die unless she received treatment in Jerusalem. I requested permission from the Israeli authorities to enter the city, which brought me into contact with Shabak and my dear friend.' He inclined his head toward Yaakov, who was now seated on the window ledge with his arms folded.

'In front of me he calls himself Solomon. I know his real name is Yaakov, but I always refer to him as Solomon. It is one of the many games we play.'

Arwish contemplated the end of his cigarette. 'Needless to say, my wife received permission to travel to Jerusalem for treatment, but it came at a steep price, the price of collaboration. Solomon jails my sons from time to time, just to keep the information flowing. He's even jailed a relative who lives on the Israeli side of the Green Line. But when Solomon truly wants to turn the screws on me, he threatens to tell my wife of my treachery. Solomon knows she would never forgive me.'

Gabriel looked up from his Caravaggio. 'Are you finished?'

'Yes, I think so.'

'Then why don't you tell me about Khaled?'

'*Khaled*,' Arwish repeated, shaking his head. 'Khaled is the least of your problems.' He paused and looked toward the darkened ceiling. '"Israel is bewildered. They have now become among the nations like an unwanted vessel, like a lonely wild ass."' His gaze settled on Gabriel once more. 'Do you know who wrote those words?'

'Hosea,' Gabriel replied indifferently.

'Correct,' said Arwish. 'Are you a religious man?'

'No,' answered Gabriel truthfully.

'Neither am I,' confessed Arwish, 'but perhaps you should heed the advice of Hosea. What is Israel's solution to her problems with the Palestinians? To build a fence. To act, in the words of Hosea, like shifters of field boundaries. The Jews complain bitterly about the centuries they spent in the ghetto, and yet what are you doing with that Separation Fence? You are building the first Palestinian ghetto. Worse still, you're building a ghetto for yourselves.'

Arwish started to raise his cigarette to his lips, but Yaakov stepped away from the window and slapped the cigarette from the Palestinian's ruined hand. Arwish treated himself to the victim's superior smile, then he twisted his head around and asked Yaakov for a cup of tea. Yaakov returned to the window and remained motionless.

'No tea today,' Arwish said. 'Only money. To get my money, I must sign Solomon's ledger and affix to it my own thumbprint. That way, if I betray Solomon, he can punish me. There is but one fate for collaboration in our part of this land. Death. And not a gentleman's death. A biblical death. I'll be stoned or hacked to pieces by Arafat's fanatical killers. That's how Yaakov ensures I tell him nothing but the truth, and on a timely basis.'

Yaakov leaned forward and whispered into Arwish's ear, like a lawyer instructing a witness under hostile questioning.

'Solomon grows irritated with my speeches. Solomon would like me to get down to business.' Arwish studied Gabriel for a moment. 'But not you, Jibril. You are the patient one.'

Gabriel looked up. 'Where's Khaled?'

'I don't know. I only know that Arafat misled you this morning. You're right. Khaled does exist, and he's taken up the sword of his father and grandfather.'

'Did he do Rome?'

A moment of hesitation, a glance toward the dark figure of Yaakov, then a slow nod.

'Is he acting at Arafat's behest?'

'I couldn't say for certain.'

'What *can* you say for certain?'

'He's in communication with the Mukata.'

'How?'

'A number of different ways. Sometimes he uses faxes. They're bounced from a number of different machines, and by the time they arrive in the Territories, they're almost impossible to read.'

'What else?'

'Sometimes he uses coded e-mails, which are routed through a number of different addresses and servers. Sometimes he sends messages to Arafat via courier or through the visiting delegations. Most of the time, though, he just uses the telephone.'

'Could you identify his voice?'

'I'm not sure I've ever heard him speak.'

'Have you ever seen him?'

'I believe I met him once, many years ago in Tunis. A young man came to visit and stayed in Arafat's compound for a few days. He had a French name and passport, but he spoke Arabic like a Palestinian.'

'What makes you think it was Khaled?'

'The way Arafat was acting. He glowed in the presence of this young man. He was positively giddy.'

'That's all?'

'No, there was something about his appearance. They always said Khaled looked like his grandfather. This man certainly bore a striking resemblance to Sheikh Asad.'

Arwish stood suddenly. Yaakov's arm swung up, and he leveled his Uzi at the Arab's head. Arwish smiled and pulled his shirt out of his trousers. Taped to his lower back was an envelope. Gabriel had missed it during his rapid search for weapons in the back of the car. Arwish removed the envelope and flipped it to Gabriel, who pried open the flap and shook the photograph out onto his lap. It showed a young man, strikingly handsome, seated next to Arafat at a table. He seemed unaware that his picture was being taken.

'Arafat has a habit of secretly photographing anyone who meets with him,' Arwish said. 'You have photographs of Khaled as a child. Perhaps your computers can confirm that this man is truly him.'

'It's not likely,' Gabriel said. 'What else do you have?'

'When he calls the Mukata, it's not his voice on the line.'

'How does he do that?'

'He has someone else do the talking. A woman – a *European* woman.'

'What's her name?'

'She uses different names and different telephones.'

'Where?'

Arwish shrugged.

'What's her native language?'

'Hard to tell, but her Arabic is perfect.'

'Accent?'

'Classical. Upper-crust Jordanian. Maybe Beirut or Cairo. She refers to Khaled as Tony.'

'Tony who?' Gabriel asked calmly. 'Tony where?'

'I don't know,' Arwish said, 'but find the woman, and maybe you'll find Khaled.'

12. Tel Aviv

'She calls herself Madeleine, but only when she's posing as a Frenchwoman. When she wants to be British, she calls herself Alexandra. When Italian, she's Lunetta – Little Moon.'

Natan looked at Gabriel and blinked several times. He wore his hair in a ponytail, his spectacles lay slightly askew across the end of his nose, and there were holes in his Malibu surfer's sweatshirt. Yaakov had forewarned Gabriel about Natan's appearance. 'He's a genius. After graduating from Cal-Tech, every high-tech firm in America and Israel wanted him. He's a bit like you,' Yaakov had concluded, with the slightly envious tone of a man who did but one thing well.

Gabriel looked out of Natan's glass-enclosed office, onto a large brightly lit floor lined with row upon row of computer workstations. At each station sat a technician. Most were shockingly young and most were Mizrahim, Jews who had come from Arab countries. These were the unsung warriors in Israel's war against terrorism. They never saw the enemy, never forced him to betray his people or confronted him across an interrogation table. To them he was a crackle of electricity down a copper wire or a whisper in the atmosphere. Natan Hofi was charged with the seemingly impossible task of monitoring all electronic communication between the outside world and the Territories. Computers did the brunt of the work, sifting the intercepts for certain words, phrases, or the voices of known terrorists, yet Natan still regarded his ears as the most reliable weapon in his arsenal.

'We don't know her real name,' he said. 'Right now she's just Voiceprint 572/B. So far we've intercepted five telephone calls between her and Arafat. Care to listen?'

Gabriel nodded. Natan clicked an icon on his computer screen, and the recordings began to play. During each call the woman posed as a foreign peace activist telephoning to express support for the beleaguered Palestinian leader or to commiserate about the latest Zionist outrage. Each conversation contained a brief reference to a friend named Tony, just as Mahmoud Arwish had said.

After listening to four of the conversations, Gabriel asked, 'What can you tell about her based on her voice?'

'Her Arabic is excellent, but she's no Arab. French, I'd say. From the South, maybe the Marseilles area. Overeducated. Oversexed. She also has a small butterfly tattooed on her rear end.'

Yaakov looked up sharply.

'I'm kidding,' said Natan. 'But listen to intercept number five. She's posing as our Frenchwoman,

167

Madeleine, head of something called the Center for a Just and Lasting Peace in Palestine. The topic of the conversation is an upcoming rally in Paris.'

'Paris?' Gabriel asked. 'You're sure it's Paris?'

Natan nodded. 'She tells Arafat that one of the organizers, a man named Tony, is predicting a turn-out of a hundred thousand. Then she hesitates and corrects herself. Tony's prediction isn't a hundred thousand, she says, it's *two* hundred thousand.'

Natan played the intercept. When it was over, Yaakov said, 'What's so interesting about that?'

'This.'

Natan opened another audio file and played a few seconds' worth of inaudible muffle.

'There was someone else in the room with her at the time. He was monitoring the conversation on another extension. When Madeleine says Tony is expecting a hundred thousand people, this fellow covers the mouthpiece and in French tells her, "No, no, not a hundred thousand. It's going to be two hundred thousand." He thinks no one can hear him, but he's put the mouthpiece right against his vocal cords. It's a real rookie mistake. We got the vibrations on tape. With a little filtering and scrubbing, I made that garble sound like this.'

Natan played the file again. This time it was audible – a man, perfect French. *'No, no, not a hundred thousand. It's going to be two hundred thousand.'* Natan clicked his mouse and pointed to the top-right corner of his computer monitor, a grid pattern crisscrossed by a series of undulating lines.

'This is a sound spectrograph. The voiceprint. It's a mathematical equation, based on the physical configuration of a speaker's mouth and throat. We've compared this print with every voice we have on file.'

'And?'

'Not a single match. We call him Voiceprint 698/D.'

'When was that call recorded?'

'Six weeks ago.'

'Do you know where the call was placed?'

Natan smiled.

There was a row, but then no Office operation was complete without one. Lev wanted to keep Gabriel locked in the basement on punishment rations of bread and water, and he briefly held the upper hand. Gabriel was blown and no longer fit for fieldwork, Lev argued. Besides, the telephone intercepts suggested Khaled was hiding in the Arab world, somewhere the Europhile Gabriel, except for his brief foray into Tunis, had never operated. As a last resort, Lev sought refuge in bureaucratic twaddle, arguing that Gabriel's committee possessed no foreign operational charter. The matter reached Shamron, as most matters eventually did. Lev sidestepped, but too late to ward off the fatal blow, for advice from Shamron had the authority of God's commandments chiseled in stone.

Having prevailed in the bureaucratic trenches, Gabriel hurriedly dealt next with his problems of identity and appearance. He decided to travel as a German, for German was his first language and remained the language of his dreams. He chose commercial interior design as his trade and Munich as his place of residence. Operations supplied him with a passport in the name of Johannes Klemp and a wallet filled with credit cards and other personal paraphernalia, including business cards engraved with a Munich telephone number. The number, if dialed, would ring in an Office safe flat, then transfer automatically to a switchboard inside King Saul Boulevard, where Gabriel's recorded voice would announce that he was away on holiday and would call back upon his return.

As for his appearance, the specialists in Operations suggested a beard, and Gabriel, who regarded any man with facial hair as distrustful and hiding something, reluctantly complied. To his everlasting disappointment, it came in very gray. This pleased the specialists, who colored his hair to match. They added a pair of frameless rectangular spectacles and a suitcase filled with fashionable monochrome clothing from Berlin and Milan. The wizards in Technical provided several innocent-looking consumer electronic devices that, in reality, were not so innocent at all.

One warm evening, shortly before his departure, he dressed in one of Herr Klemp's egregious suits and stalked the discos and nightclubs along Sheinkin Street in Tel Aviv. Herr Klemp was all that he, and by extension Mario Delvecchio, was not – a loquacious bore, a womanizer, a man who liked expensive drink and techno music. He loathed Herr Klemp, yet at the same time welcomed him, for Gabriel never felt truly safe unless wearing the skin of another man.

He thought of his hasty preparation for Operation Wrath of God; of walking the streets of Tel Aviv with Shamron, stealing wallets and breaking into hotel rooms along the Promenade. Only once had he been caught, a Romanian Jewish woman who had seized Gabriel's wrist in a Shamron-like grip and screamed for the police. 'You went like a lamb to the slaughter,' Shamron had said. 'What if it had been a gendarme? Or a carabiniere? Do you think I'd be able to walk in and demand your freedom? If they come for you, fight back. If you must shed innocent blood, then shed it without hesitation. But never allow yourself to be arrested. Never!'

Office tradition demanded Gabriel spend his final night in Israel at a 'jump site,' the in-house idiom for a departure safe flat. Without exception they are forlorn places that stink of cigarettes and failure, so he chose instead to spend the night in Narkiss Street with Chiara. Their lovemaking was strained and awkward. Afterward, Chiara confessed that Gabriel felt a stranger to her.

Gabriel had never been able to sleep before an operation, and his last night in Jerusalem was no exception. And so he was pleased to hear, shortly before midnight, the distinctive grumble of Shamron's armored Peugeot pulling up outside in the street – and to glimpse Shamron's bald head floating up the garden walk with Rami at his heels. They passed the remainder of that night in Gabriel's study, with the windows open to the chill night air. Shamron talked about the War of Independence, his search for Sheikh Asad, and of the morning he had killed him in the cottage outside Lydda. As dawn approached, Gabriel felt a reluctance to leave him, a sense that perhaps he should have taken Lev's advice and allowed someone else to go in his place.

Only when it had grown light outside did Shamron talk about what lay ahead. 'Don't go anywhere near the embassy,' he said. 'The Mukhabarat assumes, with some justification, that everyone who works there is a spy.' Then he gave Gabriel a business card. 'He's ours, bought and paid for. He knows everyone in town. I've told him to expect you. Be careful. He likes his drink.'

An hour later Gabriel climbed into an Office car outfitted as a Jerusalem taxi and headed down the Bab al-Wad to Ben-Gurion Airport. He cleared customs as Herr Klemp, endured a mind-numbing security examination, then went to the departure lounge. When his flight was called he set out across the bone-white tarmac toward the waiting jetliner and took his seat in the economy cabin. As the plane lifted off he looked out the window and watched the land sinking beneath him, gripped by a perverse fear that he would never see it or Chiara again. He thought of the journey ahead, a weeklong Mediterranean odyssey that would take him from Athens to Istanbul and finally to the ancient city on the western edge of the Fertile Crescent, where he hoped to find a woman named Madeleine, or Alexandra, or Lunetta, the Little Moon, and her friend named Tony.

13. Cairo: March 31

The gentleman from Munich was a guest the staff at the Inter-Continental Hotel would not soon forget. Mr Katubi, the well-oiled chief concierge, had seen many like him, a man perpetually ready to take offense, a small man with a small man's chip balanced precariously on his insignificant shoulder. Indeed, Mr Katubi grew to loathe him so intensely that he would wince visibly at the mere sight of him. On the third day he greeted him with a tense smile and the question: 'What is it now, Herr Klemp?'

The complaints had begun within minutes of his arrival. Herr Klemp had reserved a non-smoking room, but clearly, he claimed, someone had smoked there very recently – though Mr Katubi, who prided himself on a keen sense of smell, was never able to detect even a trace of tobacco on the air. The next room was too close to the swimming pool, the next too close to the nightclub. Finally, Mr Katubi gave him, at no additional charge, an upper-floor suite with a terrace overlooking the river, which Herr Klemp pronounced 'hopelessly adequate.'

The swimming pool was too warm, his bathroom too cold. He turned up his nose at the breakfast buffet and routinely sent back his food at dinner. The

174

valets ruined the lapels of one of his suits, his massage at the spa had left him with an injured neck. He demanded the maids clean his suite promptly at eight each morning, and he remained in the room to supervise their work – his cash had been pinched at the Istanbul Hilton, he claimed, and he was not going to let it happen again in Cairo. The moment the maids left, the DO NOT DISTURB sign would appear on his door latch, where it would remain like a battle flag for the remainder of each day. Mr Katubi wished only that he could hang a similar sign on his outpost in the lobby.

Each morning at ten Herr Klemp left the hotel armed with his tourist maps and guidebooks. The hotel drivers took to drawing straws to determine who would have the misfortune of serving as his guide for the day, for each outing seemed more calamitous than the last. The Egyptian Museum, he announced, needed a thorough cleaning. The Citadel he wrote off as a filthy old fort. At the pyramids of Giza he was nipped by a cantankerous camel. Upon his return from a visit to Coptic Cairo, Mr Katubi asked if he enjoyed the Church of Saint Barbara. 'Interesting,' said Herr Klemp, 'but not as beautiful as our churches in Germany.'

On his fourth day, Mr Katubi was standing at the entrance of the hotel as Herr Klemp came whirling out of the revolving doors, into a dust-filled desert wind.

'Good morning, Herr Klemp.'

'That is yet to be determined, Mr Katubi.'

'Does Herr Klemp require a car this morning?'

'No, he does not.'

And with that he set out along the corniche, the tails of his supposedly 'ruined' suit jacket flapping in the breeze like the mudguards of a lorry. Cairo was a city of remarkable resiliency, Mr Katubi thought, but even Cairo was no match for a man like Herr Klemp.

Gabriel saw something of Europe in the grimy, decaying buildings along Talaat Harb Street. Then he remembered reading, in the guidebooks of Herr Klemp, that the nineteenth-century Egyptian ruler Khedive Ismail had conceived of turning Cairo into 'Paris by the Nile' and had hired some of Europe's finest architects to achieve his dream. Their handi-work was still evident in the neo-Gothic facades, the wrought-iron railings, and tall rectangular shuttered windows, though it had been undone by a century's worth of pollution, weather, and neglect.

He came to a thunderous traffic circle. A sandaled boy tugged at his coat sleeve and invited him to visit his family's perfume shop. *'Nein, nein,'* said Gabriel in the German of Herr Klemp, but he pushed past the child with the detached air of an Israeli used to fending off hawkers in the alleys of the Old City.

He followed the circle counterclockwise and turned into Qasr el-Nil Street, Cairo's version of the Champs-Élysées. He walked for a time, pausing now and again to gaze into the garish shop windows to see if he was being followed. He left Qasr el-Nil and entered a narrow side street. It was impossible to walk on the pavements because they were jammed with parked cars, so he walked in the street like a Cairene.

He came to the address shown on the business card Shamron had given him the night before his departure. It was an Italianate building with a facade the color of Nile mud. From a third-floor window came the strains of the BBC's hourly news bulletin theme. A few feet from the entrance a vendor dispensed paper plates of spaghetti Bolognese from an aluminum cart. Next to the vendor a veiled woman sold limes and loaves of flat bread. Across the cluttered street was a kiosk. Standing in the shade of the little roof, wearing sunglasses and a Members Only windbreaker, was a poorly concealed Mukhabarat surveillance man, who watched as Gabriel went inside.

It was cool and dark in the foyer. An emaciated Egyptian cat with hollow eyes and enormous ears hissed at him from the shadows, then disappeared through a hole in the wall. A Nubian doorman in a lemon-colored galabia and white turban sat motionless in a wooden chair. He lifted an enormous ebony hand to receive the business card of the man Gabriel wished to see.

'Third floor,' he said in English.

Two doors greeted Gabriel on the landing. Next

to the door on the right was a brass plaque that read: DAVID QUINNELL — INTERNATIONAL PRESS. Gabriel pressed the bell and was promptly admitted into a small antechamber by a Sudanese office boy, whom Gabriel addressed in measured German-accented English.

'Who shall I say is calling?' the Sudanese replied.

'My name is Johannes Klemp.'

'Is Mr Quinnell expecting you?'

'I'm a friend of Rudolf Heller. He'll understand.'

'Just a moment. I'll see if Mr Quinnell can see you now.'

The Sudanese disappeared through a set of tall double doors. A moment turned to two, then three. Gabriel wandered to the window and peered into the street. A waiter from the coffeehouse on the corner was presenting the Mukhabarat man with a glass of tea on a small silver tray. Gabriel heard the Sudanese behind him and turned round. 'Mr Quinnell will see you now.'

The room into which Gabriel was shown had the air of a Roman parlor gone to seed. The wood floor was rough for want of polish; the crown molding was nearly invisible beneath a dense layer of dust and grit. Two of the four walls were given over to bookshelves lined with an impressive collection of works dealing with the history of the Middle East and Islam. The large wood desk was buried beneath piles of yellowed newspapers and unread post.

The room was in shadow, except for a trapezoid of

harsh sunlight, which slanted through the half-open French doors and shone upon a scuffed suede brogue belonging to one David Quinnell. He lowered one half of that morning's *Al-Ahram*, the government-run Egyptian daily, and fixed Gabriel in a lugubrious stare. He wore a wrinkled shirt of white oxford cloth and a tan jacket with epaulettes. A lank forelock of gray-blond hair fell toward a pair of beady, bloodshot eyes. He scratched a carelessly shaved chin and lowered the volume on his radio. Gabriel, even from a distance of several paces, could smell last night's whiskey on his breath.

'Any friend of Rudolf Heller is a friend of mine.' Quinnell's dour expression did not match his jovial tone. Gabriel had the impression he was speaking for an audience of Mukhabarat listeners. 'Herr Heller told me you might be calling. What can I do for you?'

Gabriel placed a photograph on the cluttered desktop – the photo Mahmoud Arwish had given him in Hadera.

'I'm here on holiday,' Gabriel said. 'Herr Heller suggested I look you up. He said you could show me something of the real Cairo. He said you know more about Egypt than any man alive.'

'How kind of Herr Heller. How is he these days?'

'As ever,' said Gabriel.

Quinnell, without moving anything but his eyes, looked down at the photograph.

'I'm a bit busy at the moment, but I think I can be of help.' He picked up the photograph and folded it into his newspaper. 'Let's take a walk, shall we? It's best to get out before they turn up the heat.'

'Your office is under surveillance.'

They were walking along a narrow, shadowed alleyway lined with shops and vendors. Quinnell paused to admire a bolt of blood-colored Egyptian cotton.

'Sometimes,' he said indifferently. 'All the hacks are under watch. When one has a security apparatus as large as the Egyptians', it has to be used for something.'

'Yes, but you're no ordinary hack.'

'True, but they don't know that. To them, I'm just a bitter old English shit, trying to scratch a living from the printed word. We've managed to reach something of an accommodation. I've asked them to tidy up my flat when they finish searching it, and they've actually done a rather good job of it.'

Quinnell released the cloth and struck out precariously down the alleyway. Gabriel, before setting off after him, glanced over his shoulder and glimpsed Members Only listlessly examining an Arabian copper coffeepot.

Quinnell's face, by the time Gabriel caught up with him, was already flushed with the late-morning heat. He'd been a star once, the roving correspondent for an important London daily, the sort of reporter who parachutes into the world's hot spots and leaves before the story turns dull and the public begins to lose interest. Undone by too much drink and too many women, he'd come to Israel on assignment during the first intifada and had washed ashore on the Isle of Shamron. Over a private dinner in Tiberias, Shamron had probed and found weakness – a mountain of debt, a secret Jewish past concealed behind a sneering, drunken English exterior. By the time coffee was served on the terrace, Shamron had made his play. It would be a partnership, Shamron had promised, for Shamron regarded as his 'partner' any man he could seduce or blackmail into doing his bidding. Quinnell would use his impressive array of Arab sources to provide Shamron with information and entrée. Occasionally he would print a piece of Shamron's black propaganda. In return, Quinnell's equally impressive debt would be quietly retired. He would also receive a few exclusive pieces of news designed to polish his fading reputation, and a publisher would be found for the book he'd always longed to write, though Shamron never revealed how he'd known Quinnell had a manuscript in his drawer. The marriage was consummated, and Quinnell, like Mahmoud Arwish, set himself on a path of betrayal for which the punishment was professional death. As public penance for his private sins, Quinnell had gone over completely to the Arab side. On Fleet Street he was referred to as the Voice of Palestine – apologist for the suicide bombers and Islamofascists. *The Imperialist, oil-guzzling West and its bastard child Israel had reaped what it had sown,* Quinnell often ranted. *There will be no security in Piccadilly until there is justice in Palestine.* He was Al-Jazeera's favorite Western commentator and much in demand on the Cairo party circuit. Yasir Arafat once called him 'a courageous man who dares to write the truth – the only man in the West who truly understands the Arab street.'

'There's a place in Zamalek you should try. It's called Mimi's. Good food, good music.' Quinnell paused and added provocatively: 'An interesting crowd.'

'Who's Mimi?'

'Mimi Ferrere. She's something of a fixture on the Zamalek social scene. Came here nearly twenty years ago and never left. Everyone knows Mimi, and Mimi knows everyone.'

'What brought her to Cairo?'

'The Harmonic Convergence.'

Quinnell, met by Gabriel's blank look, explained.

'A bloke named Jose Arguelles wrote a book some time ago called *The Mayan Factor*. He claimed to have found evidence in the Bible and Aztec and Mayan calendars indicating that August 1987 was a critical juncture in the history of mankind. The world could go one of two ways. It could enter a new age or be destroyed. To avoid destruction, 144,000 people had to gather at so-called power centers around the globe and resonate positive energy. Mimi came to the pyramids, along with several thousand other lost souls. She was quite a looker back then. Still is, if you ask me. She married a rich Egyptian and settled on Zamalek. The marriage lasted about a week and a half. When it fell apart, Mimi needed money, so she opened the café.'

'Where is she from?'

Quinnell shrugged his shoulders. 'Mimi's from everywhere. Mimi's a citizen of the world.'

'What's the crowd like?'

'Expats, mainly. A few smart tourists. Arabs with money who still like the West. There's a fellow I see there from time to time. His name is Tony.'

'Tony? You're sure?'

'That's what he calls himself. Handsome devil.' Quinnell handed Gabriel the newspaper. 'Don't go too early. The place doesn't start to get going until midnight. And watch your step around Mimi. She might be a New Age fruitcake, but she doesn't miss a trick.'

Mr Katubi booked a table for Herr Johannes Klemp at Mimi's Wine and Jazz Bar for ten o'clock that evening. At nine Gabriel came down from his room and, forsaking the taxi stand, set out across the Tahrir Bridge toward Gezira Island. Reaching the island, he turned right and headed north on the river-front road, along the fringe of the old sporting club where British colonialists had played cricket and drunk gin while the empire collapsed around them.

A string of luxury high-rise apartment buildings appeared on his left, the first evidence he had entered the most sought-after address in Cairo. Foreigners lived here; so did wealthy Egyptians who took their cues not from Islam but from the trendsetters of New York and London. It was relatively clean in Zamalek, and the incessant noise of Cairo was just a discontented grumble from the other bank of the river. One could sip cappuccinos in the coffee bars and speak French in the exclusive boutiques. It was an oasis, a place where the rich could pretend they were not surrounded by a sea of unimaginable poverty.

Mimi's occupied the ground floor of an old house just off July 26th Street. The art deco neon sign was in English, as was the entirely vegetarian menu, which was displayed under glass and framed in hand-painted wood. Next to the menu hung a large poster with a photograph of the evening's featured entertainment, five young men with silk scarves and much jewelry. It was the sort of place Gabriel would normally enter only at gunpoint. Herr Klemp squared his shoulders and went inside.

He was greeted by a dark-skinned woman dressed in orange satin pajamas and a matching head wrap. She spoke to him in English, and he responded in kind. Hearing the name 'Johannes Klemp,' she smiled warily, as though she had been forewarned by Mr Katubi to expect the worst, and led him to a table near the bandstand. It was a low, Arabesque piece, surrounded by brightly colored, overstuffed lounge chairs. Gabriel had the distinct impression he would not be spending the evening alone. His fears were realized twenty minutes later when he was joined by three Arabs. They ordered champagne and ignored the morose-looking German with whom they were sharing a table.

It was a pleasant room, long and oval-shaped, with rough whitewashed plaster walls and swaths of silk hanging from the high ceiling. The air smelled of Eastern spice and sandalwood incense and vaguely of hashish. Along the edge of the room, and barely visible in the subdued light, were several domed alcoves, where patrons could eat and drink in relative privacy. Gabriel picked at a plate of Arab appetizers and looked in vain for anyone resembling the man in the photograph.

True to Quinnell's word, the music didn't start till eleven. The first act was a Peruvian who wore a sarong and played Incan-influenced New Age pieces on a nylon-stringed guitar. Between numbers he told fables of the high Andes in nearly impenetrable English. At midnight came the featured entertainers of the evening, a group of Moroccans who played atonal Arab jazz in keys and rhythms no Western ear could comprehend. The three Arabs paid no attention to the music and spent the evening in liquor-lubricated conversation. Herr Klemp smiled and applauded in appreciation of admirable solos, yet Gabriel heard none of it, for all his attention was focused on the woman holding court at the end of the bar.

She was quite a looker back then, Quinnell had said. *Still is, if you ask me.*

She wore white Capri pants and a satin blouse of pale blue tied at her slender waist. Viewed from behind, she might have been mistaken for a girl in her twenties. Only when she turned, revealing the wrinkles around her eyes and the streak of gray in her dark hair, did one realize she was a middle-aged woman. She wore bangles on her wrists and a large silver pendant around her long neck. Her skin was olive-complected and her eyes nearly black. She greeted everyone in the same manner, with a kiss on each cheek and a whispered confidence. Gabriel had seen many versions of her before, the woman who moves from villa to villa and party to party, who stays permanently tanned and permanently thin and cannot be bothered with a husband or children. Gabriel wondered what on earth she was doing in Cairo.

The Moroccan quintet took a break and threatened to return in ten minutes. The houselights came up slightly, as did the volume of the conversation. The woman detached herself from the bar and began working the room, moving effortlessly from table to table, alcove to alcove, as a butterfly floats from one flower to the next. Old acquaintances she greeted with kisses and a whisper. New friends were treated to a long handshake. She spoke to them in Arabic and English, in Italian and French, in Spanish and respectable German. She accepted compliments like a woman used to receiving them and left no turbulence in her wake. For the men, she was an object of cautious desire; for the women, admiration.

She arrived at the table of Herr Klemp as the band was filing back onto the stage for a second set. He stood and, bowing slightly at the waist, accepted her proffered hand. Her grip was firm, her skin cool and dry. Releasing his hand, she pushed a stray lock of hair from her face and regarded him playfully with her brown eyes. Had he not seen her give the same look to every other man in the room, he might have assumed she was flirting with him.

'I'm so glad you could join us this evening.' She spoke to him in English and in the confiding tone of a hostess who had thrown a small dinner party. 'I hope you're enjoying the music. Aren't they wonderful? I'm Mimi, by the way.'

And with that she was gone. Gabriel turned his gaze toward the stage, but in his mind he was back in Natan Hofi's underground lair, listening to the recordings of the mysterious woman with a friend named Tony.

I'm Mimi, by the way.

No, you're not, thought Gabriel. You're Madeleine. And Alexandra. And Lunetta. You're the Little Moon.

Next morning Mr Katubi was standing at his post in the lobby when the telephone purred. He glanced at the caller ID and exhaled heavily. Then he lifted the receiver slowly, a sapper defusing a bomb, and brought it to his ear.

'Good morning, Herr Klemp.'

'It is indeed, Mr Katubi.'

'Do you require assistance with your bags?'

'No assistance required, Katubi. Change in plans. I've decided to extend my stay. I'm enchanted by this place.'

'How fortunate for us,' Mr Katubi said icily. 'For how many additional nights will you require your room?'

'To be determined, Katubi. Stay tuned for further updates.'

'Staying tuned, Herr Klemp.'

14. Cairo

'I never signed up for anything like this,' Quinnell said gloomily. It was after midnight; they were in Quinnell's tired little Fiat. Across the Nile, central Cairo stirred restlessly, but Zamalek at that hour was quiet. It had taken two hours to get there. Gabriel was certain no one had followed them.

'You're sure about the flat number?'

'I've been inside,' Quinnell said. 'Not in the capacity I'd hoped, mind you, just one of Mimi's parties. She lives in flat 6A. Everyone knows Mimi's address.'

'You're sure she doesn't have a dog?'

'Just an angora cat with a weight problem. I'm sure a man who claims to be a *friend* of the great Herr Heller will have no problem dealing with an obese cat. I, on the other hand, have to contend with the seven-foot Nubian doorman. How did that happen?'

'You're one of the world's finest journalists, Quinnell. Surely you can deceive a doorman.'

'True, but this isn't exactly journalism.'

'Think of it as an English schoolboy prank. Tell him the car's died. Tell him you need help. Give him money. Five minutes, and not a minute longer. Understood?'

Quinnell nodded.

'And if your friend from the Mukhabarat shows up?' Gabriel asked. 'What's the signal?'

'Two short horn blasts, followed by a long one.'

Gabriel climbed out of the car, crossed the street, and descended a flight of stone steps leading to a quay along the waterfront. He paused for a moment to watch the graceful, angular sail of a felucca gliding slowly upriver. Then he turned and walked south, Herr Klemp's smart leather satchel hanging from his right shoulder. After a few paces the upper floors of Mimi's apartment house came into view above the rise – an old Zamalek building, whitewashed, with large terraces overlooking the river.

A hundred yards beyond the building another flight of steps rose toward the street. Gabriel, before mounting them, looked down the river to see if he had been followed but found the quay deserted. He climbed the steps and crossed the street, then made his way to the entrance of a darkened alleyway that ran along the back of the apartment houses. Had it been his first time there, he might not have found his destination, but he had walked the alley in daylight and knew with certainty that one hundred and thirty normal paces would bring him to the service entrance of Mimi Ferrere's building.

Painted on the dented metal door, in Arabic script, were the words DO NOT ENTER. Gabriel glanced at his wristwatch. The walk from the car, as expected, had taken four minutes and thirty seconds. He tried the latch and found that it was locked, as it had been earlier that day. He removed the pair of thin metal tools from the side pocket of the satchel and crouched so that the latch was at eye level. Within fifteen seconds the lock had surrendered.

He eased open the door and looked inside. A short, cement-floored corridor stretched before him. At the other end was a half-open door, which gave onto the lobby. Gabriel stole forward and concealed himself behind the second door. From the other side he could hear the voice of David Quinnell, offering the Nubian doorman twenty pounds to push his disabled car from the street. When the conversation fell silent, Gabriel peered around the edge of the door, just in time to see the robes of the Nubian flowing into the darkness.

He entered the lobby and paused at the mailboxes. The box for apartment 6A bore the label: M. FERRERE. He mounted the staircase and climbed up to the sixth floor. The door was flanked by a pair of potted palms. Gabriel pressed his ear to the wood and heard no sound from within. From his pocket he removed a device disguised as an electric razor and ran it around the edge of the door. A small light glowed green, which meant the device had detected no evidence of an electronic security system.

Gabriel slipped the apparatus back into his pocket and inserted his old-fashioned lockpick into the keyhole. Just as he began to work, he heard female voices filtering up the stairwell from below. He proceeded calmly, his fingertips registering subtle changes in tension and torque, while another part of his mind turned over the possibilities. The building had eleven floors. The chances were slightly better than even that the women on the stairs were heading for the sixth floor or higher. He had two options: abandon his work for the moment and head down the stairs toward the lobby, or seek refuge on an upper floor. Both plans had potential pitfalls. The women might find the presence of a strange foreigner in the building suspicious, and if they happened to live on the top floor, he might find himself trapped with no route of escape.

He decided to keep working. He thought of the drills he'd done at the Academy, of Shamron standing over his shoulder, exhorting him to work as though his life and the lives of his team depended on it. He could hear the clatter of their high heels now, and when one of the women squealed with laughter his heart gave a sideways lurch.

When finally the last pin gave way, Gabriel put his hand on the latch and felt the gratifying sensation of movement. He pushed open the door and slipped inside, then closed it again just as the women were reaching the landing. He leaned his back against the door and, with only his lockpick as a weapon, held his breath as they passed in laughter. For an instant he hated them for their frivolity.

He locked the door. From the satchel he removed a cigar-sized Maglite and shone the narrow beam about the flat. He was standing in a small entrance hall, beyond which was the sitting room. Cool and white, with low comfortable furniture and an abundance of colorful pillows and throws, it reminded Gabriel vaguely of Mimi's nightclub. He moved slowly forward but stopped suddenly when the light fell upon a pair of neon-yellow eyes. Mimi's fat cat lay curled atop an ottoman. It looked at Gabriel without interest, then rested its chin on its paws and closed its eyes.

He had a list of targets, organized in order of importance. Highest in priority were Mimi's telephones. He found the first in the sitting room, resting atop an end table. The second he located on the nightstand in the bedroom; the third in the room she used as an office. To each he attached a miniature device known in the lexicon of the Office as a glass, a transmitter that would provide coverage of both the telephone and the room around it. With a range of roughly a thousand yards it would permit Gabriel to use his suite at the Intercontinental as a listening post.

In the office he also found the second item on his target list, Mimi's computer. He sat down, powered on the computer, and inserted a compact disk into the drive. The software engaged automatically and began collecting the data stored on the hard drive: mailboxes, documents, photographs, even audio and video files.

While the files downloaded, Gabriel had a look round the rest of the office. He leafed through a stack of post, opened desk drawers, glanced at the files. The absence of time permitted nothing more than a cursory examination of the items, and Gabriel found nothing that leapt to his attention.

He checked the progress of the download, then stood up and played the beam of the Maglite around the walls. One was covered with several framed photographs. Most showed Mimi with other beautiful people. In one he saw a younger version of Mimi, her shoulders wrapped in a kaffiyeh. In the background stood the pyramids of Giza. They, like her face, were washed in sienna by the sinking sun – Mimi, New Age idealist, trying to save the world from destruction through the power of positive thinking.

A second photograph caught Gabriel's eye: Mimi, her head resting on a lavender-colored pillow, staring directly into the camera lens. Her cheek was pressed to the face of a man feigning sleep. A hat was pulled down over his eyes, so that only his nose, mouth, and chin were visible – enough of the face, Gabriel knew, for the experts in facial recognition to make a positive identification. He produced a small digital camera from Herr Klemp's satchel and took a photograph of the photograph.

He walked back to the desk and saw that the download was complete. He removed the disk from the drive and shut down the computer. Then he glanced at his wristwatch. He'd been inside the flat for seven minutes, two minutes longer than he'd planned. He dropped the disk into his satchel, then went to the front door, pausing for a moment to make certain the landing was empty before letting himself out.

The stairwell was deserted, as was the lobby except for the Nubian doorman, who wished Gabriel a pleasant evening as he slipped past and went into the street. Quinnell, a picture of indifference, was sitting on the hood of his car, smoking a cigarette. Like a good professional, he kept his eyes to the ground as Gabriel turned to the left and started walking toward the Tahrir Bridge.

Next morning Herr Klemp fell ill. Mr Katubi, after receiving a disagreeably detailed description of the symptoms, diagnosed the disorder as bacterial in nature and predicted the onslaught would be violent but brief. 'Cairo has betrayed me,' Herr Klemp complained. 'I was seduced by her, and she repaid my affection with vengeance.'

Mr Katubi's forecast of a swift recovery proved erroneous. The storm in Herr Klemp's bowels raged on for many days and nights. Doctors were summoned, medication was prescribed, but nothing seemed to work. Mr Katubi set aside his hard feelings for Herr Klemp and personally assumed responsibility for his care. He prescribed a time-proven potion of boiled potatoes sprinkled with lemon juice and salt and delivered the concoction himself three times daily.

Illness softened Herr Klemp's demeanor. He was pleasant to Mr Katubi and even apologetic to the maids who had to clean his appalling bathroom. Sometimes, when Mr Katubi entered the room, he would find Herr Klemp seated in the armchair next to the window, gazing wearily toward the river. He spent most of his time, though, stretched listlessly on the bed. To relieve the boredom of captivity he listened to music and German-language news on his shortwave radio, on tiny earphones so as not to disturb the other guests. Mr Katubi found himself missing the old Johannes Klemp. Sometimes he would look up from his outpost in the lobby and long to see the cantankerous German pounding across the marble floor with his coattails flapping and his jaw steeled for confrontation.

One morning, a week to the day after Herr Klemp had first taken ill, Mr Katubi knocked on Herr Klemp's door and was surprised by the vigorous voice that ordered him to come in. He slipped his passkey into the lock and entered. Herr Klemp was packing his bags.

'The storm has ended, Katubi.'

'Are you certain?'

'As certain as one can be in a situation like this.'

'I'm sorry Cairo treated you so badly, Herr Klemp. I suppose the decision to extend your stay turned out to be a mistake.'

'Perhaps, Katubi, but then I've never been one to dwell on the past, and neither should you.'

'It is the Arab disease, Herr Klemp.'

'I suffer from no such affliction, Katubi.' Herr Klemp placed his shortwave radio into his bag and closed the zipper. 'Tomorrow is another day.'

It was raining in Frankfurt that evening – the Lufthansa pilot had made that abundantly clear. He'd spoken of the rain while they were still on the ground in Cairo, and twice during the flight he'd provided them with tedious updates. Gabriel had latched onto the pilot's plodding voice, for it had given him something to do besides stare at his wristwatch and calculate the hours until Khaled's next massacre of innocents. As they neared Frankfurt he leaned his head against the glass and looked out, hoping to glimpse the first lights of the south German plain, but instead he saw only blackness. The jetliner plunged into the cloud, and his window was awash with horizontal streaks of rainwater – and Gabriel, in the scampering droplets, saw Khaled's teams moving into position for their next strike. Then suddenly the runway appeared, a sheet of polished black marble rising slowly to receive them, and they were down.

In the terminal he went to a telephone kiosk and dialed the number for a freight forwarding company in Brussels. He identified himself as Stevens, one of his many telephone names, and asked to speak to a Mr Parsons. He heard a series of clicks and hums, then a female voice, distant and with a slight echo.

The girl, Gabriel knew, was at that moment seated on the Operations Control desk at King Saul Boulevard.

'What do you require?' she asked.

'Voice identification.'

'You have a recording?'

'Yes.'

'Quality?'

Gabriel, using Hebrew terms no listener could comprehend, tersely relayed to the girl the technical means with which he had captured and recorded the subject's voice.

'Play the recording, please.'

Gabriel pressed PLAY and held his recorder up to the mouthpiece of the receiver. Male voice, perfect French.

'It's me. Give me a ring when you have a chance. Nothing urgent. Ciao.'

He lowered the tape player and placed the receiver against his ear.

'No match on file,' said the woman.

'Compare to unidentified voiceprint 698/D.'

'Stand by.' Then, a moment later: 'It's a match.'

'I need a telephone number ID.'

Gabriel located the second intercept, then pressed PLAY and held the recorder up to the phone again. It was the sound of Mimi Ferrere making an international call from the phone in her office. When the last number had been dialed, Gabriel pressed pause.

The woman at the other end of the line recited the

number: *00 33 91 54 67 98*. Gabriel knew that 33 was the country code for France and that 91 was the city code for Marseilles.

'Run it,' he said.

'Stand by.'

Two minutes later the woman said: 'The telephone is registered to a Monsieur Paul Véran, 56 boulevard St-Rémy, Marseilles.'

'I need another voice identification.'

'Quality?'

'Same as before.'

'Play the recording.'

Gabriel pressed PLAY, but this time the voice was drowned out by the sound of a security announcement, in German, blaring from the speaker above his head: *Achtung! Achtung!* When it was over, he pressed PLAY again. This time the voice, a woman's, was clearly audible.

'It's me. Where are you? Call me when you can. Much love.'

STOP.

'No match on file.'

'Compare to unidentified voiceprint 572/B.'

'Stand by.' Then: 'It's a match.'

'Please note, subject goes by the name Mimi Ferrere. Her address is 24 Brazil Street, apartment 6A, Cairo.'

'I've added it to the file. Elapsed time of this call four minutes, thirty-two seconds. Anything else?'

'I need you to pass a message to Ezekiel.'

Ezekiel was the telephone code word for the Operations directorate.

'Message?'

'Our friend is spending time in Marseilles, at the address you gave me.'

'Number 56 boulevard St-Rémy?'

'That's right,' Gabriel said. 'I need instructions from Ezekiel on where to proceed.'

'You're calling from Frankfurt airport?'

'Yes.'

'I'm terminating this call. Move to another location and call back in five minutes. I'll have instructions for you then.'

Gabriel hung up the phone. He went to a news-stand, bought a German magazine, then walked a short distance through the terminal to another kiosk of telephones. Same number, same patter, same girl in Tel Aviv.

'Ezekiel wants you to go to Rome.'

'*Rome?* Why Rome?'

'You know I can't answer that.'

It was no matter. Gabriel knew the answer.

'Where should I go?'

'The apartment near the Piazza di Spagna. Do you know it?'

Gabriel did. It was a lovely safe flat at the top of the Spanish Steps, not far from the Church of the Trinità dei Monti.

'There's a flight from Frankfurt to Rome in two hours. We're booking a seat for you.'

'Do you want my frequent-flyer number?'

'What?'

'Never mind.'

'Have a safe trip,' said the girl, and the line went dead.

PART THREE
The Gare de Lyon

15. Marseilles

For the second time in ten days Paul Martineau made the drive from Aix-en-Provence to Marseilles. Once again he entered the coffeehouse on the small street off the rue des Convalescents and climbed the narrow stairs to the flat on the first floor, and once again he was greeted on the landing by the gowned figure who spoke to him quietly in Arabic. They sat, propped on silk pillows, on the floor of the tiny living room. The man slowly loaded hashish into a hubble-bubble and touched a lighted match to the bowl. In Marseilles he was known as Hakim el-Bakri, a recent immigrant from Algiers. Martineau knew him by another name, Abu Saddiq. Martineau did not refer to him by that name, just as Abu Saddiq did not call Martineau by the name he'd been given by his real father.

Abu Saddiq drew heavily on the mouthpiece of the pipe, then inclined it in Martineau's direction. Martineau took a long pull at the hashish and allowed the smoke to drift out his nostrils. Then he finished the last of his coffee. A veiled woman took away his empty cup and offered him another. When Martineau shook his head, the woman slipped silently from the room.

He closed his eyes as a wave of pleasure washed over his body. The Arab way, he thought – a bit of smoke, a cup of sweet coffee, the subservience of a woman who knew her place in life. Though he had been raised a proper Frenchman, it was Arab blood that flowed in his veins and Arabic that felt most comfortable on his tongue. The poet's language, the language of conquest and suffering. There were times when the separation from his people was almost too painful to bear. In Provence he was surrounded by people like himself, yet he could not touch them. It was as if he had been condemned to wander among them, as a damned spirit drifts among the living. Only here, in Abu Saddiq's tiny flat, could he behave as the man he truly was. Abu Saddiq understood this, which was why he seemed in no hurry to get around to business. He loaded more hashish into the water pipe and struck another match.

Martineau took another draw from the pipe, this one deeper than the last, and held the smoke until it seemed his lungs might burst. Now his mind was floating. He saw Palestine, not with his own eyes but as it had been described to him by those who had actually seen it. Martineau, like his father, had never set foot there. Lemon trees and olives groves – that's what he imagined. Sweet springs and goats pulling on the tan hills of the Galilee. A bit like Provence, he thought, before the arrival of the Greeks.

The image disintegrated, and he found himself wandering across a landscape of Celtic and Roman ruins. He came to a village, a village on the Coastal Plain of Palestine. Beit Sayeed, they had called it. Now there was nothing but a footprint in the dusty soil. Martineau, in his hallucination, fell to his knees and with his spade clawed at the earth. It surrendered nothing, no tools or pottery, no coins or human remains. It was as if the people had simply vanished.

He forced open his eyes. The vision dissipated. His mission would soon be over. The murders of his father and grandfather would be avenged, his birthright fulfilled. Martineau was confident he would not spend his final days as a Frenchman in Provence but as an Arab in Palestine. His people, lost and scattered, would be returned to the land, and Beit Sayeed would rise once more from its grave. The days of the Jews were numbered. They would leave like all those who had come to Palestine before them – the Greeks and Romans, the Persians and the Assyrians, the Turks and the British. One day soon, Martineau was convinced, he would be searching for artifacts amid the ruins of a Jewish settlement.

Abu Saddiq was pulling at his shirtsleeve and calling him by his real name. Martineau turned his head slowly and fixed Abu Saddiq in a heavy-lidded gaze. 'Call me Martineau,' he said in French. 'I'm Paul Martineau. *Doctor* Paul Martineau.'

'You were far away for a moment.'

'I was in Palestine,' Martineau murmured, his speech heavy with the drug. 'Beit Sayeed.'

'We'll all be there soon,' Abu Saddiq said.

Martineau treated himself to a smile – not one of arrogance but of quiet confidence. Buenos Aires, Istanbul, Rome – three attacks, each flawlessly planned and executed. The teams had delivered their explosives to the target and had vanished without a trace. In each operation, Martineau had concealed himself with archaeological work and had operated through a cutout. Abu Saddiq was handling the Paris operation. Martineau had conceived and planned it; Abu Saddiq, from his coffeehouse in the Quartier Belsunce, moved the chess pieces at Martineau's command. When it was over Abu Saddiq would suffer the same fate as all those Martineau had used. He had learned from the mistakes of his ancestors. He would never allow himself to be undone by an Arab traitor.

Abu Saddiq offered Martineau the pipe. Martineau lifted his hand in surrender. Then, with a slow nod of his head, he instructed Abu Saddiq to get on with the final briefing. For the next half hour Martineau remained silent while Abu Saddiq spoke: the locations of the teams, the addresses in Paris where the suitcase bombs were being assembled, the emotional state of the three *shaheeds*. Abu Saddiq stopped talking while the veiled woman poured more coffee. When she was gone again Abu Saddiq mentioned that the last member of the team would arrive in Marseilles in two days' time.

'She wants to see you,' Abu Saddiq said. '*Before* the operation.'

Martineau shook his head. He knew the girl – they had been lovers once – and he knew why she wanted to see him. It was better they not spend time together now. Otherwise Martineau might have second thoughts about what he had planned for her.

'We stay to the original plan,' he said. 'Where do I meet her?'

'The Internet café overlooking the harbor. Do you know it?'

Martineau did.

'She'll be there at twelve-thirty.'

Just then, from the minaret of a mosque up the street, the muezzin summoned the faithful to prayer. Martineau closed his eyes as the familiar words washed over him.

God is most great. I testify that there is no god but God. I testify that Muhammad is the Prophet of God. Come to prayer. Come to success. God is most great. There is no god but God.

Martineau, when the call to prayer had ended, stood and prepared to take his leave.

'Where's Hadawi?' he asked.

'Zurich.'

'He's something of a liability, wouldn't you say?'

Abu Saddiq nodded. 'Should I move him?'

'No,' said Martineau. 'Just kill him.'

Martineau's head had cleared by the time he reached the Place de la Préfecture. How different things were on this side of Marseilles, he thought. The streets were cleaner, the shops more plentiful. Martineau the archaeologist could not help but reflect on the nature of the two worlds that existed side by side in this ancient city. One was focused on devotion, the other on consumption. One had many children, the other found children to be a financial burden. The French, Martineau knew, would soon be a minority in their own country, *colons* in their own land. Someday soon, a century, perhaps a bit longer, France would be a Muslim country.

He turned into the boulevard St-Rémy. Tree-lined and split by a *payage* parking lot in the median, the street rose at a slight pitch toward a small green park with a view of the old port. The buildings on each side were fashioned of stately graystone and uniform in height. Iron bars covered the ground-floor windows. Many of the buildings contained professional offices – lawyers, doctors, estate agents – and farther up the street there were a couple of banks and a large interior-design store. At the base of the street, on the edge of the Place de la Préfecture, were a pair of opposing kiosks – one selling newspapers, the other sandwiches. During the day there was a small market in the street, but now that it was dusk the vendors had packed up their cheese and fresh vegetables and gone home.

The building at Number 56 was residential only. The foyer was clean, the stairway wide with a wood banister and a new runner. The flat was empty except for a single white couch and a telephone on the floor.

Martineau bent down, lifted the receiver, and dialed a number. An answering machine, just as he'd expected.

'I'm in Marseilles. Call me when you have a chance.'

He hung up the phone, then sat on the couch. He felt the pressure of his gun pushing into the small of his back. He leaned forward and drew it from the waist of his jeans. A Stechkin nine-millimeter – his father's gun. For many years after his father's death in Paris, the weapon had gathered dust in a police lockup, evidence for a trial that would never take place. An agent of French intelligence spirited the gun to Tunis in 1985 and made a gift of it to Arafat. Arafat had given it to Martineau.

The telephone rang. Martineau answered.

'Monsieur Véran?'

'Mimi, my love,' Martineau said. 'So good to hear the sound of your voice.'

16. Rome

The telephone woke him. Like all safe flat phones, it had no ringer, only a flashing light, luminous as a channel marker, that turned his eyelids to crimson. He reached out and brought the receiver to his ear.

'Wake up,' said Shimon Pazner.

'What time is it?'

'Eight-thirty.'

Gabriel had slept twelve hours.

'Get dressed. There's something you should see since you're in town.'

'I've analyzed the photographs, I've read all the reports. I don't need to see it.'

'Yes, you do.'

'Why?'

'It'll piss you off.'

'What good will that do?'

'Sometimes we need to be pissed off,' Pazner said. 'I'll meet you on the steps of the Galleria Borghese in an hour. Don't leave me standing there like an idiot.'

Pazner hung up. Gabriel climbed out of bed and stood beneath the shower for a long time, debating whether to shave his beard. In the end he decided to trim it instead. He dressed in one of Herr Klemp's dark suits and went to the Via Veneto for coffee. One hour after hanging up with Pazner he was walking along a shaded gravel footpath toward the steps of the galleria. The Rome *katsa* sat on a marble bench in the forecourt, smoking a cigarette.

'Nice beard,' said Pazner. 'Christ, you look like hell.'

'I needed an excuse to stay in my hotel room in Cairo.'

'How'd you do it?'

Gabriel answered: a common pharmaceutical product that, when ingested instead of used properly, had a disastrous but temporary effect on the gastro-intestinal tract.

'How many doses did you take?'

'Three.'

'Poor bastard.'

They headed north through the gardens – Pazner like a man marching to a drum only he could hear, Gabriel at his side, weary from too much travel and too many worries. On the perimeter of the park, near the botanical gardens, was the entrance to the cul-de-sac. For days after the bombing the world's media had camped out in the intersection. The ground was still littered with their cigarette ends and crushed Styrofoam coffee cups. It looked to Gabriel like a patch of farmland after the annual harvest festival.

They entered the street and made their way down the slope of the hill, until they arrived at a temporary steel barricade, watched over by Italian police and

Israeli security men. Pazner was immediately admitted, along with his bearded German acquaintance.

Once beyond the fence they could see the first signs of damage: the scorched stone pine stripped clean of their needles; the blown-out windows in the neighboring villas; the pieces of twisted debris lying about like scraps of discarded paper. A few more paces and the bomb crater came into view, ten feet deep at least and surrounded by a halo of burnt pavement. Little remained of the buildings closest to the blast point; deeper in the compound, the structures remained standing, but the sides facing the explosion had been sheared away, so that the effect was of a child's dollhouse. Gabriel glimpsed an intact office with framed photographs still propped on the desk and a bathroom with a towel still hanging from the rod. The air was heavy with the stench of ash and, Gabriel feared, the lingering scent of burning flesh. From deep within the compound came the scrape and grumble of backhoes and bulldozers. The crime scene, like the corpse of a murder victim, had given up its final clues. Now it was time for the burial.

Gabriel stayed longer than he'd thought he would. No past wound, real or perceived, no grievance or political dispute justified an act of murder on this scale. Pazner was right – the very sight of it moved him to intense anger. But there was something else, something more than anger. It made him hate. He turned and started walking back up the hill. Pazner followed silently after him.

'Who told you to bring me here?'

'It was my idea.'

'Who?'

'The old man,' Pazner said quietly.

'Why?'

'I don't know why.'

Gabriel stopped. '*Why*, Shimon?'

'Varash met last night after you checked in from Frankfurt. Go back to the safe flat. Wait there for further instructions. Someone will be in touch soon.'

And with that Pazner crossed the street and disappeared into the Villa Borghese.

But he did not return to the safe flat. Instead, he headed in the opposite direction, into the residential districts of north Rome. He found the Via Trieste and followed it west, until he arrived, ten minutes later, in an untidy little square called the Piazza Annabaliano.

Little about it had changed in the thirty years since Gabriel had first seen it – the same stand of melancholy trees in the center of the square, the same dreary shops catering to customers of the working classes. And at the northern edge, wedged between two streets, was the same apartment house, shaped like a slice of pie, with the point facing the square and the Bar Trieste on the ground floor. Zwaiter used to stop in the bar to use the telephone before heading upstairs to his room.

Gabriel crossed the square, picking his way through the cars and motorbikes parked haphazardly in the center, and entered the apartment house through a doorway marked 'Entrance C.' The foyer was cold and in darkness. The lights, Gabriel remembered, operated on a timer to save electricity. Surveillance of the building had noted that residents, including Zwaiter, rarely bothered to switch them on – a fact that would prove to be an operational asset for Gabriel, because it had virtually assured him the advantage of working in the dark.

Now he paused in front of the elevator. Next to the elevator was a mirror. Surveillance had neglected to mention it. Gabriel, seeing his own reflection in the glass that night, had nearly drawn his Beretta and fired. Instead he had calmly reached into his jacket pocket for a coin and was holding it out toward the payment slot on the elevator when Zwaiter, dressed in a plaid jacket and clutching a paper sack containing a bottle of fig wine, walked through Entrance C for the last time.

'*Excuse me, but are you Wadal Zwaiter?*'

'*No! Please, no!*'

Gabriel had allowed the coin to fall from his fingertips. Before it had struck the floor he had drawn his Beretta and fired the first two shots. One of the rounds pierced the paper sack before striking Zwaiter in the chest. Blood and wine had mingled at Gabriel's feet as he poured fire into the Palestinian's collapsing body.

Now he looked into the mirror and saw himself as he had been that night, a boy angel in a leather jacket, an artist who had no comprehension of how the act he was about to commit would forever alter the course of his life. He had become someone else. He had remained someone else ever since. Shamron had neglected to tell him that would happen. He had taught him how to draw a gun and fire in one second, but he had done nothing to prepare him for what would happen afterward. Engaging the terrorist on his terms, on his battlefield, comes at a terrible price. It changes the men who do it, along with the society that dispatches them. It is the terrorist's ultimate weapon. For Gabriel, the changes were visible as well. By the time he'd staggered into Paris for his next assignment, his temples were gray.

He looked into the mirror again and saw the bearded figure of Herr Klemp looking back at him. Images of the case flashed through his mind: a flattened embassy, his own dossier, *Khaled* . . . Was Shamron right? Was Khaled sending him a message? Had Khaled chosen Rome because of what Gabriel had done thirty years ago, on this very spot?

He heard the soft shuffle of footfalls behind him — an old woman, dressed in the black of widowhood, clutching a plastic sack of groceries. She stared directly at him. Gabriel, for an instant, feared she somehow remembered him. He bid her a pleasant morning and went back out into the sunlit piazza.

He felt suddenly feverish. He walked for a time on the Via Trieste, then flagged down a taxi and asked the driver to take him to the Piazza di Spagna.

Entering the safe flat he saw a copy of that morning's *La Repubblica* newspaper lying on the floor of the entrance hall. On page six was a large advertisement for an Italian sports car. Gabriel looked at the ad carefully and saw that it had been cut from another edition of the newspaper and glued over the corresponding page. He trimmed away the edges of the page and discovered, hidden between the two pages, a sheet of paper containing the coded text of the message. After reading it he burned it in the kitchen sink and went out again.

On the Via Condotti he bought a new suitcase and spent the next hour purchasing clothing appropriate to his next destination. He returned to the safe flat long enough to pack his new bag, then went to lunch at Nino on the Via Borgognona. At two o'clock he took a taxi to Fiumicino Airport, and at five-thirty he boarded a flight to Sardinia.

As Gabriel's plane was taxiing toward the runway, Amira Assaf rolled up to the front gate of the Stratford Clinic and showed her ID badge to the security guard. He inspected it carefully, then waved her onto the grounds. She twisted the throttle of her motorbike and sped down the quarter-mile gravel drive toward the mansion. Dr Avery was just leaving for the night, racing toward the gate in his big silver Jaguar. Amira tapped her horn and waved, but he ignored her and swept past in a shower of dust and gravel.

Staff parking was in the rear courtyard. She propped the bike on its kickstand, then removed her backpack from the seat storage compartment and left her helmet in its place. Two girls were just coming off duty. Amira bid them good night, then used her badge to unlock the secure staff entrance. The time clock was mounted to the wall of the foyer. She found her card, third slot from the bottom, and punched in: 5:56 P.M.

The locker room was a few paces down the hall. Amira went inside and changed into her uniform: white trousers, white shoes, and a peach-colored tunic that Dr Avery believed was soothing to the patients. Five minutes later she reported for duty at the window of the head nurse's station. Ginger Hall, peroxide blond and crimson-lipped, looked up and smiled.

'New haircut, Amira? Very fetching. My goodness, what I wouldn't do for that thick raven hair of yours.'

'You can have it, along with the brown skin, the black eyes, and all the other shit that comes with it.'

'Ah, rubbish, petal. We're all nurses here. Just doing our job and trying to make a decent living.'

'Maybe, but out there it's different. What have you got for me?'

'Lee Martinson. She's in the solarium. Get her back up to her room. Settle her in for the night.'

'That big bloke still hanging round her?'

'The bodyguard? Still here. Dr Avery reckons he'll be here awhile.'

'Why would a woman like Miss Martinson need a bodyguard?'

'Confidential, my sweet. Highly confidential.'

Amira set off down the corridor. A moment later she came to the entrance of the solarium. As she went inside the humidity greeted her like a wet blanket. Miss Martinson was in her wheelchair, staring at the blackened windows. The bodyguard, hearing Amira's approach, got to his feet. He was a large, heavily built man in his twenties, with short hair and blue eyes. He spoke with a British accent, but Amira doubted he was truly British. She looked down at Miss Martinson.

'It's getting late, sweetheart. Time to go upstairs and get ready for bed.'

She pushed the wheelchair out of the solarium, then along the corridor to the elevators. The bodyguard pressed the call button. A moment later they boarded a lift and rode silently upward to her room on the fourth floor. Before entering, Amira paused and looked at the guard.

'I'm going to bathe her. Why don't you wait out here until I'm finished?'

'Wherever she goes, I go.'

'We do this *every* night. The poor woman deserves a bit of privacy.'

'Wherever she goes, I go,' he repeated.

Amira shook her head and wheeled Miss Martinson into her room, the bodyguard trailing silently after her.

17. Bosa, Sardinia

For two days Gabriel waited for them to make contact. The hotel, small and ochre-colored, stood in the ancient port near the spot where the river Temo flowed into the sea. His room was on the top floor and had a small balcony with an iron rail. He slept late, took breakfast in the dining room, and spent mornings reading. For lunch he would eat pasta and fish in one of the restaurants in the port, then he would hike up the road to the beach north of town and spread his towel on the sand and sleep some more. After two days, his appearance had improved dramatically. He'd gained weight and strength, and the skin beneath his eyes no longer looked yellow-brown and jaundiced. He was even beginning to like the way he looked with the beard.

On the third morning the telephone rang. He listened to the instructions without speaking, then hung up. He showered and dressed and packed his bag, then went downstairs to breakfast. After breakfast he paid his bill and placed his bag in the trunk of the car he'd rented in Cagliari and drove north, about thirty miles, to the port town of Alghero. He left the car on the street where he'd been told to, then walked along a shadowed alleyway that emptied into the waterfront.

Dina was seated in a café on the quay, drinking coffee. She wore sunglasses, sandals, and a sleeveless dress; her shoulder-length dark hair shone in the dazzling light reflected by the sea. Gabriel descended a flight of stone steps on the quay and boarded a fifteen-foot dinghy with the word *Fidelity* written on the hull. He started the engine, a ninety-horsepower Yamaha, and untied the lines. Dina joined him a moment later and, in passable French, told him to make for the large white motor yacht anchored about a half-mile from the shoreline on the turquoise sea.

Gabriel guided the dinghy slowly out of the port, then, reaching the open water, he increased his speed and bounced toward the yacht over the gentle swells. As he drew near, Rami stepped onto the aft deck, dressed in khaki shorts and a white shirt. He climbed down to the swim step and was waiting there, hand outstretched, as Gabriel arrived.

The main salon, when they entered, looked like a substation of the team's headquarters in the basement of King Saul Boulevard. The walls were hung with large-scale maps and aerial photographs, and the onboard electronics had been augmented with the sort of technical communications equipment Gabriel had not seen since the Abu Jihad assassination. Yaakov looked up from a computer terminal and extended his hand. Shamron, dressed in khaki trousers and a white short-sleeved shirt, was seated at the galley table. He pushed his reading glasses onto his forehead and appraised Gabriel as though he were a document or another map. 'Welcome to *Fidelity*,' he said, 'combination command post and safe flat.'

'Where did you get it?'

'From a friend of the Office. It happened to be in Cannes. We took it out to sea and added the additional equipment we needed for our journey. We also changed the name.'

'Who chose it?'

'I did,' said Shamron. 'It means loyalty and faithfulness –'

'– and a devotion to duty or to one's obligations or vows,' Gabriel said. 'I know what it means. I also know why you chose it – the same reason why you told Shimon Pazner to take me to the ruins of the embassy.'

'I thought it was important that you see it. Sometimes, when one is in the middle of an operation like this, the enemy can become something of an abstraction. It's easy to forget his true nature. I thought you might need a bit of a reminder.'

'I've been doing this for a long time, Ari. I know the nature of my enemy, and I know what it means to be loyal.' Gabriel sat down at the table across from Shamron. 'I hear Varash met after I came out of Cairo. I suppose their decision is fairly obvious.'

'Khaled was given his trial,' Shamron said, 'and Varash delivered its verdict.'

Gabriel had carried out the sentences of such proceedings, but he had never actually been present at one. They *were* trials of sorts, but they were weighted profoundly in favor of the prosecution and conducted under conditions so secret that the accused did not even know they were taking place. The defendants were granted no lawyers in this courtroom; their fates were decided not by a jury of their peers but of their mortal enemies. Evidence of guilt went unchallenged. Exculpatory evidence was never introduced. There were no transcripts and no means of appeal. Only one sentence was possible, and it was irrevocable.

'Since I'm the investigating officer, would you mind if I offer an opinion about the case?'

'If you must.'

'The case against Khaled is wholly circumstantial, and tenuous at best.'

'The trail of evidence is clear,' Shamron said. 'And we started down that trail based on information given to us by a *Palestinian* source.'

'That's what concerns me.'

Yaakov joined them at the table. 'Mahmoud Arwish has been one of our top assets inside the Palestinian Authority for several years now. Everything he's told us has been proven correct.'

'But even Arwish isn't certain the man in that photograph is Khaled. The case is a house of cards. If one of the cards turns out not to be true, then the entire case collapses – and we end up with a dead man on a French street.'

'The one thing we know about Khaled's appearance is that it was said he bore a striking resemblance to his grandfather,' Shamron said. 'I'm the only person in this room who ever saw the sheikh face-to-face, and I saw him under circumstances that are impossible to forget.' Shamron held up the photograph for the others to see. 'The man in this photograph could be Sheikh Asad's twin brother.'

'That still doesn't *prove* he's Khaled. We are talking about killing a man.'

Shamron turned the photograph directly toward Gabriel. 'Will you acknowledge that if this man walks into the apartment building at 56 boulevard St-Rémy, he is, in all likelihood, Khaled al-Khalifa?'

'I will acknowledge that.'

'So we put the building under watch. And we wait. And we hope he comes before the next massacre. If he does, we get his photograph as he enters the building. If our experts are damned sure he's the same man, we put him out of business.' Shamron folded his arms across his chest. 'Of course, there is one other method of identification – the same one we used during the Wrath of God operation.'

An image flashed in Gabriel's memory.

'Excuse me, but are you Wadal Zwaiter?'

'No! Please, no!'

'It takes a very cool customer not to respond to

his real name in a situation like that,' Shamron said. 'And an even cooler one not to reach for his gun when confronted with a man who's about to kill him. Either way, if it's truly Khaled, he'll identify himself, and your mind will be at peace when you pull the trigger.'

Shamron pushed his spectacles onto his forehead. 'I want *Fidelity* in Marseilles by nightfall. Are you going to be on it?'

'We'll use the Wrath of God model,' Shamron began. '*Aleph, Bet, Ayin, Qoph*. It has two advantages. It will seem familiar to you and it works.'

Gabriel nodded.

'Out of necessity, we've made some minor alterations and combined some of the roles, but once the operation is set in motion, it will feel the same to you. You, of course, are the *Aleph*, the gunman. The *Ayin* teams, the watchers, are already moving into place. If Khaled comes to that flat, two of the watchers will switch to the role of *Bet* and cover your escape route.'

'And Yaakov?'

'You two seem to have established something of a rapport. Yaakov will be your deputy team leader. On the night of the hit, should we be so fortunate, he will be your driver.'

'What about Dina?'

'*Qoph*,' Shamron said. 'Communications. She'll consult with King Saul Boulevard on the identification of the target. She'll also serve as Yaakov's *bat leveyha.* You'll remain concealed on the boat until the hit. When Khaled is down, everyone leaves town by separate routes and makes their way out of the country. You and Yaakov will travel to Geneva and fly home from there. Dina will take the boat out of port. Once she's out in open waters, we'll put a team aboard and bring it home.'

Shamron spread a map of central Marseilles over the table. 'A slip has been reserved for you here' – he tapped the map with his stubby forefinger – 'on the east side of the old port, along the Quai de Rive-Neuve. The boulevard St-Rémy is here' – another tap – 'six streets to the east. It runs from the Place de la Préfecture, south to the Jardin Pierre Puget.'

Shamron placed a satellite photograph of the street atop the map.

'It is, quite frankly, a perfect street for us to operate. Number 56 is located here, on the east side of the street. It has only one entrance, which means that we won't miss Khaled if he comes. As you can see from the photograph, the street is busy – lots of traffic, people on the sidewalks, shops and offices. The entrance to Number 56 is visible from this large esplanade in front of the Palais de Justice. The park is home to a colony of derelicts. We've got a pair of watchers there now.'

Shamron adjusted the angle of the photograph.

'But here's the best feature, the *payage* parking lot in the median. This space here is now occupied by a car rented by one of the watchers. We have five other cars. At this moment they're all being fitted with miniature high-resolution cameras. The cameras transmit their images by scrambled wireless signal. You have the only decoder.'

Shamron nodded at Yaakov, who pressed a button. A large plasma-screen television rose slowly from the entertainment console.

'You'll keep watch on the entrance from here,' Shamron said. 'The watchers will rotate the cars at irregular intervals in case Khaled or one of his men keeps an eye on the *payage*. They've worked out the timing, so that when one car leaves, the next can pull into the same space.'

'Ingenious,' Gabriel murmured.

'Actually, it was Yaakov's suggestion. He's done this sort of thing in places where it's much more difficult to conceal the surveillance teams.' Shamron lit a cigarette. 'Show him the computer program.'

Yaakov sat down in front of a laptop computer and typed in a command. A virtual animation of the boulevard St-Rémy and the surrounding streets appeared on the screen.

'Because they know your face, you can't leave the boat until the night of the hit. That means you can't familiarize yourself with the neighborhood. But at least you can do it here. Technical created this so you can walk the boulevard St-Rémy from right here in the salon of *Fidelity*.'

'It's not the same.'

'Granted,' said Shamron, 'but it will have to suffice.' He lapsed into a contemplative silence. 'So what happens when you see an Arab man, mid-thirties, entering the apartment house at Number 56?' He allowed the question to hang on the air for a moment, then answered it himself. 'You and Dina will make a determination whether it *could* be him. If you make such a determination, you'll send a flash to King Saul Boulevard over the secure link. Then you'll transmit the video. If we're satisfied, we'll give you the order to go. You and Yaakov will leave *Fidelity* and head toward the Place de la Préfecture by motorcycle – Yaakov driving, of course, you on the back. You'll find someplace to wait. Perhaps you'll just park in the square or have a beer in a sidewalk café. If he stays for some time, you'll have to keep moving. It's a busy part of town that stays up late. You're both experienced operatives. You know what to do. When Dina sees Khaled step out that door, she'll signal you by radio. You need to be back on the boulevard St-Rémy in no more than thirty seconds.'

Shamron slowly crushed out his cigarette.

'I don't care if it's broad daylight,' he said evenly. 'I don't care if he's with a friend. I don't care if the act is witnessed by a crowd of people. When Khaled al-Khalifa steps out of that apartment house, I want you to put him on the ground and be done with it.'

'The escape route?'

'Up the boulevard Notre-Dame, over the avenue du Prado. Head east at high speed. The *Ayin* will leave a car for you in the parking lot of the Vélodrome. Then get to Geneva as quickly as possible. We'll put you in a flat there and move you when it's safe.'

'When do we leave Sardinia?'

'Now,' Shamron said. 'Head due north, toward Corsica. On the southwest corner of the island is the port of Propriano. The Marseilles ferry leaves from there. You can shadow it across the Mediterranean. It's nine hours from Propriano. Slip into the port after dark and register with the harbormaster. Then make contact with the watchers and establish the link with the surveillance camera.'

'And you?'

'The last thing you need in Marseilles is an old man looking over your shoulder. Rami and I will leave you here. We'll be back in Tel Aviv by tomorrow evening.'

Gabriel picked up the satellite image of the boulevard St-Rémy and studied it carefully.

'*Aleph, Bet, Ayin, Qoph,*' said Shamron. 'It will be just like the old days.'

'Yes,' Gabriel replied. 'What on earth could go wrong?'

Yaakov and Dina waited aboard *Fidelity* while Gabriel took Shamron and Rami ashore. Rami leapt onto the quay and held the dinghy steady while Shamron climbed slowly out.

'This is the end,' Gabriel said. 'The last time. After this, it's over.'

'For both of us, I'm afraid,' Shamron said. 'You'll come home, we'll grow old together.'

'We're already old.'

Shamron shrugged. 'But not too old for one last fight.'

'We'll see.'

'If you get the shot, don't hesitate. Do your duty.'

'To whom?'

'To me, of course.'

Gabriel brought the dinghy around and headed out into the harbor. He looked over his shoulder once and glimpsed Shamron standing motionless on the quay with his arm raised in a gesture of farewell. When he turned a second time the old man was gone. *Fidelity* was already under way. Gabriel opened the throttle and followed after it.

18. Marseilles

Within twenty-four hours of *Fidelity*'s arrival in Marseilles, Gabriel had grown to loathe the doorway of the apartment house at 56 boulevard St-Rémy. He loathed the door itself. He loathed the latch and the frame. He detested the graystone of the building and iron bars on the ground-floor windows. He resented all those who trod past on the pavement, especially Arab-looking men in their mid-thirties. More than anything, though, he despised the other tenants: the distinguished gentleman in a Cardin blazer who practiced law from an office up the street; the gray-haired grande dame whose terrier shat first thing each morning on the pavement; and the woman named Sophie who shopped for a living and bore more than a passing resemblance to Leah.

They monitored the screen in shifts – one hour on, two hours off. Each adopted a unique posture for watching. Yaakov would smoke and scowl at the screen, as though, through sheer force of will, he could compel Khaled to appear on it. Dina would sit meditatively on the salon couch, legs crossed, hands on her knees, motionless except for the tapping of her right forefinger. And Gabriel, who was used to standing for hours on end before the object of his devotion, would pace slowly before the screen, his right hand to chin, his left hand supporting his right elbow, his head tilted to one side. Had Francesco Tiepolo from Venice appeared suddenly on board *Fidelity*, he would have recognized Gabriel's pose, for it was the same one he adopted when contemplating whether a painting was finished.

The changing of the surveillance cars provided a welcome break in the tedium of the watching. The *Ayin* had perfected the sequence so that it unfolded with the precision of ballet. The replacement car would approach the entrance of the *payage* from the south. The old car would back out and drive off, then the new car would slide into the empty space. Once, the two *Ayin* purposely tapped bumpers and engaged in a convincing shouting match for the benefit of any watchers from the other side. There were always a few tense seconds when the old camera went black and the new one came on line. Gabriel would order any necessary adjustments in the angle and the focus, and then it would be done.

Though Gabriel remained a prisoner of *Fidelity*, he ordered Dina and Yaakov to behave as ordinary tourists. He pulled double and triple shifts at the screen so they could eat lunch in a quayside restaurant or tour the outer reaches of the city by motorcycle. Yaakov made a point of driving the escape route at different periods of the day to familiarize himself with the traffic patterns. Dina would shop for clothing in one of the boutique-lined pedestrian streets or don a swimsuit and sun herself on the aft deck. Her body bore the marks of the nightmare on Dizengoff Square, a thick red scar across the right side of her abdomen, a long jagged scar on her right thigh. On the streets of Marseilles she shrouded them with clothing, but aboard *Fidelity* she made no attempt to conceal the damage from Gabriel and Yaakov.

At night Gabriel ordered three-hour shifts so that those who were not watching could get some meaningful sleep. He soon came to regret that decision, because three hours seemed an eternity. The street would grow quiet as death. Each figure who flashed across the screen seemed filled with possibility. To relieve the boredom, Gabriel would whisper greetings to the *Ayin* officers on duty in the esplanade in front of the Palais de Justice – or he would raise the duty officer on the Operations Desk at King Saul Boulevard on the pretext he was testing the satellite connection, just so he could hear a voice from home.

Dina was Gabriel's relief. Once she had settled herself yoga-like in front of the screen, he would wander back to his stateroom and try to sleep, but in his mind he would see the door; or Sabri walking down the boulevard St-Germain with his hand in the pocket of his lover; or the Arabs of Beit Sayeed trudging off to exile; or Shamron, on the waterfront in Sardinia, reminding him to do his duty. And sometimes he would wonder whether he still possessed the reservoir of emotional coldness necessary to walk up to a man on a street and fill his body with chunks of searing metal. In moments of self-obsession he would find himself hoping that Khaled never again set foot on the boulevard St-Rémy. And then he would picture the ruins of the embassy in Rome, and remember the scent of burnt flesh that hung on the air like the spirits of the dead, and he would see Khaled's death, glorious and graceful, rendered in the passionate stillness of a Bellini. He would kill Khaled. Khaled had left him with no other choice, and for that Gabriel hated him.

On the fourth night he slept not at all. At 7:45 in the morning he rose from his bed to prepare for his eight o'clock shift. He drank coffee in the galley and stared at the calendar hanging from the door of the refrigerator. Tomorrow was the anniversary of Beit Sayeed's fall. Today was the last day. He went into the salon. Yaakov, wreathed in cigarette smoke, was looking at the screen. Gabriel tapped his shoulder and told him to get a couple hours' sleep. He stood in the same place for a few minutes, finishing his coffee, then he assumed his usual position – right hand to his chin, left hand supporting his right elbow – and paced the carpet in front of the screen. The lawyer stepped out of the door at 8:15. The grande dame came ten minutes later. Her terrier shat for Gabriel's camera. Sophie, Leah's wraith, came last. She paused for a moment in front of the door to fish a pair of sunglasses from her bag before floating prettily out of view.

*

'You look terrible,' Dina said. 'Take the rest of the night off. Yaakov and I will cover for you.'

It was early evening, the harbor was quiet except for the throb of French technopop from another yacht. Gabriel, yawning, confessed to Dina that he had slept little, if at all, since their arrival in Marseilles. Dina suggested he take a pill.

'And if Khaled comes while I'm lying unconscious in my room?'

'Maybe you're right.' She settled herself cross-legged on the couch and fixed her gaze on the television screen. The pavement of the boulevard St-Rémy was busy with the early-evening foot traffic. 'So why can't you sleep?'

'Do you really need me to explain it to you?'

She kept her eyes on the screen. 'Because you're worried he won't come? Because you're concerned you might not get a shot at him? Because you're afraid we'll all be caught and arrested?'

'I don't like this work, Dina. I never have.'

'None of us do. If we did, they'd run us out of the service. We do it because we have no choice. We do it because *they* force us to do it. Tell me something, Gabriel. What would happen if tomorrow they decided to stop the bombings, and the stabbings and shootings? There would be peace, right? But they don't want peace. They want to destroy us. The only difference between Hamas and Hitler is that Hamas lacks the power and the means to carry out an extermination of the Jews. But they're working on it.'

'There's a clear moral distinction between the Palestinians and the Nazis. There is a certain justice in Khaled's cause. Only his means are abhorrent and immoral.'

'Justice? Khaled and his ilk could have had peace time and time again, but they don't want it. His cause is our destruction. If you believe he wants peace, you're deluding yourself.' She pointed toward the screen. 'If he comes to that street, you have a right, indeed a moral duty, to make certain he never leaves there to kill and maim again. Do it, Gabriel, or so help me God, I'll do it for you.'

'Would you really? Do you truly think you'd be capable of killing him in cold blood, right there on that street? Would it really be so easy for you to pull the trigger?'

She was silent for a time, her gaze fixed on the flickering screen of the television. 'My father came from the Ukraine,' she said. 'Kiev. He was the only member of his family to survive the war. The rest were marched out to Babi Yar and shot to death along with thirty thousand other Jews. After the war he came to Palestine. He took the Hebrew name Sarid, which means remnant. He married my mother, and together they had six children, one child for every million killed in the Shoah. I was the last. They named me Dina: *avenged*.'

The volume of the music rose suddenly, then died away. When it was gone, all that remained was the lapping of a wake against the hull of the yacht. Dina's eyes narrowed suddenly, as if remembering physical pain. Her gaze remained on the image of the boulevard St-Rémy, but Gabriel could see that it was Dizengoff Street that occupied her thoughts.

'On the morning of October 19, 1994, I was standing at the corner of Dizengoff and Queen Esther streets with my mother and two of my sisters. When the Number Five bus came, I kissed my mother and sisters and watched them climb on board. While the doors were open, I saw him.' She paused and turned her head to look at Gabriel. 'He was sitting just behind the driver, with a bag at his feet. He actually looked at me. He had the sweetest face. No, I thought, it couldn't be possible. Not the Number Five bus on Dizengoff Street. So I said nothing. The doors closed, and the bus started to drive away.'

Her eyes clouded with tears. She folded her hands and laid them over the scar on her leg.

'So what did this boy have in his bag, this boy who I saw but said nothing about? He had the shell of an Egyptian land mine, that's what he had in the bag. He had twenty kilograms of military-grade TNT and bolts soaked with rat poison. The flash came first, then the sound of the explosion. The bus rose several feet into the air and crashed to the street again. I was knocked to the ground. I could see people screaming all round me, but I couldn't hear anything – the blast wave had damaged my eardrums. I noticed a human leg lying in the street next to me. I assumed it was mine, but then I saw that both my legs were still attached. The leg had come from someone in the bus.'

Gabriel, listening to her, thought suddenly of Rome; of standing next to Shimon Pazner and gazing at the wreckage of the embassy. Was Dina's presence aboard *Fidelity* serendipitous, he wondered, or had she been placed here intentionally by Shamron as a living reminder about the importance of doing his duty?

'The first policemen who came to the scene were sickened by the blood and the stench of burning flesh. They fell to their knees in the street and vomited. As I lay there, waiting for someone to help me, blood began to drip on me. I looked up and saw blood and scraps of flesh hanging on the leaves of the chinaberry trees. It rained blood that morning on Dizengoff Street. Then the rabbis from Hevra Kadisha arrived. They collected the largest body parts by hand, including those scraps of flesh in the trees. Then they used tweezers to pick up the smallest pieces. I watched rabbis pick up the remains of my mother and two sisters with tweezers and place them in a plastic bag. That's what we buried. Scraps. *Remnants.*'

She wrapped her arms around her legs and drew her knees beneath her chin. Gabriel sat on the couch next to her and settled his gaze on the screen to make certain they missed nothing. His hand reached out for hers. She took it as a tear spilled down her cheek.

'I blamed myself. If I'd known that the sweet-looking boy was really Abdel Rahim al-Souwi, member of Hamas's Izzedine al-Qassam Brigades, I would have been able to warn them. If I'd known that Abdel's brother had been killed in a shoot-out with the IDF in 1989, I would have understood why he was riding the Number Five bus in North Tel Aviv with a bag at his feet. I decided I would fight back, not with a gun, but with my brain. I vowed that next time I saw one of them, I would know, and I'd be able to warn the people before it was too late. That's why I volunteered for the Office. That's why I was able to make the connection between Rome and Beit Sayeed. I know them better than they know themselves.'

Another tear. This time Gabriel wiped it away.

'Why did he kill my mother and sisters, Gabriel? Was it because we stole his land? Was it because we were occupiers? No, it was because we wanted to make *peace*. If I hate them, you'll forgive me. If I beg you to show Khaled no mercy, you'll grant me leniency for my crimes. I'm Dina Sarid, the avenged remnant. I'm the sixth million. And if Khaled comes here tonight, don't you dare let him get on that bus.'

Lev had offered him use of a Jerusalem safe flat. Shamron had politely declined. Instead he'd instructed Tamara to find a folding camp bed in the storeroom and asked Gilah to send a suitcase with clean clothes and a shaving kit. Like Gabriel, he had slept little the past week. Some nights he would pace the hallways all hours or sit outside and smoke with the Shabak bodyguards. Mostly he lay on his folding cot, staring at the red glow of the digital clock on his desk and calculating the minutes that remained until the anniversary of Beit Sayeed's destruction. He filled the empty hours by recalling operations past. The waiting. Always the waiting. Some officers were driven mad by it. For Shamron it was a narcotic, akin to the first pangs of intense love. The hot flashes, the sudden chills, the gnawing of the stomach – he had endured it countless times over the years. In the back alleys of Damascus and Cairo, in the cobbled streets of Europe, and in a derelict suburb of Buenos Aires, where he'd waited for Adolf Eichmann, stationmaster of the Holocaust, to step off a city bus and into the grasp of the very people he had tried to annihilate. A fitting way for it to end, Shamron thought. One last night vigil. One final wait for a telephone to ring. When finally it did, the harsh electronic tone sounded like music to his ears. He closed his eyes and allowed it to ring a second time. Then he reached out in the darkness and brought the receiver to his ear.

The digital readout on the television monitor had said 12:27 A.M. Technically it had been Yaakov's shift, but it was the last night before the deadline, and no one was going to sleep. They had been seated on the couch in the salon, Yaakov in his usual confrontational pose, Dina in a posture of meditation, and Gabriel as though he were awaiting word of an expected death. The boulevard St-Rémy had been quiet that night. The couple who had strolled past the door at 12:27 were the first to appear in the camera shot in nearly fifteen minutes. Gabriel had looked at Dina, whose eyes had remained locked on the screen.

'Did you see that?'

'I saw it.'

Gabriel stood and went to the console. He removed the cassette from the video recorder and put a fresh tape in its place. Then he placed the cassette in a playback deck and rewound the tape. With Dina looking over his shoulder, he pressed PLAY. The couple entered the shot and walked past the doorway without giving it a glance.

Gabriel pressed stop.

'Look how he put the girl on his right side facing the street. He's using her as a shield. And look at his right hand. It's in the girl's pocket, just like Sabri.'

REWIND. PLAY. STOP.

'My God,' Gabriel said, 'he moves just like his father.'

'Are you sure?'

Gabriel went to the radio and raised the watcher outside the Palais de Justice.

'Did you see that couple who just walked by the building?'

'Yeah.'

'Where are they now?'

'Hold on.' A silence while the *Ayin* changed position. 'Heading up the street, toward the gardens.'

'Can you follow them?'

'It's dead quiet down here. I wouldn't recommend it.'

'Damn it.'

'Just a minute.'

'What?'

'Hold on.'

'What's going on?'

'They're turning around.'

'Are you sure?'

'Positive. They're retracing their steps.'

Gabriel looked up at the monitor just as they entered the shot again, this time from the opposite direction. Once again the woman was facing the street, and once again the man had his hand in the back pocket of her jeans. They stopped at the door of Number 56. The man drew a key from his pocket.

19. Surrey, England

At the Stratford Clinic it was just after ten in the evening when Amira Assaf came out of the elevator and set off down the fourth-floor corridor. Rounding the first corner, she spotted the bodyguard, sitting on a chair outside Miss Martinson's room. He looked up as Amira approached and closed the book he was reading.

'I need to make sure she's sleeping comfortably,' Amira said.

The bodyguard nodded and got to his feet. He wasn't surprised by Amira's request. She'd been stopping by the room every night at this time for the past month.

She opened the door and went inside. The bodyguard followed after her and closed the door behind him. A lamp, dimmed to its lowest setting, was burning softly. Amira went to the side of the bed and looked down. Miss Martinson was sound asleep. Hardly a surprise – Amira had given her twice her usual dosage of sedative. She'd be out for several more hours.

Amira adjusted the blankets, then opened the top drawer of the bedside table. The gun, a silenced Walther nine-millimeter, was precisely where she had left it earlier that afternoon while Miss Martinson was still in the solarium. She seized the weapon by the grip, then spun round and leveled the gun at the bodyguard's chest. He reached inside his jacket in a lightning-fast movement. Before his hand emerged, Amira fired twice, the double-tap of a trained killer. Both shots struck the upper chest. The bodyguard tumbled backward onto the floor. Amira stood over him and fired two more shots.

She drew a series of deep breaths to quell the intense wave of nausea that washed over her. Then she went to the telephone and dialed an internal hospital extension.

'Would you please ask Hamid to come up to Miss Martinson's room? There's some linen that needs to be collected before the truck leaves.'

She hung up the phone, then took the dead man by the arms and dragged him into the bathroom. The carpet was smeared with blood. Amira was not concerned by this. Her intention was not to conceal the crime, only to delay its discovery by a few hours.

There was a knock at the door.

'Yes?'

'It's Hamid.'

She unlocked the door and opened it. Hamid wheeled in a laundry cart.

'You all right?'

Amira nodded. Hamid wheeled the cart next to the bed while Amira pulled away the blankets and sheets. Miss Martinson, frail and scarred, lay motion-less. Hamid lifted her by her torso, Amira by her legs, and together they lowered her gently into the laundry cart. Amira concealed her beneath a layer of sheets.

She went out into the corridor to make certain it was clear, then looked back at Hamid and motioned for him to join her. Hamid rolled the cart out of the room and started toward the elevator. Amira closed the door, then inserted her passkey into the lock and snapped it off.

She met Hamid at the elevator and pressed the call button. The wait seemed an eternity. When finally the doors opened, they wheeled the cart into the empty chamber. Amira pressed the button for the ground floor and they sunk slowly downward.

The ground-floor foyer was deserted. Hamid went out first and turned to the right, toward the doorway that led to the rear courtyard. Amira followed after him. Outside, a van was idling with its rear cargo doors open. On the side was stenciled the name of a local laundry supply company. The usual driver was lying in a stand of beech trees two miles from the hospital with a bullet in his neck.

Hamid lifted the laundry bag out of the cart and placed it gently into the back of the van, then closed the doors and climbed into the front passenger seat. Amira watched the van roll off, then she went back inside and walked to the head nurse's station. Ginger was on duty.

'I'm not feeling terribly well tonight, Ginger. Think you can get by without me?'

'No problem, luv. Need a ride?'

Amira shook her head. 'I can manage on the bike. See you tomorrow night.'

Amira went to the staff locker room. Before stripping off her uniform she hid the gun inside her backpack. Then she changed into jeans, a heavy woolen sweater, and a leather jacket. A moment later she was walking across the rear courtyard with her bag across her back.

She climbed on the bike and started the engine, then accelerated out of the courtyard. As she rounded the back of the old mansion she glanced up at Miss Martinson's window: one light burning softly, no sign of trouble. She raced along the drive and rolled to a stop at the guardhouse. The man on duty bid her a good night, then opened the gate. Amira turned onto the road and twisted the throttle. Ten minutes later she was racing along the A24 motorway, heading south to the sea.

20. Marseilles

Gabriel slipped into his stateroom and closed the door. He went to the closet and peeled back a parcel of loose carpet, exposing the door of the floor safe. He worked the tumbler and lifted the lid. Inside were three handguns: a Beretta 92FS, a Jericho 941PS Police Special, and a Barak SP-21. Carefully he lifted each of the weapons out and laid them on the bed. The Beretta and the Jericho were both nine-millimeter weapons. The magazine for the Beretta had a fifteen-round capacity, the Jericho sixteen. The Barak – squat, black, and ugly – fired a larger and more destructive .45-caliber round, though it held only eight shots.

He field-stripped the guns, beginning with the Beretta and ending with the Barak. Each weapon appeared in perfect working order. He reassembled and loaded the weapons, then tested the weight and balance of each, deliberating over which to use. The hit was not likely to be a covert and quiet affair. It would probably take place on a busy street, perhaps in broad daylight. Making certain Khaled was dead was the first priority. For that, Gabriel needed power and reliability. He selected the Barak as his primary weapon and the Beretta 92FS as his backup. He also decided he would work without a silencer. A silencer made the weapon too difficult to conceal and too unwieldy to draw and fire. Besides, what was the point of using a silencer if the act was witnessed by a crowd of people on the street?

He went into the bathroom and stood for a moment before the mirror, examining his face. Then he opened the medicine cabinet and removed a pair of scissors, a razor, and a can of shaving cream. He trimmed the beard down to stubble, then removed the rest with the razor. His hair was still dyed gray. Nothing to be done about that.

He stripped off his clothes and showered quickly, then went back into the stateroom to dress. He pulled on his underwear and socks, then a pair of dark-blue denim trousers and rubber-soled suede brogues. He attached his radio unit to the waistband of his jeans on the left hip, then ran a wire to his ear and a second one to his left wrist. After securing the wires with strips of black tape, he pulled on a long-sleeved black shirt. The Beretta he shoved down the waistband of his jeans, at the small of his back. The Barak was compact enough to fit in the pocket of his leather jacket. His GPS tracking beacon, a small disk about the size of a one-euro coin, he slipped into the front pocket of his jeans.

He sat on the end of the bed and waited. Five minutes later there was a knock at the door. The clock read 2:12 A.M.

*

'How certain are your experts?'

The prime minister looked up at the bank of video monitors and waited for an answer. In one of the monitors was Lev's image. The director-general of Shabak, Moshe Yariv, occupied the second; General Amos Sharret, chief of Aman, the third.

'There's no doubt whatsoever,' replied Lev. 'The man in the photo given to us by Mahmoud Arwish is the same man who just walked into the apartment building in Marseilles. All we need now is your approval for the final phase of the operation to commence.'

'You have it. Give the order to *Fidelity*.'

'Yes, Prime Minister.'

'I assume you'll be able to hear the radio traffic?'

'*Fidelity* will send it to us via the secure link. We'll maintain operational control until the final second.'

'Send it here, too,' the prime minister said. 'I don't want to be the last to know.'

Then he pressed a button on his desk, and the three screens turned to black.

The motorbike was a Piaggio x9 Evolution, charcoal gray, with a twist-and-go throttle and a listed top speed of 160 kilometers per hour – though Yaakov, on a practice escape run the previous day, had topped out at 190. The saddle sloped severely downward from back to front so that the passenger sat several inches above the driver, which made it a perfect bike for an assassin, though surely its designers had not had that in mind when they'd conceived it. The engine, as usual, fired without hesitation. Yaakov headed toward the spot along the quay where the helmeted figure of Gabriel awaited him. Gabriel climbed onto the passenger seat and settled in.

'Take me to the boulevard St-Rémy.'

'You sure?'

'One pass,' he said. 'I want to see it.'

Yaakov banked hard to the left and raced up the hill.

It was a good building on the Corniche, with a marble floor in the lobby and an elevator that worked most of the time. The flats facing the street had a fine view of the Nile. The ones on the back looked down into the walled grounds of the American embassy. It was a building for foreigners and rich Egyptians, another world from the drab cinder-block tenement in Heliopolis where Zubair lived, but then being a policeman in Egypt didn't pay much, even if you were a secret policeman working for the Mukhabarat.

He took the stairs. They were wide and curved, with a faded runner held in place by tarnished brass fittings. The apartment was on the top floor, the tenth. Zubair cursed silently as he trod upward. Two packs of Cleopatra cigarettes a day had ravaged his lungs. Three times he had to pause on a landing to catch his breath. It took him a good five minutes to reach the flat.

He pressed his ear to the door and heard no sound from within. Hardly surprising. Zubair had followed the Englishman last night during a liquor-soaked excursion through the hotel bars and nightclubs along the river. Zubair was confident he was still sleeping.

He reached into his pocket and came out with the key. The Mukhabarat had a fine collection: diplomats, dissidents, Islamists, and especially foreign journalists. He inserted the key into the lock and turned, then pushed open the door and stepped inside.

The flat was cool and dark, the curtains tightly drawn against the early-morning sun. Zubair had been in the flat many times and found his way to the bedroom without bothering to switch on the lights. Quinnell slept soundly in sheets soaked with sweat. On the stagnant air hung the overpowering stench of whiskey. Zubair drew his gun and walked slowly across the room toward the foot of the bed. After a few paces his right foot fell upon something small and hard. Before he could relieve the downward pressure something snapped, emitting a sharp crack. In the deep silence of the room it sounded like a splintering tree limb. Zubair looked down and saw that he'd stepped on Quinnell's wristwatch. The Englishman, in spite of his drunkenness, sat bolt-upright in bed. *Shit,* thought Zubair. He was not a professional assassin. He'd hoped to kill Quinnell in his sleep.

'What the devil are you doing in here?'

'I bring a message from our friend,' Zubair said calmly.

'I don't want anything more to do with him.'

'The feeling is mutual.'

'So then what in God's name are you doing in my flat?'

Zubair raised the gun. A moment later he let himself out of the flat and started back down the stairs. Halfway down he was breathing like a marathoner and sweating hard. He stopped and leaned against the balustrade. The damned Cleopatras. If he didn't quit soon they'd be the death of him.

Marseilles: 5:22 A.M. The door of the apartment house swings open. A figure steps into the street. Dina's verbal alert is heard in the Operations Center of King Saul Boulevard and in Jerusalem by Shamron and the prime minister. And it is also heard in the dirty esplanade along the cours Belsunce, where Gabriel and Yaakov are sitting on the edge of a stagnant fountain, surrounded by drug addicts and immigrants with nowhere else to sleep.

'Who is it?' Gabriel asks.

'The girl,' Dina says, then she adds quickly: 'Khaled's girl.'

'Which way is she going?'

'North, toward the Place de la Préfecture.'

There follows several empty seconds of dead air. In Jerusalem, Shamron is pacing the carpet in front of the prime minister's desk and waiting anxiously for Gabriel's order. 'Don't try it,' he murmurs. 'If she spots the watcher, she'll warn Khaled, and you'll lose him. Let her go.'

Ten more seconds pass before Gabriel's voice comes back on the air.

'It's too risky,' he whispers. 'Let her go.'

In Ramallah the meeting broke up at dawn. Yasir Arafat was in high good humor. To those in attendance he seemed a bit like the Arafat of old, the Arafat who could argue ideology and strategy all night with his closest comrades, then sit down for a meeting with a head of state. As his lieutenants filed out of the room, Arafat motioned for Mahmoud Arwish to remain.

'It's begun,' Arafat said. 'Now we can only hope that Allah has blessed Khaled's sacred endeavor.'

'It is *your* endeavor, too, Abu Amar.'

'True,' said Arafat, 'and it wouldn't have been possible without you, Mahmoud.'

Arwish nodded cautiously. Arafat held him in his gaze.

'You played your role well,' said Arafat. 'Your clever deception of the Israelis almost makes up for your betrayal of me and the rest of the Palestinian people. I'm tempted to overlook your crime, but I cannot.'

Arwish felt his chest tighten. Arafat smiled.

'Did you really think your treachery would ever be forgiven?'

'My wife,' Arwish stammered. 'The Jews made me –'

Arafat waved his hand dismissively. 'You sound like a child, Mahmoud. Don't compound your humiliation by begging for your life.'

Just then the door swung open, and two uniformed security men stepped into the room, guns at the ready. Arwish tried to get his sidearm out of its holster, but a rifle butt slammed into his kidney, and a burst of blinding pain sent him to the floor.

'Today you die the death of a collaborator,' Arafat said. 'A death fit for a dog.'

The security men hauled Arwish to his feet and frog-marched him out of the office and down the stairs. Arafat went to the window and looked down into the courtyard as Arwish and the security men emerged into view. Another rifle butt to the kidney drove Arwish to the ground for a second time. Then the firing began. Slow and rhythmic, they started with the feet and worked their way slowly upward. The Mukata echoed with the popping of the Kalashnikovs and the screams of the dying traitor. To Arafat it was a most satisfying sound – the sound of a revolution. The sound of revenge.

When the screaming stopped there was one final shot to the head. Arafat drew the blind. One enemy had been dealt with. Soon another would meet with a similar fate. He switched off the lamp and sat there in the half-light, waiting for the next update.

21. Marseilles

Later, when it was over, Dina would search in vain for any symbolism in the time Khaled chose to make his appearance. As for the exact words she used to convey this news to the teams, she had no memory of it, though they were captured for eternity on audiotape: *'It's him. He's on the street. Heading south toward the park.'* All those who heard Dina's summons were struck by its composure and lack of emotion. So tranquil was her delivery that for an instant Shamron did not comprehend what had just happened. Only when he heard the roar of Yaakov's motorbike, followed by the sound of Gabriel's rapid breathing, did he understand that Khaled was about to get his due.

Within five seconds of hearing Dina's voice, Yaakov and Gabriel had pulled on their helmets and were racing eastward at full throttle along the cours Belsunce. At the Place de la Préfecture, Yaakov leaned the bike hard to the right and sped across the square toward the entrance of the boulevard St-Rémy. Gabriel clung to Yaakov's waist with his left hand. His right was shoved into his coat pocket and wrapped around the chunky grip of the Barak. It was just beginning to get light, but the street was still in shadow. Gabriel saw Khaled for the first time, walking along the pavement like a man late for an important meeting.

The bike slowed suddenly. Yaakov had a decision to make – cross over to the wrong side of the street and approach Khaled from behind, or stay on the right side of the street and loop around for the kill. Gabriel spurred him to the right with a jab of the gun barrel. Yaakov twisted the throttle, and the bike shot forward. Gabriel fastened his eyes on Khaled. The Palestinian was walking faster.

Just then a dark-gray Mercedes car nosed out of a cross street and blocked their path. Yaakov slammed on the brakes to avoid a collision, then blew his horn and waved at the Mercedes to get out of the way. The driver, a young Arab-looking man, stared coldly back at Yaakov and punished him for his recklessness by inching slowly out of their path. By the time Yaakov was under way again, Khaled had turned the corner and disappeared from Gabriel's sight.

Yaakov sped to the end of the street and turned left, into the boulevard André Aune. It rose sharply away from the old port, toward the looming tower of the Church of Notre Dame de la Garde. Khaled had already crossed the street and at that moment was slipping into the entrance of a covered passageway. Gabriel had used the computer program to memorize the route of every street in the district. He knew that the passageway led to a flight of steeply pitched stone steps called the Montée de l'Oratoire. Khaled had rendered the motorbike useless.

'Stop here,' Gabriel said. 'Don't move.'

Gabriel leapt from his bike and, with his helmet still on his head, followed the path Khaled had taken. There were no lights in the passage, and for a few paces in the center Gabriel was in pitch darkness. At the opposite end he emerged back into the dusty pink light. The steps began – wide and very old, with a painted metal handrail down the middle. To Gabriel's left was the khaki-colored stucco facade of an apartment house; to his right a tall limestone wall overhung with olive trees and flowering vines.

The steps curved to the left. As Gabriel came around the corner he saw Khaled again. He was halfway to the top and bounding upward at a trot. Gabriel started to draw the Barak but stopped himself. At the top of the steps was another apartment building. If Gabriel missed Khaled, the errant round would almost certainly plunge into the building. He could hear voices through his earpiece: Dina asking Yaakov what was going on; Yaakov telling Dina about the car that had blocked their way and the flight of steps that had forced them to separate.

'*Can you see him?*'

'*No.*'

'*How long has he been out of sight?*'

'*A few seconds.*'

'*Where's Khaled going? Why is he walking so far? Where's his protection? I don't like it. I'm going to tell him to back off.*'

'*Leave him to it.*'

Khaled gained the top and disappeared from sight. Gabriel took the steps two at a time and arrived no more than ten seconds after Khaled had. Confronting him was a V-shaped intersection of two streets. One of them, the one to Gabriel's right, ran up the hill directly toward the front of the church. It was empty of cars or pedestrians. Gabriel hurried to his left and looked up the second street. There was no sign of Khaled here either, only a pair of red taillights, receding rapidly into the distance.

'Excuse me, monsieur, are you lost?'

Gabriel turned and raised the visor of his helmet. She was standing at the head of the stairs, young, no more than thirty, with large brown eyes and short dark hair. She had spoken to him in French. Gabriel responded in the same language.

'No, I'm not lost.'

'Perhaps you're looking for someone?'

And why are you, an attractive woman, speaking to a strange man wearing a motorcycle helmet? He took a step toward her. She held her ground, but Gabriel detected a trace of apprehension in her dark gaze.

'No, I'm not looking for anyone.'

'Are you sure? I could have sworn you were looking for someone.' She tilted her head slightly to one side. 'Perhaps you're looking for your wife.'

Gabriel felt as though the back of his neck was ablaze. He looked at the woman's face more carefully and realized he'd seen it before. She was the woman who'd come to the apartment with Khaled. His right hand tightened its grip on the Barak pistol.

'Her name is Leah, isn't it? She lives in a psychiatric hospital in the south of England – at least she used to. The Stratford Clinic, wasn't that the name of it? She was registered under the name of Lee Martinson.'

Gabriel lunged forward and seized the woman by the throat.

'What have you done to her? Where is she?'

'We have her,' the woman gasped, 'but I don't know where she is.'

Gabriel pushed her backward, toward the top of the steps.

'Where is she?' He repeated the question in Arabic. 'Answer me! Don't speak to me in French. Speak to me in your real language. Speak to me in Arabic.'

'I'm telling you the truth.'

'So you *can* speak Arabic. Where is she? Answer me, or you're going down.'

He pushed her a fraction of an inch closer to the edge. Her hand reached back for the handrail but found only air. Gabriel shook her once violently.

'If you kill me, you'll destroy yourself – and your wife. I'm your only hope.'

'And if I do as you say?'

'You'll save her life.'

'What about mine?'

She left the question unanswered.

'Tell the rest of your team to back off. Tell them to leave Marseilles immediately. Otherwise we'll tell the French that you're here, and that will only make the situation worse.'

He looked over her shoulder and saw Yaakov coming slowly up the steps toward him. Gabriel, with his left hand, signaled for him to stop. Just then Dina came on the air: *'Let her go, Gabriel. We'll find Leah. Don't play it Khaled's way.'*

Gabriel looked back into the girl's eyes. 'And if I tell them to back off?'

'I'll take you to her.'

Gabriel shook her again. 'So you *do* know where she is?'

'No, we'll be told where to go. One destination at a time, very small steps. If we miss one deadline, your wife dies. If your agents try to follow us, your wife dies. If you kill me, your wife dies. If you do exactly what we say, she'll live.'

'And what happens to me?'

'Hasn't she suffered enough? Save your wife, Allon. Come with me, and do exactly as I say. It's your only chance.'

He looked down the steps and saw Yaakov shaking his head. Dina was whispering in his ear. *'Please, Gabriel, tell her no.'*

He looked into her eyes. Shamron had trained him to read the emotions of others, to tell truthfulness from deception, and in the dark eyes of Khaled's girl he saw only the abiding forthrightness of a fanatic, the belief that past suffering justified any act, no matter how cruel. He also noticed an unsettling tranquillity. She was trained, this girl, not merely indoctrinated. Her training would make her a worthy opponent, but it was her fanaticism that would leave her vulnerable.

Did they really have Leah? He had no reason to doubt it. Khaled had destroyed an embassy in the heart of Rome. Surely he could manage to kidnap an infirm woman from an English mental hospital. To abandon Leah now, after all she had suffered, was unthinkable. Perhaps she would die. Perhaps they both would. Perhaps, if they were lucky, Khaled might permit them to die together.

He had played it well, Khaled. He had never intended to kill Gabriel in Venice. The Milan dossier had been only the opening gambit in an elaborate plot to lure Gabriel here, to this spot in Marseilles, and to present him with a path he had no choice but to follow. Fidelity nudged him forward. He pulled her away from the edge of the stairs and released his grip on her throat.

'Back off,' Gabriel said directly into his wrist-microphone. 'Leave Marseilles.'

When Yaakov shook his head, Gabriel snapped, 'Do as I say.'

A car came down the hill from the direction of the church. It was the Mercedes that had blocked their path a few minutes earlier on the boulevard St-Rémy.

It stopped in front of them. The girl opened the back door and got in. Gabriel looked one final time at Yaakov, then climbed in after her.

'He's off the air,' Lev said. 'His beacon has been stationary for five minutes.'

His beacon, thought Shamron, is lying in a Marseilles gutter. Gabriel had vanished from their screens. All the planning, all the preparation, and Khaled had beaten them with the oldest of Arab ploys – a hostage.

'Is it true about Leah?' Shamron asked.

'London station has called the security officer several times. So far they haven't been able to raise him.'

'That means they've got her,' Shamron said. 'And I suspect we have a dead security agent somewhere inside the Stratford Clinic.'

'If that's all true, a very serious storm is going to break in England in the next few minutes.' There was a bit too much composure in Lev's voice for Shamron's taste, but then Lev always did place a high premium on self-control. 'We need to reach out to our friends in MI5 and the Home Office to keep things as quiet as possible for as long as possible. We also need to bring the Foreign Ministry into the picture. The ambassador will have to do some serious hand-holding.'

'Agreed,' Shamron said, 'but I'm afraid there's something we have to do first.'

He looked at his wristwatch. It was 7:28 A.M. local time, 6:28 in France – twelve hours until the anniversary of the evacuation of Beit Sayeed.

'But we can't just leave him here,' Dina said.

'He's not *here* any longer,' Yaakov replied. 'He's gone. He was the one who made the decision to go with her. He gave us the order to evacuate and so has Tel Aviv. We have no other choice. We're leaving.'

'There must be something we can do to help him.'

'You can't be any help to him if you're sitting in a French jail.'

Yaakov raised his wrist-microphone to his lips and ordered the *Ayin* teams to pull out. Dina went reluctantly down onto the dock and loosened the lines. When the last line was untied, she climbed back onto *Fidelity* and stood with Yaakov atop the flying bridge as he guided the vessel into the channel. As they passed the Fort of Saint Nicholas, she went back down the companionway to the salon. She sat down at the communications pod, typed in a command to access the memory, then set the time-code for 6:12 A.M. A few seconds later she heard her own voice.

'*It's him. He's on the street. Heading south toward the park.*'

She listened to it all again: Yaakov and Gabriel wordlessly mounting the bike; Yaakov firing the engine and accelerating away; the sound of the tires locking up and skidding along the asphalt of the boulevard St-Rémy; Gabriel's voice, calm and without emotion: *'Stop here. Don't move.'*

Twenty seconds later, the woman: *'Excuse me, monsieur, are you lost?'*

STOP.

How long had Khaled spent planning it? Years, she thought. He had dropped the clues for her to find, and she had followed them, from Beit Sayeed to Buenos Aires, from Istanbul to Rome, and now Gabriel was in their hands. They would kill him, and it was her fault.

She pressed PLAY and listened again to Gabriel's quarrel with the Palestinian woman, then picked up the satellite phone and raised King Saul Boulevard on the secure link.

'I need a voice identification.'

'You have a recording?'

'Yes.'

'Quality?'

Dina explained the circumstances of the intercept.

'Play the recording, please.'

She pressed play.

'If we miss one deadline, your wife dies. If your agents try to follow us, your wife dies. If you kill me, your wife dies. If you do exactly what we say, she'll live.'

STOP.

'Stand by, please.'

Two minutes later: 'No match on file.'

*

Martineau met Abu Saddiq one last time on the boulevard d'Athènes, at the base of the broad steps that led to the Gare Saint-Charles. Abu Saddiq was dressed in Western clothing: neat gabardine trousers and a pressed cotton shirt. He told Martineau a boat had just left the port at great haste.

'What was it called?'

Abu Saddiq answered.

'*Fidelity*,' Martineau repeated. 'An interesting choice.'

He turned and started trudging up the steps, Abu Saddiq at his side. 'The *shaheeds* have been given their final orders,' Abu Saddiq said. 'They'll proceed to their target as scheduled. Nothing can be done to stop them now.'

'And you?'

'The midday ferry to Algiers.'

They arrived at the top of the steps. The train station was brown and ugly and in a state of severe disrepair. 'I must say,' Abu Saddiq said, 'that I will not miss this place.'

'Go to Algiers, and bury yourself deep. We'll bring you back to the West Bank when it's safe.'

'After today ...' He shrugged. 'It will never be safe.'

Martineau shook Abu Saddiq's hand. '*Maa-salaamah*.'

'*As-salaam alaykum*, Brother Khaled.'

Abu Saddiq turned and headed down the steps. Martineau entered the train station and paused in front of the departure board. The 8:15 TGV for Paris was departing from Track F. Martineau crossed the terminal and went onto the platform. He walked alongside the train until he found his carriage, then climbed aboard.

Before going to his seat, he went to the toilet. He stood for a long time in front of the mirror, examining his own reflection in the glass. The Yves Saint Laurent jacket, the dark-blue end-on-end shirt, the designer spectacles – Paul Martineau, Frenchman of distinction, archaeologist of note. But not today. Today Martineau was Khaled, son of Sabri, grandson of Sheikh Asad. Khaled, avenger of past wrongs, sword of Palestine.

The shaheeds have been given their final orders. Nothing can be done to stop them now.

Another order had been given. The man who would meet Abu Saddiq in Algiers that evening would kill him. Martineau had learned from the mistakes of his ancestors. He would never allow himself to be undone by an Arab traitor.

A moment later he was sitting in his first-class seat as the train eased out of the station and headed north through the Muslim slums of Marseilles. Paris was 539 miles away, but the high-speed TGV would cover the distance in a little more than three hours. A miracle of Western technology and French ingenuity, Khaled thought. Then he closed his eyes and was soon asleep.

22. Martigues, France

The house was in a working-class Arab quarter on the southern edge of town. It had a red tile roof, a cracked stucco exterior, and a weedy forecourt littered with broken plastic toys in primary colors. Gabriel, when he was pushed through the broken front door, had expected to find evidence of a family. Instead, he found a ransacked residence with rooms empty of furniture and walls stripped bare. Two men awaited him, both Arab, both well fed. One held a plastic bag bearing the name of a discount department store popular with the French underclass. The other was swinging a rusted golf club, one-handed, like a cudgel.

'Take off your clothes.'

The girl had spoken to him in Arabic. Gabriel remained motionless with his hands hanging against the seam of his trousers, like a soldier at attention. The girl repeated the command, more forcefully this time. When Gabriel still made no response, the one who'd driven the Mercedes slapped him hard across the cheek.

He removed his jacket and black pullover. The radio and the guns were already gone – the girl had taken those while they were still in Marseilles. She examined the scars on his chest and back, then ordered him to remove the rest of his clothing.

'What about your Muslim modesty?'

For his insolence he received a second blow to the face, this one with the back of the hand. Gabriel, his head swimming, stepped out of his shoes and peeled off his socks. Then he unbuttoned his jeans and pulled them off over his bare feet. A moment later he was standing before the four Arabs in his briefs. The girl reached out and snapped the elastic. 'These, too,' she said. 'Take them off.'

They found his nakedness amusing. The men made comments about his penis while the woman made slow circuits about him and appraised his body as though he were a statue on a pedestal. It occurred to him that he was a legend to them, a beast who had come in the middle of the night and killed young warriors. *Look at him,* they seemed to be saying with their eyes. *He's so small, so ordinary. How could he have killed so many of our brothers?*

The girl grunted something in Arabic that Gabriel could not comprehend. The three men set upon his discarded clothing with box cutters and scissors and tore it to shreds. No seam, no hem, no collar survived their onslaught. Only God knew what they were looking for. A second beacon? A hidden radio transmitter? A devilish Jewish device that would render them all lifeless and permit him to escape at the time and place of his choosing? For a moment the girl observed this silliness with great seriousness, then she looked again at Gabriel. Twice more she circled his naked body, with one small hand pressed thoughtfully against her lips. Each time she passed before him, Gabriel looked directly into her eyes. There was something clinical in her gaze, something professional and analytical. He half expected her at any moment to produce a minicassette recorder and begin dictating diagnostic notes. *Puckered scarring on upper left chest quadrant, result of the bullet fired into him by Tariq al-Hourani, Allah praise his glorious name. Sandpaper-like scarring across much of the back. Source of scarring unknown.*

The search of his clothing produced nothing but a pile of shredded cotton cloth and denim. One of the Arabs gathered up the scraps and tossed them on the fireplace grate, then doused them with kerosene and set them alight. As Gabriel's clothing turned to ash they assembled around him once more, the girl facing him, the two big Arabs on either side, and the one who had served as the driver at his back. The Arab to his right was lazily swinging a golf club.

There was a ritual to situations like these. The beating, he knew, was a part of it. The girl set it in motion with a ceremonial slap to his face. Then she stepped away and allowed the men to do the heavy lifting. A well-aimed strike with the golf club caused his knees to buckle and sent him to the floor. Then the real blows began, a barrage of kicks and punches that seemed to target every portion of his body. He avoided crying out. He did not want to give them the satisfaction, nor did he want to derail their plan by alerting the neighbors – not that anyone in this part of the city would care much about three men beating the daylights out of a Jew. It ended as suddenly as it began. In retrospect it was not so bad – indeed, he had endured worse at the hands of Shamron and his goons at the Academy. They went easy on his face, which told him that he needed to remain presentable.

He had come to rest on his right side, with his hands protectively over his genitals and his knees to his chest. He could taste blood on his lips, and his left shoulder felt frozen in place, the result of having been stomped on several times in succession by the largest of the three Arabs. The girl tossed the plastic bag in front of his face and ordered him to get dressed. He made a forthright attempt at movement but could not seem to roll over or sit up or lift his hands. Finally, one of the Arabs seized him by the left arm and pulled him into a seated position. His injured shoulder revolted, and for the first time he groaned in pain. This, like his nudity, was an occasion for laughter.

They helped him to dress. Clearly they had been expecting a bigger man. The neon-yellow T-shirt with *MARSEILLES!* emblazoned across the chest was several sizes too large. The white chinos were too big in the waist and too long in the legs. The cheap leather slip-ons barely stayed on his feet.

'Can you stand up?' the girl asked.

'No.'

'If we don't leave now, you'll be late for your next checkpoint. And if you're late for your next checkpoint, you know what happens to your wife.'

He rolled over onto his hands and knees and, after two failed attempts managed to get to his feet. The girl gave him a push between the shoulder blades and sent him stumbling toward the door. He thought of Leah and wondered where she was. Zipped into a body bag? Locked into a car trunk? Hammered into a wooden crate? Did she know what was happening to her, or, mercifully, did she believe it was just another episode in her nightmare without end? It was for Leah that he remained upright and for Leah that he placed one foot in front of the other.

The three men remained behind in the house. The girl walked a half step behind him, with a leather satchel over her shoulder. She gave him another shove, this time in the direction of the Mercedes. He stumbled forward, across the dusty forecourt strewn with toys. The overturned Matchbox cars, the rusted fire truck, the armless doll and headless toy soldier — to Gabriel it seemed like the carnage wrought by one of Khaled's expertly crafted bombs. He went instinctively to the passenger side of the car.

'No,' said the woman. 'You're going to drive.'

'I'm in no condition.'

'But you must,' she said. 'Otherwise we'll miss our deadline, and your wife will die.'

Gabriel reluctantly climbed behind the wheel. The woman sat next to him. After closing the door, she reached inside the satchel and produced a weapon, a Tanfolgio TA-90, and aimed it at his abdomen.

'I know you can take this from me anytime you wish,' she conceded. 'If you choose such a course of action, it will do you no good. I assure you that I do not know the location of your wife, nor do I know our ultimate destination. We're going on this journey together, you and I. We're partners in this endeavor.'

'How noble of you.'

She hit him across the cheek with the gun.

'Be careful,' he said, 'it might go off.'

'You know France very well, yes? You've worked here. You've killed many Palestinians here.'

Greeted by Gabriel's silence, she hit him a second time. 'Answer me! You've worked here, yes?'

'Yes.'

'You've killed Palestinians here, yes?'

He nodded.

'Are you ashamed? Say it aloud.'

'Yes,' he said, 'I've killed Palestinians here. I killed Sabri here.'

'So you know the roads of France well. You won't need to waste time consulting a map. That's a good thing, because we don't have much time.'

She gave him the keys. 'Go to Nîmes. You have one hour.'

'It's a hundred kilometers, at least.'

'Then I suggest you stop talking and start driving.'

*

He went by way of Arles. The Rhône, silver-blue and swirling with eddies, slid beneath them. On the other side of the river, Gabriel pressed the accelerator toward the floor and started the final run into Nîmes. The weather was perversely glorious: the sky cloudless and intensely blue, the fields ablaze with lavender and sunflowers, the hills awash with a light so pure it was possible for Gabriel to make out the lines and fissures of rock formations twenty miles in the distance.

The girl sat calmly with her ankles crossed and the gun lying in her lap. Gabriel wondered why Khaled had chosen her to escort him to his death. Because her youth and beauty stood in sharp contrast to Leah's ravaged infirmity? Or was it an Arab insult of some sort? Did he wish to further humiliate Gabriel by making him take orders from a beautiful young girl? Whatever Khaled's motives, she was nonetheless thoroughly trained. Gabriel had sensed it during their first encounter in Marseilles and again at the house in Martigues – and he could see it now in her muscular arms and shoulders and in the way she handled the gun. But it was her hands that intrigued him most. She had the short, dirty fingernails of a potter or someone who worked outdoors.

She hit him again without warning. The car swerved, and Gabriel had to battle to get it under control again.

'Why did you do that?'

'You were looking at the gun?'

'I was not.'

'You're thinking about taking it away from me.'

'No.'

'Liar! Jewish liar!'

She raised the gun to strike him again, but his time Gabriel lifted his hand defensively and managed to deflect the blow.

'You'd better hurry,' she said, 'or we won't make it to Nîmes in time.'

'I'm going nearly two hundred kilometers an hour. I can't drive any faster without killing us both. Next time Khaled calls, tell him he's going to have to extend the deadlines.'

'Who?'

'Khaled,' Gabriel repeated. 'The man you're working for. The man who's running this operation.'

'I've never heard of a man named Khaled.'

'My mistake.'

She studied him for a moment. 'You speak Arabic very well. You grew up in the Jezreel Valley, yes? Not far from Afula. I'm told there are many Arabs there. People who refused to leave or be driven out.'

Gabriel didn't rise to her baiting. 'You've never seen it?'

'Palestine?' A flicker of a smile. 'I've seen it from a distance,' she said.

Lebanon, thought Gabriel. *She's seen it from Lebanon.*

'If we're going to make this journey together, I should have a name to call you.'

'I don't have a name. I'm just a Palestinian. No

name, no face, no land, no home. My suitcase is my country.'

'Fine,' he said, 'I'll call you Palestine.'

'It's not a proper name for a woman.'

'All right, then I'll call you Palestina.'

She looked at the road and nodded. 'You may call me Palestina.'

A mile before Nîmes, she directed him into the gravel parking lot of a roadside store that sold earthenware planters and garden statuary. For five unbearable moments they waited in silence for her satellite telephone to ring. When it finally did, the electronic chime sounded to Gabriel like a fire alarm. The girl listened without speaking. From her blank expression Gabriel could not discern whether she'd been ordered to keep going or to kill him. She severed the connection and nodded toward the road.

'Get on the Autoroute.'

'Which direction?'

'North.'

'Where are we going?'

A hesitation, then: 'Lyon.'

Gabriel did as he was told. As they neared the Autoroute tollbooth, the girl slipped the Tanfolgio into her satchel. Then she handed him some change for the toll. When they were back on the road, the gun came out again. She placed it on her lap. Her forefinger, with her short, dirty nail, lay non-committally across the trigger.

'What's he like?'

'Who?'

'Khaled,' Gabriel said.

'As I told you before, I don't know anyone named Khaled.'

'You spent the night with him in Marseilles.'

'Actually, I spent the night with a man named Monsieur Véran. You'd better drive faster.'

'He's going to kill us, you know. He's going to kill us both.'

She said nothing.

'Were you told that this was a suicide mission? Have you prepared yourself to die? Have you prayed and made a farewell videotape for your family?'

'Please drive, and don't talk anymore.'

'We're *shaheeds*, you and I. We're going to die together – for different causes, mind you, but together.'

'Please, shut up.'

And there it was, he thought. The crack. Khaled had lied to her.

'We're going to die *tonight*,' he said. 'At seven o'clock. He didn't mention that to you?'

Another silence. Her finger was moving over the surface of the trigger.

'I guess he forgot to tell you,' Gabriel resumed. 'But then it's always been that way. It's the poor kids who die for Palestine, the kids from the camps and the slums. The elite just give the orders from their villas in Beirut and Tunis and Ramallah.'

She swung the gun toward his face again. This

time he snatched it and twisted it from her grasp.

'When you hit me with this, it makes it hard to drive.'

He held out the gun to her. She took it and placed it back in her lap.

'We're *shaheeds*, Palestina. We're driving toward destruction, and Khaled is giving us directions. Seven o'clock, Palestina. Seven o'clock.'

On the road between Valence and Lyon, he pushed Leah from his mind and thought of nothing but the case. Instinctively, he approached it as though it were a painting. He stripped away the varnish and dissolved the paint, until there was nothing left but the fragmentary charcoal lines of the underdrawing; then he began building it back up again, layer by layer, tone and texture. For the moment he was unable to affix a reliable authentication. Was Khaled the artist, or had Khaled been only an apprentice in the workshop of the Old Master himself, Yasir Arafat? Had Arafat ordered it to avenge the destruction of his power and authority, or had Khaled undertaken the work on his own to avenge the death of a father and grandfather? Was it another battle in the war between two peoples or just an outbreak in the long-simmering feud between two families, the al-Khalifas and the Shamron-Allons? He suspected it was a combination of both, an intersection of shared needs and goals. Two great artists had cooperated on a single work – Titian and Bellini, he thought. *The Feast of the Gods*.

The date of the painting's commission remained elusive to him as well, though. Of one thing he was sure: the work had taken several years and much blood to produce. He had been deceived, and skillfully so. They all had. The dossier found in Milan had been planted by Khaled in order to lure Gabriel into the search. Khaled had dropped a trail of clues and wound the clock, so that Gabriel had had no choice but to desperately pursue them. Mahmoud Arwish, David Quinnell, Mimi Ferrere – they'd all been a part of it. Gabriel saw them now, silent and still, as minor figures at the edges of a Bellini, allegorical in nature but supportive of the focal point. But what was the point? Gabriel knew that the painting was unfinished. Khaled had one more coup in store, one more spectacular of blood and fire. Somehow Gabriel had to survive it. He was certain the clue to his survival lay somewhere along the path he'd already traveled. And so, as he raced northward toward Lyon, he saw not the Autoroute but the case – every minute, every setting, every encounter, oil on canvas. He would survive it, he thought, and someday he would come back to Khaled on his own terms. And the girl, Palestina, would be his doorway.

'Pull over to the side of the road.'

Gabriel did as he was told. They were a few miles from the center of Lyon. This time, only two minutes elapsed before the telephone rang.

'Get back on the road,' she said. 'We're going to Chalon. It's a –'

'I know where Chalon is. It's just south of Dijon.'

He waited for an opening in the traffic, then accelerated back onto the Autoroute.

'I can't decide whether you're a very courageous man or a fool,' she said. 'You could have walked away from me in Marseilles. You could have saved yourself.'

'She's my wife,' he said. 'She'll always be my wife.'

'And you're willing to die for her?'

'You're going to die for her, too.'

'At seven o'clock?'

'Yes.'

'Why did you make up this time? Why seven o'clock?'

'You don't know anything about the man you're working for, do you? I feel sorry for you, Palestina. You're a very foolish girl. Your leader has betrayed you, and you're the one who'll pay the price.'

She lifted the gun to hit him again, but thought better of it. Gabriel kept his eyes on the road. The door was ajar.

They stopped for gas south of Chalon. Gabriel filled the tank and paid with cash given to him by the girl. When he was behind the wheel again, she ordered him to park next to the toilets.

'I'll be back.'

'I'll be waiting.'

She was gone only a moment. Gabriel slid the car into gear, but the girl removed the satellite phone from her bag and ordered him to wait. It was 2:55 P.M.

'We're going to Paris,' he said.

'Oh, really?'

'He'll send us one of two ways. The Autoroute splits at Beaune. If we take that cutoff, we can head straight into the southern suburbs. Or we can stay to the east – Dijon to Troyes, Troyes to Reims – and come in from the northeast.'

'You seem to know everything. Tell me which way he's going to send us.'

Gabriel made a show of consulting his watch.

'He'll want to keep us moving, and he won't want us at the target too early. I'm betting for the eastern route. I say he sends us to Troyes and tells us to wait there for instructions. He'll have options if he sends us to Troyes.'

Just then the telephone rang. She listened in silence, then severed the connection.

'Get back on the Autoroute,' she said.

'Where are we going?'

'Just drive,' she said.

He asked for permission to turn on the radio.

'Sure,' she said affably.

He pressed the power button, but nothing happened. A slight smile appeared on her lips.

'Nicely played,' said Gabriel.

'Thank you.'

'Why are you doing this?'

'Surely you're joking.'

'Actually, I'm quite serious.'

'I'm Palestina,' she said. 'I have no choice.'

'You're wrong. You do have a choice.'

'I know what you're doing,' she said. 'You're trying to wear me down with your suggestions of death and suicide. You think you can make me have a change of heart, that you can make me lose my nerve.'

'Actually, I wouldn't dream of such a thing. We've been fighting each other for a long time. I know that you're intensely courageous and that you rarely lose your nerve. I just want to know why: Why are *you* here? Why not get married and raise a family? Why not live your life?'

Another smile, this one mocking. 'Jews,' she said. 'You think you have a patent on pain. You think you have the market cornered on human suffering. My Holocaust is as real as yours, and yet you deny my suffering and exonerate yourself of guilt. You claim my wounds are self-inflicted.'

'So tell me your story.'

'Mine is a story of Paradise lost. Mine is a story of a simple people forced by the civilized world to give up their land so that Christendom could alleviate its guilt over the Holocaust.'

'No, no,' Gabriel said. 'I don't want a propaganda lecture. I want to hear *your* story. Where are you from?'

'A camp,' she said, then added: 'A camp in Lebanon.'

Gabriel shook his head. 'I'm not asking where you were born, or where you grew up. I'm asking you where you're *from*.'

'I'm from Palestine.'

'Of course you are. Which part?'

'The north.'

'That explains Lebanon. Which part of the north?'

'The Galilee.'

'Western? Upper?'

'The Western Galilee.'

'Which village?'

'It's not there anymore.'

'What was it called?'

'I'm not allowed to –'

'Did it have a name?'

'Of course it had a name.'

'Was it Bassa?'

'No.'

'What about Zib?'

'No.'

'Maybe it was Sumayriyya?'

She made no reply.

'So, it *was* Sumayriyya.'

'Yes,' she said. 'My family came from Sumayriyya.'

'It's a long way to Paris, Palestina. Tell me your story.'

23. Jerusalem

When Varash convened again, they did so in person in the office of the prime minister. Lev's update took only a moment, since nothing much had changed since the last time they'd met by video conference. Only the clock had advanced. It was now five in the afternoon in Tel Aviv, and four o'clock in Paris. Lev wanted to sound the alarm.

'We have to assume that in three hours, there is going to be a major terrorist attack in France, probably in Paris, and that one of our agents is going to be in the middle of it. Given the situation, I'm afraid we have no recourse but to tell the French.'

'But what about Gabriel and his wife?' said Moshe Yariv of Shabak. 'If the French issue a nationwide alert, Khaled might very well view it as an excuse to kill them both.'

'He doesn't need an excuse,' Shamron said. 'That's precisely what he intends to do. Lev is right. We have to tell the French. Morally, and politically, we have no other choice.'

The prime minister shifted his large body uneasily in his chair. 'But I can't tell them that we sent a team of agents to Marseilles to kill a Palestinian terrorist.'

'That's not necessary,' Shamron said. 'But any way we play our hand, the outcome is going to be bad. We have an agreement with the French not to operate on their soil without consulting them first. It's an agreement we violate all the time, with the tacit understanding of our brethren in the French services. But a tacit understanding is one thing, and getting caught red-handed is quite another.'

'So what do I tell them?'

'I recommend staying as close to the truth as possible. We tell them that one of our agents has been abducted by a Palestinian terror cell operating out of Marseilles. We tell them the agent was in Marseilles investigating the bombing of our embassy in Rome. We tell them that we have credible evidence suggesting that Paris is going to be the target of an attack this evening at seven. Who knows? If the French sound the alarm loudly enough, it might force Khaled to postpone or cancel his attack.'

The prime minister looked at Lev. 'What's the status of the rest of the team?'

'*Fidelity* is out of French territorial waters, and the rest of the team members have all crossed international borders. The only one still on French soil is Gabriel.'

The prime minister punched a button on his telephone console. 'Get the French president on the line. And get a translator as well. I don't want there to be any misunderstandings.'

*

285

The president of the French Republic was at that moment meeting with the German chancellor in the ornate Lounge of Portraits in the Élysée Palace. An aide-de-camp slipped quietly into the room and murmured a few words directly into his ear. The French leader could not hide his irritation at being interrupted by a man he loathed.

'Does it have to be now?'

'He says it's a security matter of the highest priority.'

The president stood and looked down at his guest. 'Will you excuse me, Chancellor?'

Tall and elegant in his dark suit, the Frenchman followed his aide into a private anteroom. A moment later the call was routed through.

'Good afternoon, Mr Prime Minister. I take it this isn't a social call?'

'No, Mr President, it isn't. I'm afraid I have become aware of a grave threat against your country.'

'I assume this threat is terrorist in nature?'

'It is, indeed.'

'How imminent? Weeks? Days?'

'Hours, Mr President.'

'*Hours?* Why am I being told of this only now?'

'We've just become aware of the threat ourselves.'

'Do you know any operational details?'

'Only the time. We believe a Palestinian terror cell intends to strike at seven this evening. Paris is the most likely target, but we can't say for certain.'

'Please, Mr Prime Minister. Tell me everything you know.'

The prime minister spoke for two minutes. When he was finished, the French president said, 'Why do I get the sense I'm being told only part of the story?'

'I'm afraid we know only part of the story.'

'Why didn't you tell us you were pursuing a suspect on French soil?'

'There wasn't time for a formal consultation, Mr President. It fell into the category of a hot pursuit.'

'And what about the Italians? Have you informed them that you have a suspect in a bombing that took place on *Italian* soil?'

'No, Mr President, we haven't.'

'What a surprise,' the Frenchman said. 'Do you have photographs that might help us identify any of the potential bombers?'

'I'm afraid we do not.'

'I don't suppose you'd care to send along a photo of your missing agent.'

'Under the circumstances –'

'I thought that would be your answer,' the Frenchman said. 'I'm dispatching my ambassador to your office. I'm confident he will receive a full and frank briefing on this entire matter.'

'He will indeed, sir.'

'Something tells me there will be fallout from this affair, but first things first. I'll be in touch.'

'Good luck, Mr President.'

The French leader slammed down the phone and

looked at his aide. 'Convene the Group Napoleon immediately,' he said. 'I'll deal with the chancellor.'

Twenty minutes after hanging up, the president of France was taking his usual seat at the cabinet table in the Salon Murat. Gathered around him were the members of Group Napoleon, a streamlined team of senior intelligence and security officials and cabinet ministers, designed for dealing with imminent threats to the French homeland. Seated directly across the expansive table was the prime minister. Between the two men was an ornate double-faced brass clock. It read 4:35 P.M.

The president opened the meeting with a concise recounting of what he had just learned. There followed several minutes of somewhat heated discussion, for the source of the information, the Israeli prime minister, was a distinctly unpopular man in Paris. In the end, though, every member of the group concluded that the threat was too credible to ignore. 'Obviously, gentlemen, we need to increase the threat level and take precautions,' the president said. 'How high do we go?'

In the aftermath of al-Qaeda's attacks on the World Trade Center and the Pentagon, the government of France devised a four-tiered color-coded system similar to that of the United States. On that afternoon the level stood at Orange, the second level, with only Yellow being lower. The third level, Red, would automatically close vast stretches of French airspace and put in place additional security precautions in the transit systems and at French landmarks such as the Louvre and the Eiffel Tower. The highest level, Scarlet, would virtually shut down the country, including its water supply and power grid. No member of Group Napoleon was prepared to do that based on a warning from the Israelis. 'The target of the attack is likely to be Israeli or Jewish in nature,' said the interior minister. 'Even if it's on the scale of Rome, it doesn't justify increasing the level to Scarlet.'

'I concur,' the president said. 'We'll raise it to Red.'

Five minutes later, when the meeting of Group Napoleon adjourned, the French interior minister strode out of the Salon Murat to face the cameras and the microphones. 'Ladies and gentlemen,' he began, his facial expression grave, 'the government of France has received what it believes is credible evidence of a pending terrorist attack against Paris this evening . . .'

The apartment house was on the rue de Saules, in the quiet northern end of Montmartre, several streets away from the tourist morass around Sacré-Coeur. The flat was small but comfortable, a perfect pied-à-terre for those occasions when work or romantic pursuits brought Paul Martineau from Provence to the capital. After arriving in Paris, he'd gone to the Luxembourg Quarter to have lunch with a colleague from the Sorbonne. Then it was over to St-Germain for a meeting with a prospective publisher for his book on the pre-Roman history of ancient Provence. At 4:45 he was strolling across the quiet courtyard of the building and letting himself into the foyer. Madame Touzet, the concierge, poked her head out of her door as Martineau came inside.

'*Bonjour*, Professor Martineau.'

Martineau kissed her powdered cheeks and presented her with a bunch of lilies he'd bought from a stall on the rue Caulaincourt. Martineau never came to his Paris flat without bringing a small treat for Madame Touzet.

'For me?' she asked elaborately. 'You shouldn't have, Professor.'

'I couldn't help myself.'

'How long are you in Paris?'

'Only for one night.'

'A tragedy! I'll get your mail.'

She returned a moment later with a stack of cards and letters, neatly bound, as always, with a scented pink ribbon. Martineau went upstairs to his apartment. He switched on the television, turned to Channel 2, then went into the kitchen to make coffee. Over the sound of running water, he heard the familiar voice of the French Interior minister. He shut off the tap and went calmly into the sitting room. He remained there, standing frozen before the television screen, for the next ten minutes.

The Israelis had chosen to alert the French. Martineau had expected they might resort to that. He knew that the increase in the threat level would mean a change in security tactics and procedures at critical sites all around Paris, a development that required one minor adjustment in his plans. He picked up the telephone and dialed.

'I'd like to change a reservation, please.'

'Your name?'

'Dr Paul Martineau.'

'Ticket number?'

Martineau recited it.

'At the moment you're scheduled to return to Aix-en-Provence from Paris tomorrow morning.'

'That's right, but I'm afraid something has come up and I need to return earlier than expected. Can I still get on an early-evening train tonight?'

'There are seats available on the seven-fifteen.'

'First class?'

'Yes.'

'I'll take one, please.'

'Are you aware of the government's terror warning?'

'I've never put much stock in those sorts of things,' Martineau said. 'Besides, if we stop living, the terrorists win, do they not?'

'How true.'

Martineau could hear the tapping of fingers upon a computer keyboard.

'All right, Dr Martineau. Your booking has been changed. Your train departs at seven-fifteen from the Gare de Lyon.'

Martineau hung up the phone.

24. Troyes, France

'*Sumayriyya?* You want to know about Sumayriyya?
It was Paradise on Earth. Eden. Fruit orchards and
olive groves. Melons and bananas, cucumbers and
wheat. Sumayriyya was simple. Pure. Our life moved
to the rhythms of the planting and the harvest.
The rains and the drought. We were eight hundred
in Sumayriyya. We had a mosque. We had a school.
We were poor, but Allah blessed us with everything
we needed.'

Listen to her, thought Gabriel as he drove. *We ...
Our ...* She was born twenty-five years after Sumayriyya was wiped from the face of the map, but
she spoke of the village as though she'd lived there
her entire life.

'My grandfather was an important man. Not a
muktar, mind you, but a man of influence among
the village elders. He had forty dunams of land and a
large flock of goats. He was considered wealthy.'
A satirical smile. 'To be wealthy in Sumayriyya meant
that you were only a little bit poor.'

Her eyes darkened. She looked down at the gun,
then at the French farmland rushing past her window.

'Nineteen forty-seven marked the beginning of the
end for my village. In November the United Nations

voted to partition my land and give half of it to the Jews. Sumayriyya, like the rest of the Western Galilee, was destined to be part of the Arab state in Palestine. But, of course, that wasn't to be the case. The war started the day after the vote, and as far as the Jews were concerned, all of Palestine was now theirs for the taking.'

It was the Arabs who had started the war, Gabriel wanted to say – Sheikh Asad al-Khalifa, warlord of Beit Sayeed, who'd opened the floodgates of blood with his terrorist attack on the Netanya-to-Jerusalem bus. But now was not the time to quibble over the historical record. The narrative of Sumayriyya had cast its spell over her, and Gabriel wanted to do nothing to break it.

She turned her gaze toward him. 'You're thinking of something.'

'I'm listening to your story.'

'With one part of your brain,' she said, 'but with the other you're thinking of something else. Are you thinking about taking my gun? Are you planning your escape?'

'There *is* no escape, Palestina – for either one of us. Tell me your story.'

She looked out the window. 'On the night of May 13, 1948, a column of armored Haganah vehicles set out up the coast road from Acre. Their action was code-named Operation Ben-Ami. It was part of Tochnit Dalet.' She looked at him. 'Do you know this term, Tochnit Dalet? Plan D?'

Gabriel nodded and thought of Dina, standing amid the ruins of Beit Sayeed. How long ago had it been? Only a month, but it seemed a lifetime ago.

'The stated objective of Operation Ben-Ami was the reinforcement of several isolated Jewish settlements in the Western Galilee. The real objective, however, was conquest and annexation. In fact, the orders specifically called for the destruction of three Arab villages: Bassa, Zib, and Sumayriyya.'

She paused, looked to see if her remarks had provoked any reaction, and resumed her lecture. Sumayriyya was the first of the three villages to die. The Haganah surrounded it before dawn and illuminated the village with the headlamps of their armored vehicles. Some of the Haganah men wore red checkered kaffiyehs. A village watchman saw the kaffiyehs and assumed that the attacking Jews were actually Arab reinforcements. He fired shots of celebration into the air and was immediately cut down by Haganah fire. The news that the Jews were disguised as Arabs sowed panic inside the village. The defenders of Sumayriyya fought bravely, but they were no match for the better-armed Haganah. Within a few minutes, the exodus had begun.

'The Jews wanted us to leave,' she said. 'They intentionally left the eastern side of the village unguarded to give us an escape route. We had no time to pack any clothing or even to take something to eat. We just started running. But still the Jews weren't satisfied. They fired at us as we fled across the fields we had tilled for centuries. Five villagers died in those fields. The Haganah sappers went in right away. As we were running away, we could hear the explosions. The Jews were turning our Paradise into a pile of uninhabitable rubble.'

The villagers of Sumayriyya took to the road and headed north, toward Lebanon. They were soon joined by the inhabitants of Bassa and Zib and several smaller villages to the east. 'The Jews told us to go to Lebanon,' she said. 'They told us to wait there for a few weeks until the fighting ended, then we would be allowed to return. *Return?* To what were we supposed to return? Our houses had been demolished. So we kept walking. We walked over the border, into exile. Into oblivion. And behind us the gates of Palestine were being forever barred against our return.'

Reims: five o'clock.

'Pull over,' she said.

Gabriel guided the Mercedes onto the shoulder of the Autoroute. They sat in silence, the car shuddering in the turbulence of the passing traffic. Then the telephone. She listened, longer than usual. Gabriel suspected she was being given final instructions. Without so much as a word, she severed the connection, then dropped the phone back into her bag.

'Where are we going?'

'Paris,' she said. 'Just as you suspected.'

'Which way does he want me to go?'

'The A4. Do you know it?'

'I know it.'

'It will take you into –'

'– into southeast Paris. I know where it will take me, Palestina.'

Gabriel accelerated back onto the motorway. The dashboard clock read: 5:05. A road sign flashed past: PARIS 145. One hundred forty-five kilometers to Paris. Ninety-one miles.

'Finish your story, Palestina.'

'Where were we?'

'Lebanon,' Gabriel said. 'Oblivion.'

'We camped in the hills. We foraged for food. We survived off the charity of our Arab brethren and waited for the gates of Palestine to be opened to us, waited for the Jews to make good on the promises they'd made to us the morning we'd fled Sumayriyya. But in June, Ben-Gurion said that the refugees could not come home. We were a fifth column that could not be allowed back, he said. We would be a thorn in the side of the new Jewish state. We knew then that we would never see Sumayriyya again. Paradise lost.'

Gabriel looked at the clock. 5:10 P.M. Eighty miles to Paris.

'We walked north, to Sidon. We spent the long, hot summer living in tents. Then the weather turned cold and the rains came, and still we were living in the tents. We called our new home Ein al-Hilweh. Sweet Spring. It was hardest on my grandfather. In Sumayriyya he'd been an important man. He'd tended his fields and his flock. He'd provided for his family. Now his family was surviving on hand-outs. He had a deed to his property but no land. He had the keys to his door but no house. He took ill that first winter and died. He didn't want to live – not in Lebanon. My grandfather died when Sumayriyya died.'

5:25 P.M. Paris: 62 miles.

'My father was only a boy, but he had to assume responsibility for his mother and two sisters. He couldn't work – the Lebanese wouldn't permit that. He couldn't go to school – the Lebanese wouldn't allow that, either. No Lebanese social security, no Lebanese health care. And no way out, because we had no valid passports. We were stateless. We were nonpersons. We were nothing.'

5:38 P.M. Paris: 35 miles.

'When my father married a girl from Sumayriyya, the remnants of the village gathered in Ein al-Hilweh for the wedding celebration. It was just like home, except the surroundings were different. Instead of Paradise, it was the open sewers and the cinder-block huts of the camp. My mother gave my father two sons. Every night he told them about Sumayriyya, so that they would never forget their true home. He told them the story of al-Nakba, the Catastrophe, and instilled in them the dream of al-Awda, the Return. My brothers would grow up to be fighters for Palestine. There was no choice in the matter. As soon as they were old enough to hold a gun, the Fatah started training them.'

'And you?'

'I was the last child. I was born in 1975, just as Lebanon was descending into civil war.'

5:47 P.M. Paris: 25 miles.

'We never thought they would come for us again. Yes, we'd lost everything – our homes, our village, our land – but at least we were safe in Ein al-Hilweh. The Jews would never come to Lebanon. Would they?'

5:52 P.M. Paris: 19 miles.

'Operation Peace for Galilee – that's what they called it. My God, even Orwell couldn't have come up with a better name. On June 4, 1982, the Israelis invaded Lebanon to finish off the PLO once and for all. To us it all seemed so familiar. An Israeli armored column heading north up the coast road, only now the coast road was in Lebanon instead of Palestine, and the soldiers were members of the IDF instead of the Haganah. We knew things were going to get bad. Ein al-Hilweh was known as Fatahland, capital of Diaspora Palestine. On June 8, the battle for the camp began. The Israelis sent in their paratroopers. Our men fought back with the courage of lions –

alley to alley, house to house, from the mosques and the hospitals. Any fighter who tried to surrender was shot. The word went out: the battle for Ein al-Hilweh was to be a fight to the last man.

'The Israelis changed their tactics. They used their aircraft and artillery to raze the camp, block by block, sector by sector. Then their paratroopers would sweep down and massacre our fighters. Every few hours the Israelis would pause and ask us to surrender. Each time the answer was the same: never. It went on like this for a week. I lost one brother on the first day of the battle, my other brother on the fourth day. On the last day of fighting, my mother was mistaken for a guerrilla as she crawled out of the rubble and was shot to death by the Israelis.

'When it was finally over, Ein al-Hilweh was a wasteland. For the second time, the Jews had turned my home into rubble. I lost my brothers, I lost my mother. You ask me why I'm here. I'm here because of Sumayriyya and Ein al-Hilweh. This is what Zionism has meant to me. I have no choice but to fight.'

'What happened after Ein al-Hilweh? Where did you go?'

The girl shook her head. 'I've told you enough already,' she said. 'Too much.'

'I want to hear the rest of it.'

'Drive,' she said. 'It's almost time to see your wife.'

Gabriel looked at the clock: 6:00 P.M. Ten miles to Paris.

25. St-Denis, Northern Paris

Amira Assaf closed the door of the flat behind her. The corridor, a long gray cement tunnel, was in semidarkness, lit only by the occasional flickering fluorescent tube. She pushed the wheelchair toward the bank of elevators. A woman, Moroccan by the sound of her accent, was yelling at her two young children. Farther on, a trio of African boys was listening to American hip-hop music on a portable stereo. This is what remained of the French empire, she thought, a few islands in the Caribbean and the human warehouses of St-Denis.

She came to the elevator and pressed the call button, then looked up and saw that one of the cars was heading her way. Thank God, she thought. It was the one part of the journey that was completely beyond her control – the rickety old elevators of the housing block. Twice during her preparation she'd been forced to hike down twenty-three floors because the elevators weren't working.

A bell chimed, the doors screeched open. Amira wheeled the chair into the carriage and was greeted by the overwhelming stench of urine. As she sunk toward earth, she pondered the question of why the poor piss in their elevators. When the doors opened, she thrust the chair into the lobby and drew a deep breath. Not much better. Only when she was outside, in the cold fresh air of the quadrangle, did she escape the odor of too many people living too close together.

There was something of the Third World village square in the broad quadrangle that lay at the center of the four large housing blocks – clusters of men, divided by their country of origin, chatting in the cool twilight; women bearing sacks of groceries; children playing football. No one took notice of the attractive young Palestinian woman pushing a wheelchair-bound figure of indeterminate sex and age.

It took precisely seven minutes for her to get to the St-Denis station. It was a large station, a combination RER and Métro, and because of the hour, crowds were streaming out of the exits into the street. She entered the ticket hall and immediately spotted two policemen, the first evidence of the security alert. She had watched the news updates and knew security had been tightened at Métro and rail stations across the country. But did they know something about St-Denis? Were they looking for a disabled woman kidnapped the previous night from a psychiatric hospital in England? She kept walking.

'Excuse me, mademoiselle.'

She turned around: a station attendant, young and officious, with a neatly pressed uniform.

'Where are you going?'

The tickets were in her hand; she had to answer

truthfully. 'The RER,' she said, then added: 'To the Gare de Lyon.'

The attendant smiled. 'There's an elevator right over there.'

'Yes, I know the way.'

'Can I be of some help?'

'I'm fine.'

'Please,' he said, 'allow me.'

Just her luck, she thought. One pleasant station attendant in the entire Métro system, and he was working St-Denis tonight. To refuse would look suspicious. She nodded and handed the attendant the tickets. He led her through the turnstile, then across the crowded hall to the elevator. They rode down in silence to the RER level of the station. The attendant led her to the proper platform. For a moment she feared he intended to stay until the train arrived. Finally, he bid her a good evening and headed back upstairs.

Amira looked up at the arrivals board. Twelve minutes. She glanced at her watch, did the math. No problem. She sat on a bench and waited. Twelve minutes later the train swept into the station and came to a stop. The doors shot open with a pneumatic hiss. Amira stood and wheeled the woman into the carriage.

26. Paris

Where am I now? A train? And who is this woman? Is she the same one who worked at the hospital? I told Dr Avery I didn't like her, but he wouldn't listen. She spent too much time around me. Watched me too much. You're being delusional, Dr Avery told me. Your reaction to her is part of your illness. Her name is Amira. She's very kind and highly qualified. No, I tried to tell him, she's watching me. Something's going to happen. She's a Palestinian girl. I can see it in her eyes. Why didn't Dr Avery listen to me? Or did I ever really try to tell him? I can't be sure. I can't be sure of anything. Look at the television, Gabriel. The missiles are falling on Tel Aviv again. Do you think Saddam has put chemicals on them this time? I can't stand being in Vienna when missiles are falling on Tel Aviv. Eat your pasta, Dani. Look at him right now, Gabriel. He looks so much like you. This train feels like Paris, but I'm surrounded by Arabs. Where has this woman taken me? Why aren't you eating, Gabriel? Are you feeling all right? You don't look well. My God, your skin is burning. Are you ill? Look, another missile. Please, God, let it fall on an empty building. Don't let it fall on my mother's house. I want to get out of this restaurant. I want to go home and call my mother. I wonder what happened to that boy who came to the hospital to watch over me. How did I get here? Who brought me here? And where is this train going? Snow. God, how I hate this city, but the snow makes it beautiful. The snow absolves Vienna of its sins. Snow falls on Vienna while the missiles rain down on Tel Aviv. Are you working tonight? How late will you be? Sorry, I don't know why I bothered to ask. Shit. The car is covered with snow. Help me with the windows before you go. Make sure Dani is buckled into his seat tightly. The streets are slippery. Yes, I'll be careful. Come on, Gabriel, hurry. I want to talk to my mother. I want to hear the sound of her voice. Give me a kiss, one last kiss, then turn and walk away. I love to watch you walk, Gabriel. You walk like an angel. I hate the work you do for Shamron, but I'll love you always. Damn, the car won't start. I'll try again. Why are you turning around, Gabriel? Where is this woman taking me? Why are you shouting and running toward the car? Turn the key again. Silence. Smoke and fire. Get Dani out first! Hurry, Gabriel! Please, get him out! I'm burning! I'm burning to death! Where is this woman taking me? Help me, Gabriel. Please help me.

27. Paris

The Gare de Lyon is located in the 12th Arrondissement of Paris, a few streets to the east of the Seine.
In front of the station is a large traffic circle, and
beyond the circle, the intersection of two major
avenues, the rue de Lyon and the boulevard Diderot.
It was there, seated in a busy sidewalk café popular
with travelers, that Paul Martineau waited. He
finished the last of a thin glass of Côtes du Rhône,
then signaled the waiter for a check. An interval of
five minutes ensued before the bill appeared. He left
money and a small tip, then set out toward the
entrance of the station.

There were several police cars in the traffic circle
and two pairs of paramilitary police standing guard
at the entrance. Martineau fell in with a small cluster
of people and went inside. He was nearly into the
departure hall when he felt a tap at his shoulder. He
turned around. It was one of the policemen who'd
been watching the main entrance.

'May I see some identification, please?'

Martineau drew his French national identity card
from his wallet and handed it to the policeman. The
policeman stared into Martineau's face for a long
moment before looking down at the card.

'Where are you going?'

'Aix.'

'May I see your ticket, please?'

Martineau handed it over.

'It says here you're supposed to return tomorrow.'

'I changed my reservation this afternoon.'

'Why?'

'I needed to return early.' Martineau decided to show a bit of irritation. 'Listen, what's this all about? Are all these questions really necessary?'

'I'm afraid so, Monsieur Martineau. What brought you to Paris?'

Martineau answered: lunch with a colleague from Paris University, a meeting with a potential publisher.

'You're a writer?'

'An archaeologist, actually, but I'm working on a book.'

The policeman handed back the identification card.

'Have a pleasant evening.'

'Thank you.'

Martineau turned and headed toward the terminal. He paused at the departure board, then climbed the stairs to Le Train Bleu, the famed restaurant overlooking the hall. The maître d' met him at the door.

'Do you have a reservation?'

'Actually, I'm meeting someone at the bar. I believe she's already here.'

The maître d' stepped aside. Martineau made his way to the bar, then to a table in a window overlooking the platforms. Seated there was an attractive woman in her forties with a streak of gray in her long, dark hair. She looked up as Martineau approached. He bent and kissed the side of her neck.

'Hello, Mimi.'

'Paul,' she whispered. 'So lovely to see you again.'

28. Paris

Two blocks north of the Gare de Lyon: the rue Parrot. 6:53 P.M.

'Turn here,' the girl said. 'Park the car.'

'There's no place to leave it. The street's parked up.'

'Trust me. We'll find a space.'

Just then a car pulled away from the curb near the Hotel Lyon Bastille. Gabriel, taking no chances, went in nose first. The girl slipped the Tanfolgio into her handbag and swung the handbag over her shoulder.

'Open the trunk.'

'Why?'

'Just do as I say. Look at the clock. We haven't much time.'

Gabriel pulled the trunk-release lever, and the hatch opened with a dull thump. The girl snatched the key from the ignition and dropped it into the bag along with the gun and the satellite phone. Then she opened her door and climbed out. She walked back to the trunk and motioned for Gabriel to join her. He looked down. Inside was a large rectangular suitcase, black nylon, with wheels and a collapsible handle.

'Take it.'

'No.'

'If you don't take it, your wife dies.'

'I'm not going to take a bomb into the Gare de Lyon.'

'You're entering a train station. It's best to look like a traveler. Take the bag.'

He reached down and looked for the zipper. Locked.

'Just take it.'

In the tool well was a chrome-plated tire iron.

'What are you doing? Do you want your wife to die?'

Two sharp blows, and the lock snapped open. He unzipped the main compartment: balls of packing paper. Next he tried the outer compartments. Empty.

'Are you satisfied? Look at the clock. Take the bag.'

Gabriel lifted the bag out and placed it on the pavement. The girl had already started walking away. He extended the handle of the bag and closed the trunk, then set out after her. At the corner of the rue de Lyon they turned left. The station, set on a slight promontory, loomed before them.

'I don't have a ticket.'

'I have a ticket for you.'

'Where are we going? Berlin? Geneva? Amsterdam?'

'Just walk.'

As they neared the corner of the boulevard Diderot, Gabriel saw police officers patrolling the perimeter of the station on foot and blue emergency lights flickering in the traffic circle.

'They've been warned,' he said. 'We're walking straight into a security alert.'

'We'll be fine.'

'I don't have a passport.'

'You don't need it.'

'What if we're stopped?'

'I have it. If a policeman asks you for identification, just look at me, and I'll take care of it.'

'You're the reason we'll be stopped.'

At the boulevard Diderot they waited for the light to change, then crossed the street amid a swarm of pedestrians. The bag felt too light. It didn't sound right rolling over the pavement. They should have put clothing in it to weigh it down properly. What if he were stopped? What if the bag was searched and they found that it was filled with balls of paper? What if they looked inside Palestina's bag and found the Tanfolgio? *The Tanfolgio* ... He told himself to forget about the empty suitcase and the gun in the girl's bag. Instead he focused on the sensation he'd had earlier that day, the feeling that the clue to his survival lay somewhere along the path he'd already traveled.

Standing at the entrance of the station were several police officers and two soldiers in camouflage with automatic weapons slung over their shoulders. They were randomly stopping passengers, checking IDs, looking in bags. The girl threaded her arm through

Gabriel's and made him walk faster. He could feel the eyes of the policemen on him, but no one stopped them as they went inside.

The station, its roof arched and soaring, opened before them. They paused for a moment at the head of an escalator that sunk downward into the Métro level of the station. Gabriel used the time to take his bearings. To his left was a kiosk of public telephones; behind him, the stairs that led up to the Le Train Bleu. On opposite ends of the platform were two Relay newsstands. A few feet to his right was a snack bar, above which hung the large black departure board. Just then it changed over. To Gabriel the clapping of the characters sounded obscenely like applause for Khaled's perfectly played gambit. The clock read: 6:57.

'Do you see that girl using the first telephone on this side of the kiosk?'

'Which girl?'

'Blue jeans, gray sweater, maybe French, maybe Arab, like me.'

'I see her.'

'When the clock on the departure board turns to six fifty-eight, she's going to hang up. You and I will walk over and take her place. She'll pause for a moment to give us time to get there.'

'What if someone else gets there first?'

'The girl and I will take care of it. You're going to dial a number. Are you ready?'

'Yes.'

'Don't forget the number. If you do, I won't tell it to you again, and your wife will die. Are you sure you're ready?'

'Give me the fucking number.'

She recited it, then gave him a few coins as the clock turned to 6:58. The girl vacated her place. Gabriel walked over, lifted the receiver and fed coins through the slot. He dialed the number deliberately, fearful that if he made a mistake the first time he would not be able to summon the number correctly again. Somewhere a telephone began to ring. One ring, a second, a third . . .

'There's no answer.'

'Be patient. Someone will pick up.'

'It's rung six times. No one's answering.'

'Are you sure you dialed the proper number? Maybe you made a mistake. Maybe your wife is about to die because you –'

'Shut your mouth,' Gabriel snapped.

The telephone had stopped ringing.

29. Paris

'Good evening, Gabriel.'

A woman's voice, shockingly familiar.

'Or should I call you Herr Klemp? That's the name you used when you came to my club, isn't it? And the name you used when you ransacked my apartment.'

Mimi Ferrere. The Little Moon.

'Where is she? Where's Leah?'

'She's close.'

'Where? I don't see her.'

'You'll find out in a minute.'

A minute ... He looked up at the departure board. The clock rolled over: 6:59 P.M. A pair of soldiers strolled past. One of them looked at him. Gabriel turned away and lowered his voice.

'You told me if I came, you'd let her live. Now, where is she?'

'Everything will be clear to you in just a few seconds.'

The voice: he latched on to it. It drew him back to Cairo, back to the evening he'd spent at the wine bar in Zamalek. He'd been lured to Cairo for a reason – to plant a bug on Mimi's telephone, so he could overhear a conversation with a man named Tony and capture the telephone number for an apartment in Marseilles. But had he been brought to Cairo for another reason?

She started to speak again, but the sound of her voice was drowned out by the blare of a station announcement: *Train number 765 for Marseilles is now boarding on Track D* ... Gabriel covered the mouthpiece of the receiver. *Train number 765 for Marseilles is now boarding on Track D* ... He could hear it through the telephone – he was sure of it. Mimi was somewhere in the station. He spun around and glimpsed her girlish hips flowing calmly toward the exit. Walking on her left, with his hand in the back pocket of her trousers, was a man with square shoulders and dark curly hair. Gabriel had seen the same walk earlier that morning in Marseilles. Khaled had come to the Gare de Lyon to witness Gabriel's death.

He watched them slip through the exit.

Train number 765 for Marseilles is now boarding on Track D.

He glanced at Palestina. She was looking at the clock. Judging from her expression, she knew now that Gabriel had told her the truth. She was a few seconds away from becoming a *shaheed* in Khaled's jihad of revenge.

'Are you listening to me, Gabriel?'

Traffic noise: Mimi and Khaled were moving hastily away from the station.

'I'm listening,' he said – *and I'm wondering why you seated me with three Arabs in your nightclub.*

Train number 765 for Marseilles is now boarding on Track D.

Track D ... Track Dalet ... Tochnit Dalet ...

'Where is she, Mimi? Tell me what –'

And then he saw him, standing at a newspaper rack at the Relay newsstand at the east end of the station. His suitcase, a rolling rectangular bag of black nylon, identical to Gabriel's, stood upright next to him. They'd called him Bashir that night in Cairo. Bashir liked Johnnie Walker Red on the rocks and smoked Silk Cut cigarettes. Bashir wore a gold TAG Heuer watch on his right wrist and had a thing for one of Mimi's waitresses. Bashir was also a *shaheed*. In a few seconds Bashir's bag would explode, and so would several dozen people around him.

Gabriel looked to his left, toward the opposite side of the platform: another Relay newsstand, another *shaheed* with a bag identical to Gabriel's. He'd been called Naji that night. Naji: *survivor.* Not tonight, Naji.

A few feet away from Gabriel, purchasing a sandwich he would never eat, was Tayyib. Same suitcase, same glassy look of death in his eyes. He was close enough for Gabriel to see the configuration of the bomb. A black wire had been run along the inside of one arm of the pull handle. Gabriel reckoned that the release button on the handle itself was the trigger. Press the button, and it would strike the contact plate. That meant that the three *shaheeds* had to press their buttons simultaneously. But how were they to be signaled? The time, of course. Gabriel looked at Tayyib's eyes and saw they were now focused on the digital clock of the departure board. *6:59:28* . . .

'Where is she, Mimi?'

The soldiers sauntered past again, chatting casually. Three Arabs had entered the station with suitcases packed with explosives, but the security forces hadn't seemed to notice. How long would it take the soldiers to get their automatics off their shoulders and into firing position? If they were Israelis? Two seconds at most. But these French boys? Their reaction time would be slower.

He glanced at Palestina. She was growing more anxious. Her eyes were damp and she was pulling on the strap of her shoulder bag. Gabriel's eyes flickered about the station, calculating angles and lines of fire.

Mimi intruded on his thoughts. 'Are you listening to me?'

'I'm listening.'

'As you've probably guessed by now, the station is about to explode. By my calculation, you'll have fifteen seconds. You have two choices. You can warn the people around you and try to save as many lives as possible, or you can selfishly save the life of your wife. But you cannot possibly do both, because if you warn the people, there will be pandemonium, and you'll never be able to get your wife out of the station before the bombs go off. The only way to save her is to allow hundreds of other people to die – hundreds of deaths in order to save a wreck of a human being. Quite a moral dilemma, wouldn't you say?'

'Where is she?'

'You tell me.'

'Track D,' Gabriel said. 'Track Dalet.'

'Very good.'

'She's not there. I don't see her.'

'Look harder. Fifteen seconds, Gabriel. Fifteen seconds.'

And then the line went dead.

Time seemed to crawl to a stop. He saw it all as a streetscape, rendered in the vibrant palette of Renoir – the *shaheeds*, their eyes on the departure clock; the soldiers, their shoulders slung with submachine guns; Palestina, clutching the handbag that held a loaded Tanfolgio nine-millimeter. And in the center of it all he saw the pretty Arab girl walking away from a woman in a wheelchair. On the track stood a train bound for Marseilles, and five feet from the spot where the woman waited to die was an open door to the last carriage. Above him a clock read 6:59:50. Mimi had cheated him, but Gabriel knew better than most men that ten seconds was an eternity. In the span of ten seconds he had followed Khaled's father into a Paris courtyard and filled his body with eleven bullets. In less than ten seconds, on a snowy night in Vienna, his son was murdered and his wife forever lost to him.

His first move was so compact and rapid that no

317

one seemed to notice it – a blow to the left side of Palestina's skull that landed with such force that Gabriel, when he pulled the handbag off her shoulder, was not sure whether she was still alive. As the girl collapsed at his feet, he reached inside the bag and wrapped his hand around the grip of the Tanfolgio. Tayyib, the *shaheed* closest to him at the snack bar, had seen none of it, for his eyes were fixed on the clock. Gabriel drew the weapon from the bag and leveled it, one-handed, at the bomber. He squeezed the trigger twice, *tap-tap*. Both shots struck the bomber high in the chest, flinging him backward, away from the explosive-laden suitcase.

The sound of gunfire in the vast echo chamber of the station had the effect Gabriel had expected. Across the platform, people crouched or dropped to the ground. Twenty feet away, the two soldiers were pulling their submachine guns off their shoulders. And at either end of the platform the last two *shaheeds*, Bashir and Naji, were still standing, their eyes fixed on the clock. There wasn't time for both.

Gabriel, in French, shouted: 'Bomber! Get down! Get down!'

A firing lane opened as Gabriel aimed the Tanfolgio at the one called Naji. The French soldiers, confused by what they were witnessing, hesitated. He squeezed the trigger, saw a flash of pink, then watched as Naji spiraled lifelessly to the floor.

He ran toward Track D, toward the spot where Leah sat exposed to the coming blast wave. He clung to Palestina's handbag, for it contained the keys to his escape. He glanced once over his shoulder. Bashir, the last of the *shaheeds*, was heading toward the center of the station. He must have seen his two comrades fall; now he was trying to increase the killing power of his single bomb by placing it in the center of the platform where it was still most crowded.

To stop now meant almost certain death for himself and for Leah, so Gabriel kept running. He reached the entrance to Track D and turned to the right. The platform was empty; the gunfire and Gabriel's warnings had driven the passengers into the trains or toward the exit of the station. Only Leah remained, helpless and immobile.

The clock rolled over: 7:00:00

Gabriel seized Leah by the shoulders and lifted her unresisting body from the chair, then made one final lunge toward the doorway of the waiting train as the suitcase detonated. A flash of brilliant light, a thunderclap, a searing blast wave that seemed to press the very life out of him. Poison bolts and nails. Shattered glass and blood.

Black smoke, an unbearable silence. Gabriel looked into Leah's eyes. She looked directly back at him, her gaze strangely serene. He slipped the Tanfolgio into the handbag, then cradled Leah in his arms and stood. She seemed weightless to him.

From outside the shattered carriage came the first

screams. Gabriel looked around him. The windows on both sides were blown out. Those passengers who had been in their seats had been cut by the flying glass. Gabriel saw at least six who looked fatally wounded.

He climbed down the steps and made his way toward the platform. What had been there just a few seconds earlier was now unrecognizable. He looked up and saw that a large portion of the roof was gone. Had all three bombs exploded simultaneously, the entire station would likely have come down.

He slipped and fell hard to the ground. The platform was drenched with blood. All around him were severed limbs and pieces of human flesh. He got to his feet, lifted Leah, and stumbled forward. What was he stepping on? He couldn't bear to look. He slipped a second time, near the telephone kiosk, and found himself staring into the lifeless eyes of Palestina. Was it Gabriel's blow that had killed her or the shrapnel of Tayyib's bomb? Gabriel didn't much care.

He got to his feet again. The station exits were jammed: terrified passengers trying to get out, police forcing their way in. If Gabriel tried to go that way, there was a good chance someone would identify him as the man who had been firing a gun before the bomb went off. He had to find some other way out. He remembered the walk from the car to the station, waiting for the light to change at the intersection of the rue de Lyon and the boulevard

Diderot. There had been an entrance to the Métro there.

He carried Leah toward the escalator. It was no longer running. He stepped over two dead bodies and started downward. The Métro station was in tumult, passengers screaming, startled attendants trying in vain to keep the situation calm, but at least there was no more smoke, and the floors were no longer wet with blood. Gabriel followed the signs through the arched passageways toward the rue de Lyon. Twice he was asked whether he needed help, and twice he shook his head and kept walking. The lights flickered and dimmed, then by some miracle came back to life again.

Two minutes later he came to a flight of steps. He mounted them and climbed steadily upward, emerging into a thin, chill rain. He'd come out on the rue de Lyon. He looked back over his shoulder toward the station. The traffic circle was ablaze with emergency lights, and smoke was pouring from the roof. He turned and started walking.

Another offer of help: 'Are you all right, monsieur? Does that person need a doctor?'

No, thank you, he thought. *Just please get out of my way, and please let that Mercedes be waiting for me.*

He rounded the corner into the rue Parrot. The car was still there: Khaled's only mistake. He carried Leah across the street. For an instant she clung anxiously to his neck. Did she know it was him, or did she think him an orderly in her hospital in

England? A moment later she was seated in the front passenger seat, staring calmly out the window as Gabriel pulled away from the curb and rolled up to the corner of the rue de Lyon. He glanced once to the left, toward the burning station, then turned right and sped up the wide avenue toward the Bastille. He reached into the girl's handbag again and pulled out her satellite phone. By the time he rounded the traffic circle in the Place de la Bastille, King Saul Boulevard had come on the line.

PART FOUR
Sumayriyya

30. Paris

The thin rain that had greeted Gabriel upon his emergence from the Gare de Lyon had turned to a spring downpour. It was dark now, and for that he was grateful. He had parked in a quiet leafy street near the Place de Colombie and shut down the engine. Because of the darkness, and the drenching rain, he was confident no one could see into the car. He rubbed a porthole in the fogged front windshield and peered through it. The building that contained the safe flat was on the opposite side of the street and a few doors up. Gabriel knew the flat well. He knew it was apartment 4B and that the nameplate on the buzzer read Guzman in faded blue script. He also knew that there was no place to safely hide a key, which meant that it had to be opened in advance by someone from the Paris station. Usually such tasks were handled by a *bodel,* the Office terminology for local hires who do the spadework required to keep a foreign station running. But ten minutes later Gabriel was relieved to see the familiar figure of Uzi Navot, the Paris *katsa,* pounding past his window with his strawberry blond hair plastered to his large round skull and a key to the flat in his hand.

Navot entered the apartment building and a

moment later lights came on in the fourth-floor window. Leah stirred. Gabriel turned and looked at her, and for an instant her gaze seemed to connect with his. He reached out and took what remained of her hand. The hard scar tissue, as always, made Gabriel feel violently cold. She'd been agitated during the drive. Now she seemed calm, the way she always looked when Gabriel visited her in the solarium. He peered through his porthole again, toward the window on the fourth floor.

'Is it you?'

Gabriel, startled by the sound of Leah's voice, looked up sharply – too sharply, he feared, because her eyes seemed suddenly panicked.

'Yes, it's me, Leah,' he said calmly. 'It's Gabriel.'

'Where are we?' Her voice was thin and dry, like the rustling of leaves. It was nothing like he remembered it. 'This feels like Paris to me. Are we in Paris?'

'Yes, we're in Paris.'

'That woman brought me here, didn't she? My nurse. I tried to tell Dr Avery –' She cut herself off in mid-sentence. 'I want to go home.'

'I'm taking you home.'

'To the hospital?'

'To Israel.'

A flicker of a smile, a gentle squeeze of his hand. 'Your skin is burning. Are you feeling all right?'

'I'm fine, Leah.'

She lapsed into silence and looked out the window.

'Look at the snow,' she said. 'God, how I hate this city, but the snow makes it beautiful. The snow absolves Vienna of its sins.'

Gabriel searched his memory for the first time he'd heard those words and then remembered. They'd been walking from the restaurant to the car. Dani had been sitting atop his shoulders. *The snow absolves Vienna of its sins. Snow falls on Vienna while the missiles rain down on Tel Aviv.*

'It's beautiful,' he agreed, trying to prevent a note of despondency from creeping into his voice. 'But we're not in Vienna. We're in Paris. Do you remember? The girl brought you to Paris.'

She was no longer listening to him. 'Hurry, Gabriel,' she said. 'I want to talk to my mother. I want to hear the sound of my mother's voice.'

Please, Leah, he thought. *Turn back. Don't do this to yourself.*

'We'll call her right away,' he said.

'Make sure Dani is buckled into his seat tightly. The streets are slippery.'

He's fine, Leah, Gabriel had said that night. *Be careful driving home.*

'I'll be careful,' she said. 'Give me a kiss.'

He leaned over and pressed his lips against Leah's ruined cheek.

'One last kiss,' she whispered.

Then her eyes opened wide. Gabriel held her scarred hand and looked away.

*

Madame Touzet poked her head from her apartment as Martineau entered the foyer.

'Professor Martineau, thank God it's you. I was worried to death. Were you there? Was it terrible?'

He had been a few hundred meters away from the station at the time of the explosion, he told her truthfully. And yes, it was terrible, though not as terrible as he had hoped. The station should have been demolished by the destructive force of three suitcase bombs. Obviously something had gone wrong.

'I've just made some chocolate. Will you sit with me and watch the television? I do hate to watch such a horrible business alone.'

'I'm afraid I've had a terribly long day, Madame Touzet. I'm going to turn in early.'

'A Paris landmark, in ruins. What's next, Professor? Who could do such a thing?'

'Muslims, I suppose, although one never knows the motivations of someone who could commit an act as barbaric as this. I suspect we may never know the truth.'

'Do you think it might have been a conspiracy?'

'Drink your chocolate, Madame Touzet. If you need anything, I'll be upstairs.'

'Good night, Professor Martineau.'

The *bodel*, a fawn-eyed Moroccan Jew from the Marais named Moshe, arrived at the safe flat an hour later. He carried two bags. One contained a change of clothing for Gabriel, the other groceries for the pantry. Gabriel went into the bedroom and stripped off the clothing the girl had given him in the house in Martigues, then stood for a long time beneath the showerhead and watched the blood of Khaled's victims swirling down the drain. He changed into the fresh clothing and placed the old things into the bag. The living room, when he went out again, was in semidarkness. Leah was asleep on the couch. Gabriel adjusted the flowered quilt that covered her body, then went into the kitchen. Navot was standing in front of the stove, with a spatula in one hand and a tea cloth tucked into the waistband of his trousers. The *bodel* was sitting at the table, contemplating a glass of red wine. Gabriel handed him the bag of dirty clothing.

'Get rid of these things,' he said. 'Someplace where no one's going to find them.'

The *bodel* nodded, then slipped out of the safe flat. Gabriel took his place at the table and looked at Navot. The Paris *katsa* was a compact man, no taller than Gabriel, with a wrestler's heavy shoulders and thick arms. Gabriel had always seen something of Shamron in Navot, and he suspected that Shamron did, too. They'd clashed in the past, Gabriel and Navot, but Gabriel had come to regard the younger officer as a thoroughly competent field man. They'd worked together most recently on the Radek case.

'There's going to be a shit storm over this.' Navot handed Gabriel a glass of wine. 'We might as well break out the hip-waders now.'

'How much warning did we give them?'

'The French? Two hours. The prime minister called Grey Poupon directly. Grey Poupon had a few choice words, then he raised the terror alert status to Level Red. You didn't hear any of it?'

Gabriel told Navot about the disabled car radio. 'The first time I sensed any increase in security was the moment I was walking into the station.' He swallowed some of the wine. 'How much did the prime minister tell them?'

Navot relayed to Gabriel what details of the conversation he knew.

'How did they explain my presence in Marseilles?'

'They said you were looking for someone in connection with the Rome bombing.'

'Khaled?'

'I don't think they went into specifics.'

'Something tells me we need to get our stories straight. Why did they wait so long to alert the French?'

'They were hoping you'd turn up, obviously. They also needed to make sure all the members of the Marseilles team had left French soil.'

'Had they?'

Navot nodded.

'I suppose we could consider ourselves lucky the prime minister went on the record with Élysée Palace.'

'Why is that?'

Gabriel told Navot about the three *shaheeds*. 'We were at the same table in Cairo together. I'm sure someone made a very nice photograph of the occasion.'

'A setup?'

'Designed to make it look as though I was somehow involved in the conspiracy.'

Navot inclined his head in the direction of the living room. 'Will she eat anything?'

'Let her sleep.'

Navot slid an omelet onto a plate and placed it in front of Gabriel.

'Specialty of the house: mushrooms, Gruyère, fresh herbs.'

'I haven't eaten in thirty-six hours. When I'm finished with the eggs, I plan on eating the plate.'

Navot began breaking more eggs into his mixing bowl. His work was interrupted by the flashing red light atop the telephone. He snatched up the receiver, listened for a moment, then murmured a few words in Hebrew and rang off. Gabriel looked up from his food.

'What was that?'

'King Saul Boulevard. The escape plan will be ready in an hour.'

As it turned out, they had only forty minutes to wait for the plan. It was transmitted to the safe flat by way of secure fax – three sheets of Hebrew text, composed in Naka, the field code of the Office. Navot, seated next to Gabriel at the kitchen table, handled the decryption.

'There's an El Al charter on the ground in Warsaw right now,' Navot said.

'Polish Jews visiting the old country?'

'Actually, visiting the scene of the crime. It's a packaged tour of the death camps.' Navot shook his head. He had been at Treblinka that night with Gabriel and Radek and had walked among the ashes at the side of the murderer. 'Why anyone would want to go to such a place is beyond me.'

'When does the flight depart?'

'Tomorrow night. One of the passengers will be asked to volunteer for a rather special assignment – traveling home on a false Israeli passport from a different point of departure.'

'And Leah will take her place on the charter?'

'Exactly.'

'Does King Saul Boulevard have a candidate?'

'Three, actually. They're making the final decision now.'

'How will they explain Leah's condition?'

'Illness.'

'How will we get her to Warsaw?'

'*We?*' Navot shook his head. 'You're going home by a different route: overland to Italy, then a night-time pickup on the beach at Fiumicino. Apparently you're familiar with that spot?'

Gabriel nodded. He knew the beach well. 'So how does Leah get to Warsaw?'

'I'll take her.' Navot saw the reluctance in Gabriel's eyes. 'Don't worry, I won't let anything happen to your wife. I'll accompany her home on the flight. Three doctors are on the tour. She'll be in good hands.'

'And when she gets to Israel?'

'A team from the Mount Herzl Psychiatric Hospital will be ready to receive her.'

Gabriel spent a moment thinking it over. He was in no position to raise objections to the plan.

'How will I get over the border?'

'Do you remember the Volkswagen van we used in the Radek affair?'

Gabriel did. It had a hidden compartment beneath the rear foldout bed. Radek, drugged and unconscious, had been concealed there when Chiara had driven him over the Austrian-Czech border.

'I brought it back to Paris after the operation,' Navot said. 'It's stored in a garage over in the seventeenth.'

'Did you delouse it?'

Navot laughed. 'It's clean,' he said. 'More important, it'll get you over the border and down to Fiumicino.'

'Who's taking me to Italy?'

'Moshe can handle it.'

'*Him?* He's a kid.'

'He knows how to handle himself,' Navot said. 'Besides, who better than Moses to lead you home to the Promised Land?'

31. Fiumicino, Italy

'There's the signal. Two short flashes followed by a long one.'

Moshe flicked the wipers and leaned forward over the wheel of the Volkswagen. Gabriel sat placidly in the passenger seat. He was tempted to tell the kid to relax but decided instead to let him enjoy the moment. Moshe's previous assignments had involved stocking the pantries of safe flats and cleaning up the mess after the agents had left town. A midnight rendezvous on a rainswept Italian beach was going to be the highlight of his association with the Office.

'There it is again,' the *bodel* said. 'Two short flashes —'

'— followed by a long one. I heard you the first time.' Gabriel clapped the kid on the back. 'Sorry, it's been a long couple of days. Thanks for the ride. Be careful on the way home, and use —'

'— a different border crossing,' he said. 'I heard you the first four times.'

Gabriel climbed out of the van and crossed the carpark overlooking the beach, then he saddle-stepped a short stone wall and struck out across the sand to the water's edge. He waited there, the waves lapping over his shoes, and watched the dinghy drawing closer. A moment later he was seated in the prow, with his back to Yaakov and his eyes on *Fidelity*.

'You shouldn't have gone,' Yaakov shouted over the buzz of the outboard.

'If I'd stayed in Marseilles, I would have never got Leah back.'

'You don't know that. Maybe Khaled would have played the game differently.'

Gabriel twisted his head round. 'You're right, Yaakov. He *would* have played it differently. First he would have killed Leah and left her body on some road in the south of England. Then he would have sent his three *shaheeds* into the Gare de Lyon and turned it into rubble.'

Yaakov backed off on the throttle. 'That was the dumbest move I've ever seen,' Yaakov said, then, in a concessionary tone, he added: 'And by far the bravest. They'd better pin a medal on you when we get back to King Saul Boulevard.'

'I fell into Khaled's trap. They don't pin medals on officers who walk into traps. They leave them in the desert to be picked over by the vultures and the scorpions.'

Yaakov brought the dinghy to the stern of *Fidelity*. Gabriel climbed out onto the swim platform and scaled the ladder up the aft deck. Dina awaited him there. She was wearing a heavy sweater, and the wind was tossing about her dark hair. She rushed forward and threw her arms around his neck.

'Her voice,' Gabriel said. 'I want to hear the sound of her voice.'

Dina loaded the tape and pressed PLAY.

'*What have you done to her? Where is she?*'

'*We have her, but I don't know where she is.*'

'*Where is she? Answer me! Don't speak to me in French. Speak to me in your real language. Speak to me in Arabic.*'

'*I'm telling you the truth.*'

'*So you can speak Arabic. Where is she? Answer me, or you're going down.*'

'*If you kill me, you'll destroy yourself – and your wife. I'm your only hope.*'

Gabriel pressed STOP, then REWIND, then PLAY.

'*If you kill me, you'll destroy yourself – and your wife. I'm your only hope.*'

STOP. REWIND. PLAY.

'*I'm your only hope.*'

STOP.

He looked up at Dina. 'Did you run it through the database?'

She nodded. 'No match on file.'

'It doesn't matter,' Gabriel said. 'I have something better than her voice.'

'What's that?'

'Her story.'

He told Dina how the girl's story of pain and loss had virtually tumbled out of her during the final miles before Paris. How her family had come from Sumayriyya in the Western Galilee; how they had been driven out during Operation Ben-Ami and forced into exile in Lebanon.

'Sumayriyya? It was a small place, wasn't it? A thousand people?'

'Eight hundred, according to the girl. She seemed to know her history.'

'Not everyone from Sumayriyya obeyed the orders to flee,' Dina said. 'Some of them stayed behind.'

'And some of them managed to sneak back across the border before it was sealed. If her grandfather was truly a village elder, someone would remember him.'

'But even if we're able to learn the girl's name, what good will it do? She's dead. How can she help us find Khaled?'

'She was in love with him.'

'She told you this?'

'I just know it.'

'How perceptive of you. What else do you know about this girl?'

'I remember how she looked,' he said. 'I remember *exactly* how she looked.'

The notepad of unlined paper she found on the flying bridge; the two ordinary lead pencils in the junk drawer of the galley. He settled himself on the couch and worked by the glow of a halogen reading lamp. Dina tried to peer over his shoulder, but he cast her a severe look and sent her out onto the windswept deck to wait until he had finished. She stood at the rail and watched the lights of the Italian coast growing faint on the horizon. Ten minutes later she returned to the salon and found Gabriel asleep on the couch. The portrait of the dead girl lay next to him. Dina switched off the lamp and let him sleep on.

The Israeli frigate appeared off *Fidelity*'s starboard side in the afternoon of the third day. Two hours after that, Gabriel, Yaakov, and Dina were touching down on the helipad of a secure air base north of Tel Aviv. An Office greeting party awaited them. They stood in a circle and looked ill at ease, like strangers at a funeral. Lev was not among them, but then Lev could never be bothered with something as commonplace as greeting agents returning from dangerous missions. Gabriel, as he stepped off the helicopter, was relieved to see the armored Peugeot turning through the gates and coming across the tarmac at high speed. Without a word he separated himself from the others and made for the car.

'Where are you going, Allon?' shouted one of Lev's men.

'Home.'

'The boss wants to see you now.'

'Then maybe he should have canceled a meeting or two and come here to greet us personally. Tell Lev I'll try to squeeze him in tomorrow morning. I have to move a couple of things around. Tell him that.'

The rear door of the Peugeot swung open, and

Gabriel climbed inside. Shamron regarded him silently. He seemed to have aged noticeably during Gabriel's absence. His next cigarette was lit by a hand that shook more than usual. As the car lurched forward, he placed a copy of *Le Monde* in Gabriel's lap. Gabriel looked down and saw two pictures of himself – one in the Gare de Lyon, moments before the explosion, and the other at Mimi Ferrere's nightclub in Cairo, seated with the three *shaheeds*.

'It's all very speculative,' Shamron said, 'and therefore more damaging as a result. The suggestion is that you were somehow involved in the plot to bomb the train station.'

'And what might my motivation be?'

'To discredit the Palestinians, of course. Khaled carried off quite a coup. He managed to bomb the Gare de Lyon and blame us for the deed.'

Gabriel read the first few paragraphs of the story. 'He obviously has friends in high places – Egyptian and French intelligence to name two. The Mukhabarat was watching me from the moment I set foot in Cairo. They photographed me in the nightclub, and after the bombing they sent that photograph to the French DST. Khaled orchestrated the whole thing.'

'Unfortunately, there's more to the story. David Quinnell was found murdered in his Cairo apartment yesterday morning. It's safe to assume we're going to be blamed for that, too.'

Gabriel handed the newspaper back to Shamron,

who returned it to his briefcase. 'The fallout has already begun. The foreign minister was supposed to visit Paris next week, but the invitation has been rescinded. There's talk of a temporary break in relations and diplomatic expulsions. We're going to have to come clean to avoid a major rupture in our relations with France and the rest of the European Community. I suppose that eventually we'll be able to repair the damage, but only to a degree. After all, a majority of French still believe we were the ones who flew those planes into the World Trade Center. How will we ever convince them we had nothing to do with the Gare de Lyon bombing?'

'But you warned them *before* the bombing took place.'

'True, but the conspiratorialists will view that only as further evidence of our guilt. How did we know the bomb would explode at seven o'clock unless we were involved in the plot? We'll have to open our books at some point, and that includes you.'

'Me?'

'The French would like to talk to you.'

'Tell them I'll be at the Palais de Justice on Monday morning. Ask them to hold a room for me at the Crillon. I never have any luck getting a good room at the Crillon.'

Shamron laughed. 'I'll keep you away from the French, but Lev is another story.'

'Death by committee?'

Shamron nodded. 'The inquiry will begin tomorrow. You're the first witness. You should expect your testimony to take several days and that it will be extremely unpleasant.'

'I have better things to do besides sitting before Lev's committee.'

'Such as?'

'Finding Khaled.'

'And how do you intend to do that?'

Gabriel told Shamron about the girl from Sumayriyya.

'Who else knows about this?'

'Only Dina.'

'Pursue it quietly,' Shamron said, 'and for God's sake, don't leave a trail.'

'Arafat had a hand in this. He fed us Mahmoud Arwish and then killed him to cover his tracks. And now he'll reap the public relations rewards of our *alleged* involvement in the Gare de Lyon plot.'

'He already is,' Shamron said. 'The world's media are lining up outside the Mukata waiting for their turn to interview him. We're in no position to lay a finger on him.'

'So we do nothing and hold our breath every April eighteenth while we wait for the next embassy or synagogue to explode?' Gabriel shook his head. 'No, Ari, I'm going to find him.'

'Try not to think of any of that now.' Shamron gave him a paternal pat on the shoulder. 'Get some rest. Go see Leah. Then spend some time with Chiara.'

'Yes,' Gabriel said, 'an evening with no complications would do me good.'

32. Jerusalem

Shamron took Gabriel to Mount Herzl. It was beginning to get dark as he headed up the tree-lined walkway to the hospital's entrance. Leah's new doctor awaited him in the lobby. Rotund and bespectacled, he had the long beard of a rabbi and an unfailingly pleasant demeanor. He introduced himself as Mordecai Bar-Zvi, then took Gabriel by the arm and led him along a corridor of cool Jerusalem limestone. By gesture and intonation, he made it clear to Gabriel that he knew much about the patient's rather unorthodox case history.

'I must say, it appears she came through it remarkably well.'

'Is she talking?'

'A little.'

'Does she know where she is?'

'Sometimes. I can say one thing for certain she's very anxious to see you.' The doctor looked at Gabriel over the top of his smudged eyeglasses. 'You seem surprised.'

'She went thirteen years without speaking to me.'

The doctor shrugged. 'I doubt that will ever happen again.'

They came to a door. The doctor knocked once

and led Gabriel inside. Leah was seated in an arm-chair in the window. She turned as Gabriel entered the room and smiled briefly. He kissed her cheek, then sat on the edge of the bed. She regarded him silently for a moment, then turned and looked out the window again. It was as if he were no longer there.

The doctor excused himself and closed the door as he left. Gabriel sat there with her, content to say nothing at all as the pine trees outside receded gently into the gathering darkness. He stayed for an hour, until a nurse entered the room and suggested it was time for Leah to get some sleep. When Gabriel stood, Leah's head swiveled round.

'Where are you going?'

'They say you need to rest.'

'That's all I ever do.'

Gabriel kissed her lips.

'One last –' She stopped herself. 'You'll come see me again tomorrow?'

'And the next day.'

She turned away and looked out the window.

There were no taxis to be had on Mount Herzl, so he boarded a bus crowded with evening commuters. The seats were all taken; he stood in the open space at the center and felt forty pairs of eyes boring into him. On the Jaffa Road he stepped off and waited in a shelter for an eastbound bus. Then he thought better of it – he had survived one ride; a second seemed an invitation to disaster – so he set off on foot through a swirling night wind. He paused for a moment at the entrance of the Makhane Yehuda Market, then headed for Narkiss Street. Chiara must have heard his footfalls on the stairwell, because she was waiting for him on the landing outside their apartment. Her beauty, after the scars of Leah, seemed even more shocking. Gabriel, when he bent to kiss her, was offered only a cheek. Her newly washed hair smelled of vanilla.

She turned and went inside. Gabriel followed after her, then stopped suddenly. The apartment had been completely redecorated: new furniture, new carpets and fixtures, a fresh coat of paint. The table had been laid and candles lit. Their diminished length suggested they'd been burning for some time. Chiara, as she passed by the table, snuffed them out.

'It's beautiful,' Gabriel said.

'I worked hard to finish it before you arrived. I wanted it to feel like a proper home. Where have you been?' She tried, with little success, to ask the question without a confrontational tone.

'You can't be serious, Chiara.'

'Your helicopter landed three hours ago. And I know you didn't go to King Saul Boulevard, because Lev's office called here looking for you.' She paused. 'You went to see her, didn't you? You went to see Leah.'

'Of course I did.'

'It didn't occur to you to come see me first?'

345

'She's in a hospital. She doesn't know where she is. She's confused. She's scared.'

'I suppose Leah and I have a lot in common after all.'

'Let's not do this, Chiara.'

'Do what?'

He headed down the hallway to their bedroom. It too had been redecorated. On Gabriel's nightstand were the papers that, when signed, would dissolve his marriage to Leah. Chiara had left a pen beside them. He glanced up and saw her standing in the doorway. She was staring at him, searching his eyes for evidence of his emotions – like a detective, he thought, observing a person of interest at the scene of the crime.

'What happened to your face?'

Gabriel told her about the beating he'd been given.

'Did it hurt?' She didn't seem terribly concerned.

'Only a little.' He sat on the edge of the bed and pulled off his shoes. 'How much did you know?'

'Shamron told me right away that the hit had gone wrong. He kept me updated throughout the day. The moment I heard you were safe was the happiest moment of my life.'

Gabriel took note of the fact that Chiara had not mentioned Leah.

'How is she?'

'Leah?'

Chiara closed her eyes and nodded. Gabriel quoted the prognosis of Dr Bar-Zvi: Leah had come

346

through it remarkably well. He removed his shirt. Chiara covered her mouth. His bruises, after three days at sea, had turned deep purple and black.

'It looks worse than it really is,' he said.

'Have you seen a doctor?'

'Not yet.'

'Take off your clothes. I'll run a hot bath for you. A good soak will do you good.'

She left the room. A few seconds later he heard water splashing against enamel. He undressed and went into the bathroom. Chiara examined his bruises again, then she ran her hand through his hair and looked at the roots.

'It's long enough to cut now. I don't want to make love to a gray-haired man tonight.'

'So cut it.'

He sat on the edge of the bath. As always Chiara sang to herself while she cut his hair, one of those silly Italian pop songs she loved so much. Gabriel, his head bowed, watched as the last silvered remnants of Herr Klemp fluttered to the floor. He thought of Cairo, and how he had been deceived, and the anger welled within him once more. Chiara switched off the shears.

'There, you look like yourself again. Black hair, gray at the temples. What was it Shamron used to say about your temples?'

'He called them smudges of ash,' Gabriel said. *Smudges of ash on the prince of fire.*

Chiara tested the temperature of the bath. Gabriel

unwrapped the towel from his waist and slid into the water. It was too hot – Chiara always made it too hot – but after a few moments the pain began to retreat from his body. She sat with him for a time. She talked about the apartment and an evening she had spent with Gilah Shamron – anything but France. After a while she went into the bedroom and undressed. She sang softly to herself. Chiara always sang when she removed her clothing.

Her kisses, usually so tender, pained his lips. She made love to him feverishly, as though trying to draw Leah's venom from his bloodstream, and her fingertips left new bruises on his shoulders. 'I thought you were dead,' she said. 'I thought I'd never see you again.'

'I was dead,' Gabriel said. 'I was dead for a very long time.'

The walls of their bedroom in Venice had been hung with paintings. Chiara, in Gabriel's absence, had hung them here. Some of the works had been painted by Gabriel's grandfather, the noted German expressionist Viktor Frankel. His work had been declared 'degenerate' by the Nazis in 1936. Impoverished, stripped of his ability to paint or even teach, he had been deported to Auschwitz in 1942 and gassed on arrival along with his wife. Gabriel's mother, Irene, had been deported with them, but Mengele had assigned her to a work detail, and she'd managed to survive the women's camp at Birkenau until it was evacuated in the face of the Russian advance. Some of her work hung here in Gabriel's private gallery. Tormented by what she had seen in Birkenau, her paintings burned with an intensity unmatched by even her famous father. In Israel she had used the name Allon, which means oak tree in Hebrew, but she'd always signed her canvases *Frankel* to honor her father. Only now could Gabriel see the paintings for themselves instead of the broken woman who had produced them.

There was one work that bore no signature, a portrait of a young man, in the style of Egon Schiele. The artist was Leah, and the subject was Gabriel himself. It had been painted shortly after he returned to Israel with the blood of six Palestinian terrorists on his hands, and it was the only time he ever agreed to sit for her. He had never liked the painting, because it showed him as Leah saw him – a haunted young man, aged prematurely by the shadow of death. Chiara believed the painting to be a self-portrait.

She switched on the bedroom light and looked at the papers on the bedside table. Her examination was demonstrative in nature; she knew that Gabriel had not signed them.

'I'll sign them in the morning,' he said.

She offered him the pen. 'Sign them now.'

Gabriel switched off the light. 'Actually, there's something else I want to do now.'

Chiara took him into her body and wept silently through the act.

'You're never going to sign them, are you?'

Gabriel tried to silence her with a kiss.

'You're lying to me,' she said. 'You're using your body as a weapon of deception.'

33. Jerusalem

His days quickly acquired shape. In the mornings he would wake early and sit in Chiara's newly decorated kitchen with coffee and the newspapers. The stories about the Khaled affair depressed him. *Ha'aretz* christened the affair 'Bunglegate,' and the Office lost its battle to keep Gabriel's name out of print. In Paris the French press besieged the government and the Israeli ambassador for an explanation of the mysterious photographs that had appeared in *Le Monde*. The French foreign minister, a blow-dried former poet, threw gasoline on the fire by expressing his belief that 'there may indeed have been an Israeli hand in the Holocaust of the Gare de Lyon.' The next day, Gabriel read with a heavy heart that a Kosher pizzeria on the rue des Rosiers had been vandalized. Then a gang of French boys attacked a young girl as she walked home from school and carved a swastika into her cheek. Chiara usually awakened an hour after Gabriel. She read of the events in France with more alarm than sadness. Once a day she phoned her mother in Venice to make certain her family was safe.

At eight Gabriel would leave Jerusalem and make the drive down the Bab al-Wad to King Saul Boulevard. The proceedings were held in the top-floor conference room so Lev would not have far to walk when he wished to pop in and observe them. Gabriel, of course, was the star witness. His conduct, from the moment he'd returned to Office discipline until his escape from the Gare de Lyon was reviewed in excruciating detail. Despite Shamron's dire predictions, there was to be no bloodletting. The results of such investigations were usually preordained, and Gabriel could see from the outset that he was not going to be made the scapegoat. This was a collective mistake, the committee members seemed to be saying by the tone of their questions, a forgivable sin committed by an intelligence apparatus desperate to avoid another catastrophic loss of life. Still, at times the questions became pointed. Did Gabriel have no suspicions about the motivations of Mahmoud Arwish? Or the loyalty of David Quinnell? Would things not have gone differently if he'd listened to his teammates in Marseilles and turned back instead of going with the girl? At least then Khaled's plan to destroy the credibility of the Office would not have succeeded. 'You're right,' Gabriel said, 'and my wife would be dead, along with many more innocent people.'

One by one, the others were brought before the committee as well, first Yossi and Rimona, then Yaakov and lastly Dina, whose discoveries had fueled the investigation into Khaled in the first place. It pained Gabriel to see them in the dock. His career was over, but for the others the Khaled affair, as it had become known, would leave a black mark on their records that would never be expunged.

In the late afternoon, when the committee had adjourned, he would drive to Mount Herzl to spend time with Leah. Sometimes they would sit in her room; and sometimes, if there was still light, he would place her in a wheelchair and push her slowly round the grounds. She never failed to acknowledge his presence and usually managed to speak a few words to him. Her hallucinatory journeys to Vienna became less apparent, though he was never certain precisely what she was thinking.

'Where is Dani buried?' she asked once, as they sat beneath the canopy of a pine tree.

'The Mount of Olives.'

'Will you take me there sometime?'

'If your doctor says it's all right.'

Once, Chiara accompanied him to the hospital. As they entered, she sat down in the lobby and told Gabriel to take his time.

'Would you like to meet her?' Chiara had never seen Leah.

'No,' she said, 'I think it's better if I wait here. Not for my sake, for hers.'

'She won't know.'

'She'll know, Gabriel. A woman always knows when a man's in love with someone else.'

They never quarreled about Leah again. Their battle, from that point onward, was a black operation, a covert affair waged by long silences and remarks edged with double meaning. Chiara never entered their bed without first checking to see whether the papers had been signed. Her lovemaking was as confrontational as her silences. *My body is intact,* she seemed to be saying to him. *I'm real, Leah is only a memory.*

The apartment grew claustrophobic, so they took to eating out. Some evenings they walked over to Ben-Yehuda Street – or to Mona, a trendy restaurant that was actually located in the cellar of the old campus of the Bezalel Academy of Art. One evening they drove down Highway One to Abu Ghosh, one of the only Arab villages along the road to survive the expulsions of Plan Dalet. They ate hummus and grilled lamb in an outdoor restaurant in the village square, and for a few moments it was possible to imagine how different things might have been had Khaled's grandfather not turned the road into a killing zone. Chiara marked the occasion by buying Gabriel an expensive bracelet from a village silversmith. The next evening, on King George Street, she bought him a silver watch to match. Keepsakes, she called them. Tokens by which to remember me.

When they returned home that night, there was a message on the answering machine. Gabriel pressed the playback button and heard the voice of Dina Sarid, telling him that she'd found someone who had been there the night Sumayriyya fell.

*

The following afternoon, when the committee had adjourned, Gabriel drove to Sheinkin Street and collected Dina and Yaakov from an outdoor café. They drove north along the coast highway through dusty pink light, past Herzliyya and Netanya. A few miles beyond Caesarea, the slopes of Mount Carmel rose before them. They rounded the Bay of Haifa and headed for Akko. Gabriel, as he continued north toward Nahariyya, thought of Operation Ben-Ami – the night a column of Haganah came up this very road with orders to demolish the Arab villages of the Western Galilee. Just then he glimpsed a strange conical structure, stark and gleaming white, rising above the green blanket of an orange grove. The unusual building, Gabriel knew, was the children's memorial at Yad Layeled, a museum of Holocaust remembrance at Kibbutz Lohamei Ha'Getaot. The settlement had been founded after the war by survivors of the Warsaw Ghetto uprising. Adjacent to the edge of the kibbutz, and barely visible in the tall wild grass, were the ruins of Sumayriyya.

He turned onto a local road and followed it inland. Dusk was fast approaching as they entered al-Makr. Gabriel stopped on the main street and, with the engine still running, entered a coffeehouse and asked the proprietor for directions to the house of Hamzah al-Samara. A moment of silence followed while the Arab appraised Gabriel coolly from the opposite side of the counter. Clearly he assumed the Jewish visitor to be a Shabak officer, an impression Gabriel made no effort to correct. The Arab led Gabriel back into the street and, with a series of points and gestures, showed him the way.

The house was the largest in the village. It seemed several generations of al-Samaras lived there, because there were a number of small children playing in the small dusty courtyard. Seated in the center was an old man. He wore a gray galabia and white kaffiyeh and was puffing on a water pipe. Gabriel and Yaakov stood at the open side of the courtyard and waited for permission to enter. Dina remained in the car; the old man, Gabriel knew, would never speak forthrightly in the presence of a bareheaded Jewess.

Al-Samara looked up and, with a desultory wave of his hand, beckoned them. He spoke a few words to the oldest of the children and a moment later two more chairs appeared. Then a woman came, a daughter perhaps, and brought three glasses of tea. All this before Gabriel had even explained to him the purpose of his visit. They sat in silence for a moment, sipping their tea and listening to the buzz of cicadas in the surrounding fields. A goat trotted into the courtyard and gently butted Gabriel's ankle. A child, robed and barefoot, shooed the animal away. Time, it seemed, had stopped. Were it not for the electric lights coming on in the house, and the satellite dish atop the roof, Gabriel would have found it easy to imagine that Palestine was still ruled from Constantinople.

'Have I done something wrong?' the old man asked in Arabic. It was the first assumption of many Arabs when two tough-looking men from the government arrived uninvited at their door.

'No,' Gabriel said, 'we just wanted to talk to you.'

'About what?'

The old man, hearing Gabriel's answer, drew thoughtfully on his water pipe. He had hypnotic gray eyes and a neat mustache. His sandaled feet looked as though they had never seen a pumice stone.

'Where are you from?' he asked.

'The Valley of Jezreel,' Gabriel replied.

Al-Samara nodded slowly. 'And before that?'

'My parents came from Germany.'

The gray eyes moved from Gabriel to Yaakov.

'And you?'

'Hadera.'

'And before?'

'Russia.'

'Germans and Russians,' al-Samara said, shaking his head. 'Were it not for Germans and Russians, I'd still be living in Sumayriyya, instead of here in al-Makr.'

'You were there the night the village fell?'

'Not exactly. I was walking in a field near the village.' He paused and added conspiratorially: 'With a girl.'

'And when the raid started?'

'We hid in the fields and watched our families walking to the north toward Lebanon. We saw the

Jewish sappers dynamiting our homes. We stayed in the field all the next day. When the darkness came again, we walked here to al-Makr. The rest of my family, my mother and father, my brothers and sisters, all ended up in Lebanon.'

'And the girl you were with that night?'

'She became my wife.' Another puff on the water pipe. 'I'm an exile, too – an *internal* exile. I still have the deed to my father's land in Sumayriyya, but I cannot go back to it. The Jews confiscated it and never bothered to compensate me for my loss. Imagine, a kibbutz built by Holocaust survivors on the ruins of an Arab village.'

Gabriel looked around at the large house. 'You've done well for yourself.'

'I'm far better off than those who went into exile. It could have been like this for all of us if there'd never been a war. I don't blame you for my loss. I blame the Arab leaders. If Haj Amin and the others had accepted the partition, the Western Galilee would have been part of Palestine. But they chose war, and when they lost the war, they cried that the Arabs had been victims. Arafat did the same thing at Camp David, yes? He walked away from another opportunity at partition. He started another war, and when the Jews fought back, he cried that he was the victim. When will we learn?'

The goat came back. This time al-Samara gave it a whack on the nose with the mouthpiece of his water pipe.

'Surely you didn't come all the way here to listen to an old man's story.'

'I'm looking for a family that came from your village, but I don't know their name.'

'We all knew each other,' al-Samara said. 'If we were to walk through the ruins of Sumayriyya right now, I could show you my house – and I could show you the house of my friend, and the houses of my cousins. Tell me something about this family, and I'll tell you their name.'

He told the old man the things the girl had said during the final miles before Paris – that her grandfather had been a village elder, not a *muktar* but an important man, and that he'd owned forty dunams of land and a large flock of goats. He'd had at least one son. After the fall of Sumayriyya, they'd gone north, to Ein al-Hilweh in Lebanon. Al-Samara listened thoughtfully to Gabriel's description but seemed perplexed. He called over his shoulder, into the house. A woman emerged, elderly like him, her head covered by a veil. She spoke directly to al-Samara, carefully avoiding the gaze of Gabriel and Yaakov.

'You're certain it was *forty* dunams?' he asked. 'Not thirty, or twenty, but *forty*?'

'That's what I was told.'

He made a contemplative draw on his pipe. 'You're right,' he said. 'That family ended up in Lebanon, in Ein al-Hilweh. Things got bad during the Lebanese civil war. The boys became fighters. They're all dead, from what I hear.'

'Do you know their name?'

'They're called al-Tamari. If you meet any of them, please give them my regards. Tell them I've been to their house. Don't tell them about my villa in al-Makr, though. It will only break their hearts.'

34. Tel Aviv

'Ein al-Hilweh? Are you out of your fucking mind?'

It was early the following morning. Lev was seated at his empty glass desk, his coffee cup suspended midway between his saucer and his lips. Gabriel had managed to slip into the Office while Lev's secretary was in the ladies' room. The girl would pay dearly for the lapse in security when Gabriel was gone.

'Ein al-Hilweh is a no-go zone, period, end of discussion. It's worse now than it was in eighty-two. A half-dozen Islamic terror organizations have set up shop there. It's not a place for the faint of heart – or an Office agent whose picture has been splashed about the French press.'

'Well, someone has to go.'

'You're not even sure the old man's still alive.'

Gabriel frowned, then sat, uninvited, in one of the sleek leather chairs in front of Lev's desk.

'But if he *is* alive, he can tell us where his daughter went after she left the camp.'

'He might,' Lev agreed, 'or he might know nothing at all. Khaled certainly told the girl to deceive her family for security reasons. For all we really know, the entire story about Sumayriyya might be a lie.'

'She had no reason to lie to me,' Gabriel said. 'She thought I was going to be killed.'

Lev spent a long moment pondering his coffee. 'There's a man in Beirut who might be able to help us with this. His name is Nabil Azouri.'

'What's his story?'

'He's Lebanese and Palestinian. He does a little of everything. Works as a stringer for a few Western news outlets. Owns a nightclub. Does the odd bit of arms dealing and has been known to move the odd shipment of hashish now and again. He also works for us, of course.'

'Sounds like a real pillar of his community.'

'He's a shit,' Lev said. 'Lebanese to the core. Lebanon incarnate. But he's exactly the kind of person we need to walk into Ein al-Hilweh and talk to the girl's father.'

'Why does he work for us?'

'For money, of course. Nabil likes money.'

'How do we talk to him?'

'We leave a message on the phone at his nightclub in Beirut and an airline ticket with the concierge of the Commodore Hotel. We rarely talk to Nabil on his turf.'

'Where does he go?'

'Cyprus,' Lev said. 'Nabil likes Cyprus, too.'

It would be three days before Gabriel was ready to move. Travel saw to his arrangements. Larnaca is a popular Israeli tourist destination, and so it was not necessary to travel on a forged foreign passport. Traveling under his real name was not possible, though, so Travel issued him an Israeli document under the rather unexceptional name of Michael Neumann. The day before his departure, Operations let him spend an hour perusing Nabil Azouri's file in a secure reading room. When he had finished, they gave him an envelope with ten thousand dollars in cash and wished him luck. The next morning, at seven, he boarded an El Al plane at Ben-Gurion Airport for the one-hour flight to Cyprus. Upon arriving he rented a car at the airport and drove a short distance up the coast to a resort called the Palm Beach Hotel. A message from King Saul Boulevard awaited him. Nabil Azouri was coming that afternoon. Gabriel spent the remainder of the morning in his room, then, a short time after one o'clock, he went down to the poolside restaurant for lunch. Azouri already had a table. A bottle of expensive French champagne, drunk below the label, lay chilling in a silver bucket.

He had dark curly hair, frosted with the first strands of gray, and a thick mustache. When he removed his sunglasses, Gabriel found himself gazing into a pair of large sleepy brown eyes. On his left wrist was the obligatory gold watch; on his right, several gold bracelets that chimed when he lifted his champagne glass to his lips. His cotton shirt was cream-colored, his poplin trousers wrinkled from the flight from Beirut. He lit an American cigarette with a gold lighter and listened to Gabriel's proposition.

'Ein al-Hilweh? Are you out of your fucking mind?'

Gabriel had anticipated this reaction. Azouri treated his relationship with Israeli intelligence as though it were just another one of his business enterprises. He was the bazaar merchant, the Office was the customer. Haggling over the price was part of the process. The Lebanese leaned forward and fixed Gabriel in his sleepy stare.

'Have you been down there lately? It's like the Wild West, Khomeini style. It's gone to hell since you boys pulled out. Men in black, praise be to Allah the most merciful. Outsiders don't stand a chance. Fuck it, Mike. Have some champagne and forget about it.'

'You're not an outsider, Nabil. You know everyone, you can go everywhere. That's why we pay you so lucratively.'

'Tip money, Mike, that's all I get from your outfit – cigarettes and champagne and a few bucks to waste on the girls.'

'You must have expensive taste in girls, Nabil, because I've seen your pay stubs. You've made a rather large sum of money from your relationship with my firm.'

Azouri raised his glass in Gabriel's direction. 'We've made good business together, Mike. I won't deny that. I'd like to continue working for you.

That's why someone else needs to run down to Ein al-Hilweh for you. It's too rich for my blood. Too dangerous.'

Azouri signaled the waiter and ordered another bottle of the French champagne. Refusing an offer of work wasn't going to keep him from having a good meal on the Office tab. Gabriel tossed an envelope onto the table. Azouri eyed it thoughtfully but made no move for it.

'How much is in there, Mike?'

'Two thousand.'

'What flavor?'

'Dollars.'

'So what's the deal? Half now, half on delivery? I'm just a dumb Arab, but two thousand and two thousand add up to four thousand, and I'm not going into Ein al-Hilweh for four thousand dollars.'

'Two thousand is only the retainer.'

'And how much for delivery of the information?'

'Another five.'

Azouri shook his head. 'No, another ten.'

'Six.'

Another shake of the head. 'Nine.'

'Seven.'

'Eight.'

'Done,' said Gabriel. 'Two thousand in advance, another eight on delivery. Not bad for an afternoon's work. If you behave yourself we'll even throw in gas money.'

'Oh, you'll pay for the gas, Mike. My expenses are

always separate from my fee.' The waiter brought the second bottle of champagne. When he was gone again, Azouri said, 'So what do you want to know?'

'I want you to find someone.'

'There are forty-five thousand refugees in that camp, Mike. Help me out a little bit.'

'He's an old man named al-Tamari.'

'First name?'

'We don't know it.'

Azouri sipped his wine. 'It's not a terribly common name. It shouldn't be a problem. What else can you tell me about him?'

'He's a refugee from the Western Galilee.'

'Most of them are. Which village?'

Gabriel told him.

'Family details?'

'Two sons were killed in eighty-two.'

'In the camp?'

Gabriel nodded. 'They were Fatah. Apparently his wife was killed, too.'

'Lovely. Go on.'

'He had a daughter. She ended up in Europe. I want to know everything you can find out about her. Where she went to school. What she studied. Where she lived. Who she slept with.'

'What's the girl's name?'

'I don't know.'

'Age?'

'Early thirties, I'd say. Spoke decent French.'

'Why are you looking for her?'

'We think she may have been involved in the attack on the Gare de Lyon.'

'Is she still alive?'

Gabriel shook his head. Azouri looked out at the beach for a long moment. 'So you think that by tracing the background of the girl, you're going to get to the big boss? The brains behind the operation?'

'Something like that, Nabil.'

'How do I play it with the old man?'

'Play it any way you want to,' Gabriel said. 'Just get me what I need.'

'This girl,' the Lebanese said. 'What did she look like?'

Gabriel handed Azouri a magazine he'd brought down from his room. Azouri opened it and leafed through the pages until he came upon the sketch Gabriel had made aboard *Fidelity*.

'She looked like that,' Gabriel said. 'She looked exactly like that.'

He heard nothing from Nabil Azouri for three days. For all Gabriel knew, the Lebanese had absconded with the down payment or had been killed trying to get into Ein al-Hilweh. Then, on the fourth morning, the telephone rang. It was Azouri, calling from Beirut. He would be at the Palm Beach Hotel in time for lunch. Gabriel hung up the phone, then he went down to the beach and took a long run at the water's edge. His bruises were beginning to fade, and much of the soreness had left his body. When he had finished, he returned to his room to shower and change. By the time he arrived at the poolside restaurant, Azouri was working on his second glass of champagne.

'What a fucking place, Mike. Hell on earth.'

'I'm not paying you ten thousand dollars for a report on conditions at Ein al-Hilweh,' Gabriel said. 'That's the UN's job. Did you find the old man? Is he still alive?'

'I found him.'

'And?'

'The girl left Ein al-Hilweh in 1990. She's never been back.'

'Her name?'

'Fellah,' said Azouri. 'Fellah al-Tamari.'

'Where did she go?'

'She was a smart girl, apparently. Earned a UN grant to study in Europe. The old man told her to take it and never come back to Lebanon.'

'Where did she study?' Gabriel asked, though he suspected he already knew the answer.

'France,' Azouri said. 'Paris first, then she went somewhere in the south. The old man wasn't sure. Apparently there were long periods with no contact.'

'I'm sure there were.'

'He didn't seem to fault his daughter. He wanted a better life for her in Europe. He didn't want her wallowing in the Palestinian tragedy, as he put it to me.'

'She never forgot about Ein al-Hilweh,' Gabriel said absently. 'What did she study?'

'She was an archaeologist.'

Gabriel remembered the appearance of her fingernails. He'd had the impression then that she was a potter or someone who worked with her hands outdoors. An archaeologist certainly fit that description.

'*Archaeology?* You're certain.'

'He seemed very clear on that point.'

'Anything else?'

'Yeah,' Azouri said. 'Two years ago she sent him a very strange letter. She told him to destroy all the letters and photographs she'd sent from Europe over the years. The old man disobeyed his daughter's wishes. The letters and photos were all he had left of her. A couple of weeks later, a bully boy shows up in his room and burned the things for him.'

A friend of Khaled, Gabriel thought. Khaled was trying to erase her past.

'How did you play it with him?'

'You got the information you wanted. Leave the operational details to me, Mike.'

'Did you show him the sketch?'

'I showed him. He wept. He hadn't seen his daughter in fifteen years.'

An hour later, Gabriel checked out of the hotel and drove to the airport, where he waited until the evening flight to Tel Aviv. It was after midnight by the time he returned to Narkiss Street. Chiara was asleep. She stirred as he climbed into bed, but did not wake. When he pressed his lips against her bare shoulder, she murmured incoherently and rolled away from him. He looked at his nightstand. The papers were gone.

35. Tel Megiddo, Israel

Next morning Gabriel went to Armageddon.

He left his Skoda in the parking lot of the visitors' center and hiked up the footpath to the top of the mount through the searing sunlight. He paused for a moment to gaze out across the Jezreel Valley. For Gabriel the valley was the place of his birth, but biblical scholars and those obsessed by endtime prophecies believed it would be the setting for the apocalyptic confrontation between the forces of good and evil. Regardless of what calamity might lay ahead, Tel Megiddo had already witnessed much bloodshed. Located at the crossroads between Syria, Egypt, and Mesopotamia, it had been the site of dozens of major battles over the millennia. Assyrians, Israelites, Canaanites, Egyptians, Philistines, Greeks, Romans, and Crusaders – all had shed blood beneath this hillock. Napolean defeated the Ottomans there in 1799, and a little more than a century later General Allenby of the British army defeated them again.

The soil on the top of the hill was cut by a labyrinth of trenches and pits. Tel Megiddo had been under intermittent archaeological excavation for more than a century. So far, researchers had discovered evidence that the city atop the mount had been destroyed and rebuilt some twenty-five times. A dig was under way at the moment. From one of the trenches came the sound of English spoken with an American accent. Gabriel walked over and looked down. Two American college students, a boy and a girl, were hunched over something in the soil. Bones, thought Gabriel, but he couldn't be sure.

'I'm looking for Professor Lavon.'

'He's working in *K* this morning.' It was the girl who'd spoken to him.

'I don't understand.'

'The excavation trenches are laid out in a grid pattern. Each plot is lettered. That way we can chart the location of every artifact. You're standing next to *F*. See the sign? Professor Lavon is working in *K*.'

Gabriel made his way over to the pit marked *K* and looked down. At the bottom of the trench, two meters below the surface, crouched an elfin figure wearing a broad-brimmed straw hat. He was scratching at the hard subsoil with a small pick and appeared thoroughly engrossed in his work, but then he usually did.

'Find anything interesting, Eli?'

The picking stopped. The figure looked over his shoulder.

'Just a few pieces of broken pottery,' he said. 'How about you?'

Gabriel reached down into the trench. Eli Lavon

took hold of Gabriel's hand and pulled himself out.

They sat in the shade of a blue tarpaulin and drank mineral water at a folding table. Gabriel, his eyes on the valley below, asked Lavon what he was doing at Tel Megiddo.

'There's a popular school of archaeological thought these days called biblical minimalism. The minimalists believe, among other things, that King Solomon was a mythical figure, something of a Jewish King Arthur. We're trying to prove them wrong.'

'Did he exist?'

'Of course,' said Lavon, 'and he built a city right here at Megiddo.'

Lavon removed his floppy hat and used it to beat the gray-brown dust from his khaki trousers. As usual he seemed to be wearing all of his clothing at once – three shirts, by Gabriel's count, with a red cotton handkerchief knotted at his throat. His sparse, unkempt gray hair moved in the faint breeze. He pushed a stray lock from his forehead and appraised Gabriel with a pair of quick brown eyes.

'Isn't it a little soon for you to be up here in this heat?'

The last time Gabriel had seen Lavon, he'd been lying in a hospital bed in the Hadassah Medical Center.

'I'm only a volunteer. I work for a few hours in the early morning. My doctor says it's good therapy.'

Lavon sipped his mineral water. 'Besides, I find this place provides a valuable lesson in humility.'

'What's that?'

'People come and go from this place, Gabriel. Our ancestors ruled it briefly a very long time ago. Now we rule it again. But one day we'll be gone, too. The only question is how long will we be here this time, and what will we leave behind for men like me to unearth in the future? I hope it's something more than the footprint of a Separation Fence.'

'I'm not ready to give it up just yet, Eli.'

'So I gather. You've been a busy boy. I've been reading about you in the newspapers. That's not a good thing in your line of work – being in the newspapers.'

'It was your line of work, too.'

'Once,' he said, 'a long time ago.'

Lavon had been a promising young archaeologist in September 1972 when Shamron recruited him to be a member of the Wrath of God team. He'd been an *ayin*, a tracker. He'd followed the Black Septembrists and learned their habits. In many ways his job had been the most dangerous of all, because he had been exposed to the terrorists for days on end with no backup. The work had left him with a nervous disorder and chronic intestinal problems.

'How much do you know about the case, Eli?'

'I'd heard through the grapevine you were back in the country, something to do with the Rome bombing. Then Shamron showed up at my door one evening and told me you were chasing Sabri's boy. Is it true? Did little Khaled really do Rome?'

'He's not a little boy anymore. He did Rome, and he did Gare de Lyon. And Buenos Aires and Istanbul before that.'

'It doesn't surprise me. Terrorism is in Khaled's veins. He drank it with his mother's milk.' Lavon shook his head. 'You know, if I'd been watching your back in France, like I did in the old days, none of this would have happened.'

'That's probably true, Eli.'

Lavon's street skills were legendary. Shamron always said that Eli Lavon could disappear while shaking your hand. Once a year he went to the Academy to pass along the secrets of his trade to the next generation. Indeed, the watchers who'd been in Marseilles had probably spent time sitting at Lavon's feet.

'So what brings you to Armageddon?'

Gabriel laid a photograph on the tabletop.

'Handsome devil,' Lavon said. 'Who is he?'

Gabriel laid a second version of the same photo on the table. This one included the figure seated at the subject's left, Yasir Arafat.

'Khaled?'

Gabriel nodded.

'What does this have to do with me?'

'I think you and Khaled might have something in common.'

'What's that?'

Gabriel looked out at the excavation trenches.

A trio of American students joined them beneath the shade of the tarpaulin. Lavon and Gabriel excused themselves and walked slowly around the perimeter of the dig. Gabriel told him everything, beginning with the dossier discovered in Milan and ending with the information Nabil Azouri had brought out of Ein al-Hilweh. Lavon listened without asking questions, but Gabriel could see, in Lavon's clever brown eyes, that he was already making connections and searching for further avenues of exploration. He was more than just a skilled surveillance artist. Like Gabriel, Lavon was the child of Holocaust survivors. After the Wrath of God operation, he had settled in Vienna and opened a small investigative bureau called Wartime Claims and Inquiries. Operating on a shoestring budget, he had managed to track down millions of dollars in looted Jewish assets and had played a significant role in prying a multibillion-dollar settlement from the banks of Switzerland. Five months earlier a bomb had exploded at Lavon's office. Lavon's two assistants were killed; Lavon, seriously injured, had been in a coma for several weeks. The man who planted the bomb had been working for Erich Radek.

'So you think Fellah al-Tamari knew Khaled?'

'Without question.'

'It seems a bit out of character. To remain hidden

all those years, he must have been a careful chap.'

'That's true,' Gabriel said, 'but he knew that Fellah would be killed in the bombing of the Gare de Lyon and that his secret would be protected. She was in love with him, and he lied to her.'

'I see your point.'

'But the most compelling piece of evidence that they knew each other comes from her father. Fellah told him to burn the letters and the photographs she'd sent over the years. That means Khaled must have been in them.'

'As Khaled?'

Gabriel shook his head. 'It was more threatening than that. She must have mentioned him by his other name – his *French* name.'

'So you think Khaled met the girl under ordinary circumstances and recruited her sometime after?'

'That's the way he'd play it,' Gabriel said. 'That's how his father would have played it, too.'

'They could have met anywhere.'

'Or they could have met somewhere just like this.'

'A dig?'

'She was an archaeology student. Maybe Khaled was, too. Or maybe he was a professor, like you.'

'Or maybe he was just some good-looking Arab guy she met in a bar.'

'We know her name, Eli. We know she was a student and that she studied archaeology. If we follow the trail of Fellah, it will lead us back to Khaled. I'm sure of it.'

'So follow the trail.'

'For obvious reasons, I can't go back to Europe just yet.'

'Why not turn it over to the Office and let their searchers do the job?'

'Because after the fiasco in Paris there's not going to be an appetite for having another go at Khaled on European soil – at least not officially. Besides, I *am* the Office, and I'm giving it to you. I want you to find him, Eli. Quietly. That's your special gift. You know how to do these sorts of things without making a racket.'

'True, but I've lost a step or two.'

'Are you fit enough to travel?'

'As long as there's no rough stuff. That's your department. I'm the bookish one, you're the muscle Jew.'

Lavon dug a cigarette from his shirt pocket and lit it, cupping his hand against the breeze. He looked out over the Valley of Jezreel for a moment before speaking again.

'But you always were, weren't you, Gabriel?'

'What's that?'

'The muscle Jew. You like to play the role of the sensitive artist, but deep down you're more like Shamron than you realize.'

'He's going to kill again. Maybe he'll wait until next April, or maybe a target will come along sooner – something that will allow him to temporarily quench his thirst for Jewish blood.'

'Maybe you suffer from the same thirst?'

'A little,' Gabriel conceded, 'but this isn't about revenge. It's about justice. And it's about protecting the lives of innocents. Will you find him for me, Eli?'

Lavon nodded. 'Don't worry, Gabriel. I'll find him – *before* he can kill again.'

They stood in silence for a moment, looking down at the land.

'Did we drive them out, Eli?'

'The Canaanites?'

'No, Eli. The Arabs.'

'We certainly didn't ask them to stay,' Lavon said. 'Maybe it was easier that way.'

A blue sedan was idling in Narkiss Street. Gabriel recognized the face of the man seated behind the wheel. He entered the apartment house and climbed quickly up the stairs. Two suitcases stood on the landing, outside the half-open door. Chiara was seated in the living room, dressed in a smart black European two-piece suit and high-heeled shoes. Her face had makeup on it. Gabriel had never seen Chiara with makeup before.

'Where are you going?'

'You know better than to ask me that.'

'A job?'

'Yes, of course a job.'

'How long will you be gone?'

Her silence told him she was not coming back.

'When it's over, I'm going back to Venice.' Then she added: 'To take care of my family.'

He stood motionless and looked down at her. Chiara's tears, when they spilled down her cheeks, were black with mascara. To Gabriel they looked like streaks of dirty rain on a statue. She wiped them away and examined her blackened fingertips, angry at her inability to control her emotions. Then she straightened her back and blinked hard several times.

'You look disappointed in me, Gabriel.'

'For what?'

'Crying. You never cry, do you?'

'Not anymore.'

He sat down next to her and tried to hold her hand. She drew it away from him and dabbed at her smudged makeup with a tissue, then she opened a compact case and looked at her reflection in the mirror.

'I can't get on a plane looking like this.'

'Good.'

'Don't get any ideas. I'm still leaving. Besides, it's what you want. You would never tell me to leave – you're far too decent for that – but I know you want me to go.' She snapped the compact shut. 'I don't blame you. In a strange way, I love you more. I only wish you hadn't told me that you wanted to marry me.'

'I did,' he said.

'*Did?*'

'I *do* want to marry you, Chiara' – he hesitated – 'but I can't. I'm married to Leah.'

'Fidelity, right, Gabriel? Devotion to duty or to one's obligations. Loyalty. Faithfulness.'

'I can't leave her now, not after what she's just been put through by Khaled.'

'In another week, she won't remember it.' Chiara, noticing the color in Gabriel's face, took his hand. 'God, I'm sorry. Please forget I ever said that.'

'It's forgotten.'

'You're a fool to let me walk out of here. No one will ever love you the way I've loved you.' She stood up. 'But we'll see each other again, I'm sure. Who knows, maybe I'll be working for you soon.'

'What are you talking about?'

'The Office is swirling with rumors.'

'It usually is. You shouldn't pay attention to rumors, Chiara.'

'I once heard a rumor that you'd never leave Leah to marry me. I wish I'd paid attention to that one.'

She slung her bag over her shoulder, then bent down and kissed Gabriel's lips.

'One last kiss,' she whispered.

'At least let me drive you to the airport.'

'The last thing we need is a tearful good-bye at Ben-Gurion. Help me with my bags.'

He carried the suitcases down and loaded them in the trunk of the car. Chiara climbed into the backseat and closed the door without looking at him. Gabriel stood in the shade of a eucalyptus tree and watched the car drive off. As he walked upstairs to the empty apartment, he realized he hadn't asked her to stay. Eli had been right. It was easier that way.

36. Tiberias, Israel

A week after Chiara's departure Gabriel drove to Tiberias for dinner at the Shamrons'. Yonatan was there, along with his wife and three young children. So was Rimona and her husband. They both had just come off duty and were still in uniform. Shamron, surrounded by his family, seemed happier than Gabriel had seen him in years. After supper he led Yonatan and Gabriel onto the terrace. A bright three-quarter moon was reflected in the calm surface of the Sea of Galilee. Beyond the lake, black and shapeless, loomed the Golan Heights. Shamron liked it best on his terrace, because it faced east toward his enemies. He was content to sit quietly and say nothing for a time while Gabriel and Yonatan talked pessimistically about the *matsav* – the situation. After a while, Shamron gave Yonatan a look that said he needed to speak to Gabriel privately. 'I get the message, Abba,' Yonatan said, getting to his feet. 'I'll leave you to it.'

'He is a colonel in the IDF,' Gabriel said, when Yonatan had gone. 'He doesn't like it when you treat him like that.'

'Yonatan has his line of work, and we have ours.'

Shamron adroitly shifted the focus from his personal problems to Gabriel's. 'How's Leah?'

'I'm taking her to the Mount of Olives tomorrow to see Dani's grave.'

'I assume her doctor has approved this outing?'

'He's coming with us, along with half the staff of the Mount Herzl Psychiatric Hospital.'

Shamron lit a cigarette. 'Have you heard from Chiara?'

'No, and I don't expect to. Do you know where she is?'

Shamron looked theatrically at his wristwatch. 'If the operation is proceeding as planned, she's probably sipping brandy in a ski lodge in Zermatt with a certain Swiss gentleman of questionable character. This gentleman is about to ship a rather large consignment of arms to a Lebanese guerrilla group that doesn't have our best interests at heart. We'd like to know when that shipment is leaving port and where it's going.'

'Please tell me Operations isn't using my former fiancée as bait in a honey trap.'

'I'm not privy to the details of the operation, only the overarching goals. As for Chiara, she's a girl of high moral character. I'm sure she'll play hard to get with our Helvetian friend.'

'I still don't like it.'

'Don't worry,' Shamron said. 'Soon *you'll* be the one deciding how we use her.'

'What are you talking about?'

'The prime minister would like a word with you. He has a job he'd like you to take.'

'Javelin-catcher?'

Shamron threw back his head and laughed, then suffered a long, spasmodic fit of coughing.

'Actually, he wants you to be the next director of Operations.'

'Me? By the time Lev's committee of inquiry has finished with me, I'll be lucky to get a job as a security guard at a café in Ben-Yehuda Street.'

'You'll come out of it just fine. Now is not the time for public self-flagellation. Leave that for the Americans. If we have to tell a few half-truths, if we must lie to a country like France that is not interested in our survival, then so be it.'

'By way of deception, thou shalt do war,' Gabriel said, reciting the motto of the Office. Shamron nodded once and said, 'Amen.'

'Even if I come out of it in one piece, Lev won't allow me to have Operations.'

'He won't have a say in the matter. Lev's term is ending, and he has few friends in King Saul Boulevard or Kaplan Street. He won't be invited to stay for a second dance.'

'So who's going to be the next chief?'

'The prime minister and I have a short list of names. None of them are Office. Whoever we select, he'll need an experienced man running Operations.'

'I knew it was leading to this,' Gabriel said. 'I knew it the moment I saw you in Venice.'

'I admit my motives are selfish. My term is coming to an end, too. If the prime minister goes, so do I. And this time there won't be a return from exile. I need you, Gabriel. I need you to keep watch over my creation.'

'The Office?'

Shamron shook his head, then lifted his hand toward the land.

'I know you'll do it,' Shamron said. 'You have no choice. Your mother named you Gabriel for a reason. Michael is the highest, but you, Gabriel, you are the mightiest. You're the one who defends Israel against its accusers. You're the angel of judgment – the prince of fire.'

Gabriel, silent, looked out at the lake. 'There's something I need to take care of first.'

'Eli will find him, especially with the clues you've given him. That was a brilliant piece of detective work on your part. But then you always did have that kind of mind.'

'It was Fellah,' Gabriel said. 'She doomed him by telling me her story.'

'But that's the Palestinian way. They're trapped in their narrative of loss and exile. There's no escaping it.' Shamron leaned forward, resting his elbows on his knees. 'Are you really sure you want the job of turning Khaled into a martyr? There are other boys who can do it for you.'

'I know,' he said, 'but I need to do it.'

Shamron sighed heavily. 'If you must, but it's

going to be a private affair this time. No teams, no surveillance, nothing Khaled can manipulate to his advantage. Just you and him.'

'As it should be.'

A silence fell between them. They watched the running lights of a fishing boat steaming slowly toward Tiberias.

'There's something I need to ask you,' Gabriel said.

'You want to talk to me about Tochnit Dalet,' Shamron said. 'About Beit Sayeed and Sumayriyya.'

'How did you know?'

'You've been wandering in the wilderness of Palestinian pain for a long time now. It's only natural.'

He asked Shamron the same question he'd put to Eli Lavon a week earlier at Megiddo. Did we drive them out?

'Of course we did,' Shamron said, then hastily he added: 'In a few places, under specific circumstances. And if you ask me, we should have driven more out. That was where we went wrong.'

'You can't be serious, Ari.'

'Let me explain,' he said. 'History dealt us a losing hand. In 1947, the United Nations decided to give us a scrap of land to found our new state. Remember, four-fifths of Mandatory Palestine had already been cut away to create the state of Transjordan. Eighty percent! Of the final twenty percent, the United Nations gave us half – ten percent of Mandatory

Palestine, the Coastal Plain and the Negev. And still the Arabs said no. Imagine if they'd said yes. Imagine if they'd said yes in 1937, when the Peel Commission recommended partition. How many millions might we have saved? Your grandparents would still be alive. My parents and my sisters might still be alive. But what did the Arabs do? They said no, and they aligned themselves with Hitler and cheered our extermination.'

'Does that justify expelling them?'

'No, and that's not the reason why we did it. They were expelled as a consequence of war, a war *they* initiated. The land the UN gave us contained five hundred thousand Jews and four hundred thousand Arabs. Those Arabs were a hostile force, committed to our destruction. We knew that the minute we declared our independence we were going to be the target of a pan-Arab military invasion. We had to prepare the battlefield. We couldn't fight two wars at the same time. We couldn't fight the Egyptians and the Jordanians with one hand while battling the Arabs of Beit Sayeed and Sumayriyya with the other. They had to go.'

Shamron could see that Gabriel remained unconvinced.

'Tell me something, Gabriel. Do you think that if the Arabs had won the war that there would be any Jewish refugees? Look at what happened in Hebron. They brought the Jews to the center of town and cut them down. They attacked a convoy of doctors and nurses heading up Mount Scopus and butchered them all. To make certain no one survived, they doused the vehicles with gasoline and set them alight. This was the nature of our enemy. Their goal was to kill us all, so we would never come back. And that remains their goal today. They want to kill us all.'

Gabriel recited to Shamron the words Fellah had spoken to him on the road to Paris. *My Holocaust is as real as yours, and yet you deny my suffering and exonerate yourself of guilt. You claim my wounds are self-inflicted.*

'They *are* self-inflicted,' Shamron said.

'But was there a blanket strategy of expulsion? Did you engage in ethnic cleansing as a matter of policy?

'No,' Shamron said, 'and the proof is all around us. You had dinner the other night in Abu Ghosh. If there was a blanket policy of expulsion, why is Abu Ghosh still there? In the Western Galilee, why is Sumayriyya gone but al-Makr still there? Because the residents of Abu Ghosh and al-Makr didn't try to butcher us. But maybe that was our mistake. Maybe we should have expelled them all instead of trying to retain an Arab minority in our midst.'

'Then there would have been more refugees.'

'True, but if they had no hope of ever returning, perhaps they might have integrated themselves into Jordan and Lebanon, instead of allowing themselves to be used as a propaganda tool to demonize and delegitimize us. Why is Fellah al-Tamari's father still in Ein al-Hilweh after all these years? Why didn't any of his brother Arab states – nations with whom he shares a common language, culture, and religion – why didn't any of them take him in? Because they want to use him as a tool to question my right to exist. I'm here. I live, I breathe. I *exist*. I don't need anyone's permission to *exist*. I don't need anyone's approval. And I certainly have nowhere else to go.' He looked at Gabriel. 'I just need you to watch over it for me. My eyes aren't what they used to be.'

The lights of the fishing boat disappeared into the port of Tiberias. Shamron seemed suddenly weary. 'There will never be peace in this place, but then there never was. Ever since we stumbled into this land from Egypt and Mesopotamia, we've been fighting. Canaanites, Assyrians, Philistines, Romans, Amalekites. We deluded ourselves into believing our enemies had given up their dream of destroying us. We have prayed for impossible things. Peace without justice, forgiveness without restitution.' He looked provocatively at Gabriel. 'Love without sacrifice.'

Gabriel stood and prepared to take his leave.

'What shall I tell the prime minister?'

'Tell him I have to think about it.'

'Operations is only a way station, Gabriel. One day you'll be the chief. The *Memuneh*.'

'You're the *Memuneh*, Ari. And you always will be.'

Shamron gave a satisfied laugh. 'What shall I tell him, Gabriel?'

'Tell him I have nowhere else to go, either.'

*

The telephone call from Julian Isherwood provided Gabriel with the excuse he'd been looking for to remove the last traces of Chiara from the flat. He contacted a charity for Russian immigrants and said he wished to make a donation. The following morning, two skinny boys from Moscow came and removed all the furniture from the living room: the couches and chairs, the end tables and lamps, the dining room table, even the decorative brass pots and ceramic dishes that Chiara had selected and placed with such care. The bedroom he left untouched, except for the sheets and the duvet, which still bore the vanilla scent of Chiara's hair.

During the days that followed, Narkiss Street was visited by a succession of delivery trucks. The large white examination table arrived first, followed by the fluorescent and halogen lamps with adjustable stanchions. The venerable art supply shop of L. Cornelissen & Son, Great Russell Street, London, dispatched a shipment of brushes, pigment, medium, and varnish. A chemical firm in Leeds sent several cases of potentially dangerous solvents that aroused more than the passing interest of the Israeli postal authorities. From Germany came a costly microscope on a retractable arm; from a workshop in Venice two large oaken easels.

Daniel in the Lions' Den, oil on canvas, dubiously attributed to Erasmus Quellinus, arrived the following day. It took Gabriel the better part of the afternoon to disassemble the sophisticated shipping crate, and only with Shamron's help was he able to man-euver the enormous canvas onto the twin easels. The image of Daniel surrounded by wild beasts intrigued Shamron, and he stayed late into the evening as Gabriel, armed with cotton swabs and a basin of distilled water and ammonia, began the tedious task of scrubbing more than a century's worth of dirt and grime from the surface of the painting.

To the degree possible he duplicated his work habits from Venice. He rose before it was light and resisted the impulse to switch on the radio, lest the daily toll of bloodshed and constant security alerts break the spell the painting had cast over him. He would remain in his studio all morning and usually worked a second shift late into the night. He spent as little time as possible at King Saul Boulevard; indeed he heard of Lev's resignation on the car radio while driving from Narkiss Street to Mount Herzl to see Leah. During their visits together, her journeys to Vienna were shallower and shorter in duration. She asked him questions about their past.

'*Where did we meet, Gabriel?*'

'*At Bezalel. You're a painter, Leah.*'

'*Where were we married?*'

'*In Tiberias. On Shamron's terrace overlooking the Sea of Galilee.*'

'*And you're a restorer now?*'

'*I studied in Venice, with Umberto Conti. You used to visit me there every few months. You posed as a German girl from Bremen. Do you remember, Leah?*'

One searing afternoon in June, Gabriel had coffee with Dr Bar-Zvi in the staff canteen.

'Will she ever be able to leave this place?'

'No.'

'What about for short periods?'

'I don't see why not,' the doctor said. 'In fact, I think it sounds like a rather good idea.'

She came with a nurse the first few times. Then, as she grew more comfortable being away from the hospital, Gabriel brought her home alone. She sat in a chair in his studio and watched him work for hours on end. Sometimes her presence brought him peace, sometimes unbearable pain. Always, he wished he could set her upon his easel and re-create the woman he had placed in a car that snowy night in Vienna.

'Do you have any of my paintings?'

He showed her the portrait in the bedroom. When she asked who the model had been, Gabriel said it was him.

'You look sad.'

'I was tired,' he said. 'I'd been gone for three years.'

'Did I really paint this?'

'You were good,' he said. 'You were better than me.'

One afternoon, while Gabriel was retouching a damaged portion of Daniel's face, she asked him why she had come to Vienna.

'We'd grown apart because of my work. I thought my cover was secure enough to bring you and Dani along. It was a foolish mistake, and you were the one to pay for it.'

'There was another woman, wasn't there? A French girl. Someone who worked for the Office.'

Gabriel nodded once and returned to work on the face of Daniel. Leah pressed him for more. 'Who did it?' she asked. 'Who put the bomb in my car?'

'It was Arafat. I was supposed to die with you and Dani, but the man who carried out the mission changed the plan.'

'Is he alive, this man?'

Gabriel shook his head.

'And Arafat?'

Leah's grasp on the present situation was tenuous at best. Gabriel explained that Yasir Arafat, Israel's mortal enemy, now lived a few miles away, in Ramallah.

'Arafat is *here*? How can that be?'

From the mouths of innocents, thought Gabriel. Just then he heard footfalls in the stairwell. Eli Lavon let himself into the flat without bothering to knock.

37. Aix-en-Provence: Five Months Later

The first stirrings of a mistral were prowling the ravines and gorges of the Bouches-du-Rhône. Paul Martineau, climbing out of his Mercedes sedan, buttoned his canvas field coat and turned the collar up round his ears. Another winter had come to Provence. A few more weeks, he thought, then he'd have to shut down the dig until spring.

He retrieved his canvas rucksack from the trunk, then set out along the edge of the ancient stone wall of the hill fort. A moment later, at the point where the wall ended, he paused. About fifty meters away, near the edge of the hilltop, a painter stood before a canvas. It was not unusual to see artists working atop the hill; Cézanne himself had adored the commanding view over the Chaine de l'Étoile. Still, Martineau reckoned it would be wise to have a closer look at the man before starting to work.

He transferred his Makarov pistol from his rucksack to the pocket of his coat, then walked toward the painter. The man's back was turned to Martineau. Judging from the attitude of his head he was gazing at the distant Mont Sainte-Victoire. This was confirmed for Martineau a few seconds later when he glimpsed the canvas for the first time. The work was very much in the style of Cézanne's classic landscape. Actually, thought Martineau, it was an uncanny reproduction.

The artist was so engrossed in his work he seemed not to hear Martineau's approach. Only when Martineau was standing at his back did he cease painting and glance over his shoulder. He wore a heavy woolen sweater and a floppy wide-brimmed hat that moved with the wind. His gray beard was long and unkempt, his hands were smeared with paint. Judging from his expression he was a man who did not enjoy being interrupted while he was working. Martineau was sympathetic.

'You're obviously a devotee of Cézanne,' said Martineau.

The painter nodded once, then resumed his work.

'It's quite good. Would you be willing to sell it to me?'

'I'm afraid this one is spoken for, but I can do another if you like.'

Martineau handed him his card. 'You can reach me at my office at the university. We'll discuss the price when I see the finished canvas.'

The painter accepted the card and dropped it into a wooden case containing his paints and brushes. Martineau bid him a good morning, then set off across the site, until he arrived at the excavation trench where he'd been working the previous afternoon. He climbed down into the pit and removed the blue tarpaulin spread over the bottom, exposing a stone-carved severed head in semi-profile. He opened his rucksack and removed a small hand trowel and a brush. Just as he was about to begin working, a shadow darkened the base of the pit. He rose onto his knees and looked up. He had expected to see Yvette or one of the other archaeologists working on the dig. Instead, he saw the hatted silhouette of the painter, lit from behind by the bright sun. Martineau lifted his hand to his brow and shielded his eyes.

'Would you mind moving away from there? You're blocking my light.'

The painter silently held up the card Martineau had just given him. 'I believe the name on this is incorrect.'

'I beg your pardon.'

'The name says Paul Martineau.'

'Yes, that's me.'

'But it's not your real name, is it?'

Martineau felt a searing heat across the back of his neck. He looked carefully at the figure standing at the edge of the trench. Was it really him? Martineau couldn't be sure, not with the heavy beard and floppy hat. Then he thought of the landscape. It was a perfect imitation of Cézanne in tone and texture. Of course it was him. Martineau inched his hand toward his pocket and made one more play for time.

'Listen, my friend, my name is –'

'Khaled al-Khalifa,' the painter said, finishing the sentence for him. His next words were spoken in

397

Arabic. 'Do you really want to die as a Frenchman? You're Khaled, son of Sabri, grandson of Asad, the Lion of Beit Sayeed. Your father's gun is in your coat pocket. Reach for it. Tell me your name.'

Khaled seized the grip of the Makarov and was pulling it from his pocket when the first round tore into his chest. The second shot caused the gun to slip from his grasp. He toppled backward and struck his head against the rocklike base of the pit. As he slipped toward unconsciousness, he looked up and saw the Jew, scooping a handful of earth from the mound at the edge of the trench. He tossed the soil onto Khaled's face, then raised his gun for the final time. Khaled saw a flash of fire, then darkness. The trench began to spin, and he felt himself spiraling downward, into the past.

The painter slipped the Beretta back into the waist-band of his trousers and walked back to the spot where he'd been working. He dipped his brush in black paint and signed his name to the canvas, then turned and started up the slope of the hill. In the shadow of the ancient wall he encountered a girl with short hair who bore a vague resemblance to Fellah al-Tamari. He bid her a good morning and climbed into the saddle of his motorcycle. A moment later he was gone.

Author's Note

Prince of Fire is a work of fiction. That said, it is based heavily on real events and was inspired in large measure by a photograph – a photograph of a young boy at the funeral of his father, a master terrorist killed by agents of Israeli intelligence in Beirut in 1979. The terrorist was Black September's Ali Hassan Salameh, architect of the Munich Olympics massacre and many other acts of murder, and the man upon whose lap the boy sits in the photograph is none other than Yasir Arafat. Students of the Israeli-Palestinian conflict will recognize that I borrowed much from Ali Hassan Salameh and his famous father to construct the fictional Asad and Sabri al-Khalifa. There are key differences between the Salamehs and the al-Khalifas, far too many to enumerate here. A search of the Coastal Plain will produce no evidence of a village called Beit Sayeed, for no such place exists. Tochnit Dalet was the real name of the plan to remove hostile Arab population centers from land allocated for the new State of Israel. There was once a village called Sumayriyya in the Western Galilee. Its destruction occurred as described in the pages of this novel. Black September was indeed a covert arm of Yasir Arafat's Palestine Liberation Organization, and the consequences of its brief, bloody reign of terror live on today. It was Black September that first demonstrated the utility of carrying out spectacular acts of terrorism on the international stage, and evidence of its influence is all around us. It can be seen in a school in Beslan, in the wreckage of four trains in Madrid, and in the empty space in lower Manhattan where the twin towers of the World Trade Center once stood.

Yasir Arafat fell ill and died as I was completing this novel. Had he chosen the path of peace instead of unleashing a wave of terror, it would have never been written, and thousands of people, Israeli and Palestinian, would still be alive today.

Acknowledgments

This novel, like the previous four books in the Gabriel Allon series, could not have been written without the assistance of David Bull. David truly is among the finest art restorers in the world, and his friendship and wisdom have enriched both my life and my work. Jeffrey Goldberg, the brilliant correspondent of *The New Yorker*, generously shared with me his wealth of knowledge and experience and was kind enough to read my manuscript and offer several helpful suggestions. Aviva Raz Schechter of the Israeli embassy in Washington provided me with a unique window on Israel in a turbulent time. Louis Toscano twice read my manuscript, and it was made better by his sure editorial hand. My friend and literary agent, Esther Newberg of International Creative Management, read each of my early drafts and quietly pointed me in the right direction.

I consulted hundreds of books, articles, and Web sites while preparing this manuscript, far too many to cite here, but I would be remiss if I did not mention a few. I am deeply indebted to the great Israeli scholar Benny Morris, whose groundbreaking *The Birth of the Palestinian Refugee Problem* helped to shape my views on the nature and scope of the Arab expulsions that took place in 1947 and 1948. Morris's towering history of the Arab-Israeli conflict, *Righteous Victims*, also proved to be an invaluable resource, as was Martin Gilbert's *Israel*. My own impressions of contemporary Israeli society were sharpened by three works in particular: *The Israelis* by Donna Rosenthal, *Still Life with Bombers* by David Horowitz, and *War Without End* by Anton La Guardia. *The Quest for the Red Prince* by Michael Bar-Zohar and Eitan Haber is a telling account of the Salameh family's violent history. It was Yaron Ezrahi of the Israeli Democracy Institute in Jerusalem, not the fictitious Colonel Yonatan Shamron, who first compared the Separation Fence to the Wailing Wall, and with far more eloquence and passion than I managed here. Those familiar with the Yom Kippur evening service will recognize that I have borrowed four lines of prayer, composed originally for the British edition of *Gates of Repentance*, and placed them in the mouth of Ari Shamron in the penultimate chapter.

None of this would be possible without the support and dedication of the remarkable team of professionals at Putnam: Carole Baron, Daniel Harvey, Marilyn Ducksworth, and especially my editor, Neil Nyren. They are, quite simply, the very best at what they do.

Finally, my wife, Jamie Gangel, skillfully read each of my early drafts, served as a sounding board for my ideas, and, as always, helped drag me across the finish line. I cannot overstate her contribution, nor can I thank her enough.